"I know you have secrets, Briar."

Questions sped through her eyes. "My secrets are my concern."

Now was the time to tell her, but while Ivo hesitated, she moved yet closer, and lifting one hand, rested it lightly upon his shoulder. *Now what?* When he simply stared down at her, she moved her other hand and slid it behind his head, tugging. He bent lower, to accommodate her.

"Briar," he tried again, but now it was a groan.

She pressed her mouth to his, her lips soft and warm. Ivo drew her into his arms, raising her so that her feet came off the floor and her entire body was pressed against his. His tongue slid between her lips, his mouth almost rough in his passion. She clung to him, kissing him back, clearly enjoying being in his arms as much as he liked having her there.

Then she drew back, and pressed her hot face against his neck. "Do you want me?" she murmured into his skin.

Other **AVON ROMANCES**

SARA BENNETT

ONCE HE LOVES

AVON BOOKS
An Imprint of HarperCollins*Publishers*

This is a work of fiction. Names, characters, places, and incidents are products of the author's imagination or are used fictitiously and are not to be construed as real. Any resemblance to actual events, locales, organizations, or persons, living or dead, is entirely coincidental.

AVON BOOKS
An Imprint of HarperCollins*Publishers*
10 East 53rd Street
New York, New York 10022-5299

Copyright © 2003 by Sara Bennett
ISBN: 0-06-051970-3
www.avonromance.com

First Avon Books paperback printing: April 2003

Avon Trademark Reg. U.S. Pat. Off. and in Other Countries, Marca Registrada, Hecho en U.S.A.
HarperCollins® is a registered trademark of HarperCollins Publishers Inc.

Printed in the U.S.A.

10 9 8 7 6 5 4 3 2 1

Prologue

York, the north of England
Late summer, 1072

Briar lifted aside the heavy tapestry screen
and peered cautiously through the narrow
gap. The large, well-lit room beyond was filled
with smoke and noise. Lord Shelborne's daughter
had made a worthy alliance, and the celebrations
were to be stretched over several days. Presently
the merry guests were finishing the last course of
a sumptuous feast, but soon the trestle tables
would be cleared, and the entertainments would
begin.

Briar cast her gaze over the crowd. She dismissed the women—Lord Shelborne's toothy
daughter and her ladies, the important wives of
the important men, the lowly serving wenches.

The man Briar sought was on his own.

She had hated him for full two years, and now she thought of little else. Without that consuming and single-minded hatred, she sometimes thought she would long ago have died of hunger or cold or simply walked into the sea and let the saltwater take her. In a strange way, her hatred of this man had kept her alive.

Briar's eyes moved over the room, noting the assembled barons and knights and their servants, as well as the merchants and the clerics and the other important men of York. Some had obviously overimbibed, and sat with heads nodding, while others pawed drunkenly at the serving wenches who moved between the tables. There were those who huddled together in conversation, or sweated on the fall of the dice, or roared laughter at a bawdy joke. And then there were the men who neither drank too much, nor said too much. The men who watched and listened and waited.

In Briar's experience, these were the men to be taken seriously, to be feared, the ones who held authority over the rest. And it did not surprise her that it was among them that she found the man she sought.

He was standing beside a rowdy group, half listening to their conversation, and yet he was apart. Alone. He was big, a wolfskin cloak draped about his broad shoulders, while his wild and tangled dark hair framed a fierce face. There was something lost about him, an air of abandonment. And his eyes, brooding and passionate, were as black as his soul. Aye, mayhap that was it; he had long ago sold his soul to the devil.

Her breath checked in her throat. Her fingers tightened upon the embroidered curtain that separated the chill, dank passageway where she stood from the welcoming warmth of the other room. The candles spun dizzily, the laughter faded, and for a brief moment Briar was catapulted back to Castle Kenton in 1070, a girl bereft, and yet trying to be brave, while the armed men bluntly informed her that now her father was dead her home was no longer hers . . .

It was but a moment of despair, and then Briar was herself again.

Impatiently, she shook her head. *Enough!* This was no time for weakness. Tonight of all nights she must be strong. Briar focused her eyes once more, and this time she controlled her reaction, taking her time as she examined the shape of him, the look of him, the essence of him.

Her heart gave a single, hard thump.

It *was* the man she sought; she couldn't possibly be mistaken. Jocelyn had said he had been invited here tonight, and there was no one else in the room who drew her eyes like he. So big, so dark, so fierce. It was as if a certain power emanated from him and touched her, surrounded her. Her body tensed and goose bumps rose on her skin. This was the man who had begun that terrible chain of events, which had blighted her young life, her future and all her hopes. Aye, it was *he*. There was no doubt in her mind.

"Jesu, protect me, and allow me to complete my task," Briar whispered, and then shuddered uncontrollably.

Strangely, the shudder wasn't due to fear, or

dread, or terror of what was to come. It was a
shudder of anticipation, almost of . . . longing.
Her mind was full of all she had plotted for, since
her world became this bleak struggle for survival.
She wanted to grasp this culminating moment in
her hands. And hold on to it.

"Briar?"

A soft voice behind her, the sweet scent of rose-
mary in fine hair, a warm, gentle hand against her
shoulder. Briar turned and faced her younger sister, Mary, trying to school her features into seren-
ity when her heart was thundering and her throat
felt tight. Those familiar dark eyes searched her
own.

"Briar, what is it?"

Mary had seen at once that something was
wrong, and even as Briar prepared to soothe her,
she resigned herself to her sister's empathy. They
had been through much together; she would be
foolish to think she could dupe Mary easily. Still,
Briar gave a reassuring smile as she took Mary's
hand in hers.

" 'Tis nothing, sister. I am spying on the company tonight, that is all. What think you, will we
sooth these savages with our songs?" And she
lifted aside the screen again, to reveal the noise
and laughter.

Mary gazed dutifully into the room. "You will
have them quiet as mice, Briar, as you well know,"
she replied, with an unusual touch of asperity.

Briar smiled a secretive smile. "We shall see."

Mary gave her a puzzled glance and opened
her mouth to ask more questions, but Briar fore-
stalled her. "Remember, sister, that after we have

sung you must go to the kitchens and wait with Jocelyn. Sleep by the fire, if you wish. I will come for you when it is time for us to go home. Can you remember that?"

Jocelyn would keep her safe. Jocelyn, some eight years older than Briar, had always been more like a mother than a sister. The cataclysmic events that had caused them all to flee Castle Kenton as outcasts could not change the roles each played within the family.

Jocelyn had always been the one who saw to details like hot food and warm clothing, who could turn a bare dwelling into a home, and now she stood like a rock of constancy in this sea of change.

Briar had always been the leader, the fighter, the strong one, and now she was the sister who swore vengeance against the powerful man who had taken all that was theirs.

Mary, at seventeen, had always been the gentle one, the youngest, and so the one who must be looked after, and the need to protect and shelter her had only grown in her sisters as their situation deteriorated.

Mary lifted an eyebrow. "I am not a lackwit, sister, I remember. But you have not told me where you are going. Why will you not tell me?"

" 'Tis something I must do, that is all. I will come to you when I can, and then we will go home together."

She could never tell Mary what she was planning, that she had persuaded one of the servants to secretly prepare her a chamber at the back of Lord Shelborne's house, and that Briar meant to share that chamber with the man in the other room. Give him false kisses and caresses, and coldly cleave her body to his. Tonight, she would use her womanhood to tempt him. As her only weapon, it would serve her well.

'Tis just, she thought. *A woman began this calamity, and now a woman will end it.*

Mary was hovering, obviously wanting to ask more. But at heart she had always been a biddable girl, and now, with a sigh, she acquiesced.

"Very well, Briar. I will wait in the kitchen with Jocelyn. It is warm there, and Odo will be in the stables, helping with the horses. She is lonely without him. Do you think, Briar, that I will ever find a man to love as Jocelyn loves her Odo?"

Jocelyn loved Odo, it was true, even though he was not the strong husband he had once been. Something had broken him, and without Jocelyn to care for him, Briar doubted Odo would live a week. And yet without Odo to care for, Jocelyn would be lost and alone. They were bound together by ties of need as strong as any marriage vows.

Briar shook her head at Mary's wistful question— she did not want to think of love. Not when her whole being was consumed with hate. Tonight was the culmination of two years of blind rage, smoldering and fermenting inside her, hot and angry. Briar had lived her need for vengeance, worn it like a heavy dark cloak about her shoulders. It had subjugated all other emotions, until she had rarely thought of anything else.

Tonight would end it.

Out in the other room the level of noise was rising, like a tide flooding up through the floor and walls, all the way to the ceiling beams. The guests were growing impatient. They had eaten and drunk, and now they were expecting to be entertained. And Briar and Mary were the entertainment.

A vision filled Briar's mind, so strong and real she physically flinched. That pale, angular face, too fierce and too intense to be handsome, and those brooding black eyes: He was not to be taken lightly, her enemy. She did not underestimate him, but nor did she underestimate herself. She did not accept the tales that would have her believe he was more than flesh and blood. He was but a man, the same as any other. And tonight she would wind her carnal spell about him, binding him so fast, so tight that he would not escape.

And then she would destroy him.

Chapter 1

Ivo de Vessey half smiled as Sweyn murmured a joke in his ear. A serving girl paused before them, filling their tankards with more warm ale, and returned Sweyn's grin. Outside the late summer evening was fading into darkness, drawing shadows down upon the city of York, but here in Lord Shelborne's hall the company was jolly and the food good, and Ivo had drunk far too much.

Ivo had come north with Lord Radulf, in response to yet another skirmish within the northern lands of Radulf's wife, the Lady Lily. The north of England seethed with subversion like a many-headed monster, and despite King William's brutality in putting down each rebellion, no matter how small, there was always another to take its place.

Sweyn, a fellow mercenary, had accompanied

Ivo, and along with a large troop of Radulf's men, they had reached York as the bells for Vespers began to toll. Lord Radulf, missing his wife and best left to his own company, had retired, but Ivo had been in favor of going at once to the castle and asking the garrison for information on this latest act of lawlessness. Before he could set out, a messenger had arrived at the door with a request for Lord Radulf and his men to come and feast at the hall of Lord Shelborne. Sweyn had promptly set about persuading Ivo to bathe and change his travel-stained clothing, and attend Lord Shelborne's hall instead of the possibly dubious repast they would find among the soldiers of the garrison.

"The invitation is for Lord Radulf," Ivo had argued.

"Aye, but he is like a surly bear tonight and best left undisturbed. A warning, my friend, never let a woman make her home in your heart."

"I need no warning," Ivo had retorted. "But will this Lord Shelborne not think it strange that we have left Lord Radulf behind?"

"Not if he saw him, Ivo. He would be grateful we had not brought him." Sweyn strode impatiently to the door. "Come, there will be time enough for talk of rebellions tomorrow! Enjoy yourself tonight, my friend. Lord Shelborne's messenger says there will be dancing and singing, and one of the women has the voice of an angel. An angel, he says, who can heal a sick man, and make a broken man whole. And there will be dice, Ivo! I am desperate to replenish my coin."

Ivo had snorted. "Do you think of nothing but women and dice, Sweyn?"

Sweyn had stopped and pretended to consider.
"No."

So Ivo had laughed, and allowed himself to be
bullied into going to Lord Shelborne's hall. And
Sweyn had been right, Ivo admitted it now. There
was such a thing as being too dedicated to one's
tasks, too serious, too willing to forgo pleasure for
the sake of duty. Tomorrow would be soon
enough to apply themselves to Radulf's problems
in the north. Surely even a disgraced knight was
allowed an occasional evening of leisure.

Ivo had been sipping his ale, deep in his
thoughts, and it was a moment before he became
aware that all had gone quiet. An expectant hush.
He glanced up, and as he did he heard the voice.

It was low and slightly husky; deeper than that
of the women he was accustomed to hearing sing.
The timbre of it brushed over his skin, soft as fur,
warm as blood, making him instantly aware. His
body tightened, hardened, as if he were preparing
for battle, every sense alerted. Ivo narrowed his
eyes and turned his head, searching for the singer
in a room made smoky from ill-drawing fires and
shadowy from candles that flickered in the many
drafts.

And found her.

She sat upon a small dais, and as he stared, the
vapor in the hall seemed to clear from before his
eyes.

Long chestnut hair lay smooth and heavy over
her back and shoulders. Too heavy for her pale
and piquant face and wide, slanting eyes. She was
a small woman, slender, but with a voice at once
powerful and moving. The notes she sang vi-

brated through him, caught like a small fist in his chest, and made his heart ache.

Dear God, what was this?

Ivo blinked, and stared at her, and realized then that the woman was gazing directly back at him. As if she were singing for *him*, and *him* alone. He took a shaky breath.

Beside him, Sweyn leaned over to whisper in his ear. "The messenger had it aright, Ivo. She *is* an angel."

"Aye," Ivo said, wondering if he sounded as bemused as he felt.

Was he sick, to be healed?

Mayhap, but he doubted even *she* could heal him. As that voice soared and dipped, filling the quiet room, permeating it like rich, heady wine, Ivo wondered if he was alone in his abstraction, or whether every man and woman here felt the same. Her voice was drawing emotions from him that he had thought—hoped—forgotten. Love and happiness, sorrow and pain, inextricably mixed. Emotions, memories, he had long ago put aside. For how could a disgraced knight and a mercenary lay claim to such luxuries as feelings?

How could he dare?

Ivo gritted his teeth, forcing the rapid beating inside his chest to calm, forcing the heat in his blood to cool. *Look again,* he told himself. *'Tis but a woman, singing.* A small woman in a dark gown with her chestnut hair loose about her and her pale hands clasped in her lap. 'Twas nothing amazing.

He realized, as he fought off the spell, that there was a harpist accompanying her. He stared at the

instrument, as if that would help rebuild his barricades, and saw 'twas one of the small harps used
by the Welsh. The harp was being played by a girl
with hair of a darker hue and a taller figure than
the songstress, and her expression was utterly serious as she concentrated upon her notes. Despite
their differences, the two looked similar enough
to be sisters.

Aye, singing sisters, Ivo thought, with relief. No
magic there! He had dreamed the sensation of that
small hand inside his chest, squeezing his heart,
of course he had. Perhaps something in her song
had unconsciously reminded him of the past,
enough to slice through his usually reliable protective walls.

It would not happen again.

But even as he made his vow, the woman's
voice soared one last time, and the poignancy of
that single, pure note brought tears stinging to
Ivo's eyes. He blinked angrily, wondering why *he,*
who should know better, could be so weak. A
grown man toughened by battle and despair, a
soldier who had not wept since he was a boy of
eleven. How could this stranger so easily unlock
his burdened heart with her key?

As if the songstress had read his thoughts,
the woman's gaze settled upon him once more.
Her eyes were large and dark, and with very
little effort he feared he could drown in them. And
then she smiled—a small, secretive smile—and
smoothed her plain gown over her hips with a
slow, sensual movement.

Ivo's hand closed hard on the tankard, so hard
that he felt the metal ease beneath his strong fin-

gers. There was no mistaking the woman's look, or the smile that went with it—he had too many years and too much experience behind him to do that. She had just issued him an invitation.

Ivo was not in the habit of attracting his women this way, but just for a moment all he felt was another rush of relief. There had been no magic here after all, nothing bizarre or bewildering. Just a flesh and blood woman, who, for whatever reason, was desirous of his company. He let his gaze linger on the curves of her body beneath the drab gown, the way her hair caught fire in the sputtering candlelight. Ivo's body stirred, hardened. It had been many a long month since he had last lain with a woman, and even longer since he had been fortunate enough to find one so comely as this songstress.

"She likes you," Sweyn said with a laugh. "Tell me now that you would have preferred an evening in the castle garrison, with the stench of unwashed soldiers to accompany your meal."

Ivo shrugged, and set his tankard down carefully. "Tonight she smiles at me. Tomorrow it might be you." His voice was dry and noncommittal, but desire beat like a pulse within him.

"You underrate yourself," Sweyn retorted. "If you get the chance to enjoy her, my friend, think not of the morning. The garrison will still be there." He gave Ivo a none-too-gentle push, and went off to find himself a game of dice.

Ivo was crossing the room before he knew it. He hadn't realized until he started walking how light-headed he was—it must be the ale. His boots seemed barely to touch the rush-strewn floor. The dais was before him and he vaguely noted that the girl with the harp had gone.

But the angel was there, waiting.

"You sing wondrously well, demoiselle." He heard his own voice, deep and quiet, as if it were that of a stranger. "I am bewitched."

She laughed, and cast him a flirtatious glance.

Her eyes were not brown as he had thought, but hazel. Watchful and secretive, and framed with thick dark lashes, they were set wide apart and slanted upward like a cat's eyes. There was something familiar in those eyes, something distant and yet part remembered. *I know her, but from where . . .* Even as his mind was turning, his gaze moved on. Her mouth was small and lush, her chin a point for her heart-shaped face, and her skin was smooth and unmarked apart from a small scar on her right cheekbone. That long chestnut-colored hair fell about her, curling at the ends, rippling over her shoulders like a smooth waterfall.

There is something about her eyes, and the scar on her right cheekbone. Something about the scar . . .

Why had he drunk so much? His mind must be fogged with ale fumes.

"You like my songs, sir?" Her French was flawless—this was no English peasant.

Ivo blinked, brought his thoughts back to the here and now. "Aye, demoiselle, I like them very much."

Her eyes smiled up at him, like the brown and green shadows in a forest, tempting him onward into places he had never been before. She reached out a slender hand and rested it upon his arm. Her hand looked pale and fragile against his dark sleeve, and he hesitated to cover it with his own.

"Mayhap you would like a private audience?"

Were the words truly spoken? Or had he dreamed them because they were so much what he wanted to hear?

Ivo knew he was sobering up fast.

He gazed down intently into her face, and saw her lick her lips nervously with the tip of her pink tongue. There was a flicker of doubt in her eyes, as though she feared he would say her nay. He wanted to laugh—*nay* was the last thing he would say her right now! She was beautiful, and her song still held him in its spell. And if he wasn't either mad, or badly mistaken, she was offering herself to him.

All of herself.

Lust soared through him, tightening every muscle. To his surprise, his manhood began to thicken—he had thought he had better control than that. Ivo was no brutish soldier, willing to forgo all niceties for a hasty roll in the hay. He had been taught courtesy and respect, and although he may not always have abided by them, he knew the right from the wrong. To suddenly feel so totally out of control, like a lusty stallion in a paddock of mares, confused him.

But there was more than lust here. Ivo felt a poignancy that was in one part the suppressed emotions she had stirred up with her song, and in the other part a memory of his past. It was as if this angel really would in some way heal him, repair the broken man.

Make him whole again.

He clenched the fist he had kept hidden in the wolfpelt cloak at his side, his maimed flesh warm inside the leather-and-steel glove he always wore in the company of others. He had learned to use his damaged hand as well as any man whose hand was whole—he had had no choice. Still he was proud of the accomplishment. Miles had thought to cripple him and render him useless, but he had failed.

"You are a stranger here."

The woman interrupted his introspection. Her voice was as low and husky as it had been when she sang, and again he felt the shiver of its touch on his skin. Like the brush of velvet, soft and sensual.

"I am come from the south."

No need to tell her more, thought Ivo. Indeed, he was wary to open his mouth in case all that he was, and hoped and dreamed, gushed out. His mind felt wide open and echoey, his body hummed with desire. And atop that he had the sensation of familiarity—as if he had known her before.

Ivo held out his hand to her, the good one—no need to frighten her with his deformity just yet. The touch of her soft skin made him even more crazy to have her—images of her naked body in his arms sliced his brain like a red-hot blade—and his voice came out sharper than he had intended.

"To answer your question, demoiselle, I would very much like a private audience. Do you have a room?"

He could have bitten off his tongue. *Do you have a room?* What sort of enticing lovetalk was that for a man who was once a knight? He needed his friend Gunnar Olafson here, with his smooth ways and magic smile. Why could Ivo not be more like Gunnar, wooing her delicately into his arms, instead of his usual blunt and impatient self?

She was gazing up at him—she barely came to his shoulder. She smiled a little smile, mayhap reading the anguish in his eyes, but she was not angry and not insulted. If anything, she looked pleased. Before Ivo could consider what might be the reasons for this, she spoke again.

"Aye, I have a room."

She was not even pretending to misunderstand him. Then, just as he was again doubting the whole business, she gave a soft, reckless laugh, and held out her hand. "Come and we will sing together, my lord."

He wanted to tell her he was not anyone's lord, that he did not know her at all, that this was not wise. But when had Ivo ever cared about *wise*? Tonight his body had a will of its own. He lifted his hand and she caught his fingers tightly in her own cold ones, then she led him through an arras-covered doorway. Into the shadows.

It was chill here, and the sounds from the hall were abruptly muted. Ivo knew from long experience that he should be wary, and yet still he went with her, as though entranced. Deep inside him, there lay mistrust—the years of living in his brother's dark shadow had made him cautious—but he did not mistrust her enough to deny himself the pleasure of her. She had offered, and Ivo meant to take.

'Twas as simple and as brutal as that.

* * *

Briar felt dizzy, as if this were not real at all.
How could it have been so simple? So easy? Not
even Briar at her most optimistic had believed her
enemy would fall so willingly into the net she
cast. But he had, and now she held him in the
palm of her hand. Literally. Briar's fingers tightened their grasp about that warm, broad hand,
feeling the ridges of calluses and scars that told of
many years of battle.

His hand.

The great Lord Radulf, the King's Sword.

Before he died, Briar's father had cursed
Radulf, blaming him for the death of Anna,
Briar's stepmother, whose murder was still un-
solved. Anna's murder had precipitated the destruction of the Kenton family. Thus, in Briar's
mind, Radulf had begun this terrible calamity.
Aye, he had destroyed her family, taken from her
her home and wealth, her life and all she had
taken for granted. Until it was no more.

"Radulf did this," she had said dully, the day
they were cast out from Castle Kenton because
their father was branded a traitor. They had
trudged into the tiny village, but no one there had
dared to help them or shelter them—they were all
too afraid of the consequences. So they had
walked on, with nowhere to go.

"Radulf did this!" She had screamed it out the
second time, her voice echoing across the moors.
Radulf. Her feverish mind had found a focus, a
thing to hate and blame for all that had befallen
them. A way to keep her alive.

Her elder sister, Jocelyn, had looked at her

while Odo ambled along to the side like a great, mindless bear. Jocelyn's blue eyes were reddened and swollen, her face puffy and blotched from crying. "'Tis over and done. We must make our way as best we can, Briar, and not look backward."

"'Tis not over and done! Father swore to take vengeance, and now *I* swear to fulfill his wish."

Jocelyn had gazed back at her, her thin face intent. "Put this behind you, Briar. It is wrong to seek to heal evil with more evil. I beg you, put this behind you."

Briar had shaken her head angrily. How could she put such things behind her, forget what had happened to their father and to them? Go on as if nothing had happened? She was not like Jocelyn—her anger could not be dampened with a trickle of water.

Briar had meant what she had said that day, but in the meantime they had wandered far, eventually all the way to York, living like peasants. And no one came to their aid. They were Richard Kenton's daughters, the traitor's children, and therefore safer forgotten.

But Briar had not forgotten, and the need for vengeance had grown; a blind, desperate need that gave her no rest. Nor would it, until it was satisfied. The answer to her prayers came when she had heard Radulf was traveling into the north to deal with a rebellion on his wife's lands. By then, Briar had known much of the King's Sword, and his love for his wife. And she had known exactly how she would repay him for what he had done to her and her family.

"And what will happen then? When you have

lain with Radulf, and soured Lily's love for him?
Will that content you, Briar?"

Jocelyn had been less than impressed when
Briar had divulged her intended plan to her sister
some weeks past. Her blue eyes had been hard
and watchful as she demanded answers. Jocelyn
had still not given up trying to persuade Briar to
put the past behind her, and Jocelyn was no gentle
flower, unlike Mary.

These days Jocelyn was employed as Lord Shelborne's cook, and he treasured her for her fine
pastries and bread, and the succulent dishes she
placed before him. It was Jocelyn who had given
Briar the important news that Radulf was to be invited to the marriage celebrations at Lord Shelborne's hall.

"I don't know if I will be content, sister," Briar
had said in answer to Jocelyn's questions. "But at
least I will have fulfilled our father's last wish."

Jocelyn had shaken her head impatiently. "You
have thought only of the moment, Briar, as usual.
I know you well. You are headstrong and brave
and determined, but you fail to think beyond the
moment. What do you believe Radulf will do with
you when you tell him who you are? Think carefully, Briar, before you act. Remember, morning
always follows night."

"So you will not help me?"

"No, I will not help you! You go to your own
destruction by such behavior. Briar, I, too, have
many reasons to hate Radulf. But will that bring
our father back? Or our lands and wealth and the
joy we knew? Will it bring my Odo back to the
man he used to be? What do you hope to achieve

by making Radulf suffer, Briar? Methinks it will only increase your own suffering . . ."

Now, as Briar tightened her grip, her small hand in his, Jocelyn's warnings rang in her head. She had refused to listen to Jocelyn then, and she did not want to remember her words now. They made her feel uneasy, edgy. Radulf *must* suffer, just as they had suffered. Aye, Briar was right and Jocelyn was wrong, and she must damp down all doubts within her, be cold as winter on the moors about her home at Castle Kenton. That was why she had not said another word to Jocelyn about tonight, why she had turned instead to Grisel, one of the maidservants. It was simple enough to spin Grisel a tale about a man for whom Briar was lovesick, to beg her to prepare her a room, to swear her to silence.

The chamber that Grisel had found for her was at the back of Lord Shelborne's house. Quickly Briar pulled her enemy inside the chamber after her, and closed the door. Her gaze darted about the room, assuring herself that everything was in place. Grisel had left a single candle on a wooden chest, and its flame shivered in the draft, sending shadows dancing upon the low-beamed ceiling. The bed was large and thick with sumptuous furs and soft cushions. It looked most inviting, as it was meant to.

Grisel had made a tempting trap, with Briar herself as the bait.

"This is your room?"

He was watching her, those gleaming black eyes piercing her own. She had never seen such eyes, so expressive, so wounded, so ancient. As if

he had seen things she could only dream of . . .
Again Briar shook herself. She could read desire
in them, and that was all she needed to see. Aye,
he wanted her. She had known it from the moment they exchanged glances across Lord Shelborne's hall. So much for Radulf's famed fidelity
to the Lady Lily! And yet . . .

Something struck her amiss, like a sour note on
Mary's harp.

Breathless, Briar struggled with her doubt and
fear. *Not now.* She pressed the emotions down inside herself, deep, deep down. She could not allow her feelings to sway her now, not when
vengeance was within her grasp. This was the
time for a cool, clear head and a cold heart. If
Radulf was willing to betray his wife, then Briar
told herself she was more than willing to help him
do it.

"Wine?" she asked calmly, moving to pour
some into a goblet from the jug Grisel had placed
earlier.

"Aye, demoiselle." He reached out his hand.

When she saw the black glove upon it, Briar
hesitated. "One glove?" she asked, with a breathy
laugh. "Is this an affectation, my lord?"

He shook his head, the humorless smile barely
curling the edges of his wide mouth. "No affectation, demoiselle. My hand is injured and I wear
the glove so that it will not frighten pretty ladies
like yourself. That is all."

Briar shrugged, but her gaze was curious. Had
Radulf hurt himself? She had not heard of any serious injury, and she always had her ears open for
talk of the King's Sword. " 'Twould take more than

that to frighten me, my lord," she said grimly, without thinking.

His gaze sharpened at her tone. "Oh?" he asked. "Are you not the fearful sort?"

But Briar had control of herself, and she laughed again, her deceit once more firmly in place. She poured some wine for herself and drank deeply, letting the slightly sour, heady brew relax her. He moved closer. His fingers brushed against her neck, lifting a lock of hair and feeling its texture. His touch made her shiver, but it was not from fear or revulsion. This was something more, something new, something unexpected. Startled, she lifted her head and met his gaze.

His eyes were mesmerizing.

"You are very beautiful," he murmured, and stepped so close that her body was almost touching his. She felt his heat, smelled his scent, saw the flicker deep in his eyes. He smiled then, his wide mouth curling up and completely transforming the fierce angles of his face. His was a face made for smiling, and yet she could see by the lines upon it that such moments were rare.

Briar could not look away. Not even when he set both their goblets upon the chest and leaned down and kissed her, his lips smooth and unhurried against hers.

"Demoiselle," he whispered, and rubbed his rough cheek against hers, before capturing her lips once more with his. His mouth was hot and seductive, and Briar went still, confused by the sensations that were cudgeling her mind and body. This was not how she had imagined it! She had meant to seduce him, playing at feelings she could not possibly feel, disguising her distaste and bitter triumph beneath the soft cries of a woman enjoying her man. Leading her enemy further and further into the maze until it was too late, until he was utterly lost in its tangled paths, and willingly hers.

I am Briar, she would tell him then. *The daughter of Lord Richard Kenton. I am here to avenge my father and stepmother.*

Or maybe she would simply arrange to have someone discover them in bed, someone who would report back to Lily. Radulf would be shattered by his guilt and her pain, aye, destroyed.

That was the problem with loving someone. Love could so easily become a weapon . . .

Dear God, his mouth was hot! He gripped her upper arms, pulling her closer against his hard body. Briar found that she was leaning into him, her own hands slipping about his waist beneath the wolfpelt cloak. His body was big and strong, and his touch was as perfect as it was startling. As was the realization that she wanted this.

Where was the distaste for what she was doing? Where was the resignation? She should be grimly suffering even as she triumphed over this man, her enemy. She had plotted so long to punish him; she had never expected to enjoy it!

Nay, this was not how it was meant to be. This was *her* moment, and if anyone should grow weak from their kisses, then it should be *he.*

Briar stepped away from him, taking a breath, watching him warily now. He smiled again, coming after her, backing her toward the bed. "We will

sing together," he said softly. "An old song, demoiselle, but a good one."

"I know many old songs," she replied, and he
laughed, a low seductive sound. For a brief,
shaken moment Briar wondered if she could go
through with it.

Have you waited so long just to turn tail now? she
asked herself angrily. *Just because something in his
looks tugs at your womanly emotions, just because his
kisses are not as repulsive as you expected. Remember,
this is the man who stole from you the life you loved. He
deserves to be punished. Whether you enjoy the punishment or not is immaterial.*

But these were things Briar had never expected
to feel in such circumstances—pleasure, desire,
need. She *had* lain with a man. Once. Two years
ago. There had been no pleasure then. The memory was a montage of pain and sorrow, and she
fully expected this night to be similar. That so far
it was not had unsettled her, momentarily distracted her, but now she stiffened her resolve and
set doubts aside. She would do this, she *would* . . .

But he must have seen something in her face.
When she met his eyes again, they were even more
intense than before. And there was a new reserve
about him, as if he no longer quite believed in her.

"Drink," she urged him softly, pouring more
wine into his goblet and handing it to him.

He took the vessel from her, but did not drink.
Perhaps he no longer trusted her enough to do so.
The shadows played games with his face, making
him more handsome than he really was, smoothing out the irregular features and straightening the
broken nose. His hair grew in wild, untrimmed

curls about his face, and the wolfskin cloak added to his barbaric appearance. This was not a man who played games, and if she did this thing now—and later betrayed him to his lady—then he might very well kill her.

Despite herself, Briar shivered.

"You are cold."

That deep, quiet murmur; the voice of a Norman knight of breeding and education. Such was Radulf. A great man.

And yet do not be deceived, she reminded herself. *Do not fall under his spell. Remember the injury he has done you. Remember and take your vengeance and find your justice, even if it is two years too late. Do not lose sight of what you have set out to do here tonight.*

"What is your name, demoiselle?"

"Briar," she said, knowing he would not recognize it. Why should he? She was nothing to him, and two years ago she had been but a girl, kept safe on her father's estate, content with her present and her future, not realizing that soon her world would be destroyed. Again the memory sobered her, strengthened her.

He was still watching her through the shadows; his eyes so intent, it felt as if they were inside her head.

"Briar. 'Tis a prickly name, demoiselle. Are you thorny like the wild briar?"

Briar smiled, hoping he would not read its falseness. She reached down with a trembling hand and began to unknot her girdle.

"I am tough like the briar, sir. Even when my enemies think me vanquished, I can spring up again in the most unlikely of places."

She had amused him, mayhap even delighted him—she read it in his eyes.

"And yet you sing like a nightingale."

"You are kind." She disposed of the compliment, suddenly impatient. They were wasting time. The sooner he had bedded her, the sooner this thing would be done.

The girdle was unknotted, and Briar put it aside. Her gown was loose enough to slide down over her shoulder, displaying smooth, rounded flesh. He went still, watching her as she brought her arm out of the gown, and then slowly repeated the action with her other shoulder and arm. Grasping firmly the worn, brown cloth, she held it up against her breasts.

His rapt attention pleased her. A moment ago she had felt as if she had lost control of the situation; now she had it back again. That black, brooding gaze moved slowly upward, to her face, examining her lips, her tumbling hair, before his eyes fastened on hers. The silence in the chamber stretched out. Something in the tension of his body, the crackle in the air about him, told Briar that if she wanted to turn back then she should do it now. Before it was too late.

Slowly, her eyes on his, she let the gown fall.

Had he groaned aloud? Ivo would not have been surprised if he had. He had never seen a woman so beautiful.

Her long chestnut hair curled over her pale shoulders and down over the curve of her back. It made a pretty screen for her small, rounded breasts with their tawny nipples. Her hazel eyes took on a secretive slant, as she watched him through her dark lashes, and her pink lips tilted enigmatically at the corners.

Ivo still didn't understand why of all the men in the hall she had chosen *him*, but it was often so with women. Sweyn laughed and said they were intrigued by his warriorlike looks coupled with his nobleman's voice. He no longer cared. The elusive thought that he knew her from somewhere still tugged at him, but he cared not for that, either. His body was hard and ready, the wench was lovely and very desirable, and he was not fool enough to question his good fortune.

He felt its touch rarely enough these days.

Ivo took a step closer. The color of her eyes deepened. With lust? Or was it something else that ran swiftly through the green and brown? Surely not fear? For if she were afraid of him, why would she be here, now?

Still, it was with a cautious gentleness that Ivo reached out his good hand, instinctively keeping the other one hidden at his side. He touched her cheek, feeling the soft smoothness of her skin, the slight indentation of her scar. He cupped her chin, his thumb tracing the shape of her lips, memorizing the feel of them.

Her lips parted and she sighed and swayed a little, eyes shutting. Ivo smiled, pleased by the faint blush staining her skin, the tightening of her nipples into hard little cherries, begging for the comfort of his tongue. Aye, there was desire here, and she felt it as much as he.

He caught her long hair in his hand, using it to tilt her face back for his mouth. The kiss was long and hot, and while he kissed her his hand sought her breasts and caressed them. She shuddered, moaning into his mouth. Her dark lashes fluttered wildly and she drew back a little, hands clasping his forearm, as if she sought to steady herself.

He bent and kissed her again, opening her mouth with his, probing with his tongue. She was hot inside, and needy. She, too, felt the fire burning between them. He sensed it, knew it, and suddenly it no longer mattered to him what her reasons might be. This was a moment out of time; the drab and brutal world he lived in had been left behind. There was only the disgraced knight and the songstress, and together they would make the stars burn.

Ivo slid to his knees before her, and took her nipple in his mouth.

She arched back with a gasping cry, hands tangling in his hair and tugging painfully. He didn't care. He pulled the gown down from her hips, knowing he was rough but the need to see her naked drove him beyond gentleness. Here was more pale, smooth flesh—the swell of her belly and buttocks, the white length of her thighs and the tawny hair between.

She was small, but most definitely a woman. A little thin, mayhap, a little delicate, but the curves were in their rightful places. For a moment Ivo just looked, feeling like a blind man who has suddenly begun to see. And then he slid his hands down over her thighs, and bending forward placed a kiss on the soft hair at their juncture.

She started and stepped back, forgetting perhaps that the bed was so close, for with a squeak she fell back upon it. Helpless, hampered by her long hair, she struggled to sit up. And then, as he firmly gripped and parted her legs with his strong hands, she stiffened anxiously.

But he only wanted to look. Amused, he met her eyes, sensing her uncertainty beneath the headiness of her passion. And then shocked surprise, as he grinned at her and stooped to run his tongue along her inner thigh. Until he found the hot core of her.

"Oh!" She jerked as if he had shot her with an arrow, and then groaned in her husky, sensual voice.

Ivo decided he liked this song the best of any she had sung tonight.

"Sing to me, demoiselle," he murmured wickedly, and used his tongue again, seeking out the places that gave her the most enjoyment. She tried to tense, to pull away, but he would have none of it. With another groan, she gave herself up to pleasure.

Briar felt the passion rippling over her, washing away all her thoughts of vengeance, of the past, of her so-carefully constructed plan. She was left with only one thing—the need for release. Briar gasped, her eyes blind to the dim, candle-lit room as that questing tongue set off a myriad of sparks within her.

Why could she not remember Filby, who had hurt her when he took her, his only interest finding his own pleasure upon her, before he had risen and straightened his clothing. He had stared down at her then, with cold eyes, with a look she would never, ever forget. As though she were not the daughter of a great man, and the woman that until this moment he had courted and pretended to cherish.

Why could she not remember Filby?

Because the ripples of passion were turning into pounding waves. All control gone, Briar cried out, arching against him, dimly aware of the surging undertow within her own body.

Jesu, she had not meant it to be like this! She had wanted to be cold, to feel discomfort, even pain, and most of all she had wanted to hate him as he deserved. Instead she lay upon the sumptuous bed, weak and tumbled, her whole body throbbing from the pleasure he had just given her. Why could this man not have been cruel like Filby? And why could Filby not have lavished the same care upon her as this man?

To Briar, dazed and bewildered, the world seemed all turned about.

When the warm wash of pleasure had finally faded a little, Briar opened her eyes. He was grinning at her again, his chin resting familiarly against her belly. With an effort Briar bestirred herself.

"You . . ." She swallowed, tried again. "You are very good at what you do, my lord."

"Aye, 'tis my one true vocation."

She giggled. God help her, she giggled like a silly maid!

He smiled back, and then proceeded to crawl up onto the bed beside her, slipping and sliding on the furs, and then rolling her into his arms. Before she could think to protest, his mouth was on hers, hot and tasting of her, something she found shocking and yet curiously exciting. The heat of his lips and tongue were stirring the tide within her again. How could that be, when he had only just sated her?

He was pressed against her from shoulder to hip, and she realized she could feel him, big and hard inside his breeches. Without thought, as naturally as if his body was as familiar to her as her own, Briar stretched down her hand and stroked him. He groaned, burying his face against her warm throat. She cupped the bulge of his manhood, trying again to remind herself of Filby, trying to bring forth the old, bitter memories of their mating.

"We are not finished yet," she said firmly. Her vengeance could not be complete until he had lain with her, inside her, and proved himself as faithless to his wife as he had been to her stepmama.

The thought chilled Briar, enough to cool the desire building within her.

"No, demoiselle, we are not finished yet." Evidently he did not sense the change within her. Rising up onto his knees on the bed, he began swiftly to disrobe, pulling his tunic and shirt over his head.

He was a big man, in all ways, and Briar watched him with reluctant admiration. Sunbrowned skin, a body broad and hard-muscled, the body of a warrior. Her eyes moved of their own accord, over the wondrous planes and curves and hollows. Numerous scars covered him, testimony to the many battles in which he had fought. He had been hurt many times, mayhap faced death many times. Briar touched a long white scar on his ribs, testing the puckered flesh.

Aye, she told herself with satisfaction, *many have tried to take his life, but they have used the wrong weapons. Sharpened wood and iron and steel are of no use—he is too wily a warrior. No, the way to harm him is from* within. *To find the weakness in him. To slay him by breaking his heart.*

Almost unwillingly, uneasy from what he was making her feel, Briar ran her fingertips up the hard muscles of his stomach to his chest, rough with a dusting of dark hair. His nipples were hidden there, and she found them, feeling them tighten with her touch. More eagerly now, she folded her hands over the heavy curves of his shoulders, aware of their breadth and strength, before she slid them down, over his sizeable upper arms. He was indeed a creature of myth and legend. She could enjoy the sight and touch and feel of him, no matter what emotions lay in her heart.

He tugged his breeches down over his narrow hips, stripping them quickly from his strong legs. He was naked now, every curving muscle, every scar, every wonderful inch of him. Briar had never felt desire like this before—it was new and heady and completely unexpected. Her fascinated gaze followed the line of dark hair from his belly, down to his groin. His manhood jutted out, big and bold; he could not pretend indifference, even had he wanted to. And Briar could not resist stretching out her hand and grasping him, closing her hand gently upon him. So potent, so male. Beneath the velvet softness of his skin there was a hot, steely strength.

He had gone very still.

Drawn at last from her preoccupation of his magnificent body, Briar looked up at him. His eyes flared with burning desire, and yet he did not move. Clearly a battle was going on within him while he fought to subdue his lust. He was, she realized in surprise, trying to be careful, trying not to frighten her. He wanted her, and the same lustful beast she had seen in Filby was there, lurking inside his tense face and brooding gaze, but he was, unlike Filby, trying to rein it in. 'Twas the man in control of the beast and not the other way around.

And as she watched him struggle, Briar realized something more.

She wanted *him*.

Wanted him inside her, as she could never remember wanting any man. She *wanted* to take the beast she saw in his eyes, that fierce, wild wanting, and tame it. Make it her own.

I feel this way because I am so close to taking the vengeance I have dreamed of for so long, she tried to tell herself.

But it was a lie.

Even as she repeated the words to herself, she knew she was avoiding the truth. Briar wanted him. Her body craved his. What had begun as playacting, a cold-blooded pretense, was now real desire, real lust. And explain it to herself in whatever manner she may, it was unexplainable.

As if he had sensed her need, he had begun to kiss her. Long, passionate kisses that made her mindless. Briar pressed against him, her arms about his neck, her fingers tangled in his black hair. As he kissed her, he was caressing her breasts, plucking at the taut nipples, causing her body to burn and ache. The cleft between her legs was swollen and hot, and when his manhood prodded at the juncture of her thighs, instinctively she opened them, giving him access. She should be frightened, or at least wary, because he was so big—but she was not.

Nevertheless, Briar braced herself.

But instead of thrusting himself brutally inside her, as Filby had done, he began to play with her. He ran his tongue slowly down one side of her throat, tasting her, enjoying her as if she were one of Jocelyn's honey cakes.

The comparison made her giggle, and then quickly gasp in shocked surprise. "Ouch!" Briar pressed back into the furs, so that she could look at him, her face slack with amazement. "You bit me!"

"Just a little," he admitted, with an unrepentant smile. "You taste so good, demoiselle."

"I do?"

"Aye," he mocked. "Inside and out." And, sliding his hands beneath her, he raised his body over hers, lifted her, and with a thrust of his hips, entered into her slippery depths.

Briar's eyes grew wider as she stared up at him.

Ivo felt the little movements inside her, the adjustments to his size, the grasp of her body about his. She was tight, though no virgin. But neither was she much used—Ivo knew the signs. In truth he cared not what she was, only that at this moment she was *his*. Ivo threw his head back with a groan of ecstasy, thrusting himself into her a little more, and a little further, unashamedly enjoying her. He withdrew, and thrust again, deep this time, and she quivered from her head to her toes.

"Oh, demoiselle," he whispered hoarsely, gazing down at her with blurred black eyes, his hair a dark aureole in the candlelight. "Tell me I am not dreaming."

And just like that, a wild storm of pleasure swept through her. Briar cried out and arched against him. He held her firm, allowing her to ride the tempest, content to let her have her moment while he kept his own pleasure in check. When she was still again, gasping, a sheen of perspiration covering her body, her hair sticky against his skin, he gently kissed her face. Little, light kisses across her cheeks and nose and brow; soft kisses against her eyelids, and the tiny scar.

A child's cry. The bark of a hound. Voices raised in consternation.

The memory was there and gone, too quick for him to grasp it. Besides, his senses were clamoring for release, to take what she offered so freely. Whomever she was.

Ivo gazed down at her, at her mouth, reddened now, lush and swollen from his kisses. He nibbled it with his teeth while thrusting slowly between her thighs, feeling the tight sheath grasping him, holding him. It felt so good and yet he was wild to finish it—the two longings tugged him in opposing directions, an agony that was like ecstasy.

This wasn't going at all as Briar had imagined it.

She had thought he would take her brutally, guiltily, and then toss her aside. She had thought to find joy in it, yes, but only because it was a culmination of two years of yearning and plotting. She had certainly not expected to be thrown into such a wild, passionate storm by his embrace. And she had not imagined to feel such delight in the joining of his body to hers.

More than that.

Such a sense of rightness, as if she had been born to be here.

Sweet Jesu, how could that be?

Briar's anxious thoughts scattered as he moved again, stroking her deep inside each time he moved his hips. Oh, it felt so good when he did that. Felt so wonderful. Caught up again in her own rising passion, and completely in thrall to his tender teasing, Briar lifted her own hips to meet him. She could feel his entire body rigid with his need to let go, and yet he did not. Incredibly he held himself back, he waited, and Briar knew instinctively he was waiting for her to soar once more, before he would allow himself to join her.

"Sing, demoiselle." His husky breath stirred the damp curls on her brow. "Sing our song."

No, she thought, no, I must not, I *will* not . . . But it was already too late. Briar heard her own voice, harsh with pleasure and longing, as he tipped her over the edge once more. And this time, as she reached completion, he drove hard, once, twice, and followed, shouting his joy to the shadows, planting his seed deep within her, and shuddering his contentment in her enfolding arms.

Chapter 2

Briar lay quiet, her head rested upon his chest, with her hair spilling about them both. She could feel the steady thud of his heart, as well as every breath. He was stroking her back, his fingers gentle against her heated skin, while his gloved hand rested, relaxed, upon his hard-muscled stomach. She gazed at the black leather, idly wondering what was so terrible about the hand that he must keep it covered even at such a time as this.

Beyond the chamber, the noise from the hall was faint and far away. Other musicians were entertaining the crowd—the sound of flute and drums rose and fell—but they were not so successful as she and Mary had been, if the catcalls were anything to go by. Briar tried to smile, but her lips felt frozen.

Where was her sense of triumph? There should be a wondrous sense of triumph after her two years of planning and plotting for this fateful day. Two years in which she and Mary and Jocelyn had lived like peasants—*starving* peasants at that!— barely staying alive. Two years in which they had been outcast from all they had loved and held dear. If it had not been for her ability to sing and Mary's to play the harp, they would surely have perished long since. But they *had* survived, somehow. Each day had been a new quest to find food to eat and somewhere to sleep. The worst times had been when they were newly outcast, when she and Mary had been separated from Jocelyn and Odo, and Briar had felt as if she were truly alone.

Revenge was the only thing that had kept her from perishing.

And, of course, there was Mary.

Briar loved her younger sister very much, but every morning when she awoke it was to the knowledge that Mary was her responsibility. Jocelyn had Odo, and therefore it fell to Briar to protect Mary. If there were ever any sacrifices to be made, then Briar made them without complaint. 'Twas the way it should be, the way it must be.

Before they reached York, theirs had been a grim, day-to-day existence, and sometimes Briar had caught sight of her reflection in a puddle or a pond, and was shocked by her thin, stark appearance. The girl in the water had been a stranger. Aye, she had been thinner and paler—that was to be expected—but she had changed in essence, too. The dark emotions that had begun to burn in her eyes were very different from those that had brought her only smiles when her father was alive.

Briar was the second daughter of Lord Richard Kenton, once one of the most powerful men in England, and a loyal subject to King William the Conqueror of England and Duke of Normandy. Richard Kenton, a minor baron in Normandy, had seen an opportunity for wealth and advancement when William had asked for men to follow him and fight for him in England.

The lands of the newly named Kenton estate had been extensive, although the country was wild and strange. Briar had loved it. Her father had owned other estates—King William liked to spread the lands of his powerful barons about the countryside in case they grew too strong and set up small kingdoms of their own—but Kenton had been his favorite, too. Father and second daughter had shared that bond, despite a stepmama who was beautiful and demanding.

And then everything had gone wrong.

All because her father was wed to a woman whom Lord Radulf had once loved. And when the great Radulf had seen Anna, at his wedding ceremony to the Lady Lily in York, he wanted her again. Greedily, in the selfish manner of a child, wanted what he could not have. And when it was clear that he could not have her, he had her killed.

Briar's father had been beside himself with grief and rage, believing he knew the truth of the matter, and yet unable to convince the king, Radulf's friend from childhood, that it was so. In his blind fury, Richard Kenton rebelled against

William—and lost his lands, his wealth, and his army when Radulf won the battle. It was then that Briar's father, distraught, abandoned by former friends and supporters, knowing he must face the traitor's noose, took his own life.

Perhaps he thought by doing so he would free his three daughters of the taint of his treason. That, despite his actions, they would be allowed to continue living the life to which they were accustomed. That his disgrace would stop with his death.

But it was not to be.

At the time that news of her father's death came, Briar had been within weeks of making an advantageous marriage to their neighbor, Lord Filby. Filby had seemed smitten with her, and had sworn he wanted nothing more than to make her happy—her father would never have considered his suit if that were not the case, for he was a loving man when it came to his family. Briar had expected Filby to stand by her in her time of trouble, to marry her despite her father's misfortunes, and to take care of her and Mary. It was simply the way in which things were done in the Kenton family, and Briar—sheltered, pampered—had imagined everyone else was the same.

What an innocent she had been!

Filby had soon ripped that innocence asunder and taught her the cold, harsh reality. He had replied to her desperate message with a blunt refusal. No, he would not ride to Castle Kenton, he would not enter the stronghold of a traitor, and as she was now a traitor by association, he would not marry her.

Bewildered, believing her betrothed had some-how mistaken the matter or did not fully under-stand her dilemma, Briar had stated her intention of riding to Filby. Jocelyn and Odo were at Castle Kenton—Odo so ill he could not leave his cham-ber, and Jocelyn unable to see further than her husband's health. Mary, who had never been asked to do more than smile and embroider, could only stare big-eyed at Briar. Neither of them were of any help.

Briar had felt she had no choice. She had her mare saddled and rode out. To her relief Filby's gate had been opened to allow her entry, but the man who granted her audience was very different from the besotted suitor who had sought her hand.

He was cold. He was unfeeling. He was un-moved.

When her pleading had no effect upon him, in a moment of wild desperation, Briar had offered him her body in exchange for his help. Surely, she had thought in some fevered part of her mind, once he had lain with her, loved her, he would not be able to desert her?

The memory of those short moments with Filby still made Briar curl up and shrivel inside. For he had indeed taken what she offered him, but bru-tally, without conscience or consideration, and it had made not the slightest difference. Filby still abandoned her to her fate, and Briar had ridden home, even more broken than before.

A fortnight later, Filby's men had come to Cas-tle Kenton to make a proclamation. Briar and Mary and Jocelyn had the choice of remaining at the castle and being taken prisoner, locked up until Filby decided what to do with them, or to leave and become formally known as outcasts. Briar, aware of what Filby would make of her if she stayed, chose the latter. Odo, who would once have given his life to protect them, was now unable even to feed himself, and Jocelyn was terrified of what would happen if she remained with him at Castle Kenton.

They had left their past behind them.

The world beyond Castle Kenton was harsh, a foreign land ruled by a Norman king. Without the safety provided by their money and power, they had to rely upon the conquered English folk to stay alive. There was kindness, more than Briar would have believed, but they could not beg forever. They must find an honest way to make money.

It was Mary who had hid her little harp beneath her cloak before she left Castle Kenton, who took to playing for a coin here and there. And then Briar had begun to sing an accompaniment, and found her voice was much admired. One evening, as they sang and played, some of the king's soldiers rode up. Jocelyn and Odo had fled one way, and Mary and Briar had fled the other. After that, the two younger sisters were alone.

They had continued to travel, making their way as best they could, dressing as men for safety. After they reached York, they continued to play and sing, and became sought after. Accordingly, their talent had risen in value. They had begun to sing in the halls of those Norman families where once they might have been guests, and that was how they had been reunited with Jocelyn and Odo, now servants of Lord Shelborne.

No one remembered them; no one wished to, Briar thought bitterly. Lord Kenton was long dead, but who would be foolish enough to claim an acquaintance with a traitor, dead or otherwise? It was almost like being invisible. She sang and entertained, was cheered and feted, but no one really saw her. Comments were made, secrets passed about, and all in her presence as if she were a deaf-mute. It amused her, and angered her, and fed her blind need for vengeance.

For it was vengeance more than anything else that had kept her alive these past months and years. The need to pay Radulf—the great Lord Radulf!—back for what he had done to them. For it was Radulf she blamed. Filby had his place in her black thoughts, but he was dead now, killed in an uprising on his lands. Briar could not revenge herself upon a dead man, and besides, Radulf was the true instigator of their downfall. And when she had heard he was to come to York, she had made her plan.

It was a simple one, and turned on Radulf's lady, Lily. For who had not heard of the special bond of love that existed between Radulf and his lady wife?

Rumor also had it—so said the gossips in the halls where she sang—that Lily would not come north with him. She had been lately brought to bed of a son and was still weak from the birthing. Radulf would come by himself. It was logical that he would be lonely, vulnerable to the charms of a sympathetic woman, an easy target for seduction. It seemed only just that Radulf should fall by the same means he had used to bring about the destruction of Briar's father. So Briar had decided then that she would take away that which he treasured most—the love and trust of his wife.

He would not die, but as Briar well knew, there were worse things than dying.

She had not realized just how easy it would be.

Briar had known, as she had prepared to sing tonight, that Radulf would be in Lord Shelborne's hall. He had been invited—Jocelyn had let slip to her that the messenger had gone out shortly after Radulf arrived in York. Of course he would come—a lonely man, missing his wife, with an opportunity to forget himself in the conversation of others? Aye, he would come.

And she had known something of his appearance. Didn't everyone know what the great Radulf, the King's Sword, looked like? A big, dark man with a brooding gaze. A man who caught the eye and kept it with the mesmerizing quality of his presence.

She had known him at once.

As if it had been meant to be.

Briar combed her fingers through the dark whorls of hair that formed a crucifix on the broad chest of the man beside her. Her body ached and tingled from his use of her—she felt betrayed by her own senses, but there would be time to consider that later. For now, she had what she wanted. Vengeance. How would the Lady Lily enjoy hearing such news? Aye, then she would know how it felt to be betrayed and abandoned, and Radulf would learn what it was to lose all and yet remain breathing.

She had much about which to be pleased, and yet . . .

Briar listened to the heavy thud of the man's heartbeat beneath her cheek, and wondered again why she could not exult. Despite all, the sense of triumph eluded her. Why hadn't the smoldering need for vengeance, that had begun to burn inside her the day her father died, turned to a clear, cleansing flame? If anything, the black smoke was even thicker and more acrid.

She had won!

Why then did she feel as if she had lost?

A big hand covered hers, stilling her when she had begun to tug mindlessly at the hairs on his chest. "You mean to pluck me bald, demoiselle?" he asked her with quiet humor.

Briar lifted her head. He was smiling, and as she gazed at him, she was once more puzzled by her fascination for a face which, taken feature by feature, was not all that fascinating. The broken nose and sharp, angular lines of cheekbones and jaw and brow. The wild, dark hair that was in desperate need of a comb. He was watching her, his black eyes brooding, expectant, secret.

Suddenly Briar felt a senseless, almost unstoppable urge to confess to him what she had done. The words had already begun to thicken her tongue, but she gulped them back, terrified by her own lack of control.

Remember who this is! Remember what he can do to

you! Have you not learned well in the past two years that you can trust no one?

Great men had no hearts, only cold ambition and self-interest. Witness what Radulf and Filby and the king had done to her family.

And what of your father? Was he not a great man? And yet he loved you.

That was true, he had loved her. He was also kind and generous, and see where it had gotten him?

"Demoiselle?" His voice brushed over her skin, making her shiver. "You are deep in thought."

Should she tell him now? How she meant to destroy him? Was it wise to do so, when he had her alone? Best to wait, to choose her moment, to make sure of her own safety first. Men like Radulf, Briar had learned, would not think twice about removing an annoying obstacle in their path. Men like Radulf spoke sweet words, even while they were plotting evil deeds.

"My lord—"

He leaned over her, his mouth smiling, his eyes like dark stars. " 'Tis best I tell you now, lady. I am no lord."

The timid knock on the door was an unwelcome interruption. He was no lord? What did he mean by that? Did he intend to try and hide his identity from her? Mayhap he was already planning when he could use her again . . .

Her heart bumped, and Briar knew to her horror that she wanted him to.

Yes, yes, if you lie with him again you will draw him

*in further! So deep that he will forget where he ends and
you begin, until there is no escape.*

The thought was feverish. Briar did not trust
herself. She wanted him again, aye, but were her
reasons pure? From the moment she saw him in
Lord Shelborne's hall, her body had cried out to
his in a manner that was as old as time. Was that
vengeance? Was that revenge? Nay, surely 'twas
lust and desire!

"Jesu," she whispered in anguish.

Radulf had stiffened at the knock upon the
door, and now he glanced at Briar with a frown
that would have made a lesser woman flinch. He
grasped her in one arm, reaching down with the
other to the floor by the bed, where he had lain his
sword.

"Do not fret," Briar managed, her throat dry.
She tried for a smile and felt her mouth stretch un-
naturally. " 'Tis probably only a servant come to
see whether we are in need of more wine. . . ."

The knock was repeated, louder this time. Not a
servant then, thought Briar. A servant would
never pound upon a door so vigorously. No, this
fist sounded masculine, and large.

"Ivo?" A deep voice, muffled by the wood. "Ivo
de Vessey!"

Briar had opened her mouth to reply that there
was no Ivo de Vessey in here, when Radulf sat up.
He ran his fingers down her arm, and then
cupped her breast in a possessive fashion she
wasn't at all sure she liked, especially when her
nipple perked up in instant response.

"Aye, Sweyn?" shouted her tormentor. "What

do you want? I warn you, you have chosen a most inconvenient time."

The door opened and the owner of the voice peered in. He was tall and fair, a handsome man Briar vaguely remembered seeing standing in the group beside Radulf, in the hall. Sweyn—was that his name?—raised a blond eyebrow as he took in the scene before him. Belatedly Briar ducked behind her lover, using him as a cover for her nakedness.

Ivo smiled, enjoying feeling her warm body and her warm breath upon his bare back. A strand of her hair lay upon his hip, the curled end tickling his thigh. He twined it lazily about his finger, examining the smooth fineness of it.

Sweyn was grinning at him, but Ivo was in no mood to put up with his friend's humor.

"Well?" he demanded in a surly tone.

Ivo had no intention of leaving Briar just yet. Aye, his body was insatiable where she was concerned, but it was the manner in which he satisfied it that surprised him. Not just with a selfish need to take her, although he had enjoyed the taking very much. There was more to it. He had wanted it to last forever, and had brought her again and again to her fulfillment. He had found pleasure and pride in gazing into her hazel eyes as they darkened with desire, flared with surprise, then blurred with ecstasy.

Aye, and she was as surprised by the situation as he. If Ivo was not mistaken, here was a woman who had not known much joy. Her unhappiness made a bond between them, more so than he had felt with any woman for a great many years. He didn't know why she had brought him here, allowed him the use of her inexperienced body and showed him her passion, but he felt a longing to protect her, to keep her from harm, to be her knight. Ivo was not one to believe in fate, but it seemed to him, as he lay with Briar in his arms, that their lives had come together for a reason, a purpose. And before this night was through, he meant to discover what it was.

Unfortunately, Sweyn had other plans.

"We are needed," he said, the humor subdued to a spark in his blue eyes. "You know I wouldn't have disturbed you otherwise, Ivo."

Ivo gave a sullen grunt, followed by a resigned nod of his head. "Aye, 'tis clear you are most upset, Sweyn. Go. I will meet you in the hall."

Sweyn chuckled at his friend's display of bad humor, and closed the door.

During his conversation, Ivo had been aware of Briar's warm presence at his back. Now she was clinging to his shoulders, and her fingers dug into his flesh so hard that her nails were surely drawing blood. Was she so upset that he must leave her? The thought pleased him, and he was gentle as he eased himself away from her nails, and shifted his body on the bed, the better to see her.

She was white, her hazel eyes enormous in her heart-shaped face, and her breasts were rising and falling deliciously fast. Ivo frowned; this was more than a small upset, far more.

"Demoiselle," he said carefully, "I must go. I am

called away by my lord. But I swear to you that I will return—"

"What did he call you? What is your name?" Her voice was low, almost a whisper.

He frowned, puzzled, and reached to touch her cheek. She shook her head desperately, scooting away from him on the rumpled cushions and furs. What was wrong with her? This was beyond strange. The niggling sense of doubt grew within him, and Ivo's frown blackened. 'Twas time they cut through this nonsense, and got to the heart of the matter—he had never been one for prevarication.

He pushed aside the wild tangle of his hair with his black leather glove. "I am Ivo de Vessey," he said with barely concealed impatience. "I am here in the service of Lord Radulf, to put down the skirmish on his northern borders. I was once a Norman knight, demoiselle, but am one no longer. Disgrace has tainted me. Now I fight for coin instead of glory. Is that introduction enough? If you require one after what has taken place in this bed tonight!"

Briar wondered if she was going to scream. She could feel the sound building up inside her, like a roaring tempest in a small room, whirling around and around in the tiny space, and threatening to destroy all within.

I have given myself to the wrong man! She felt little, vulnerable, as she had not felt in two years. Her hatred, her plots, had helped keep her safe from the full extent of her grief and loss, and suddenly, now, she was back in that pit.

I have given myself to the wrong man!

It could not be so. She had been so positive this man was Radulf . . . so *positive* she had recognized him in some elemental way. She had not even thought to ask anyone! This man was Radulf! The dark hair and eyes, the impressive size, his war-like air. Who else could it have been?

Shadows drew in from the corners of the room, fluttering at the edges of her vision. Briar felt close to fainting.

He is not Radulf!

So much plotting and planning, all her dreams of vengeance, all that had kept her going through the long, long weeks and months. She felt herself beginning to crumble, turning to nothing but fine, choking dust. Ashes. She had built herself protective walls of hatred and revenge, keeping herself safe with dreams of what she would do to Radulf when she found him. And now they were falling down, blowing away in the hot wind of disaster.

Sweet Jesu, she had given herself to the wrong man!

Briar was distraught, more shaken than she could ever remember. The grief she had felt when her father died and all was taken from her, when Filby used her and then heartlessly discarded her to her fate, came sweeping over her, fresh and raw as ever. The single-minded dream of vengeance had helped to keep her living and breathing, and now for it to go so terribly, terribly wrong . . .

It was beyond bearing.

Hot and angry tears sprang from her eyes. Forgetting her nakedness, forgetting what they had just done together, Briar rose up on her knees, her hair streaming about her body, and shook her clenched fists in his face.

"No, no! It cannot be, I do not believe it! You are Radulf, say you are! I wanted Radulf in my bed, Radulf's body in mine. 'Tis a trick, a lie, yes, yes, it must be a lie!"

He looked shocked, but almost at once he was reaching for her, trying to subdue her. Briar would not be subdued. She struck out at him, screaming wildly and struggling, until he covered her mouth with his hand and held her fast against his big body. Still she squirmed and wriggled and cried, but now her sounds were muffled and her movements were hampered by his great strength.

"Demoiselle," he said, trying to penetrate the fit that had come upon her. There was agony in her cries, a pain that went deep. Ivo knew pain, he understood it, and he wanted to understand what was happening with Briar. "Tell me what ails you, lady! Hush, you are safe, you are safe with me . . ."

And then, as the meaning of her words finally became clear, he frowned down at her and said more sharply, "Did you seek to lure *Radulf* to your bed? Lady, he would never come. He is in thrall to his wife, how could you not know that? Everyone knows that! Come, come, compose yourself. What is Lord Radulf to you? Will I not do instead? For truly, my angel, I am more than willing to lie with you again. We two were made to be one."

It was true. Never had Ivo lain with a woman who gave him more pleasure, who had so easily found a place in his mind and his senses. Already

Ivo felt the desire stir anew at the thought of having her, even though his angel had turned into a wildcat. Strangely, he was not jealous. What they had experienced together was too remarkable. Whatever this nonsense with Radulf meant, he would untangle it to his own advantage.

She had stilled, suddenly, and now lay limp in his embrace. Carefully, watching for signs of a renewal of her mad struggles, Ivo removed his hand from over her mouth and, when she said not a word, eased his grip on her. She was unmoving in his arms, shuddering off and on, as if she were very cold. And yet she did not feel cold.

Musingly, Ivo gazed down at her. Here was a woman who had been hurt in some way—mayhap not physically, but nevertheless she had been injured. He sensed it, tasted it, recognized it. Gently, he smoothed back her hair, so that he could better see her face. It was white and drawn, and tears leaked through the spiky clumps of her dark lashes, oozing down her cheeks. Ah, such pain, such anguish, was etched into her sweet features! Ivo felt his heart squeeze with tender feelings he had long thought beyond him.

She had brought them back to life again. After all these years, she had jolted his frozen heart into a response. Ivo did not know whether to be furious with her, or grateful. In truth, he was bewildered, and feared he would soon be more so. Was it true what they had said, then, that this woman could heal a sick man and make a broken man whole?

Time to think of that later. Just now it was clear that there was something very wrong with the lady Briar, and Ivo must do his best to discover what it was.

"Demoiselle," he said gently, "do not grieve. Whatever saddens you so, I will help you to overcome it."

He meant it, more than he had ever meant anything in his life, but she shook her head and her mouth turned down.

"You cannot," she said. "No one can. I am truly lost."

"No, angel, you are not lost. I have found you and you are not lost." He bent and kissed her lips, tasting the salt of her tears.

Slowly she responded, her lips opening on a sigh, the heat coursing through her. He deepened the kiss; he could not help it. Her body pressed against him and he groaned, his hand sliding down her soft belly to the juncture of her thighs. In response, her arms tightened around his waist, drawing him closer. He moved over her, the head of his manhood probing her entrance.

"You are not lost," he whispered again, running quick hot kisses across her breasts, before drawing her nipple deep into his mouth.

She arched with a moan of sheer pleasure. The tears were still wet on her cheeks, but her pain had been forgotten, or at least put aside, by her need for him. Ivo looked down at her in wonder, amazed he had turned her so easily from agony to ecstasy. With a practiced thrust, he entered her, smoothly and fully.

Her eyes opened wide.

"Briar," he murmured, and smiled.

Dazed, she smiled back at him, gasping as he

thrust again, deeper this time, but slowly, carefully. Her fingers crept up his arms, clinging to
him as his muscles shifted and tightened, feeling
the tension in him as he held himself back, moving so tenderly, so gently.

Time stood still, as he drowned in her eyes.

And then passion caught them unawares, and
she cried out, her mouth hot against his throat as
his hips pumped harder and faster, seeking obliv-
ion. Afterward, he wrapped his arms about her,
tucking her safely to his side, as the tremors eased.

*The hound barked. The child cried. "Briar! Sweet
Jesu, she is hurt!" The boy reached the little girl first,
bending to help her back onto her uncertain feet. Blood
trickled down one side of her plump, baby face, mingling with hot, angry tears. The child gazed up at him
with a trembling lip, hazel eyes deep and solemn. And
in that instant Ivo, himself only nine years old, lost his
heart.*

The memory was there, fully formed in his
head. Amazed, Ivo stared down at the sated
woman in his arms.

"Briar," he breathed. " 'Tis Briar."

It was as if her name in his mouth pulled her
from her voluptuous exhaustion. Briar's dark
lashes lifted, her hazel eyes opened very wide.
She stared at him blankly, and then with a small
scream, she sat up. A knee in his side, an elbow in
his chest, and she had launched herself across the
bed, away from him, wiping the back of her hand
across her mouth as if he were foul.

"Go, go!" she screamed, and pointed to the
door. She dragged herself to the very end of the
bed, her body trembling, her face still swollen and

tear-streaked. "I do not want you to touch me again! I . . . I cannot think when you touch me. Go now! And never return, Ivo de Vessey. Never!"

Ivo hesitated. He had been about to tell her what he had remembered, but short of holding her physically captive . . . And he did not think she would look upon him kindly if he pinned her down and shouted at her. Nay, it was plain she was not to be reasoned with, not now, not in this state. Whatever had upset her, it was not something she would confide to him, not tonight.

Now that Ivo knew who she was, there was time to consider. Aye, he must think hard on this before he took any further steps. Better that he go, as she demanded. He would think on what he had learned, and resume this business later. Besides, Sweyn had said they were wanted, and Ivo knew he had neglected his duty as long as he dared.

With a little shrug, he began to dress, hastily pulling up his breeches and slipping his shirt and tunic over his head. All the while she crouched upon the bed, shaking, her face turned so far from him that he could see the strained cords of her neck. As if the sight of him was acutely painful to her. Or repulsive.

Ivo was not insulted. He knew she had felt no such thing earlier. She had wanted him; she had enjoyed what he did to her. He had felt her body tremble in release, had tasted her desire. He knew it to the marrow of his bones. Aye, she had wanted him. Whatever was wrong now was not because of that. For some inexplicable reason she had imagined him to be Radulf—he remembered now that she had not asked him for his name. Why was

his being Radulf so important to her? He did not
believe she was the sort to be fascinated by a man
because of his wealth and power, the sort who
would give herself to a man just for what he could
give her materially.

Mayhap he was being a fool for trusting a
woman he did not know, except for some childhood memory . . . And yet, he could not, *would*
not, let her go. He remembered again the way she
had looked up at him as he took her, the trusting,
dreaming expression in her eyes. She had not held
back; there had been no deceit in her desire for
him, whatever her lips might say. And she had let
him take her that last time, even when she knew
he was *not* Radulf.

Aye, there was much here to think on.

She had given him back his heart—for better or
worse, he did not know yet. Nay, he would not
desert her now, just as he had not deserted her on
that long ago day when she received her scar. His
decision was made, burnt into his flesh, like the
remembrance of her touch.

"Farewell, demoiselle." He turned to her at last,
fully dressed, and strapped his sword about his
hips. The two green stones gleamed dully in the
sputtering candlelight; they were the eyes of the
snarling creature, half beast and half bird, that
had been fashioned into the hilt. A griffin. It was
his family emblem, and he had received and worn
it with great pride when he became a knight.

Long ago, long gone.

She may have brought his heart back to life, but
she could not give Ivo back that burning sense of

self-worth and pride he had felt when he was made a knight. Could she?

Briar had not answered his farewell. Instead she continued to tremble against the bed where they had just made love. He watched her a moment more, and his newly revived heart ached for her. *You are mine, now.* The words were on the tip of his tongue, but Ivo was too wise to speak them. Women were strange creatures, and sometimes 'twas best just to leave them be.

Ivo closed the door softly behind him.

Briar held her breath, but his footsteps moved away, faded into the echoes of music and laughter from the hall. She collapsed into the furs, her body going limp, and sobbed her heartache in hot, scalding tears. The aching silence was filled with her pain. Anger, too. She was angry with herself for making such a blunder, and with Ivo de Vessey for not making her aware of that blunder, and with Radulf for not being where he should be. But most of all she felt despair, because she feared she would never be able to carry out her plan now. She had set her mind to seduce Radulf, and instead had lain with Ivo de Vessey, who by his own tongue was a disgraced knight and a mercenary.

And she had lain with him again, after he had told her who he was.

How could she have been so foolish?

But something about Ivo de Vessey had called to her, drawn her in like a bee to poison nectar. Aye, a willing victim! She had believed he was Radulf. She had *wanted* to believe it, she realized now, because she had felt an instant attraction to him. More than that—a meeting of flesh and blood, bodies and minds, such as she had only heard of in songs. She had never looked for such a thing to happen to her; her mind had been too full of dark dreams of vengeance. Was that dream over now? How could she seek out Radulf and seduce him after Ivo de Vessey?

Briar groaned aloud.

Her tears had stopped, and she swallowed down any lingering sobs. This situation was even graver than she had first thought. It had only just occurred to her how grave. The fact that her joining with Ivo had not been unpleasant, or degrading, or in any way like the brief moments with Filby—that it had been one of the most wondrous nights of her life, rung a desperate warning peal in her mind.

Briar groaned again and covered her flushed, swollen face with her shaking hands. *No, no, no!* She needed to be calm and cold and single-minded. She could not lust after a stranger, a man who had no part in her life, or her dreams of vengeance. He was nothing to her, and so it must remain. How could she continue to survive if it were otherwise?

Impatiently, Briar brushed the tears from her cheeks. Jocelyn had been right, she had not considered the consequences of her action, and now they seemed particularly dire. She had lain with Ivo de Vessey and made a bond with him, and even if she tried to sever that bond, she sensed Ivo would fight to stop her.

No, angel, you are not lost. I have found you.

He had held her with such tenderness, such concern, feelings she would never have imagined such a big, warlike man could possess. And then he had kissed her again, and even after she knew he was not Radulf, she had kissed him back. She had let him touch her. Lie upon her and enter her body with his. Aye, when she should have been cold as rock toward him, she had melted and burned and sobbed with desire.

Briar's breath quickened, and she closed her eyes and squeezed her hands into fists. No, no, she could not think of it now. Her mind was a whirling mass of confusion, and her throat was raw from crying. The grief she had thought long past her had returned, and as for her dreams of vengeance . . . Because of her wild lovemaking and her wild regrets, Briar had hardly enough strength remaining to dress herself, let alone consider what to do about the ruin of her plan.

Mary.

She must fetch Mary, and take her home.

The thought of her sister stilled the chaos inside her, and helped restore Briar to some semblance of the strong and resilient woman she had believed herself to be. Wearily, she used the bedding to mop at her face, ignoring the signs of passion. A vision of his naked body, lying upon the furs, strong-limbed and hard-muscled, languorous from their lovemaking, filled her mind like a warm breeze on a cold night. She banished it.

Mary would be worrying. Briar would make up some story—mayhap she had had a private audience for her songs? A widow, grieving for her one true love, who had wished to hear her sing in pri-

vate. Mary would believe her, and they would go
on as they had before.

Well, not quite. Briar wondered, miserably, if
she would ever be as she was before. Ivo de
Vessey had changed her, she wasn't sure just how,
but she knew it was so. Like a bolt of dark lightning he had split the old Briar asunder. And she
was very much afraid the change was forever.

"Was she as sweet as she looked?"

Ivo ignored Sweyn, kicking his horse into a gal-
lop through the still, moonlit streets of York. The
sky was clear and starry, a wondrous arc above,
and he wished suddenly he could show it to Briar.
It had been long since Ivo had wanted to share
anything with a woman, and the realization gave
him pause.

"Did she sing to you?" Sweyn would not stop
his teasing.

Ivo made an impatient sound. "What she and I
did is private between us. You said we were
wanted, what did you mean?" He had not even
thought to ask until now, being otherwise occupied.

"Radulf sent word."

Ivo frowned, thinking of this. The King's Sword
had been in a foul mood ever since they left
Crevitch. 'Twas rumored he had wanted to bring
his wife, Lily, but with her baby son so new she
had not felt it wise to come. Ivo did not blame her
for preferring the safety and comfort of Crevitch
Castle to a horse's back. But mayhap Radulf did
not quite see it that way.

"Radulf did not say what he wanted?"

"No, lackwit. That is what we go to find out."

Ivo scowled at his friend, but Sweyn only gave him a grin in return. Sweyn was one of the most even-tempered men he knew. Nothing ever rumpled his good humor. Ivo, passionate and with a temper uneven at best, found that being in Sweyn's company could be extremely difficult at times.

"I was not supposed to come north," he grumbled now.

"Aye, 'twas Gunnar Olafson who was meant to come," Sweyn pretended to sympathize. "But he got himself wed to Lady Rose of Somerford Manor, and so you came in his stead. Think you he should have left the lady alone in the chapel, to ride up to York? So that you could remain at Crevitch and sulk?"

"I am not sulking."

"No? Then what ails you, Ivo? You should be glad you came to York. If you had not, you wouldn't have heard the angel sing."

That was true. "The angel," however, was going to be a bigger problem than he had first imagined. Briar, daughter of Lord Richard Kenton, wealthy and powerful baron, traitor, and dead by his own hand.

He looked up at the sky again. It was a long, long time since he had yearned for a woman. He had learned at an early age that love was not wise, that it could be twisted and mangled, and that sometimes it hurt so unbearably it was like dying inside and yet continuing to breathe. Since then, he had tried not to love. Of course, it could be a difficult task to keep your heart encased in iron,

and Ivo was a passionate man. He had made
friends, good friends, like Gunnar Olafson and
Sweyn. But he had loved no woman, wanted no
woman, beyond fulfilling the more basic of his
urges. He had needed no woman to make him feel
whole.

Until now.

Ivo tried not to groan aloud. What was wrong
with him that he coveted Briar, with her big hurt
eyes and hot needy mouth? When he had every
reason to be suspicious and wary of her? Why did
he have this terrible, intense desire to play the
chivalrous knight for her? When he knew, better
than anyone, that his days as a knight were long
dead.

Chapter 3

"**B**riar?"

Briar blinked. Her body felt heavy, and she didn't want to move from the soft furs that cradled her. She had been dreaming of hard, strong arms and sharp pleasures, and the images lingered in her mind. With a sigh, she opened her eyes.

The room was dark, apart from the wavering light of a candle at the door. The shapes and spaces around her were unfamiliar. She sat up, her body protesting, and looked about her. *Where am I?* And then she remembered. *Jesu!* She was in one of Lord Shelborne's chambers! A moment, that was all it had taken. She had closed her eyes, briefly, readying herself to go and find Mary and take her home, and . . .

I must have fallen asleep.

"Briar?"

She peered through her tangled hair, her eyes still tender from crying. The bleary candlelight by the door flared, showing Jocelyn's face and, behind her, the young maid, Grisel.

Jocelyn spoke over her shoulder. "You may go now, Grisel."

Grisel, eyes huge in the trickle of light, bobbed a shaky curtsy and scuttled away into the darkness.

The silence was profound.

Briar brushed her hair out of her face and smoothed her gown down. Her mind was working again, but slowly, creakily, like an old waterwheel. She set her shoulders in preparation for a scene.

Jocelyn moved forward, the candle wavering before her. A tall and stately woman, she looked very much the daughter of Lord Kenton and a very unlikely cook. Briar knew her sister, although normally even-tempered, did have a temper. Perhaps not the fiery, quick temper that was Briar's, but a temper nevertheless.

"When you didn't come to fetch Mary I realized what you had done. Grisel was behaving so guiltily, 'twas a simple matter to make her tell me."

She didn't *sound* angry, yet, but it was difficult to tell with Jocelyn—she held her emotions inside. Unlike Briar, who sparked with them like steel striking stone.

"I will come now. I—I fell asleep—"

Jocelyn was beside the bed now, the candle flame reflected in her blue eyes. Briar could see the knowledge, as if it were written there.

She knew.

Briar told herself she should stand up hotly for what she had done—wasn't she seeking vengeance for them *all*, not just herself? But right now she was simply too beaten, too exhausted to justify herself to her sister. In truth, Briar, who was usually so independent and so headstrong, felt as if something vital inside her had shattered.

As if sensing her weakness, Jocelyn pressed her advantage, her voice trembling now with anger.

"I have learned that you gave a private audience to a man, Briar. Are you going to tell me about it? I know 'twas not Radulf. He did not come to the hall tonight. Rumor has it he was missing his wife, and stayed away."

"Please, do not—"

"Aye, please do! You brought a man here, sister. You tricked Grisel into preparing this chamber for you, telling the simple wench some lying tale! And all the time you meant to bring Radulf here— it *was* Radulf you had set your sights on, wasn't it? You asked after him so many times, I cannot be mistaken in that. I was a fool not to realize you had not given up your foolish plot, Briar. Who was here with you? Tell me!"

Resigned, Briar said, "He was one of Radulf's men. His name was Ivo de Vessey. He was tall and dark-haired, and I thought . . . I thought I recognized him." Tears stung her eyes, but she blinked them back. "I *thought* he was Radulf."

Jocelyn made a sound like a groan. "I told you to take care, Briar. I warned you to leave well alone. 'Tis Filby all over again."

Briar shook her head slowly, back and forth.

Her blue eyes wide now with worry, Jocelyn

caught her sister's chin to hold her still, the candle dipping wildly in her other hand. "You destroy yourself with your own hatred, Briar! Now what have you done? This man, did he hurt you?"

Briar swallowed. "No, he did not hurt me."

Jocelyn stared at her a moment, blankly. Under her gaze, the color crept slowly, tellingly, into Briar's face. Jocelyn frowned, then stepped back awkwardly. "I do not understand you."

Briar felt her cheeks burn even hotter. "This man, this Ivo de Vessey, he was not like Filby."

Jocelyn continued to gaze at her as if she were mad, and then realization made her catch her breath. "You liked what he did to you."

"Whether I liked it or not is irrelevant—"

"You liked it! Dear God, I should be horrified, but instead I am strangely glad. You are safe and unharmed, and this man . . . But what is it, Briar? You are different. Something in you has changed."

Briar turned away. "It was the wrong man," she whispered in anguish. "I meant to punish Radulf for all he has done to us, and instead . . . I failed us all."

"You mistake me," Jocelyn said, more gently. "I am not angry with you, well . . . I was. Sister, I have always regretted not stopping you from going to Filby. He was callous and unfeeling, and he wounded you deeply. I never did like him. If Odo had not been so ill, and I had not had other thoughts to fill my head, I would have stopped you. Instead you went off in your own headstrong way, certain you could change the mind of such a man. Briar, we cannot always change the way of the world, just because we wish to. Surely tonight has shown you that, if nothing else?"

"I admit I have made a mistake," Briar replied bluntly. Tears tightened her throat, but she tried to swallow them back down. "I-I don't know what to do."

The admission sapped her limited strength, and she slumped down upon the bed, covering her face with trembling hands. "I don't know what to do," she repeated with all the bewilderment of a wounded child. "I thought it would feel so good that I had succeeded at last, but I felt . . . empty. I had stolen Radulf from his wife, just as he stole Anna from our father, and it was *right* and *just*. But instead I felt tainted. And then I learned the man I had lain with was not even Radulf! I had let the wrong man use my body. I had given myself to the wrong man and achieved nothing!"

"Oh Briar—"

"No, no, you were right. Even though it was not Radulf, and I realized my ridiculous mistake, I knew then that I had *wanted* Radulf to be this man because I was . . . he was . . . Jocelyn, you were right. I *did* like what we did. He made me feel such things! He was like no other man. But then I realized that, being with him, had ruined everything. I cannot even think of . . . of . . . with Radulf. Not now. And my plot, my vengeance, is all broken up and confused in my mind. What will I do? I feel such pain, such emptiness and loss. Jocelyn, if I cannot honor my father by defeating his enemy, what am I to do?"

Jocelyn wrapped her arms around Briar and

held her tightly as she wept. The sobs were painful to hear, but Jocelyn felt only relief. Briar had held herself aloof for so long, ever since they left Castle Kenton. She had professed her hatred and sought her revenge, but it had been a barricade behind which she hid from the stark truth—that nothing could ever be the same again. And now that barricade seemed to have suffered some major damage.

Was that the doing of this man? This Ivo de Vessey? Had he breached her sister's defenses when all else had failed? Or was it simply that, now that Briar's plot had fallen in a heap, she found herself at a crossroads she had never faced before? To go on hating, as she had for two years, or to strike out in a new direction.

Whatever the case, Jocelyn felt that Ivo de Vessey deserved her gratitude.

"Will you see him again?" she asked quietly.

Her sister lifted her ravaged face and gave her a wild look. "Nay, I must not! I must never see him again!"

Jocelyn hugged her closer, her mind working. Clearly Briar was suffering, but if this Ivo de Vessey had wrought one miracle, he may be able to perform another.

"Tell me about him," she said coaxingly. "Humor me. What was he like? I worry, Briar, that this man had not seen a woman for some time. You are fair; he probably could not believe his good luck. Was that all there was to it?"

Briar snuggled down against her sister's shoulder. She had not been held like this since she was a child, and it felt good. Was Jocelyn right? she wondered. Was it that Ivo had merely been eager for a woman, and any woman would do? But if that were the case, would he have held her so tenderly? Would he have kissed her mouth as if it were all he had ever wanted? Called her his angel? And, come to think of it, he had not looked like the sort of man who would have any trouble finding a woman for his bed. Nay, he had not thrown himself onto her like a starving man a loaf of bread! He had held back, kept his passion in check until she had reached her own peak. Were they the actions of an oaf who cared nothing for the needs of women?

"He was a knight, once," she said at last, softly, as if she were confiding something rare and sweet. "He is no unlearned fool, Jocelyn. He speaks well, and his mind is sharp and clever. He acts like a noble, although now he is disgraced and fights for coin to feed himself—even so, much of his past remains."

"I see. Do you think he is smitten with you? Or is he weak-minded? Aye, why else did he fall into disgrace. Mayhap he is easily corrupted?"

Briar shook her head. "I don't know if he is smitten or not. He . . . he enjoyed what we did. He said he had found me and I think he will not easily let me go. And weak-minded or easily corrupted? Nay, I think not."

"Better and better."

The satisfaction in Jocelyn's voice made Briar search her face. Her sister's eyes were gleaming in a manner rare these days.

"You lay with the wrong man," Jocelyn explained patiently, "but you may turn that to your advantage."

"What do you mean? I told you, I must never see him again."

"You say this Ivo de Vessey is one of Radulf's men? Isn't that what you want? A way into Radulf's camp. Mayhap you can bend this Ivo de Vessey to your will?"

Briar frowned, remembering how he had subdued her with his great strength and kissed her into passion. Bend *him* to *her* will? Could she resist him? Could she gain the upper hand? And even if she could, did the determination to fulfil her vow still exist within her?

"You mean I could use him to get at Radulf?" Briar asked suspiciously. This did not make sense; Jocelyn was always trying to talk her out of her plots, not into new ones.

Jocelyn was nodding enthusiastically. "But he would need to be very enamored of you. So desirous of your body that he would be willing to do anything for you. Do you believe you could make this man so crazed with lust that he would be your willing slave, Briar?"

Did she? The thought of trying caused a treacherous warmth to curl in the pit of her stomach. Guiltily, Briar glanced at Jocelyn, in time to see her sister's half smile of satisfaction.

"I do not understand why you are trying to help me now, when all along you have tried to stop me taking revenge on Radulf."

Jocelyn looked innocent. "Mayhap I think your mind needs to take a new direction, sister."

Briar did not feel convinced. The idea was a good one; it was the motive behind it that concerned her.

"You liked him," Jocelyn said. "I can see it in your face when you speak of him. You talk of plots and vengeance, but I wonder if your liking for this man will overcome your obsession for what is over and done, and now cannot be undone. I pray 'tis so, Briar, for your sake."

"My obsession? I plotted for us *all*, sister. We all deserve justice. You, Mary, our father, and Anna."

"Aye, Anna." Jocelyn looked away, watching as wax rolled down the stub of candle. "Mayhap justice has been done, Briar, and you just cannot see it. I want to forget what happened. I am not like you."

This time when the silence stretched on, neither of them broke it.

Briar took a deep breath. She was beginning to throw off her depression; she was never one to allow her mind to remain stagnant for long. 'Twas true, she told herself now, her original plan to hurt Radulf was ruined, but Jocelyn's idea had merit, no matter what her hidden motive may be. Mayhap it was possible, after all, to pick up those shattered pieces . . .

Briar remembered again the sensation of his warm, strong arms about her, and his mouth seeming to steal her very soul as he kissed her. There had been an intensity between them, a clashing and melding of minds and bodies. If he had felt the same as she, then *he* would seek *her* out again.

And then all I have to do is make him so crazed with lust, he will turn traitor for me.

And then what? Steal up on Radulf with an assassin's dagger? Briar shuddered at the thought. Well, she would think of something when the time came. She always did.

The structure appeared sound, but the foundations needed some work. Briar had been fully prepared to martyr herself, to suffer to achieve her revenge. Indeed, suffering and martyrdom had been an integral part of her plan. This new Jocelyn-inspired plot seemed far too much like pleasure-seeking. Where was the pain in making Ivo de Vessey desire her? The very thought of it sent shivers of anticipation through her.

Jocelyn was watching her again, her eyes sharp, but when she spoke her voice was gentle. "You are tired. Sleep in my bed tonight, there is room enough for Mary, too. I will go to the stables with Odo—it will be like old times."

Briar wanted to protest, but weariness was stealing her ability to argue. She allowed Jocelyn to lead her from the chamber and down the dark, cold passage toward the kitchen.

When Briar and Mary were settled, Jocelyn stood a moment and gazed upon them.

They are young, despite all their hardship. I feel old in comparison. My burdens are so heavy, my back feels bowed, but I do not begrudge them. How can I? Sometimes love is the heaviest burden of all.

She smiled. Briar had looked so woebegone, so bereft. She had needed a new scheme to see her through her anguish, and Jocelyn had found it for her. Briar could not know that it was her happiness that Jocelyn was really plotting. This man, this Ivo de Vessey, had spun her sister like a top. If Jocelyn could throw them together, grow that tiny spark into something more lasting, mayhap Briar could finally put away her destructive dreams of revenge.

For all their sakes.

Ivo woke to Sweyn's snores and a chorus of dawn birdsong. He had only had a couple of hours' sleep, and they had been restless, but still he rose and began to dress. Sweyn would think him scrambled in the head when he knew where he was going.

Ivo and Sweyn and the rest of Radulf's men had spent much of the night discussing the situation in the north. Matters were grim, according to one of Lady Lily's vassals, who had ridden hard to reach York when he had learned Lord Radulf was coming. The vassal informed them that a large band of Scots had crossed the border to join with the rebels. They were ravaging the land—already much depleted by previous rebellions—to feed themselves, and seemed intent upon carnage. Plans had to be made to fight them, support had to be gained from other barons and vassals, and all as swiftly as possible. This small skirmish now had the capacity to expand into another full-blown war in the north.

Ivo had listened to the talk of fighting and death, and all the while he was aware of the ache in his heart. The heart Briar had stripped bare of its shield, made vulnerable again. And he knew, foolish as it was, that he could not go north without saying farewell to her.

"We are leaving as soon as Radulf has broken his fast and written a letter to his lady."

It was Sweyn, sitting up on his mattress, his bare chest gleaming in the pale light. He was eyeing Ivo with weary amusement.

"You must be here when we go, Ivo."

"I will be. I need to speak with her. To tell her."

"To tell her what? That you bedded her and enjoyed her? What else is there to say? 'Twas one night, Ivo. Let it go now. Move on. 'Tis the way of men like us. We do not settle, we do not grow fond of any woman, for we may be dead on the morrow."

Ivo looked grim. "Do you think I do not know that better than any man, Sweyn?"

"But still you need to speak with her?" Sweyn shook his head, and for once he was not smiling. "Beware, Ivo."

Ivo knew that Sweyn was right, but being right was not enough to stop him. How could he explain to his friend that the need to see her again was stronger than the clear knowledge that she could hurt him?

Instead of sleeping, he had been remembering the past. Replaying that brief memory over and over again in his mind. And wondering why she had wanted him to be Radulf. Obviously there were reasons for what she had done. And still he could not forget how she had clung to him, given herself to him, *after* she knew who he really was.

That made all the difference.

Ivo strapped on his sword. The need to see her was twisting inside him, and if he did not give in to it before he left York, he would not have a moment's peace while he did his work under Radulf's banner. He had to tell her where he was going and why, he had to make her believe he meant to return. He could not ride away and leave her thinking their moments together were nothing more to him than a soldier's lust.

And what of the rest? Will you tell her that you know who she is?

That was more difficult.

Ivo was well aware that those tied by blood to Lord Kenton were traitors by association. Bringing her demons into the light might help her. Or she may turn from him. Mayhap 'twas better to wait. He did not want her to push him away—she had seemed so desperate last night, so alone. He didn't want her to be alone anymore. The chivalrous knight in him—the part of him he had thought dead—would simply not allow it.

I should know better, he thought.

But this new, frightening need to protect, to comfort, to hold Briar outweighed Ivo's slender stock of caution.

Briar opened her eyes.

Sometimes, even now, she still awoke and thought she was at Castle Kenton. That when she rose she could gaze out at the mist-sodden moors, and the day would stretch comfortably before her. That nothing had changed.

And then she would remember, and grieve all over again.

But this morning was different.

At first Briar didn't understand why. Where had this sense of lightness come from? This sense of something new, of something anticipated.

Puzzled, she drew the curtain a little, and peered from her shadowy bed, set into the thick wall of the kitchen, out into the room itself. A young maid with tangled hair raked the burning coals from the oven, leaving it hot enough for the baking of the day's batch of bread. Another girl kneaded the dough for the loaves, while at the same time keeping an uneasy eye on the big man who sat at the far end of the table, his shoulders hunched and his head bowed as if he were asleep.

Odo.

All was as it should be. She was curled up with Mary in the bed that was Jocelyn's, because last night Jocelyn had insisted she and Mary remain here rather than walk home in the dark and the cold. And for once Briar had been too overcome to argue.

Her mind probed cautiously at memories of the scene in the bedchamber, finding pain and confusion, but acceptance, too. She knew now she would never be able to take the real Radulf to her bed—the idea sickened her, as if it were a betrayal. Mayhap it was. To do such a thing would go against her own strong sense of right and wrong. Was Jocelyn correct, did the end not always justify the means?

Has Ivo de Vessey made me understand this? Has he immersed himself so deeply within me, and in such a short time?

Briar remembered the way he had looked at her, so intense, as if he was seeing everything about her there was to see. Those black eyes of his had made her feel wrung out, invaded, turned upside down. As if he saw *her*, the real Briar. It was not a comfortable sensation.

Had he also read in her eyes the real reason she had taken him to that chamber?

Briar hoped not. He had been puzzled by her behavior at the end, but before that he had been well pleased. He had held her and called her angel. Aye, there was still a chance she could turn last night to her advantage, turn failure into success. Jocelyn was right. Mistake or not, Ivo de Vessey *was* Radulf's man.

Ivo de Vessey could be the key that opened the door into Radulf's world.

Was vengeance not entirely dead to her, then? Could she resurrect that all-consuming desire to make one man pay for their suffering? Briar had told Jocelyn last night that she had meant to see justice done for all of them, and so she had. Briar had been arrogant and single-minded enough to believe that what she was doing was important. Jocelyn may want to bury her head in the sand, put the past behind her, as she was so fond of saying, but Briar could not forgive. Radulf had wronged them, and so he should pay. Oh, not in the way she had meant him to pay last night. That was unthinkable. But she *could* use Ivo de Vessey, follow Jocelyn's advice.

Make him crazy with lust for you? Make him want you?

The voice in her head was sly and knowing; Briar was grateful when Jocelyn noticed she was awake and interrupted it.

"You are feeling better?"

Jocelyn had come to stand beside her husband. Her wiry dark hair hung in a long plait down her slim back, her sharp blue gaze shifted from Briar to rest upon Odo's bent head, and softened with love and devotion. Jocelyn was a striking woman, her features strong rather than pretty, except when she looked upon Odo—*then* she was beautiful.

"Aye, Jocelyn, I am better now." Different, though, in a manner she was yet to explain to herself satisfactorily. But there was no need for Jocelyn to know that.

Her sister nodded and, brushing her fingers lightly on Odo's shoulder as she passed, poured some milk from a jug into a wooden bowl. She brought the bowl over to Briar and handed it to her. Mary slept on, her dark lashes brushing her pale cheeks, her fingers curled like a child's against her lips. At seventeen years, Mary was more than old enough to have been married and have children of her own—girls in their privileged world were often betrothed as babies. But Briar still thought of Mary as the little sister who must be cosseted; mayhap she always would.

"You seem more like your old self," Jocelyn said, and then lowered her voice so the servants could not hear. "Are you still determined to go on with this foolishness?"

" 'Tis not foolishness. This time the idea was yours, sister, and it was a good one."

Jocelyn grinned like a young girl. "It was, wasn't it?"

Briar's eyes narrowed.

Jocelyn went on. "You needed your dark plot. It was what kept you alive, Briar. I know that. But 'tis true, I think the time has come for you to put it aside and get on with your life. Mayhap this Ivo de Vessey will help you to do that."

Frustration and anger filled Briar. "My life is vengeance; 'tis what I live for!" she said. But even as she spoke the familiar words, the doubts were circling like birds of prey.

Beside her, Mary yawned and stretched, and turned over onto her back. She rubbed her eyes, her voice husky from sleep. "I dreamed I was home, Briar. And everything that has happened to us, *that* was the dream."

"Oh, Mary," whispered Briar, moisture stinging her eyes. Jesu, she had not cried so much in years. Irritated at her own lack of control over her emotions, she bit her lip and forced back the tears.

Jocelyn's brisk voice dispelled the gloom. "I have milk for you to drink, and soon the bread will be baked. You can feast before you go." As she spoke she set about pouring another, larger bowl of milk for Odo, setting it by the big man. Once he would have turned and smiled at his wife, taken her hand in his, kissed her fingers. Now he made no movement toward her, nor gave any sign that he even knew anyone else was in the room.

Briar remembered Odo from before, big and hearty, always with a smile on his face. He had stood by their father, and if he had not been so ill when Lord Kenton rebelled against the king, mayhap things would have turned out differently. Odo would never have let his father-by-marriage commit so hasty an act, or risk so much. Odo would have made him wait, until emotion had cooled, until any decision made could be made with a clear head. And then, if Lord Richard had still wanted to take such a grave step, then Odo would have led his army.

Aye, Odo had always been a good and loyal man. 'Twas a pity Jocelyn's husband should have been reduced to this. Surely even death was preferable to being a broken shell without a mind? Although Briar did not think Jocelyn would agree—for Jocelyn, even this empty creature with Odo's face and body was better than no husband at all.

"Will Lord Shelborne mind our feasting on his bread?" Mary asked.

Jocelyn shrugged and spoke with some of the old Kenton arrogance. "I care not what Lord Shelborne minds."

Briar smiled.

Jocelyn ignored her and held the bowl of milk to Odo's lips, murmuring encouragement to him as if he were a babe.

After Odo had been struck down by his illness, he had lost the ability to speak, nor did he understand what others said to him. And one side of his face had lost all movement, sagging like dead flesh, while the same side of his body no longer moved to his command but jerked and stuttered as if Odo were now a puppet with strings. Gradually body movement had returned, but his face remained fixed and his gaze empty; the Odo of old was gone.

Mary and Briar rose and washed their faces in the warm water provided. Then they dressed behind the screen stretched across the corner, smoothing their crumpled clothing as best they could before they pulled on their well-worn stockings and shoes. And all the time, the kitchen maids continued with their tasks, as if the Kenton sisters did not exist.

It was apt, thought Briar. Because in many ways it was true that they did not exist, not any longer. And that was why the past sometimes seemed like a dream to them all. Briar remembered the comfortable wealth of Castle Kenton, with its newly built stone keep and strong wooden barricades, and before that, the house in Normandy where they had lived together. When she thought of those times, it was as if they had happened to someone else.

Her mother was even more of a dream. She had died when Briar was a child, shortly after Mary was born. Her father had remained alone, until he had wed Lady Anna, in Normandy. Briar had not known her stepmother well, but she had found her amusing company, and certainly she was very beautiful. Once they were in England, Anna and Richard had often been away in London at court, or else in York. Anna preferred gaiety and gossip to the isolation of Castle Kenton, where Briar and Mary had spent much of their time. Sometimes Jocelyn and Odo had stayed, too, but more often they were busy overseeing Richard's estates.

84

Their father had trusted Odo to stand in his shoes, while he himself kept his beautiful wife happy.

They had been privileged.

Why was it that one only realized the full extent of one's good fortune when it was lost?

"Where were you last night?"

Mary was combing her long dark hair, but her curious gaze was fixed upon Briar.

"I was asked to sing privately."

"Oh." Mary frowned for a moment as if she would ask more questions, and then smiled wistfully instead. "You sing so beautifully, Briar. I once overheard it said that your voice could heal the sick."

Briar laughed bitterly. "I am become a holy relic! Mayhap the desperate will take pilgrimages to my door."

"You should be thankful for such a gift." Mary sounded disapproving, and not at all like her usual meek self.

Briar looked at Mary. Now that she thought of it, Mary's behavior *had* been odd recently. Mayhap there was something wrong? Mary was always so biddable and quiet that Briar hardly noticed her. Had she been too intent upon her own problems to notice Mary's?

"I *am* thankful for it," she said matter-of-factly. "It has helped to keep us alive."

"Sometimes . . ." Mary hesitated, setting down her comb. "Sometimes, Briar, I think I do not do enough."

Briar was surprised. "You play your harp, Mary."

"But there must be more I can do! You and Jocelyn coddle me as if I were still a baby."

"You are a baby to us," Jocelyn retorted, mopping the milk from Odo's gray-flecked beard while he continued to stare vacantly before him.

"If our father had not died, I would be wed now."

Briar smiled grimly. "If our father had not died, we would all have been wed now, Mary."

"Do you think you would have been happy with Filby?" Jocelyn asked her curiously. "Mayhap you would have had the good fortune never to have learned what he really was."

"How could I not have? I would have grown to hate him, I think."

"Well, at least you discovered the truth about him, before it was too late."

"Not quite too late."

Jocelyn looked stricken, but before she could answer, another of the maidservants came hurrying into the kitchen. It was young Grisel, her small round face almost wild. Her voice burst out in a high-pitched whine.

"Thereisaman."

The sisters looked to each other, startled. Mary giggled, and covered her mouth with her hand. Jocelyn frowned. "Speak more slowly, Grisel."

The maid took a deep breath. "There is a man."

"And?"

"He demands to speak with Briar, with the songstress."

"He wants to speak to me?" Briar ran nervous hands over her hair, still uncombed and hanging tangled down her back. "Did you tell him I was not here?"

The girl shifted from foot to foot. "I tried to tell him you were not within, but he said you were. He was so big and so stern . . . I was frightened to say him nay! And he had such eyes . . . I think he could read inside my head, lady."

Briar felt the floor tip beneath her own feet.

"So you told him she was here." Jocelyn answered for her, with evident disgust.

"Aye." The girl mumbled it apologetically.

"And has he a name, this frightening man?" Jocelyn asked, glancing sharply at Briar.

Grisel nodded. "He says he is Ivo de Vessey, of Lord Radulf's household."

Briar feared her face betrayed her. He had come to see her! She felt very peculiar, as if she were made of colored glass—that precious stuff that some of York's newly built churches displayed in their windows. It was beautiful, there was no doubt, but so easily broken. Briar wondered if she too might shatter with disappointment, if it turned out that Ivo de Vessey was here for some other, more prosaic purpose.

"Grisel, go and tell this man the songstress will see him. And then take him to the alcove off the hall. And bring him some wine."

Grisel ducked a curtsy, and reluctantly retreated.

Briar snatched the comb from Mary and began to work on her hair, tugging through the painful knots with her usual stubborn determination. But her hands were trembling, and that made her angry.

"He has returned very quickly," Jocelyn said. "Why do you think that is?

"How should I know?" Briar retorted.

Jocelyn gave her a little, knowing smile. "Mayhap he is caught in your spell already, Briar."

"Is this the man you sang to last night?" Mary asked the question with such studied innocence that it gave Briar pause. There was a cunning gleam in Mary's eyes.

For a brief moment, Briar wondered if her young sister was really as naïve as she seemed. And then she dismissed the doubt as ridiculous, and took Mary's hands in hers. "I will go and see. Stay here and have something to break your fast. When I return, we can go home."

Mary nodded, but Briar sensed her suspicion.

"Take care," Jocelyn warned.

"Do not worry. I know what I am about."

"Do you?" Jocelyn replied softly. "Every vixen will meet her match one day, Briar. Mayhap you have met *your* fox . . ."

Ivo paced back and forth in the alcove, his boots scattering wine-soaked straw left over from last night's revelries. Where was she? He knew she was somewhere within this household, for last night he had put a guard on Lord Shelborne's house to follow the singing sisters. Only they had never left. And so he had told the maidservant, who had tried to pretend she had never heard of Briar. The girl, already terrified at the sight of him, had crumbled like stale cheese before his determined questioning.

Where was she? Had she sneaked out through a

back way? Was she even now running down
York's narrow lanes, trying to escape him? Didn't
she realize yet that she couldn't? Ivo smiled to
himself. She was *his*.

A slight sound outside the alcove drew his attention. Ivo turned to face her, the wolfpelt cloak
settling about his shoulders. She was coming toward him, rumpled, her big hazel eyes sleepy and
wary at the same time, her face pale and strained,
her hair unbound about her shoulders. Something
in his chest clenched, hard and painful, and he
took a sharp breath.

The childhood memory was there, blurring the
edges of the present. The little girl falling, cutting
her cheek on the hound's half-chewed bone, her
family running in response to her cries. And he,
young and gentle, yet to learn the harsh realities
of being Miles's brother, lifting her up. Earning
her gratitude and her childish love. She had followed him about, to the amusement of all, until
the day he left the Kenton household. And he had
allowed it, perhaps because he missed his mother
and his sister, and perhaps because he was a little
in love with her himself.

She was still beautiful.

But now she was a grown woman, and he was a
man. The innocence had gone. Aye, she was indeed a woman. Ivo almost groaned aloud, and his
groin tightened instantly with lust, while his
blood began to heat. It didn't matter. Whatever
she wanted from him, he would find some way to
give it to her, without compromising his loyalty to
Radulf and his integrity as a de Vessey. He would
do it. And at the same time he would protect her

from Lord Radulf, from the enemies of her father, even from herself.

Silently, Ivo swore it.

She had reached him. There were shadows under her eyes and her mouth was closed tight, but he could see a pulse jumping in her throat.

"Briar."

Her name was like honey in his mouth.

Her gaze slid warily over his chain-mail tunic, the wolfpelt cloak tied over it, and the big sword strapped at his side. He had removed his helmet, leaving his head bare.

"You surprise me, de Vessey." Her voice sounded cool and distant. "I thought never to see you again."

"Why? Because you mistook me for another?"

She came even closer—unwillingly, he thought, but she was clearly determined not to let him know she was afraid. Her scent caught in his nostrils, adding to his yearning, and he had to force himself not to reach out and pull her against him, although his body throbbed with his need.

"I know you have secrets, Briar."

Questions sped through her eyes. "My secrets are my concern."

Now was the time to tell her, but while Ivo hesitated, she moved yet closer, and lifting one hand, rested it lightly upon his shoulder. *Now what?* When he simply stared down at her, she lifted her other hand and slid it behind his head, tugging. He bent lower, to accommodate her.

"Briar," he tried again, but now it was a groan.

She pressed her mouth to his, her lips soft and warm. Ivo drew her into his arms, lifting her so that her feet came off the floor and her entire body was pressed against his. His tongue slid between her lips, his mouth almost rough in his passion. She clung to him, kissing him back, clearly enjoying being in his arms as much as he liked having her there.

Then she drew back, and pressed her hot face against his neck. "Do you want me?" she murmured into his skin.

He half laughed, half groaned, as he lowered her back to her feet. "What do you think?"

"Is that why you came, de Vessey, because you couldn't stay away from me?"

Ivo wondered what the questions were for. Wasn't it clear enough to her that he was burning up with desire for her? That he would do almost anything for a brush of her fingers on his fevered brow, a smile from her lush mouth? But mayhap not. She had seemed innocent in many ways, mayhap she was innocent in this, too. Or was she just cautious? Needing him to tell her that he really did care for her. She had been hurt—he had felt it last night, and felt their kinship because of it.

Ivo wondered, grimly, just what lessons she had learned since her father had died. And how they had been taught to her.

"I cannot keep away from you, Briar," he said, looking with quiet intensity into her face. "You are right in that. I desire you. I do not think that will change until I have had you many, many times, and even then . . . But I get ahead of myself. There is another reason why I have come here to speak with you."

Instantly she was watchful, the heat fading from her eyes.

That was good, he told himself. She was no fool, his songstress, and in her tenuous position she needed all her wits about her. He wanted her to listen to him, and listen well.

"I go north with Lord Radulf, to fight the Scots and their friends."

She surprised him with an, "Oh?" before she looked away, shrugging her shoulders as if she did not care. As if she was wondering to herself why he would feel the need to tell her such a thing. Even after their passionate embrace, Ivo could not help but experience a moment of doubt. Had he been mistaken? Was he as much of a fool as Sweyn had thought? Had he allowed feeling back into his poor, wounded heart, only to be struck a fatal blow?

And then she glanced up at him through her dark lashes. A quick look, secretive, but full of doubt and uncertainty. And loss.

Ivo knew then that he had not been mistaken. He grinned, and watched the temper flare in her. Color climbed into her cheeks, anger flashed in those slanting eyes, until it seemed that at any moment she would claw him like an angry little cat.

"Why do you tell me this?" she asked him, and tossed her untidy hair like the pampered and spoiled child she had probably once been. "Men come and go; I forget them in a week."

Ivo's smile broadened. "But you will not forget *me*, demoiselle."

"How can you be so sure?" The look dared him,

and yet she was wary. She did not believe herself untouchable then. Whatever lesson she had learned had been well taught.

Ivo reached out and captured her chin in strong but gentle fingers. She glared up at him, daring him to do more. He did, brushing his thumb back and forth against her lips. They were reddened and swollen from their kisses of moments before, and suddenly his thumb wasn't nearly enough. Ivo bent his head and claimed her mouth once more with his.

The spark caught, and began quickly to burn. She clung to him, her fingers tugging painfully in his hair. Their mouths fused and melded, wanting more and yet knowing that this was not the time nor the place. Ivo enjoyed the feel of her, the knowledge that she was no longer holding back. He had pushed beyond her wariness, beyond whatever plans were seething in that hot little head of hers, to the place where nothing existed but him and her, together.

"I *will* come back."

She blinked, and for a moment stared up at him blindly. And then, gradually, the knowledge returned. Her arms dropped to her sides, and she stepped back. The silence between them was painful, but he did not break it.

"Is that a vow?" she asked, her voice low and husky.

"Do you want it to be?"

She shrugged with pretended indifference, suddenly cooling. "I did not expect you to plight your troth to me, not because of a single night. I gave you my body, and you gave me yours. Was it so special? Surely it happens all the time between men and women?"

Impatience gripped him, but Ivo held it down. This was no time to lose his temper with her. She was playing games, but he did not have to join in.

"I will come back, Briar, because I am so hot for you that I burn. Just as you burn for me. Why pretend it is not so? In time the flames may well turn cold, but for now we can warm ourselves with their heat."

She looked up at him, paler than ever, and he felt her trembling. "Good. As long as you do not think it is forever. Love is for fools, de Vessey."

"Aye, demoiselle," he said in agreement.

"Good," she said again, but she did not look as if she thought it was good.

"I will return when the fighting is over. Wait for me." She looked so lost and miserable, Ivo sought for something else to say, to rekindle the coals of her anger. He allowed his expression to grow stern. "And do not think to take any other strangers to your bed, no matter *who* you believe them to be."

Instantly she was glaring up at him, bristling like a wildcat. "Oh, and why not? You cannot stop me taking the whole garrison to my bed, if I wished it!"

He had spoken the words on purpose, to bring some life back into her beautiful face, but still jealousy washed over him. "I will know, lady," he growled. "You are mine."

She was startled, mayhap even a little confused, by his answer. But as he watched she swallowed both down, then narrowed her eyes at him. Anger flashed again in the flecks of brown and green, and color stung her white cheeks. "*Yours?* I am no man's, and certainly not the belongings of a disgraced knight. Go! Go and fight, and I hope the Scots cut you into pieces!"

As soon as she had spoken she caught her breath, like a child who expects to be punished. But Ivo did not find her words insulting or painful—he admired courage, and it was clear his woman had plenty, no matter what had been done to her. Aye, she was brave, but someone, at some time, had hurt her. The flinch she gave betrayed her as he reached up to smooth back a long curl of her hair.

"Ah, demoiselle," he said quietly, gazing deep into her eyes. "We both know that your prayers will keep me safe until I return to you."

When he bent his head for another kiss, she tried to pull away from him, cursing him beneath her breath. But as soon as his mouth closed on hers, all fight was forgotten. She responded desperately, clinging and hot, her body pressed hard to his. All too soon, he had to set her away, his eyes sweeping one last time over her face and figure, planting her image firmly in his mind.

And then he was gone, his boots ringing out on the wooden floor. The door banged hollowly, the sound echoing down the hall to where Briar still stood in the entrance to the alcove, staring after him.

Alone.

"I did not mean it," she whispered, her trembling fingers digging into her palms, her nails drawing blood. "I did not mean what I said. Jesu, do not let him die . . . do not let him *die* . . ."

Chapter 4

Several weeks later

York's Sunday market was an organized muddle beneath a cloudswept sky. Vendors raucously called out their wares, children squealed, buyers bargained, and farmers' animals lowed, squawked, and squealed. Stalls and tables, some sheltered by canvas, jostled for space with penned animals and pushing, gaping townsfolk. Two fellows, who had obviously overimbibed at the aleseller's stall, were shouting insults at each other. An enterprising housewife was selling hot broth to keep out the cold, and the cabbagy smell of it mingled with that of bread baking and meat roasting, and the underlying earthy odor of livestock.

The market opened every Sunday, selling the

necessaries of life to the townsfolk and those who had traveled in from the countryside. For a time after William's harrowing of the north, the market had been a sorry place indeed, but gradually, like York itself, it was rebuilding.

When Briar and Mary first arrived in York, they were two of the many performers who came here every Sunday to sing and play, and hopefully be thrown enough coins to buy their supper.

Briar smiled now at the memory, and felt her spirits lift for the first time in weeks. She had been like a ghost, knowing she was worrying Mary and Jocelyn with her wane state, but refusing to discuss with them what ailed her. Her pride prevented her, as well as the knowledge that she was being foolish. And the niggling doubt that she may have imagined the whole thing.

He was in the north, fighting the Scots.

But at least he was alive!

Briar had overheard a conversation while performing in a York merchant's home the night before.

"Radulf has put to flight the rebels who thought to make merry on his land," one large and important-looking man announced, *"and without the loss of even one of his own men!"*

"The rebels were mainly Scots," put in another, not willing to be thought less well informed.

"Then these Scots are either very brave or very foolish!"

Laughter erupted, but the merriment was soured by envy. Radulf was a great man, but not everyone liked a man who was greater than they.

Briar had not cared to dwell on the problems of

being a great man. She was too elated by what she had heard. Ivo had told her he would return—she remembered his mouth on hers with an ache in her heart—but her experience with Filby had made her doubt him, and as time passed, she had doubted her memories of him more.

Besides, her hasty words as they parted had weighed heavily upon her. There were nights since, when she had woken from bloody, fearsome dreams, where Ivo de Vessey lay dead upon the ground, his wonderful eyes dulled, his smile gone, his voice silent. And then, her heart pounding, Briar would stare wide-eyed into the darkness, until dawn came to comfort her. How could he have gotten into her mind so quickly, and yet so completely?

You are mine.

Even while she fought against such an arrogant belief on his part, Briar wondered whether it was not, in some way, so. Perhaps the pleasure she had felt in the joining of their bodies, that hot, burning, bone-deep pleasure, had given him a special power over her? A power that no other man had ever had.

She wanted him back. It was an endless, aching yearning. And Briar knew she would do almost anything to see him again.

He had been right in that, too.

Her prayers since he left had been all for his safe return.

Briar and Mary wandered freely through the busy, noisy crowd, enjoying the fact that they had nothing to do and nowhere to go. Sometimes, thought Briar, 'twas a blessing to be poor. Because you didn't matter, you became almost invisible, and being invisible certainly had its uses.

A nearby table was set out with leather goods, each carefully tooled. A villainous-looking woman fixed her eyes on them, and instinctively Briar moved closer to her sister and urged her on to a fruit vendor's stall. Always a shy and timid girl, Mary had naturally leaned heavily upon Briar since their father's death and their fall from grace. Briar had gotten used to the role of Mary's protector, of standing between her youngest sister and a harsh world.

She never complained of the burden. She loved her sister, and she did not for a moment consider Mary should do more to lighten the load. Without Mary, and the need to care for her, Briar was not sure she would have survived, even with her dark dream of vengeance.

Briar frowned and fingered a basket of very ripe wild plums, lifted a skeptical brow when the vendor named his price. "They are rotten," she said flatly.

Five minutes later, she had haggled the price down considerably, and the two girls moved off with their bounty. Briar bit into one of the plums, and the juice spurted out and ran down her chin. With a giggle, Mary did the same.

"You drove a hard bargain with that man," she ventured, but her dark eyes were sparkling.

"He was a badling. I gave him a fair price."

Mary finished the plum and fastidiously licked her sticky fingers, drying them off on her worn kirtle. "You call every male a badling these days, Briar. There are some good men among the bad."

"Pooh! They are all badlings and fleshmongers. Name one who is not, sister."

Mary wrinkled her brow. "Odo. He is . . . was a good man."

Briar laughed. "That was because Jocelyn would not allow him to be otherwise. Name me another."

"What of the man who came to see you at Lord Shelborne's? The man you sang to, Briar. Was he a badling and a fleshmonger?"

Briar blinked, wondering for a surprised moment whether her sister's expression was really as innocent as it appeared. The doubt shocked her. What was she thinking? Mary was a child.

"*He* is the worst badling and fleshmonger I have ever met," she said uncomfortably.

But Mary did not hear her; her fickle attention had been captured by something far more interesting. "Look, sister!"

Briar looked, while the dark, sweet syrup from the plum trickled down her pointed chin and stained the front of her coarse brown gown. With her chestnut hair loose about her shoulders, and her feet bare, Briar felt like a young girl. Gone was the world-weary woman who often dwelt in her heart. A sense of optimism filled her, and she smiled when she saw the direction of Mary's interest.

Her younger sister was gazing in rapture at a clothseller's stall. The man was clearly no York native, but one of the foreign merchants who had taken the journey to England in the hope of making a fortune. Bolts of beautiful materials spilled over the wooden board, some so exquisite they were surely only fit for the highest in the land—or the highest in York, anyway. The rolls of cloth were complemented by trays of ribbons, beads, and other trimmings. York's matrons were already gathering, like crows at a feast, eagerly discussing styles and colors, shouldering out the dreamers.

Briar followed after her sister. In her opinion, 'twas not always good sense to wish for luxuries it was no longer in their power to obtain, but Mary was so entranced. And besides, Briar reminded herself, *he* was alive and she was happy. Why not pretend, just this once?

And then a length of green wool caught her eye, and it was no longer pretense.

The cloth was very dark. The deep, deep green of a pond, when you look into its secret depths. And it was so soft and so fine—her fingers itched to stroke. If she had a gown made of such stuff, Briar told herself, she could do anything. Radulf would beg her pardon, the king would return Castle Kenton, Filby would grovel at her feet. Indeed, the whole of York would be at her feet, bare or otherwise!

Ivo among them. Aye, especially Ivo!

Unthinking, Briar stretched out her hand to touch . . . and caught the baleful eye of the cloth-seller. He scowled at her. Clearly he thought she had the plague, at the very least! Aye, and so she did, to him. She was poor; what would such a poor creature as she want with fine wool, if it was not to spoil it for others, or steal it to sell? Briar knew that he would not hesitate to shout for help, and she would be fined.

Her spirits, which had been on the rise, plummeted.

"Come, sister, we are not wanted here," she said, more sharply than she meant.

Mary sighed. "Do you think, one day, Briar, we might wear fine clothes again? I know it is wrong of me to long for such petty nonsense, when our other needs are so great, but sometimes I just cannot help it. If we had not once lived very differently from this, then I would not feel the lack, I am sure. But we did, and I do."

There were tears in the younger girl's eyes and, forgetting her stern demeanor, Briar gave her a quick, fierce hug. " 'Tis not wrong, and one day we will dress better than queens, you will see. That clothmonger will be begging us to touch his wares then."

Mary smiled, as Briar had meant her to.

Hand in hand, they continued on through the crowded market, until Mary's excited cry stopped them once more. "Oh, Briar, look!" A pair of acrobats were performing, twisting and turning their slim bodies into bizarre shapes. "As if they have no bones!" Mary gasped, clapping her hands. They stood and watched, and again Briar put aside their many troubles and lost herself in her sister's simple joy.

We are still alive, she told herself, *that is the miracle. Despite all Radulf and Filby and the king have done to destroy us, the daughters of Richard Kenton remain.*

And as long as she, Briar, was alive, those great men best beware!

One of the acrobats bent over backward and peeped at them through his legs. The crowd

clapped and laughed. The other acrobat put his
feet behind his head, as if they were tied in a knot.

Laughing, engrossed, Briar was completely unprepared when that quiet, deep voice spoke just
behind her.

"Demoiselle."

She froze. Her heart began to pound like a ham-
mer. The amusing scene before her shifted, faded.
She was looking at a bed of soft furs and cushions,
and in it, a big naked man, who lay back and
gazed at her with the most intense black eyes she
had ever known. His hands were on her body, his
mouth on hers, and she was filled with the wonderful ache of completion.

*Jesu, how many times have I woken in the night,
dreaming of this? How many times during each day
have I found myself thinking of our brief time together?
And now, he is here, his mesmerizing voice as smug as
a well-fed cat because he has found me . . .*

"Briar, look at me."

Briar shivered. Her skin felt thin as breath, sensitive to the softest touch, the briefest brush of his
gaze. She was aglow, like a lantern with a bright
candle inside. Aglow, because he had found her,
and he was alive!

Only a brief moment had passed, and her wild
emotions were settling. Or so she thought, until
she turned, and found the reality of him so much
more than she had imagined. She was over-
whelmed by the sheer sense of his size, his presence, the brooding beauty of his smile beneath the
shadow of his helmet, and his eyes, like black
stars gleaming down into hers.

"Ivo de Vessey." She sounded breathless. At her

side, Mary was looking from one to the other with an interest that did not seem entirely guileless.

Ivo's smile broadened, and there was a satisfied twist to his lips that immediately irritated Briar. "As you see, I am returned to York, demoiselle, just as I promised I would. Are you pleased to see me?"

It was not a question that Briar felt able to answer without giving herself away. Pleased to see him? She had thought of nothing else but Ivo de Vessey since he left! Instead of making plans for Radulf's fall, for the justice that was long denied her dead father and stepmother, Briar had been dreaming of kisses and cuddles like a lovesick maid. It was madness, and she did not wish to admit it to herself let alone him. He must never know just how deeply he had possessed her. *Never.*

With difficulty Briar stilled the agitation afflicting her and lifted her chin, examining him with a carefully assumed casualness.

"I am indifferent, de Vessey."

He snorted his disbelief.

He wore the chain-mail tunic he had gone away in, but now there were rents and tears in it that had not been there before. There was a stain over his thigh the rusty color of dried blood. The familiar wolfpelt cloak was tossed carelessly over one shoulder, giving him that barbarous appearance. His untamed hair was covered by the close-fitting metal helmet with its thick nasal, but Briar could see a bruise, beginning to fade now, on his cheek and jaw—as though someone had struck him a violent blow.

He was alive, but clearly not without some new trophies to mark his participation in this latest battle.

He still looked very dangerous. Was it that, or his sheer size that was making him so very conspicuous here in the market? People were shuffling away from him, or else staring in slack-jawed wonder. And that being so, why had she not noticed him earlier? Curse the acrobats for distracting her. If she had seen him approaching, she would have been much better prepared.

Those brooding black eyes were fixed on her, trying to read her thoughts. Again, as if to mock her own lack of self-control, memories of their cleaved bodies and fused mouths swam in her head. Angrily, she thrust them away. There was no time for make-believe—this was real, this was here and now, and she needed all her wits about her.

"I said I would return," he told her. "And as you see, I am not cut into pieces, although 'tis not from lack of the Scots trying. Tell me, were your prayers answered, demoiselle? What did you pray for, I wonder?"

"I did not pray at all. I forgot."

He didn't believe her, the arrogant brute. She could see it in his smile.

"How do you know I did not find someone else, while you were away?"

That stung. His gaze narrowed. Then, with an impatient sigh, Ivo de Vessey reached up and removed his helmet.

Briar's mouth fell open. "You have cut your hair!" she cried out in dismay.

Where had they gone? The wonderful, wild curls that she remembered, that dark aureole about his fierce face? They had been chopped into submission. Now his hair lay shorter about his skull, hardly a curl in it, like a true Norman knight. The change accentuated even more the angles and planes of his face.

"Aye. It needed to be cut." He gave her a puzzled frown, no doubt questioning her sanity.

Of course he had cut his hair! Annoyed, Briar clamped down on her shocked dismay. He was a soldier, a warrior, and anything that might interfere with his fighting, with his ability to do his job and to stay alive, would have to be dealt with. His hair had grown long, it would be uncomfortable under his tight-fitting helmet, therefore he had cut it short.

"Sister?"

Mary stood protectively at her side. Her dark eyes were worried, and a line creased the smooth skin between her brows.

"Briar, who is this man?"

Briar blinked. *Protectively?* It was always Briar who protected Mary, never the other way around. What was happening to her? With an effort, Briar pulled herself together, burying her confusion of thoughts for later examination.

"Mary, this is Ivo de Vessey. Mary is my sister."

Ivo shot one of his searching glances at Mary, and then he smiled. It was the sort of nonthreatening, courtly smile that a knight might bestow upon a fragile creature, and therefore nothing like the smile he gave Briar. His bow to Mary was

equally courtly. "I am enchanted, demoiselle. I
have heard your playing upon the harp and ad-
mire it very much."

Mary flushed pink with pleasure. "Oh! I thank
you, sir. I am not very good, not really, but I practice."

"Then your practice has been well rewarded,
lady."

"I," Mary glanced at Briar, momentarily
tongue-tied, "I am not a lady, sir."

"And I am not a sir. Call me Ivo and I will call
you Mary."

Mary gave him her shy smile, clearly capti-
vated by his manner. "Very well, Ivo."

Briar couldn't bear it any longer. His easy con-
quest of her sister was almost a betrayal, and certainly very irritating. Her voice was tart and
somewhat shrewish, but she could not stop the
words.

"You may have lost your knighthood, de
Vessey, but your tongue remembers well that tra-
dition of flattery."

Ivo raised his eyebrows, and anger glittered in
his eyes. He held it at bay, but Briar was pleased to
think she had struck home with her barb. Un-
masked the real Ivo from beneath the polite pretense. Somehow she did not think him a man
made for calm conversation and measured argument. One glance at Ivo de Vessey was enough to
tell her he was either passion or anger, joy or sadness, one thing or the other. There would be no
middle ground with him. He was a man who
would love you or hate you, and maybe both.

He pinned her with his gaze, like an insect against a wall, and then leaned down, his breath warm against her cheek.

"I have been seeking answers to my questions about you, Briar," he said, and it was almost a threat. "I would know what kind of woman barters her body to strangers, and yet speaks the French tongue like a lady born."

He had asked about her! Pried into her past? Perhaps even laughed with his friends about her passion, describing in detail what they had done. Suddenly, Briar felt ill and frightened, and more. The only way to deal with the pain was to replace it with something hotter, and Briar allowed her anger to engulf her.

Ivo had the satisfaction of seeing rage cloud those lovely eyes, before her dark lashes swept down and hid them. She had lit his temper, so he had repaid her in kind. They both had secrets. Proud areas of flesh they would rather not have prodded. She best remember that, next time she wanted to wound him.

And yet . . . Ivo's gaze slid over her, and he felt his anger melting before the picture she made. Plum juice had stained her chin, and her hair, loose about her shoulders, was windblown and untidy. She wore an old darned gown and no shoes upon her feet. And she was the most beautiful woman he had ever seen.

He was filled with an aching longing. How could he miss someone so much, when he had only held her in his arms so briefly? They had joined bodies, but her mind was still very much a mystery. And her motives . . . Well, he had still to clarify them, although he was moving closer.

When Ivo had first reached the market, and spotted Briar, he had sat upon his horse for a long moment, just watching her go from stall to stall, hand in hand with her sister. Like two children. The sight had delighted and puzzled him. When he had remembered Briar it had been her body in his arms, or her sobs, or her stubborn refusal to admit what was between them.

Certainly not this sweet innocence she was displaying now.

There was much he did not know about her. While Ivo had fought in the north, taking on the grim task of subduing rebels, he had spent his few spare moments dreaming of Briar. While he lay, soaked by rain and muddy from fighting, trying to sleep, he had warmed himself with the memory of her voice as she sang. While he rode hard through rugged country, searching for the straggling remains of the rebel force, he had remembered her eyes, blurred with passion, as he joined his body with hers.

She was in his blood. Whether he willed it or not, she was now a part of him. And he needed to understand what secret game she played, so that he could save her from the consequences. And mayhap save himself, too.

Immediately upon his return to York, Ivo had gone to Lord Shelborne's house to inquire of the singing sisters. After a time, and much whispering beyond the curtained doorway, a tall woman with blue eyes and dark hair had come to speak with him. She had looked long at him, without any shyness or fear.

"*You* are Ivo de Vessey," she had said at last, with satisfaction.

"Aye, lady. I seek the songstress, Briar. Do you know where I can find her?"

The woman had smiled a little smile and nodded, a gleam in her eyes. "It is market day. She will be there with her sister."

The information had been gained so easily—Ivo had felt puzzled and a little suspicious. "I do not mean to hurt her." He had meant to reassure and instead had blurted it out.

That smile again. "I can see that, Ivo de Vessey." Then, a frown had creased her brow, and she had said, "Your name is familiar to me. Why is that?"

"I am a soldier in Lord Radulf's household."

"And before that?"

Her questions had been sharp, impertinent, but Ivo had not thought to refuse her her answers. There had been something in her manner—the same sense he had had with Briar—that it was her *right* to ask such questions, and his duty to reply to them. This woman was no ordinary servant, and his wits had sharpened.

"I was a knight, once. And long ago, when I was a young boy, I was a squire in the household of Richard Kenton."

She had blinked. "Aye. Now I remember it. My sister was your shadow for one whole summer. Does she know that yet?"

Her sister! Ivo had examined her more carefully

and memory gave him his answer—a girl of ten, a vague remembrance of her kindness. The older sister, Jocelyn. "No," he had said at last, "she does not know. I would ask you not to tell her, lady, not yet. I need time."

Jocelyn had laughed. "Aye, I'm sure you do. I will not tell her, sir. I wish you well, truly I do. Now go to the market or you will miss her."

A strange conversation, but as he rode to do her bidding, Ivo had felt as if he had a friend in Briar's camp.

"You dress like a ragamuffin, but you are far from that."

He spoke so abruptly that Mary jumped, but Briar just glared at him like an angry she-cat, her eyes more green than hazel.

"You are impertinent."

He laughed out loud, for those words, more than anything else, had given her away. No simple songstress would say such a thing to a knight, even if he *were* a disgraced knight. Briar had more layers than an onion, and Ivo would enjoy unpeeling each one.

She was watching him suspiciously, as if she was aware she had betrayed herself but did not know how. "I do not like your look, de Vessey. You are altogether too pleased with yourself."

"I am trying to work you out, demoiselle, 'tis all. Are you the Queen of Norway, in hiding here in York?"

Briar scowled at him. "You are being foolish, I am no queen!"

"Ah, then a Princess of Scotland, fleeing from your father and seeking love in England."

Mary giggled, and earned herself a warning glare from her sister.

"Then you must be a noblewoman, wronged and seeking redress."

It was too close to the mark, and both girls paled. Briar began to turn away, but Ivo's gloved hand snaked out and caught her arm, holding her with ease. Anger colored Briar's face red and her eyes shone with fury, but before she could utter the demand that he release her, a deep and friendly voice called from nearby.

"Ivo? I had thought you lost among the cabbages and cattle!"

It was Sweyn, his fair head bright in the gloom, sitting bestride his horse and leading Ivo's. He edged closer to the small group, scattering onlookers. His blue gaze slid curiously over Briar and Ivo, and rested momentarily upon Mary. The girl was looking up at the Dane upon his horse, like a Norse god against the cloudy sky, and her dark eyes were wide and grave, her cheeks still flushed from feeling Briar's displeasure. Ivo thought he saw something pass over Sweyn's face, something he had never seen there before, but the next moment the Dane was smiling his usual lazy smile, ready to be amused.

"Sweyn, you are here just in time to make yourself useful. I would speak privately with this lady. Will you remain here with her sister, Mary?"

Sweyn glanced again at Mary, now with her head bowed, fingers nervously fiddling with her girdle, and raised a questioning eyebrow at his friend. But his voice was amiable enough. "Aye, if you wish it, Ivo. Lady, are you agreeable to that?"

Mary murmured something incomprehensible, which Ivo chose to take as consent.

He held out his hand to Briar. "Demoiselle?"

Briar hesitated. There had been a formality in his gesture, as if he meant to have more than a simple conversation with her, and she seemed to recognize it. One moment Ivo read refusal in her eyes, mixed with a flash of fear, but the next she had placed her hand reluctantly in his.

He wasted no time in leading her away through the busy market.

For a time they walked in silence. Briar pretended an interest in the passing stalls she no longer felt, and ignored the curious and sometimes nervous glances of their fellows. At some time during his absence, she had convinced herself that Ivo de Vessey was the one and only path to Radulf, and therefore she had no choice but to bind him to her. It was a sacrifice she must make if she still wanted vengeance.

If she still had the will and the courage to seek an end to this calamity that had befallen the Kenton family.

The fire that had possessed her before the night spent in Ivo's arms had cooled. 'Twas true. No matter how she tried to fan it into life again, it did not seem to want to burn as brightly. But it could not have gone out, not completely. There was still a glow deep inside her—there must be!—and mayhap in time Briar could rekindle it.

Ivo would supply that spark.

That was why she was going with him. For the purposes of her dark plot. Not because she had missed him and yearned for him. No, no, never that. She had wanted to tell Mary these very things, but the girl had not looked at her, not once. Again, worry for Mary clouded her thoughts, before the memory of Jocelyn's voice pushed it out.

You must make him crazy with lust for you.

Briar wriggled uncomfortably, feeling the warmth trickle through her body. She was prepared to do that. More than prepared, she was eager to do it. And wasn't that a little worrying? That this particular part of her plot was of more interest to her than any other? Had Ivo worked some sort of spell on her? For she was having great difficulty keeping a clear and cold head . . .

"If you tell me what secrets burden you, Briar, I can help."

"Help?" He sounded sincere, but she did not trust him. She did not trust herself. Briar would have pulled her hand from his, but he would not let her go, gripping her fingers more tightly in his calloused ones. "I have no secrets, de Vessey," she told him sharply. "I do not know what you speak of. I am a simple songstress, that is all."

He gave a skeptical laugh, and followed her through the jostling, indifferent crowd. "You did not answer my question before, Briar. Did you miss me while I was gone?"

Briar turned her head to glance up at him. His expression was unreadable, but she thought he would not have asked the question had he been as sure of her as he pretended. What should she do? Abuse him further, or play at being indifferent? Neither would gain her the result she was seeking. To bind him to her, she must give him a part of herself. No matter how grudgingly.

"I missed you, aye, and I prayed for you."

The words came surprisingly easily—something else to worry her!

He smiled, lips curving, his black gaze slipping from hers to play on her mouth. "What part of me did you miss the most?"

Briar made an impatient sound. "What sort of question is that, de Vessey?"

"A fair one, demoiselle. I will answer the same question for you. I missed your mouth. Your lips are so soft and so sweet, but inside you feel hot and my head spins when your tongue mates with mine. Aye, 'twas your mouth I missed most. And yet . . ." He examined her face and body, making Briar squirm. "And yet, there are other things about you I missed just as much. Will I list them?"

"No, you will not!" She tossed her head so that her chestnut hair danced in the fitful sunlight. "I was sorry to see that bruise upon your face, but now I think it well deserved."

"You are cruel, lady. Will you not heal me with a kiss?"

In Briar's opinion, that didn't deserve a reply.

They had reached one of the many snickleways that linked the streets of York. Shadowed and narrow, the lane was suitably private. Briar walked ahead and Ivo followed her through, uncomplaining, but clearly prepared for trouble. His free hand closed on the decorated hilt of his sword, and he turned his head from side to side, carefully examining each doorway and each shadow.

Briar smiled secretly to herself.

He was suspicious of her, and yet he still came with her. He was willing to put himself at risk, to be with her. Surely that boded well?

Briar had never tried to ensnare a man before; she had not believed it in her nature. There were some women who found such things enjoyable, to whom the capture of a man's mind and heart was a pleasant day's sport. Briar had never been one of their number. She had been betrothed to Filby, and thought to wed him and eventually be his wife, but there had been no attempt on her part to ensnare him. No talk of desire or love, not by her, although Filby had played at being the besotted bridegroom once or twice, more to her amusement than her delight. A woman in Briar's position took the husband her family chose for her. Filby had suited because his estates abutted hers, and he was a Norman of some wealth and power. He was not as wealthy or as powerful as Richard Kenton, but Briar's father had thought to keep her close and make her happy, and for that he had been willing to forgo a brilliant marriage.

She would not marry now.

Who in her old world would want her? And she could not see herself wed to a fleshmonger in the Shambles, or a beltmaker in Girdlergate. She walked among these people as if she were one of them, but Briar knew deep in her heart that she was not, and never could be. Nay, she was neither one thing nor the other.

They had reached a particularly dark spot in the snickleway. Briar stopped, and Ivo paused a little way behind her, wary, watchful. Instinctively he loosened his sword in its scabbard, glancing around, searching for enemies.

"What do we here?" he asked her. " 'Tis the sort of place where men's throats are slit."

He wondered if it were a trap, if she intended to do harm to him. He might desire her, she thought, but he was not a fool.

"I thought you wanted private words with me," Briar replied airily, and turned a face to him that she knew was pale and a little wild. This was the very spot where Anna, her stepmama, was murdered, but Ivo de Vessey could not know that. It seemed to Briar somehow apt that her seduction of him should begin here. How could she possibly lose sight of her real objective, in this place? How could she feel any pleasure in it, while such a memory was raw at her feet?

"Your choice of scene lacks something, Briar." He spoke dryly, but he took his hand from his sword.

She shrugged. "Take it or leave it."

A chill breeze drifted up the snickleway, a reminder that they were well into autumn. Briar shivered. Or mayhap it was the spirit of Anna? Beautiful Anna, who, it was said, broke men's hearts with impunity—although that, Briar reminded herself, had been before she married Richard Kenton. Still, if anyone could give Briar lessons in making a man crazed with lust, then surely it was Anna?

Ivo made an impatient sound and, taking her by surprise, grabbed up her hand and led her firmly out of the snickleway, and into Goodramgate. Abruptly, at the same moment, the sun shone, throwing aside its covering of clouds. Briar closed her eyes, feeling its welcome warmth against her skin. When she opened them again, she could see beyond the uneven rooftops, to where ladders and scaffolding had been thrown up by the men usually hard at work reroofing and rebuilding York's Saxon Minster.

The Minster had stood upon that spot for over three hundred years. During the most recent rebellion in the north, King William's men had burned much of the city, including the Minster, to prevent the rebels from overtaking it. Aye, York had suffered much from the wars between men, and the new Norman Archbishop of York, Thomas of Bayeux, was determined to restore the Minster to God's glory.

Ivo hurried her along, closer to the great church. The precincts were still much in ruin and deserted. An arched section of wall stood alone, warmed by the sun, and a barrier against the cold breezes.

"This is better." Ivo stopped, and promptly pulled her into his arms.

Briar started to struggle, before she remembered she was supposed to be compliant. Though not *too* compliant, not *too* easily won, she reminded herself. Men appreciated the hunt, the chase, and the capture, in that order. Briar rested her hands against Ivo's mailed chest, feeling his heat even through the layers of clothing and the woven iron rings of his armor. He seemed almost a stranger. It was his hair, she told herself. She had dreamed so often of that wild hair, and her fingers in it, that its lack unsettled her.

"You spoke of my bruised face, demoiselle. A man struck me with the flat of his sword. If it had been the edge I would not be standing here now."

The sun was no longer warm enough; somehow the chill wind had seeped through the wall. Briar stared up at him, and knew her own face was white. "But he did not," she said, and her voice shook only slightly. "You are whole."

"Your prayers kept me safe, Briar," he said softly, and stroked his rough finger down her soft cheek.

"Then I am glad, Ivo." She meant it. Slowly, carefully, as if such a thing were entirely foreign to her nature, Briar leaned into him and rested her cheek against his heart. It beat hard and strong. The sound calmed her, and she did not protest as he tightened his own hold about her.

He desired her. That part of him she remembered so well was nudging her belly. She ignored it. She had never realized before just how comforting a man's arms could be.

And yet Ivo de Vessey is a man, the same as any other. Why should he be different?

His breath fanned her temple, his lips brushed her skin, gentle but promising more. Instinctively, Briar lifted her face to him, and his mouth closed on hers.

He stilled, as if taken by surprise, and then with a low groan he returned her kiss, his mouth no longer tender, but eager and hot. Ah, here was something she understood! Lust, desire, these things she could deal with. Relieved, Briar met his eagerness with enthusiasm. Her tongue tangled with his, and when he slid his hands down to cup her bottom, bringing her closer to the point of his need, she did not demur, but wriggled against him.

It was Ivo who broke the kiss. His breath was warm against her cheek; he was panting as if he had run a race.

"I will not take you against the wall, Briar. Is that what you want?"

Surprised, she looked up at him, and was at once captured by that dark, brooding gaze. She licked her lips, and watched him follow the movement with rapt attention. Confidence returned to her, and Briar smiled.

"I do not know whether such a thing would be flattering or not, Ivo. But you are right, 'tis not what I want."

"Then you had best not push me too far, demoiselle. I think you are not accustomed to the ways of men, though you pretend."

Annoyed, she tried to pull away from him, but he held her easily, allowing her only to lean back in his arms. Laughter warmed his smile and his eyes, as if he thought her struggles comical. Briar wanted to slap him and demand he release her, but she knew to do either would be to undo all the magic she had worked so far.

"And you think *you* are accustomed to the ways of *women*, de Vessey? You could no more see into a woman's head than weave a stocking!"

To her surprise he didn't bristle, he laughed. "I can read some women, but you are different, Briar. Have you ever *loved* a man, demoiselle?"

The blunt question gave her pause. Briar hesitated, and then decided upon honesty. "Nay, apart from my father, I have loved no man."

Ivo's laughter was gone. "I will be the first, then."

"Jesu! You are arrogant, Sir Disgraced Knight. I do not love you, why should I? What do you have, that would tempt me to love such as you?"

He ran his hand gently through her hair, his gloved fingers strangely stiff and unresponsive. "I can give you safety, Briar. A place to come and know you will not be harmed or hurt, where you no longer need to be the brave one. A place where you need not be alone."

She went cold, suddenly afraid of his words, and the feelings they caused to well up within her. What he had described was a place she longed for with all her heart, but she had not known it, until now. How could *he* know? Was he truly able to see into her mind?

And what if he abandons you once he has had his fill of you? Be very careful how much you give him. Step back. Keep your distance. He might sink deep but you must not.

Briar made herself smile—one of Anna's teasing smiles.

"I ask only one thing of you, Ivo."

He was watching her intently. "And what is that, demoiselle?"

"That you do not cut your hair again. I prefer it the way it was."

He stared at her a moment, totally blank, and then he threw back his head and laughed loudly.

"I will grow my hair to my toes, then, Briar, before I cut it again." He spoke at last, humor gleaming in his eyes. "Does that please you?"

She smiled. "Aye, it does. Do you seek to please me, Ivo?"

"Always, demoiselle."

The moment stretched. His fierce black gaze almost undid her, but she held on. Her voice was breathless. "Tell me why you were disgraced?"

A door closed within him; she saw it happen. His eyes went blank, cold, distant. He shut her out as effectively as if he really had stepped inside a room. "I, too, have my secrets," he said.

She was tempted to push him further, to try and learn that which he did not want her to know. But then she remembered it was none of her business—nor did she want it to be. Better he keep his hurts to himself. She was not interested in his past, was she? She did not want to know him too well; she dared not begin to care for him. Ivo de Vessey was to be a means to an end. Nothing more.

"Very well. We will share our bodies but keep our feelings removed."

The statement sounded so cold.

Ivo was watching her closely, but then he spoke the words she had been waiting to hear.

"It will all be just as you wish, demoiselle."

Chapter 5

Mary watched with relief her sister and the big, dark man make their way toward her. It was cold. The sunshine had vanished, and dark clouds loomed over York. The thinning crowds were in a hurry to be home before the storm came, and Mary didn't blame them.

"Their reunion does not appear to have been a happy one." Sweyn had dismounted, and was standing beside Mary.

She agreed—Briar's expression was guarded, while Ivo de Vessey looked grim. "My sister is cautious where men are concerned, and with reason."

Sweyn seemed amused by her answer. "Ivo is careful of women," he explained. "With reason."

"Oh. Then mayhap they are well matched." She sounded prim and self-conscious.

"Aye. Love makes the strangest bedfellows . . ."

The humor seemed to have gone from him and they stood side by side, both longing, Mary was sure, for the other to be gone.

It had not been like this a moment ago.

After the first awkwardness of two strangers being left alone together, they had found they conversed easily enough. Sweyn's manner was so easy, so comfortable; shy Mary had blossomed. And Sweyn, too, seemed to be delighted by her. They had been enjoying their brief, unexpected moment, and then something had happened. Sweyn had fallen quiet, and when he tried to recapture something of their previous ease, he had been almost clumsy.

Mary had not thought him a clumsy man, far from it. He was a man who did not take himself too seriously, and he had seemed so tolerant, so indulgent, so truly interested in her. The sort of man any woman would be flattered to be with.

And now this.

Had she done something wrong? Said something very foolish? Why else would the big, handsome Dane lose interest in her? It was as if, she thought bleakly, he had shone a golden light on her and then turned it off.

Anxious, upset, Mary greeted Briar, fully expecting her sister to notice her wounded feelings and comfort her, as she always did.

But for once Briar did not notice her dilemma. Her gaze kept flicking to Ivo de Vessey, almost as if to assure herself he was still there. Ivo looked even graver this close up, but he gave Mary a courtly bow before he swung himself up onto his horse. He was clearly impatient to be gone, but his impatience had the flavor of someone who was being hunted. Chased by his own demons.

Looking at Ivo's dark, commanding gaze, Mary thought his demons must be great indeed.

Sweyn remounted more slowly, the lines about his blue eyes crinkling as he looked at the sky. Rain was close now; she could smell it in the air. And so, she realized, could he.

"I must go."

He sent a half smile in Mary's direction, something far removed from the lazy grin he had worn earlier. Mary nodded, pretending to fiddle with a thread on her sleeve, her heart lodged in her throat as she asked herself again what she had done wrong. Then she heard the clatter of his horse's hooves as he followed Ivo from the market.

Only then did Mary, her face bright with color, lift her head to watch him go.

The two sisters stood close together, waiting by silent consent until the horses were no longer visible. Mary turned reluctantly to her sister, but Briar remained still, her face pale and set. Strangely, even in her stillness, she seemed to thrum with tension, a little like the strings on Mary's harp. There was something between Briar and Ivo de Vessey, something serious, but whether it was good or bad, Mary could not guess. Nor did she expect her sister to tell her. Briar still thought of her as a child, and until recently Mary had been content to allow herself to be so treated.

It had been simpler, somehow.

While Briar and Jocelyn had cared for her, she did not have to think. She did not have to take upon herself the burden of finding food and shelter. She played her harp, aye, there was that, but the rest she left to them.

Recently that had begun to change. Now that they were more settled in York, Mary had felt a growing need to take a step away from her sisters. To be herself. It was difficult. Sometimes she wanted nothing more than to creep back into the warm safety of their arms, but with a firm and gentle determination she was persisting. She was not a child, although it pleased them to treat her so. How could she be, after all that had happened? She knew much, and had suffered much; they all had. How could she begin to repay them, unless they would allow her to grow up and take her proper place in their little family?

The handsome blond mercenary with the clear blue eyes, Sweyn, *he* had not thought her a child. Mary had known it, instinctively, by the manner in which he looked at her. His gaze had slid over her body, and he had smiled into her eyes. He had looked at Mary and seen a woman, and he had even flirted with her, a little. That had been fun. She had enjoyed very much the sensation of being looked upon as a grown woman, and not a helpless child.

And then he had told her a silly joke that made her laugh, and after that the sweet moment had turned sour.

Mayhap she had laughed too long and too hard? Mayhap he had seen her for the pretender she was? The joke had not even been that funny, but she had still laughed, lit up by his attention like a burning coal. By the time she had stopped laughing, it had been too late. He had been staring at her, oddly, as if he had never seen a girl like her before. He had stared at her until she grew uncomfortable.

Mary had not understood the look in his blue eyes, or the way he had seemed to withdraw from her without actually moving. He had not stopped speaking with her, but his words had grown stilted, uncomfortable, clumsy. Strange behavior in such an urbane man.

He had thought her childish and silly. Aye, that must be it. She *was* childish and silly. Suddenly Mary felt her frustration bitter in her mouth. She didn't *want* to be a child any longer—it was well past time she grew up. If she had been a proper woman, confident in herself and her body, then mayhap Sweyn would have wanted to stay with her a little longer.

But then again, he *had* smiled at her as he rode away.

A smile that was almost a promise . . .

"You were gone a long time." Mary broke into her own thoughts, and glanced bright-eyed at Briar.

"Was I?"

"Ivo seemed very pleased to see you, sister."

"How would you know?" Briar snapped. "I do not want to speak of him."

She set off at a brisk pace through the market, head held high, as if her gown were not patched and her feet not bare and dusty. Ignoring the demanding calls of the vendors, Mary sighed and hurried after her. Briar had a hot temper, though it was not often that she turned it on Mary. Something must be very wrong for her to do so now.

Mary wanted to remind Briar that she was a grown woman, that there was no need to shelter her from unpalatable truths any longer. That Briar could talk to her about Ivo de Vessey, or anything else. But even as she opened her mouth to do so, one look at Briar's angry face made her close it again. Perhaps this was not the right time to exert her independence.

They were all so different, the three daughters of Lord Kenton. Jocelyn, sensible and tranquil and loving. Mary, shy and gentle. And Briar, the strong one, the hurt one, the angry one. Briar had burned with her hatred these past two years; she had been determined to revenge their father by punishing Lord Radulf. The terrible events of two years ago had wounded them all, but it was Briar who could not seem to put it behind her. Jocelyn said she wanted the past forgotten—she had Odo to concern her. Mary, coddled and cared for, had missed the privilege that had been hers, but nevertheless would try to make a new life.

But not Briar. She was too hurt by what had happened to her at the hands of those powerful men. It was as if she was unable to look forward, without looking backward.

Would Ivo de Vessey help Briar find a happier future? Would Sweyn help Mary to be a woman? The Dane was very handsome. Mary had found herself wondering, as they stood together in the marketplace, whether he might kiss her.

"Mary?"

Mary blinked. Briar touched her arm, concerned. They were standing in the entry to one of the many snickleways that crisscrossed York, narrow thoroughfares between the more important streets. Mary flushed bright red, as if she had done something wrong, which surprised Briar. What could an innocent girl like Mary be thinking . . . to make her blush?

"I am sorry, sister," Mary spoke breathlessly. "I was woolgathering. Did you say something?"

" 'Twas nothing," Briar replied, eyeing her curiously and a little anxiously. Perhaps, she thought, Mary was unwell. York was not the healthiest of places, with its open drains and mounds of debris in the streets. "Come, let us hurry home. The air grows chill."

It *was* chill. Briar glanced up at a sky that was no longer blue but a dark gray, lowering over the city. Quickening her steps, she instinctively reached for her sister's hand. Mary smiled. She tried to hide it, but Briar noticed.

"What is it? Mary?"

Mary met her eyes wryly. "I am a full head taller than you, Briar."

"So?"

" 'Tis just . . . The way you hold my hand in yours, 'tis as if I were still a child."

"It does not matter how tall you grow, Mary," Briar reminded her brusquely. "That changes nothing. You are still a child to me."

Mary's cheeks pinkened and her eyes narrowed. She looked for a moment as if she wanted to say more, a great deal more. And then she sighed, and allowed herself to be tugged along after her sister, past a ruined church, into Coppergate. The two girls took to their heels and ran as the wind rose and threatened to toss their hems over their heads. Mary shrieked and Briar laughed, holding down her gown as they ran, and the first big raindrops splattered the ground around them.

The image of Ivo de Vessey leaning over her to kiss her, his lips smooth and warm, once more filled Briar's mind. She gasped and lifted her face to the rain, feeling its cold daggers against her skin. Why did he possess her thoughts so? Always, before, she had been able to order them, keep a part of herself locked away. Now it was as if he had permeated every single inch of her.

Aye, she had enjoyed what he did to her. In her secret heart, she wanted him to do it again. But at what cost? Would it be too high? And what if, in the end, she wasn't able to separate her mind from her senses? If she wasn't able to remain cold and distant from him, her mind free from the contamination of his kisses, how could she do what she had sworn to?

Was it really possible to give him her body, and take his, and then forget him?

When her stepmother had died, and then her father, when Filby had taken her, Briar had drawn on her cloak of vengeance. She could not have survived else. But Ivo de Vessey had come, and he had rent and torn that cloak, and now the cold breeze of doubt was assailing her. She had begun to wonder if there really was nothing more to her life than this weighty task she had set herself. And she had begun to wonder if she really was the sort of woman who could use a man for her own ends, and then abandon him.

I have my secrets, too, demoiselle.

How had he been hurt? His hand, always covered—what had happened to it? What lay behind that dark and brooding gaze? She wanted to know; the need was as fierce within her as her body's need for his. She wanted him, and she understood that that want was not going to go away easily.

For the first time in a very long time, Briar was living in the present.

And it hurt.

The rain increased, drumming down upon them. The storm closed over York like Ivo's mysterious black glove, thunder muttering, lightning slashing across the leaden sky. King William's second castle rose like a gloomy warning on its motte, on the other side of the Ouse. Along either side of the river, near the wooden bridge, were the staithes, where the ships went on loading and unloading their cargoes in the rain. Smoke billowed from the roof of a small hospice, a shelter for the poor and homeless.

Thankfully Briar and Mary were no longer classed among them.

Home, for them, was one of a cluster of ancient and crumbling buildings that hugged the very edges of the River Ouse, beyond the busy staithes. These dwellings were relics of the days when the Vikings ruled here and called it Jorvik. Many buildings in York had been abandoned or burned through William's determination to occupy it; and many were being rebuilt. But areas like this old Viking outpost would never be reoccupied.

The Ouse had turned into an angry rush of gray water, winding its way down to the deeper places.

The wasted houses looked closer to collapse than
ever, roofs dipping, blackened timbers bulging.
The place looked so grim that no one would ever
have thought to look for two women there.

But inside their chosen shelter, it was warm and
dry, and they had done their best to make it their
own. The oak beams in the walls were sound, and
where the roof sagged, they had found a solid
support to prop under it. This particular dwelling
was larger than the rest; mayhap it had once been
the home of a leader or a Viking prince—even tall
Odo was able to stand upright within it. It be-
spoke of the Kenton sisters' inborn arrogance that
they would chose the largest and grandest hovel
for themselves.

Briar hurried to the hearth, and finding a spark
among the coals, carefully fed it into a blaze of
heat. Soon her face was pink and shining with
sweat, and she and Mary stripped off their sodden clothing and hung them by the fire to dry.
They wrapped themselves in blankets, and Briar
found some of the bread Jocelyn had given them
the day before while Mary poured water to drink.

It was a poor sort of meal, but they did not com-
plain. They had long ago learned to be grateful for
what they had. There had been many days after
their father died and they had been outcast by
Filby, when they hadn't eaten. At the memory of
her betrothed, Briar found a spark of her own—a
reminder of her burning hatred. Filby had once
kissed her fingers and swore his undying love to
her, but it had been all lies.

Nothing was real.

No one could be trusted.

How could she ever place her life in the hands of a man again, knowing of what they were capable? How could she believe Ivo when he promised her peace and safety? Surely 'twas better not to take the risk?

A knock on the door heralded Jocelyn and Odo. "How cozy it is in here! Odo, see how warm it is."

Jocelyn led her husband gently into the room, settling him by the fire, still speaking to him as if he understood every word she said. Odo stared blankly before him, the ruined side of his face immobile, the red flames coloring his graying hair and pale eyes. His hair had begun to go gray after he was struck down with his illness, now it was almost all gray, and he looked haggard and far older than his years. How much longer could he go on like this, even with Jocelyn's loving care?

"Sister, you should not come out in such weather!" Mary scolded her, hurrying to take Jocelyn's sodden cloak.

Jocelyn smiled and shook the raindrops from her hair. "Why should I be afraid of a little rain? Besides, I came because I had something to say."

Her glance to Briar was a warning, and Briar groaned inside. She knew what her sister was going to say before she even said it.

"Ivo de Vessey came to Lord Shelborne's home to ask questions about you."

"You are too late," Briar retorted. "He found us at the market."

Jocelyn's eyes narrowed. "And?"

"He—" She glanced at Mary and stopped.

Mary sighed loudly and rose to her feet. "Something I must not hear? Are my seventeen-year-old ears so innocent that they cannot be sullied? Oh, never mind! I will go and fetch more wood from the pile outside. But do not be too long in your gossip; it is cold out there and I do not want to get soaked again."

When she had gone, with much muttering, the two sisters exchanged a look.

"What ails her?" asked Jocelyn. " 'Tis not like Mary to speak so."

"I know not. She has been strange. Not herself at all. I wonder if she is catching a chill."

"Then tell me quickly, so that she can come back into the warm," Jocelyn demanded.

"He is smitten, I think. At least . . . he wants me, but he is cautious. He has secrets of his own, so he will not pry too deeply into mine in case he has to tell me his."

"So neither of you trusts the other," Jocelyn mocked. "Not quite true love."

Briar's eyes flashed. "Who said aught about love? This is a matter of our usefulness to each other, that is all."

Jocelyn looked like she would like to argue, but bit the words back. "When will you meet him again?"

"I know not."

"You have caught your man, Briar, but methinks he might be more than you can handle."

"We shall see." Briar hid her doubts beneath a confident exterior.

Just then Mary opened the door, her face sullen, raindrops glittering like pearls in her dark hair.

She dumped her armful of wood by the fire and, ignoring her sisters, set about rebuilding the blaze. Jocelyn rose to help her, speaking softly, teasing Mary to smile back, and then to laugh.

Briar watched them in silence. Once, they would have sat in their hall and servants would have performed their every command. Once, she had dressed in fine clothes, with jewels upon her fingers, and ridden her mare through the crisp mornings upon the moors.

Others had spoken jealously of the Kentons. Her father had too much, they said. He did not deserve his wealth and power, they said. Well, they would be happy now! At least he had treated the people he ruled with fairness and generosity, for all the good it had done him. Those same people had not lifted a hand to help his daughters when they had been outcast and desperate.

Jocelyn had brought food, and she and Mary were preparing a meal. Odo sat, head bowed, sunk into his own thoughts. Watching him, Briar wondered what he reflected on, so deep inside himself. Did he remember the past, and the hearty, good-natured man he had once been? Did he remember the love between him and Jocelyn, when they had wed in Normandy? They had been in York when Anna was murdered, but Odo had fallen dangerously ill—struck down as if by a lightning bolt—and there had been nothing he could do to help Briar's father. Jocelyn, too, had been fully occupied with her husband. At the time she had believed he would get better. He *had* recovered somewhat in body, although one side of his face remained distorted; it was his mind that had left him, like smoke through a hole in the thatch. Would it ever return?

Briar did not think so. Her sister may still hope, but every day Briar saw Odo growing more drawn and aged. As if the years were being sucked from him by whatever had taken his mind. She thought it would be a release for him when he died. Jocelyn would be the one to suffer; Jocelyn would be destroyed all over again.

There is danger in loving a man so completely.

Briar knew that was so, and she did not intend to give any man her heart.

Is it something you can stop from happening? Is it something you can control?

The question made her uneasy. She had never been so uncertain of herself before she met Ivo de Vessey. She had always seen her way clearly, chosen her path carefully. Now the candle she had lit—her candle of vengeance—was no longer bright enough to light her through the dark maze. She felt lost; she felt a tremendous urge to place her faith in Ivo de Vessey.

How could that be a good thing?

Ivo lifted the goblet and drank the contents down. The wine was good and he wished he could drink enough to cloud his thoughts, and to send Briar away.

From his place beside Ivo, Sweyn nodded at the room full of important men.

"They all come when Radulf calls."

It was true, they had all come. Some to do him homage, some just to gaze on the famous King's

Sword, and others because they feared his anger if they did not. He was more hated than he was loved. Did Briar hate him? Ivo asked himself. Was that why she had meant to take him to her bed? As some sort of revenge? Or was she like so many others, wanting to possess Radulf in the hope that some of his power would come off on her.

Ivo did not think so. Briar was a woman of strong passions. When she hated, she would hate with a single-minded determination, and from what he had heard of her past, she had much reason to hate. Aye, if he were a gambling man, like Sweyn, he would bet on hatred. Ivo understood hate, he knew how it could corrode and destroy, but he was also sure that hate could be turned around. Healed. Briar had opened his heart again—surely it was for a reason?

If a man could capture *her* fierce heart, would she bind herself to only him?

Ivo realized that the room had fallen silent. There was a group about Radulf, but he dominated them, standing head and shoulders above them. But that wasn't the reason for the hush. Just now Radulf did not look best pleased. A short, stout man cringed before him, as if he feared that Radulf was about to tear him limb from limb.

"My Lord Radulf." His voice was shaky as he swept a deep bow. "My lord, I only meant, my lord, that it might be as well if Lady Lily were here, my lord. The people trust her. My lord." The little man was clearly wishing himself anywhere but before the black stare of Radulf. "They need to know for themselves that she is hale and hearty."

"Hale and hearty!" roared Radulf. "Why in

God's name should she *not* be hale and hearty?
She is at Crevitch with our children. She cannot
come jolting all over the country, just because
some peasants think she should wipe their
noses!"

The vassal stammered something completely
incomprehensible, bowing so low he was almost
touching his own nose on the floor. "I meant no
offense, my lord," he added in a squeak.

"Then do not speak it!"

Still bowing, the stout little man eased himself
away.

"Our lord is in a quandary." Ivo spoke quietly,
not wishing Radulf to overhear him and deal him
the same fate. "His lady is safer in the south,
locked up at Crevitch, but without her visible
presence her lands in the north will continue to
seethe. And while the north hovers on the brink of
war, Radulf cannot go home to her."

Sweyn chuckled. "I see his problem. Will he
send for her, do you think?"

Ivo shrugged. "If he cannot make peace soon,
he may have no choice. The king will want to
know what is amiss, and 'tis doubtful he will scru-
ple to bring the lady north."

"Women are not as fragile as we think, although it pleases some men to treat them thus."

"Perhaps it would be better if it were the truth,"
Ivo retorted. "If they said aye and nay and did
what they were told, I for one would be much
happier."

Sweyn measured his friend with sparkling blue
eyes. "You speak of one lady in particular?"

"Aye." Ivo glowered.

"Is she not biddable enough for you?"

"She plays a deep game, but soon enough I will have all her secrets from her."

"Perhaps her sister will be easier to unlock?"

As he spoke the words, Sweyn's smile faded and he shook his head. It was as if the thought of Mary unsettled him in some way.

"What is it?" Ivo asked curiously. He had never seen Sweyn unsettled by a woman before.

"She is young, untried." Sweyn hesitated, and then laughed at his own thoughts. "I grow strange, my friend, pay me no mind. You know that I am never serious—life is a jest, to be enjoyed and gambled upon, and women are sweetmeats to make its passing more palatable."

But the words were spoken with an effort, and full of self-mockery. As if Sweyn made fun of himself.

"Take care, Sweyn, that you do not fall headfirst into my lady Mary's dark eyes and drown!" He frowned. "At least she seems sweet and gentle. Her sister is a frustrating baggage. Hot tempered, stubborn . . ."

And just as her songs had tugged at his heart, the brave tilt of her chin made Ivo want to ride out and slay dragons for her.

"Has she told you yet what game she plays?"

Ivo shook his head. He had told Sweyn he knew that they had once been the daughters of an important man, but not who that man was. Sweyn had shrugged and said it mattered not to him, as long as Ivo did not involve him in anything treasonous. Ivo had forborne to answer, for that may well be the case.

"While I was waiting for you at the market today, Mary told me where she and her sister lived."

"And?"

"Does the address interest you?"

"You know it does. Tell it to me, Sweyn."

Sweyn rubbed his brow. "I have so many things to think of, I may have forgotten it. What will you give me to remember?"

Ivo glowered at him. "Tell it to me or face me tomorrow in the training yard."

"Now I am afraid," Sweyn mocked, ostentatiously loosening the muscles of his shoulders and rolling his arms. "I am half inclined to refuse to tell you, just so that you have to fight me for it. And you would, Ivo, we both know that." He grinned at his friend's angry expression. "Do not strike me down. I will tell you where your songstress lives. 'Tis a place by the river. The houses are old Viking dwellings, and they are falling down, although the one they have chosen seems sturdy enough. Still ... 'tis not a good place, Ivo. The staithes are closeby, and such locations are rife with cutthroats."

Ivo shook his head in disgust, his hand clenching on the hilt of his sword. Briar, in such a place? He had the wild urge to ride there right now and bring her to safety. But he knew if he did such a thing she would refuse him, and abuse him, and enjoy doing so. Frustrated, he ground his teeth, and then a thought occurred to him. He turned to stare at his friend.

"How do you know about the state of their abode, Sweyn?"

Sweyn's gaze slid from his.

Ivo blinked. Could there be a hint of color in the Dane's tanned cheeks? Could Sweyn actually be blushing? Now it was Ivo's turn to play teasing games.

"You went there, didn't you? You wanted to see for yourself whether or not they were safe? Ah, Sweyn, what of your boast that no one woman would ever be enough for you?"

Sweyn lifted his eyes, and for once they lacked their laughing sparkle. Indeed, Sweyn looked confused, and Ivo felt almost sorry for him.

" 'Tis true, Ivo. One woman would not be enough. That is why I cannot think of having her, I dare not think of having her. This madness will pass. I *know* it will pass."

Ivo nodded with mock solemnity. "Of course it will pass, my friend. It is like a fever—you either survive it or you don't."

If it were possible, Sweyn appeared even more miserable.

"Ivo!"

It was a voice he knew. "Lord Henry!" Ivo turned to greet one of Radulf's oldest and closest friends. Broad of shoulder and strikingly handsome, Henry was also the owner of a clever and diplomatic tongue, and accordingly spent most of his time at court.

"I have news for you," Henry said to Ivo, when the greetings were done. "And you will not like it."

"Then tell me quickly, my lord."

"Your brother, Miles, is come to York. I saw him near Bootham Bar two days ago, but he slipped away before I could stop him."

Miles!

For a moment Ivo couldn't move, couldn't think, couldn't feel. And then it was as if a great dark cloud fell over him, taking his breath and filling him with despair. Miles, his brother, who hated him and wished him dead. Who, all his life, had given Ivo nothing but misery. The last time they had come close to meeting, Gunnar Olafson had been there to shield him from Miles's malevolence. Now Gunnar was in the south, and Ivo was in York.

And so was Miles.

"But there is a warrant for him—he is to be arrested for his treason at Somerford." Sweyn was speaking the words Ivo was thinking. Miles had, under Lord Fitzmorton's orders, overtaken the manor at Somerford and threatened the overlordship of Radulf and, through him, King William himself. Lord Fitzmorton had managed to wriggle his way out of trouble, but he had used Miles as his scapegoat, blaming him for most of what had occurred.

Ivo had thought, at the time, it was convenient that Miles had vanished so completely. Fitzmorton would not want Miles de Vessey questioned, in case he told the truth about the affair. Although, if he did tell the truth, it would be the first time!

Lord Henry was speaking. "Nevertheless, warrant or no warrant, I have seen him. Lord Fitzmorton may claim all he likes that, after Miles left Somerford, he vanished from sight, but I do not believe him. Miles is too clever, too valuable for Fitzmorton to lose him entirely. And he knows too much. Fitzmorton will have sent him up here, to his lands in the north, to wait until the king can be persuaded to pardon him. 'Tis a misfortune for us all that Radulf has also come north."

"Miles will be certain to make Ivo's time here dangerous and uncomfortable," Sweyn said with a frown. "I have never known two brothers less similar."

Ivo just shook his head. Miles, here! After what had happened in the summer, he had hoped his brother had taken ship to Normandy or perhaps France. Was Miles to follow him about forever, like an evil shadow? He would never be safe while Miles lived, and he had known that for a long time. But knowing something and acting upon it were two different things, particularly when it was his own brother. Hate him or not, Ivo had an aversion to killing members of his own family.

And yet it may come to that.

"I will have to find him and make him leave. He will not go, so then I will have to fight him. And if we fight, he will try to kill me, so I will have to kill him."

When he looked up, he caught the tail end of the glance Sweyn and Lord Henry had exchanged between them. They thought that Miles might kill *him*. He could see the fear in their eyes. Aye, he told himself bleakly, mayhap Miles would triumph. He had always triumphed before. But whatever the outcome, Ivo sensed the day of battle was fast approaching.

"You saw him two days ago?" he asked Lord Henry, while his stomach churned.

"Aye."

"Does Lord Radulf know?"

"I have told him, but at the moment he has other matters on his mind."

Ivo nodded grimly. "Then 'tis up to me to deal with Miles's evil. I will see to this, Lord Henry. Leave it with me."

Henry gave him a searching glance, and then nodded, content that it was so. "Good man!"

When he had gone, Sweyn said hopefully, "Perhaps Miles has taken fright from York. Perhaps seeing Lord Henry has hurried him onto a ship away from England. Far away."

"I pray 'tis so, Sweyn. I pray 'tis so."

But Ivo knew it wasn't. He sensed Miles's presence, like some foul miasma. Aye, he and his brother would have their day of reckoning, and soon.

Chapter 6

Ivo steadied his horse and narrowed his eyes against the glare off the water. The staithes, or landing stages, toward Ouse bridge were busy with boats and their cargoes. More craft moved upon the river, taking advantage of the still, morning air. Voices drifted from the two Norman castles, the shouts of soldiers who had been up since the Angelus bell, preparing for the day.

But here, where Briar lived, it was an island of solitude. Flotsam had collected in the mud along the shore, and most of the dwellings had fallen into heaps of wood and straw. There was a sense of decay and neglect. Of damp despair.

Ivo did not like to think of her living here, not without his protection. He knew he had no rights to her, but still he felt as if he did. In his mind she was his, and his knightly duty was clear. 'Twas a pity he was no longer a knight.

That had been Miles's doing.

"We are brothers, after all," Miles said. *"Let us try, this once, to stand side by side as we fight our lord's enemy."*

"How can you expect me to forget our sister? How can I fight beside Matilda's murderer?"

Miles's eyes filled with tears. *"Do you not think her death lodges in my heart, too, Ivo? I do not need you to remind me of what I caused. She was my sister, too."*

And Ivo, horrified and suspicious to find Miles in the pay of the same lord as himself, had nevertheless swallowed both in the hope that maybe, just maybe, Miles had changed. That maybe they might be truly brothers, at last.

But Miles hadn't been interested in protecting his lord, or fighting his lord's enemy. He had wanted only to hurt Ivo. At the crucial moment he had struck. He had lulled Ivo into dropping his guard, persuaded him to drink from a poisoned cup—or, at least, wine tainted with a sleeping draft. Ivo had slept deeply, and while he slept, the attack upon the lord had come. Miles had fought well, brilliantly, sending the enemy about, but the lord Ivo had been meant to play bodyguard to had been killed by a stray arrow bolt.

That was suspicious enough, Ivo later thought, but by then it was too late to prove anything against Miles. No one would have believed him.

Ivo still clearly remembered the moment he had awoken. Head pounding and mouth dry, he had stumbled out into the bailey, only to realize what had happened. The rest of the garrison had turned to him, silently condemning. And then Miles, quiet, restrained, but unable to hide from Ivo the evil gleam of triumph in his eyes.

"Shame upon you, Ivo. You were drunk, and now you have let us all down. I have forgiven your cowardice before, but I will not do so again. From this moment, you are no longer my brother."

Ivo had been stripped of his knighthood and sent out into the world, disgraced. At first he had been too bitter to care what became of him. He had lived with outlaws in the forest and fully expected to be hanged. Then, after robbing a cart belonging to a bishop, he had had the good fortune to be pursued and captured by Gunnar Olafson. Gunnar had been paid by the bishop to return his goods, and this he had done.

Ivo he had kept.

Ivo never understood why. What redeeming feature had Gunnar seen in the wild-haired, black-bearded creature he had become? Whatever it was, Gunnar had never swerved in his belief in Ivo, and Ivo knew he owed him his life. He had fought at Gunnar's side up and down the country, and at some stage during that time, he had fought his way out of the abyss. Ivo had been with Gunnar Olafson's little band of misfits ever since. In a way, it had been his home—the only home he had.

But now Gunnar had wed Lady Rose of Somerford Manor, and no longer called himself a mercenary. He had given his men a choice—they could remain at Somerford with him or take what was owed them and go their own ways.

One of Gunnar's five mercenaries, Alfred, had remained at Somerford, mainly because of the miller's pretty daughter. Reynard and Ethelred were still deciding, and were currently at Crevitch with Lady Lily, and Ivo and Sweyn had opted to continue as mercenaries in the employ of Lord Radulf.

Ivo could not see himself getting fat at Somerford Manor, although he would miss Gunnar. Miss him far more than he had ever missed Miles.

He still did not understand why Miles hated him so. They had different mothers, but Miles had always been the favored elder son in his father's eyes. Ivo knew he had done nothing to his brother—apart from observe his evil actions. Perhaps that had been enough. Perhaps Miles did not want any witnesses. Would Miles live more easily with himself once Ivo was dead?

It was a puzzle to Ivo. And now Miles was in York, and it seemed as if the end to their bitter story might be fast approaching. Could he defeat his brother? Each and every other time they had met in anger, Miles had won. Would this time be different?

He would know that soon enough.

With a grim smile, Ivo urged his horse forward, toward the dilapidated dwelling that was the home of Briar, songstress and second daughter of Lord Richard Kenton.

Briar had washed her hair. She was seated, drying it by the fire and running her fingers through the long, chestnut strands. There were times, after she was outcast, when she had been tempted to cut her hair. Especially when she and Mary had been on their own, and had had to dress as men for their own protection. There was a freedom in being a man, and one time Briar held a knife blade to her long locks. What was the use in having such hair when she was a lady no more? she had asked herself. She had no servants to help her care for it. Hair such as hers was for admiration and homage, and Briar had lost both.

But an inner stubbornness had prevented her. If she cut her hair, she had reasoned, then *they* would have won. And that would never do.

Briar was wearing her old linen chemise—why get her clothes all wet? Mary was dressed, however, and was busy setting out their bowls, about to serve up the mess of boiled grain and water and the few crumbled pieces of goat's cheese that was their breakfast. The smell of the steaming pot in the warm room was not unpleasant. Briar ran her fingers through her hair again, relaxed, unprepared.

The loud knock against their door made both women look up, startled.

"Is it Jocelyn?" Wide-eyed, Mary turned to Briar for confirmation.

But Briar shook her head. "Jocelyn does not knock like that."

"Then who . . . ?"

Fumbling down beside her stool, Briar searched until her fingers found, and gripped, the sword. *Her* sword. The weapon was only half the size of the swords worn by fighting men, and very much lighter. When, as a girl, Briar had shown an interest in learning the skill of defending herself with a sword, it had amused her father to have one made especially for her. Briar had been delighted with it, and spent many hours practicing. When Mary had smuggled her harp from Castle Kenton, Briar had taken her sword. The detail said something about each of them.

"Who is it?" Briar called out loudly, with all the bravado she could muster.

"Ivo de Vessey!"

The two women stilled. "What does he want?" Mary whispered.

Briar had a good idea what Ivo wanted. Her question was, "How did he know we live here?"

Mary flushed bright red. "Oh, Briar! I did not think. When Sweyn asked me, I did not think to deny him."

Briar frowned. She did not blame her sister— she was young and innocent—but it seemed that Ivo de Vessey was encroaching upon her private life more and more, and that had no part in her plan.

" 'Tis too late now," she told Mary with wary eyes. "If we do not let him in, I fear he will break down our door."

Mary nodded and went to the door. She heaved up the heavy bar that held it fast shut, and set it aside. Light spilled in, although the half-open door gave some shelter.

Briar held her breath.

"Lady Mary, I beg pardon for my early visit. Is your sister here?"

His voice, quiet and deep, sent shivers across Briar's skin, and started a burning in the pit of her stomach. The attraction was almost too strong to resist, and she shivered. Why was it this one man seemed so easily able to stir the fire in her blood?

"Briar?"

Mary, half blinded by the sunlight, had her hand still resting on the door as she awaited Briar's signal to say him yay or nay. But before Briar was able to decide to give her either, the door was inexorably forced wide open, causing Mary to take a hasty step backward. Ivo was a big, dark shadow against the early light.

Briar did not need to see the details of him to know he stared directly at her. His body seemed to go very still . . .

Jesu, she wore only her old chemise!

Briar took a shaky breath, and berated herself for being too fazed by his arrival to remember to cover herself. Could he see her skin through the thin cloth? And her hair was half wet and loose all about her. If it were any other man, Briar would have been embarrassed and appalled to be seen in such a state. But it was Ivo, and she was oddly excited. She *wanted* him to see her, she *wanted* him to desire her.

Jesu, what is happening to me? Have I turned into a whore after just one night with him?

Nay, she thought wryly, just a fool who yearned for Ivo de Vessey's attention. Well, she certainly seemed to have it now. Her face felt flushed by the heat of the fire, but in contrast her voice was frozen with reproof. Lady Briar at her best.

"Your manners are wanting, de Vessey."

Mary hovered closeby. "Is your friend with you, Ivo?"

Ivo took his eyes from Briar with an effort. Tall and slim, dark-haired and dark-eyed, Mary was pretty enough in a timid and unassuming manner.

She had none of the fire of her sister, and she was nothing like Sweyn's usual doves. The fact that he had given Mary more than a single glance was astounding, for Sweyn liked his women buxom with come-hither eyes and easy smiles. He was not a man for hard work when it came to women, and Mary looked like a lot of hard work to Ivo.

He smiled at her kindly—people, he thought, would always be kind to Mary. "Sweyn is here. We thought 'twas best for someone to stay with you, while your sister and I are away. But Sweyn will not come inside—he asked me to tell you that he is quite happy to remain on guard outside."

In fact Sweyn had been adamant, and the expression in his eyes had turned almost hunted.

The girl looked thoughtful, and a little disappointed. Ah, thought Ivo, does the wind blow that way then?

"Then I will leave him there, if that is what he wishes."

Ivo smiled. "You will be safe, Mary. Sweyn is good at protecting pretty ladies."

Briar's sharp tongue sliced at him.

"Do not think to beguile my sister. She is far too fine for a *disgraced* knight."

Ivo's body stiffened as he felt the wound reopen. Disgraced, aye, that was what he was. She had cut him in the reminding, but he would not give her the satisfaction of knowing it. Briar, the firebrand, spat flame at all about her, but Ivo was determined to make her burn for another reason entirely.

He took a stride into the room, ducking his head beneath the lintel, and closed the door behind him. Inside, the dwelling was bigger than he had imagined, and the ceiling was not pressing down upon his head.

With the light quenched, Briar was able to see him.

Her heart flopped like a fresh-caught fish.

The bruise on his jaw was fading, but if anything he appeared even more dangerous. There was an added gravity to him today, as if he had come bearing bad news.

He is leaving again.

The words froze her, and she stared at him, waiting for the pain to ease.

But all he said was, "My name is Ivo. Why do you not use it?"

Briar felt relief pour through her, making her dizzy. He was not going away. He had not come to tell her that.

Ivo seemed unaware of her inner turmoil, as his gaze wandered over her in a leisurely way. He took in her skimpy chemise, only coming to her knees, and her bare legs showing below it, and her bare arms, and her long, damp hair. More quickly, he took note of the pot bubbling over the coals, and the clothing, wet from yesterday, steaming to the side. It was a very domestic scene, a place of women, and safe for a man like him. Or so he would think.

Briar actually saw him relax. His shoulders loosened, his hand dropped away from the hilt of his sword, and his serious air vanished as his wide mouth curled into a smile. Aye, she thought, annoyed now, he has set aside his vigilance because he sees no need for it here. Two women,

alone and undefended? He would think himself
far the superior if it came to a fight.

The urge to shake that male arrogance was too
strong to resist, and Briar did not even try.

She tightened her grasp on her sword hilt, and
lifted it into clear view. From the corner of her eye
she saw him pause. Slowly, enjoying the moment,
she turned the blade, admiring the manner in
which the firelight glinted upon it.

"You are armed?"

Briar glanced at him, saw his brows lifted in
surprise. "Aye," she retorted smugly, "and I know
how to use it."

His surprise didn't turn to instant terror, as she
had hoped. At least, not yet. "You would defend
yourself with that?"

"To the death."

He laughed, his face turning handsome.
"Whose death, that is the question. You are blood-
thirsty for a wench. I will not fight you today. Today, I have other plans for you."

Briar didn't even try to hide her annoyance.
Why could he not behave as she wanted? "I am
not going anywhere with you, de Vessey! Mary
and I must play and sing tonight at Lord Shelborne's hall. 'Tis important I rest my voice," she
added, and used one hand to stroke her throat.

For a moment he simply watched the movements of her long fingers against her smooth
flesh, as if he found it impossible to look away. His
voice sounded hoarse. "You can rest your voice
later, demoiselle. Dress yourself, for I have something to show you."

His arrogance was really beyond bearing! "I don't want to see anything you have to show me."

"Ah, but you will. Do as I say."

Briar stood up to her full height—which unfortunately was not terribly tall. The hem of the chemise brushed her knees, and she shook back her hair, until it hung out of the way, down her back. She took up a fighting stance, gripping her sword in both hands in the manner in which she had been taught.

"Nay, de Vessey. I do no man's bidding!"

Something shifted in his eyes. Amusement, certainly, and confidence in his own abilities to best her, but something else, too. Before she could decide what it was, Ivo took the two steps needed to reach her, neatly avoiding the drying clothing strung out near the fire.

Jesu, he was tall. And *big*. He looked down at her with a flicker of a smile, as if he found her determination to defend herself a pleasant diversion on an otherwise dull morning. And there again was that other thing in his black eyes . . .

Briar realized then that it was interest, excitement. He found her behavior curious, but he was enjoying it. Well she would show him!

Briar made a lunge at him, never intending to connect. He froze, eyes widening with surprise.

"You are bold, demoiselle."

"I will fight you if I must." She waved the sword blade in front of his nose, but he didn't even flinch.

"You will not hurt me."

He said it with such surety her temper boiled.

"You are wrong! I am more than happy to slice you end to end, de Vessey!"

He grinned. His eyes gleamed. There was no hiding their expression now. She was challenging his male strength and superiority, and he liked it. Jesu! He *liked* it . . .

Her concentration slipped, and before she knew it he had snaked out his hand and covered hers; they gripped the sword hilt together. His grip was relentless. He smiled into her eyes and slowly, with little effort, he pushed the sword away and down. Briar's muscles strained against him, arms shaking, but it was no use. The blade tilted until it pointed harmlessly to the ground.

That deep voice murmured in her ear.

"I have enough bruises for now, demoiselle. I beg you will not hurt me."

He was laughing at her! But Briar had felt his strength, and knew in her fury that he was barely exerting himself, while she was pushing against him with all her might. Time for another approach.

With a shrug of her shoulder, Briar let herself relax, the sword loose in her fingers.

"I did not want to hurt you," she retorted.

He grinned at her like a boy, and she saw in his eyes that he really was enjoying himself. But not in the manner she had expected. He wanted to kiss her. And more. *I want you.* She could see it in his eyes. The need thrummed in him, making his body hard, and starting an answering need in her. Her skin heated, her breasts tightened, and that place between her legs ached. And all that from just being close to him! Warily, for her own protec-

tion, Briar backed away from him . . . and put her
bare foot into a bowl of breakfast.

The mushy grain squished up between her
toes, like warm, soft mud. With a gasp of disgust,
Briar leapt forward, and straight into his arms. Ivo
caught hold of her, his surprised gaze meeting
hers. And then surprise turned to laughter as he
realized what had happened, and the laughter
burst from him.

Angry and embarrassed, Briar pulled away.

"You are an oaf," she hissed furiously. "Fight
me, you coward! We will see who is the winner
here."

Ivo wiped his eyes. He shouldn't have laughed.
He knew it. But she had looked so funny, standing
there with her foot in the bowl. So sweetly funny.
Laughter threatened again, but he held it back,
and cleared his throat. When he looked up, the
younger sister, Mary, was watching him, face
slack in amazement. Did men not laugh in her
life? Or had the humor simply been beaten out of
the Kenton sisters?

Abruptly Ivo lost the urge to laugh. "Briar," he
began, trying for patience, "dress yourself, or do
you wish me to carry you off in your shift?"

"I wish nothing of the sort!" she told him furiously. She had that small sword in her hands, and
Ivo silently cursed himself for not removing it
from her when he had the chance. And she was
thrusting it at him, as if she fully intended to fight
him.

The blade did look sharp and well polished, despite its lack of size. She had obviously been taught

to use it, but would she? Even when she was in a
temper, like now? Would she really hurt him? Ivo
did not think so, but as his own temper flared up,
he decided that if she wanted to play at soldier,
then he would oblige.

Slowly, watching her eyes, he drew his own
sword from its scabbard.

A flicker of unease lit the hazel of her eyes, a
moment of doubt, but she subdued it, adjusting
and tightening her grip on her weapon. Aye, she
was brave. Foolish, mayhap, but no coward, he
would give her that. Did she really think to best a
man like him, who had been fighting mock battles
since he was eight? And with that puny weapon?
He was a big man, and his weapon reflected it.
With intimidating ease, he raised his own sword
in front of him, and the firelight caused the green
stone eyes of the griffin to gleam and the mighty
blade to catch fire.

Briar held her ground, but now he could see the
tremor in her hands. Slowly, giving her plenty of
time, he brought his blade down in a sweeping
arc, and she stopped him. He could have sliced
right through her blocking movement—he was
bigger and heavier—but he didn't, instead swinging his blade to her other side and allowing her to
block him there, too.

She smiled, pleased with her small victories.
Quickly, she swung at his right, stepping in close.
Ivo blocked now, needing to retreat so that he
could wield his larger weapon in the small space.
The clang of steel was loud. Briar came on, striking out at him again and again. Ivo defended, and
with each stroke his admiration for her tactics and

her skill grew. Aye, she was good, but not good enough to best him.

Time she realized it.

So quickly she had no chance to stop him, Ivo brought his sword up with a numbing blow, knocking her blade away from him. He reached out, and snatched her weapon from her. He had tossed it aside, far into the shadows, before she could even catch her breath.

She was shocked and dismayed, and mayhap a little humiliated. He had won. But to his surprise, Ivo did not enjoy a sense of victory. He did not like to see her beaten, despite knowing it had needed to be done. Aye, he preferred to allow her her victories over him. But in this matter he could not give way, not even in a mock battle. If Ivo was to be Briar's protector, then she must trust in his ability to fight for her. And win.

"I suppose you will run me through now, de Vessey."

Her furious little face glowered up at him as she stood up straight in her worn chemise, her fists clenched by her sides.

Ivo's mouth twisted. "I do not kill women, demoiselle."

"But you are a disgraced knight, de Vessey, surely they kill anyone?"

Fury roared into him, like floodwaters through an open sluice. Somehow he controlled it. He had grown better at self-control since he met Briar. He had had no choice. One of them must display some maturity, he told himself self-righteously.

Slowly, Ivo slid his sword back into its scabbard, never once taking his gaze from hers. She didn't look away but he could tell she wanted to. Aye, she was hasty and impetuous, arrogant and stubborn. But he understood why she was striking out at him. It was because she felt so helpless and impotent, because of the need to *do* something in her own defense.

Briar was not used to feeling helpless.

He wanted to tell her that there was no need for her to feel like that. He would fight her battles for her; he would stand strong at her side.

"Can you not speak?" she demanded.

Her eyes shot darts into his. But her body was warm and scented through her thin undergarment, the skin of her legs and arms smooth and rosy in the firelight, her breasts heaving from emotion and exertion. Her chestnut hair had almost dried, curling thickly about her. Her mouth was lush and full . . .

He wanted her. More than any woman he had ever known, he wanted her. Desire hardened his body.

"I can speak," he said, his voice husky with need, "but do you want to hear my words?"

Her eyes narrowed in suspicion, the thick dark lashes sweeping down. She must have read his intentions in his gaze, because she made to turn and run. But it was too late. Ivo reached out and caught her about the waist, hauling her in against his body. The feel of all that soft flesh was almost his undoing, and Ivo bit back a groan. She pushed her palms against his chest, twisting away, but he was too strong for her and they both knew it.

Ivo leaned closer, breathing in the scent of her newly washed hair. His hands tightened on her waist, sliding around to her back, feeling the pull of flesh and muscle. He knew the moment she felt his desire, hard against her stomach, for she went still. Her eyes widened and flew to his.

"You make me want you," he whispered, slowly and deliberately, for her ears only. "I know you are as hot on the inside as you are on the outside. Send your sister away, demoiselle, and we will spend the morning in your bed."

She considered it! Just for a moment, he saw the indecision in her face, a flash of hot need to match his own. His heart jolted in anticipation. But then she had conquered it, and the brief weakness vanished beneath a new wave of her ever-present temper.

"Burn in hell, de Vessey!"

"I fear, Briar, that is something I may well do."

He sighed. There was a world of regret in that sigh; it was the sound of a man who wanted what he could not have. He let her go, and moved to open the door, then paused, outlined by the light. His voice had turned cold and brusque.

"Get dressed, demoiselle. I will wait outside for you. But do not make me wait too long."

"Curse him!" Briar gasped, swinging about, pulling at her hair like one demented.

One moment she was so furious with him for his arrogant confidence that she longed to scratch out his eyes, and then the next she could weep and rail with disappointment because he had given up too easily. What was wrong with her?

Briar knew now, when it was too late, that she should have softened sooner. Wasn't she supposed to be winning him to her side? Spitting at him and daring him to fight her was hardly the way to a man's heart . . . Was it? And yet, sometimes, she wondered if it might be the way to Ivo's. When she had raised her sword and challenged him to do battle with her, he had looked at her in such a way. As though his lust for her was so great, he wanted to have her there and then.

Aye, he lusted after her. She was not mistaken in that. But she had best take care she did not play too hard to catch—if she ran too fast and too hard, she might outrun him altogether.

Slowly Briar became aware that Mary was staring at her with big, dark eyes. As if Briar had grown an extra head.

"You deliberately made him angry," her sister said, with a mingling of fear and amazement. "Aren't you afraid of what he will do, Briar, if you make him angry?"

Briar shrugged as if she didn't care. "He is all bluff, Mary. He will not hurt me."

Mary frowned. "But how do you know for certain?"

Briar began to pull on her gown with impatient fingers. "I just do." She tied the girdle with sharp, angry jerks, and then drew on her cloak. The garment was still warm despite its hard wear; it had served her well, though the Lincoln green wool had faded almost to gray.

How do I know for certain?

Briar didn't know *how* she knew, she just . . . *knew*. Mayhap she was stupid to believe as she did—her past had shown her that men were not to be trusted. And yet there was a solid core of cer-

tainty inside her, that told her Ivo de Vessey
would never hurt her. A moment ago she had
been in a temper with him, she had fought him,
but it was not a real fight. Instead, there had been
a kind of excitement in it, as if she were testing her
mettle, setting the limits she could go with him.
And he had been willing to let her have her
way . . . for a time. When he had had enough, he
had put an end to it.

He indulged me.

The realization should irritate her. Instead Briar
felt warm and comfortable, a sensation very like
the feelings she had had when she was safe and
secure at Castle Kenton.

He wants me, she reminded herself brusquely,
and while he wants me, I am safe from him. She could
manipulate him to her will, take what she wanted,
use him for her own ends. And he would allow it.

*And then? What will happen once it is over? Will he
let me walk away from him so easily? And will I want
to go?*

Aye, there was a question!

Briar couldn't answer it, and thought it best not
to try. She firmed her lips, and set about the task of
binding her hair into one long braid before she
twisted it up under the fur-lined hood of her
cloak. Then she sat down on the stool to pull on
her woollen, oft-darned stockings and cast-off
shoes.

Mary watched her dress, clearly still not satisfied. "You don't even know this man," she reminded Briar, "and yet you trust him with your
life. Why is that, sister?"

"That is no concern of yours, Mary."

"But it is, Briar. What if he had killed you just now with his sword? What would have become of me then?"

"*Killed* me?" Briar spluttered. "Ivo de Vessey will not *kill* me. Nay, 'tis not my death he wants from me. You are too young to understand—"

"But I am not too young!" Mary cried, and she looked flushed and cross. "I am seventeen, Briar. I am a woman. Why will you not speak to me like one?"

Her words gave Briar pause, but there was no time now for long discussions with Mary on what it was and was not good for her to hear. She sighed, and made her voice gentler, calmer. "We will speak of it later."

Mary groaned and threw up her hands. "Now you talk to me as if I were a lackwit! Go then, Briar. I can see you are like a mare at the stallion's gate. Go to your stallion. In truth, I would welcome some time on my own."

Briar had stopped, her hand on the door. She was shocked at her sister's earthy words. What did Mary know of mares and stallions? Clearly she needed to sit down with her young sister and have a serious talk.

But not now.

Ivo de Vessey was waiting, and the tingle up and down her spine made her wonder if there was some truth in Mary's fanciful observations after all.

Mary was standing with her back to Briar, arms folded tight about herself, almost as if she were keeping her emotions from spilling out. Briar could read the tension in her rigid shoulders and back.

"I do not know where I am going, but I will try not to take too long." Her voice sounded almost pleading, as if she were asking Mary's permission. Briar cleared her throat, and tried for a firmer tone. "Do not fret, Mary. The Dane is outside, on watch. You will be safe until I return."

"As you say, sister." Mary did not turn around, but she sounded softer, more her usual self. "I will be quite safe with Sweyn."

"Good." Briar hesitated a moment longer, knowing her disgraced knight awaited her. She admitted to herself that she was curious to see where he meant to take her, and her blood ran hotter at the thought of spending time alone with him. But Mary was her sister . . .

Mary glanced over her shoulder, her face pale. "Go, Briar," she said impatiently. "I do not need you."

Briar smiled, relief conquering the guilt in her heart. She opened the door and went outside.

Chapter 7

The river was gray today, a shiny steel-gray that dazzled her eyes. A pair of dippers floated upon its surface, their feathers sleek and wet, while a heron searched among the rubbish along the shore. Ivo waited by his horse, looking stiff and uneasy. Briar knew, as if he had told her, that he did not feel safe in this place. He was wrong; it was safe enough if a person was careful. She and Mary had had only one unpleasant encounter: a man had tried to get inside their home, but had soon fled when Briar came at him with her sword, and he realized they weren't the helpless women he had thought them. They had not been molested since.

Their dwelling was warm and dry, better than many of the other accommodations they had found since they left Castle Kenton. It would do.

And besides, what choice had they? Despite their popularity they were lowly women entertainers, and the money they earned was barely enough for food and clothes. They could not afford to live high. And Jocelyn could not jeopardize her, and above all Odo's, place in Lord Shelborne's household by smuggling in her sisters. They had agreed on that. Odo always came first with Jocelyn.

Briar walked up to Ivo and tilted her head to see his face. It was closed, watchful, but he did not move back, not even when the toes of her shoes touched his and her cloak brushed his legs. She realized then that she liked that about him, the fact that he didn't back down from her.

"What do you want to show me?"

Something moved in his closed face. Pain? Regret? But even as her suspicions were aroused, he had resumed his intent, black stare.

"You will see soon enough, demoiselle."

She narrowed her eyes at him. "I do not like surprises, de Vessey."

"Come," he said impatiently, and held out his linked hands for her foot, to throw her into the saddle.

Briar glanced behind her. "What of my sister? Where is the Dane? I cannot leave her here, alone."

Ivo's expression turned superior. "You think *you* are strong enough to stand between her and any cutthroats who lurk here? Briar, you delude yourself. You are a small woman, and although I am sure you would fight to the death, you would soon be overcome if the man were determined."

"I do well enough," she replied, refusing to be drawn.

After giving her another long look, he nodded his head in the direction of one of the fallen cottages. The big blond man leaned against a crumbling wall, arms crossed, as still as if he were asleep. He did not appear to be keeping watch, thought Briar, and yet something in his very stillness made her think of a hawk hovering, waiting to dive upon its prey.

Mary was in good hands, then.

Briar hitched up her skirt to show her darned stockings and old shoes, and was amused at the blind expression that came into Ivo's eyes. He was good at protecting his feelings—or was he protecting hers? With a mental shrug, she set her foot in his hands, and he threw her up into the saddle as easily as if she had been a feather.

As he prepared to mount behind her, Briar looked down, into his upturned face. Their eyes met and locked.

To her surprise, he smiled.

As if he was pleased simply to be in her company.

Ivo rode through the quiet streets of York, with Briar tucked securely into his arms. At first she had tried to hold herself apart, her body stiff and ungiving, but gradually she had relaxed and slipped further into the curve of his body. It was more comfortable for her, but not so much for him. Her haughty demeanor did little to alleviate his desire for her.

His body ached.

When he had seen her before the fire, her long hair glowing, her body near enough to naked, he had felt as raw as a youth with his first wench. If Mary hadn't been there, Ivo doubted he would have been able to stop himself from grabbing her up, carrying her to her bed, and making her his again. And again.

The memories of their night together were as fresh and new in his mind as if they had just happened. She might resist him at every turn—he smiled to himself as he remembered her attempts to fight him with her puny sword—but it made no difference to how he felt. He wanted her. More than that—he wanted to protect her, defend her, carry the memory of her kisses into battle, and win for her sake.

Why wouldn't she see that?

But of course she could not, he reminded himself bitterly. What woman would want the services of a disgraced knight? No wonder she thought it best to protect herself. She did not trust him, and who could blame her?

The king's castle rose high and solemn above the newly constructed rooftops, while a flag flapped wildly in the breeze. During the last siege of York all the buildings surrounding the castle had been burned by William's men, so that the rebels should have no protection on their approach. Now that there was peace again, the area was gradually being reestablished.

The woman in his arms shifted. Ivo felt all the softness leave her body as she realized where they were going. Like a wild creature scenting danger, Briar stiffened.

"You are safe," he said firmly, slowing his horse as they made the approach. "There is a man I want you to see. He is a prisoner here. He knows you."

"He knows *me*?"

" 'Twas he who gave me this fine bruise upon my face."

"And you want me to congratulate him?" she asked cautiously, her eyes gleaming.

He laughed. Jesu, he admired her. She was making jokes, when he well knew she was terrified. The king was her enemy and this was his castle— how could she not think the worst?

"Aye, you can do that if you wish."

They had been admitted through the gate and into the bailey without any problems. Now Ivo dismounted and, reaching up, grasped Briar's waist, bringing her down beside him. She stepped closer and he hid a smile. *Now* he was her protector, disgraced or not.

Without asking first, he took her cool fingers in his and led her toward the place where the prisoners were held.

It was cold and forbidding here, but little different to most dungeons. Ivo had seen many, though rarely from the inside. Briar, he suspected, had seen none; indeed, it appeared she did not like the look of this one at all. Perhaps she was imagining herself in here, imagining what it would be like if she were locked up by the king's order.

" 'Tis a dreary place," she murmured.

He wanted to pull her closer, to kiss her, to tease her in his arms until she was warm and feisty again. His sharp-tongued lady. But there were too many eyes upon them, and he did not wish to make her a cause for gossip. With a murmured word to the guard, he led her into a cell.

The man he sought was master of a gloomy corner. He sat on a bench before a smoky brazier, one of his legs heavily bandaged. Graying hair hung long about his shoulders, and pale eyes adorned a tanned and wrinkled face. He peered at them as if he had trouble seeing them.

"I have the lady you asked for," Ivo said clearly, and drew Briar forward.

She resisted but then, with a deep breath, allowed it.

The prisoner began to struggle to his feet.

"Nay, do not stand," Briar said hastily. She took a step and stopped. A sense of recognition swept over her, ousting the sickness in her belly. 'Twas this wretched place, she thought, 'twould make anyone bilious.

Briar glanced at Ivo, but he stood to one side, as if he had no part in the conversation. His eyes were fierce, glowing with some strong emotion, but she could not read it.

"Do I know you?" she asked the prisoner uncertainly. "Why have you asked for me, old man?"

"Aye, you know me, lady." The pale eyes lifted to hers, and froze her in place. Nausea twisted within her again, while that well-remembered voice said, "I am Anthony the traitor, lady, but once I was called Sir Anthony Delacourt."

Sharp memory, like the sting of a whip to her flesh.

Sir Anthony, vassal and friend, stood by her father at Castle Kenton, his face as grim as Lord Richard's, as the two men prepared to make treason against the king.

"I thought you died at the hands of Radulf's men," Briar said, her voice oddly devoid of feeling. The cell was growing dark around her, as if night had come suddenly and without warning.

"No, my lady, I did not die."

For a single, insane moment she thought: If Sir Anthony is alive, then mayhap so is my father! And then she remembered that that could not be. Her father had died at his own hand and she had prayed over his poor, cold body . . .

Dizziness assailed her. Briar reached out, blindly, her legs giving way. A hard, strong arm came around her, and cool, gloved fingers closed over her own grasping ones. Eyes shut, she clung to him, soaking up his strength and support, while the world faded in and out, and sickness threatened to humiliate her.

Gradually everything stilled and righted. Her breathing returned to normal, and her stomach stopped doing a jig. He was, she realized, holding her up, his voice a soft, urgent murmur in her ear.

"My angel, my sweet lady, please, be strong . . ."

There was a temptation to simply remain where she was and listen to his endearments. No man had ever called her such things before, and again that warm and wonderful feeling filled her. But to play at helplessness was not Briar's way. He was right, she was strong, and she must be strong now.

"I am recovered."

Instantly he stilled, his breath ragged against her hair, waiting.

She swallowed, and licked her dry lips. " 'Twas

just a moment, when I . . . I remembered . . ."

"I understand."

He said it as if he really did.

Her fingers tightened on his as she straightened, regained her footing, and then she released them. He stepped back, but not very far.

Sir Anthony was watching her warily, his face more haggard even than before.

"You say you did not die." She sounded cold, emotionless—it was necessary to be both.

"I escaped and fled north, to Scotland."

"Then what do you *here? Now?*"

"I have lost all I had in England, so I made a life by fighting for whoever wanted me. I was part of the recent rebellion on Lady Lily's lands, but this time I did not escape. De Vessey here has brought me to justice, lady. He beat me in fair fight, and treated me kindly in defeat. On the journey to York, we spoke of many things, and one of them was you."

De Vessey. The realization squeezed her, dangerously tight, so that for a moment she could hardly breathe. She fought back, refusing to collapse before him like one of the foolish, hysterical women she had always despised. She dare not show any more weakness, not now.

Now, when he knew who she was.

Ivo de Vessey, Radulf's man, knows me. Can anything be more disastrous?

Sir Anthony's voice droned on. "When de Vessey told me you were in York, lady, I asked to see you again. Lady Briar, I think often on those days. Your father was a great man."

"Aye," she whispered, tears spilling from her eyes, though her voice did not tremble. "So he was."

Behind her the silence was palpable, but she could not turn, she dared not.

"I asked to see you again, Lady Briar, because I wanted to make sure you did not blame your father for what occurred. 'Twas never his fault. He found the king's justice wanting, and in his pain and grief, sought to make his own justice."

"I know this, Sir Anthony," she said, and now it was anger that made her voice shake. "I do not blame my father. I well know who to blame for our calamity."

Anthony eased his wounded leg with a grimace. "I tried to tell him, lady, but he would not listen to me. If Odo had been well, mayhap he would have listened to him, but Odo was close to death." The pale eyes lifted and fixed on hers. "'Tis not something one man can easily tell another. That he is a cuckold."

Briar blinked, her anger turning colder.

What was this? Cuckold? Had the man been wounded in the head, as well as the leg?

There had been talk, afterward, of Anna's unfaithfulness, but Briar had always dismissed it. Her father had loved his beautiful wife so much; how could Anna betray devotion such as that? Briar could not imagine being loved in such a single-minded way, and if she was, she knew she would never wantonly destroy it. That was why she had chosen the form of vengeance against Radulf that she had—to destroy his wife's love and faith in him. It was the worst punishment Briar could imagine.

"But I thought 'twas only talk!" she cried out now. "I know Radulf lusted after Anna, but I believed she resisted his importunings, and that was why he had her killed. Are you telling me, Sir Anthony, that they were lovers? No wonder my father was so bitter!"

Sir Anthony shook his head. He looked as if he were sorry for what he was about to say—there was something in his eyes that spoke of deep regret. But there was also a recklessness in the set of his head, a strong need to speak, to set himself free. Whatever the cost to her.

"Anna was faithless, lady, but I do not know if Radulf was her partner. There were . . . others. I heard mention of both Lord Fitzmorton and Lord Shelborne. Your father did not know—or pretended not to. I think, if he had been forced to recognize her for what she was, it would have destroyed him. As it did. Nay, lady, *she* was the reason he died. He fought for her, seeking justice for her death, when she had been all too happy to besmear his reputation while she was alive. If anyone killed your father, Lady Briar, then it was Anna."

The silence was deep; a dark hollow sound.

What does it matter whether she was faithful or not? screamed a shrill voice in her head. *Radulf still ordered Anna to be murdered, and it was that murder which began the whole downward spiral of the Kenton family. Whether she was a faithful wife or not changes nothing!*

But it did.

Sir Anthony had spoken of matters Briar had never heard before. Mayhap it was simply that she had been too young, and too sheltered, to grasp the meaning of them at the time. Whatever the explanation, hearing them now had left her shocked and shaken. She needed time to be alone, to lick at her wounds, to recover herself.

And to convince herself she had been right to waste two years of her life seeking vengeance at Radulf's door.

"I do not know who killed her." Sir Anthony's already wrinkled face creased in thought. "Perhaps 'twas Radulf, perhaps 'twas some other who desired her and could not own her, not wholly. Even I let her use me. You do not know how persuasive she could be."

Shamefaced, he turned away, and Briar felt the hot sickness return. Suddenly she knew she did not want to hear any more.

"Take me away, de Vessey."

He reached out as if to comfort her, but Briar pulled back, standing rigid and alone. Aye, alone, as it should be. It seemed that no man was to be trusted after all.

Turning, blindly, Briar all but ran out of the dark cell, past the guard, and up the stairs. Her chest was heaving from more than physical exertion as she burst into the light.

Cold, gray day surrounded her. She took deep gulps of the frigid air, desperately attempting to still the queasiness in her stomach.

She would not be sick before Ivo, she would not!

It was a long moment before she sensed he was standing right behind her. Silent, waiting, so attuned to her that he knew exactly what she wanted from him. Tears stung her eyes and she gave a shaken laugh. He was playing at being her loyal knight. Aye, her very own *disgraced* knight.

" 'Tis all lies," she said, recovering a little. "You have had much time on the journey to bring Sir Anthony to your side, and to help him in the telling of his tale."

When he did not answer, Briar took another deep, steadying her breath, and turned at last to face him.

Had she expected to see distrust, because she was a traitor's daughter? Mayhap even triumph, that he had kept this information from her so completely. Sir Anthony must have made him aware on the journey to York of who she really was, but he had waited until now to tell her. Briar had not thought Ivo de Vessey a naturally cautious man, who would keep such information to himself longer than necessary, but mayhap she was wrong.

But as she looked into his dark eyes, all she could see was compassion and understanding, and the hot flicker of temper that she had lit.

"Why would I feed him lies?" he asked her evenly, but with an edge to his voice. "Sir Anthony is dying—his leg is beyond healing—and seeks to lighten the burden on his conscience. He thinks that if he had forced your father to accept the truth, that his wife was a whore, then your father might well be alive today. Anthony was weak when it mattered, he thought only of his own shame where Anna was concerned and what telling your father would mean to their friendship, and his future. He accounted his own skin more important than that of Sir Richard. *That* is what he seeks to redress now."

"It doesn't make any difference." Woodenly, Briar repeated the words she had spoken to Sir Anthony. "Radulf still had Anna killed—mayhap she had threatened to tell Lily. He still deserves to suffer for what he did to her . . . to *us*."

"Nay, Briar," he said softly.

"Aye! He did! Now take me home."

He hesitated, but he must have sensed she was on the verge of breaking down completely. How could he not? Briar asked herself wildly. She was clutching onto self-control with her fingernails, and even now they were slipping.

Ivo nodded and moved toward his horse.

Briar took two shaky steps before she stopped again. The words almost choked her.

"You *knew*, de Vessey. May you rot in hell, you knew who I was, and did not tell me."

Ivo paused—she could see him setting his shoulders, preparing himself for the tempest, before he turned. His face wore a resigned look. "Let us leave this place first, demoiselle, and then we will talk."

Briar was tempted to have it out with him at once. She wanted to shout and scream. He knew it, too. The watchfulness was there in his eyes, but he gave a wry grin.

"Later, Briar," he promised softly, "you can tear

my flesh off in strips. But not here, not in front of the king's guard where questions may well be asked."

Briar glanced about and realized that they had gathered quite a deal of interest from the other occupants of the castle bailey. With a stiff nod, she led the way to Ivo's horse and allowed him to help her to mount before him. Together they rode in silence, beyond the sturdy walls and into the city of York.

Their surroundings meant nothing to her. Her eyes were blind. Her mind kept running back and forth, trapped; over and over she heard Anthony's words, but she could not concentrate. She could not *think*. Her father's face filled her vision, and Anna, beautiful Anna.

Why did I not know? Was I so blind that I could not see what was happening? Or mayhap I preferred not to? Am I so like my father? Wilfully blind . . .

"I was protected and innocent," she whispered. "And a fool. I should have seen. I should have spoken to my father, made him listen, made him stop—"

"Lady, I know a private place." His voice cut through her soft mutterings as he turned into a narrow snickleway. There was a small hostelry at the farther end. At this time of day there were few inside, and Briar waited, head aching, stomach roiling, while Ivo called for the host.

"Ah, good sir!" The man came forward eagerly. "The private room you wanted is—"

"Aye, I will have a private room," Ivo cut him short, glancing uneasily at Briar. She stared back, knowing she should be suspicious of their exchange but too shocked to take it in properly.

"Of course, of course." The man winked, broadly and unmistakably. "This way."

The private chamber was small, barely large enough for the table and stool and narrow bed that filled it. Ivo had to stoop his head beneath the ceiling beams. Briar held herself still, hands clenched at her sides, impatience making her skin twitch. Ivo kept one watchful eye on her as he instructed the host to bring food and drink, and then at last they were alone.

Briar barely waited until the door was closed.

"Tell me now, de Vessey," she said, and her voice was husky with the strain of being calm.

"I will. But first, come and sit down."

She sighed, but did as she was told. 'Twould save time, she reasoned, if she didn't argue. And besides, her legs were weak and shaky, and it was a relief to sink down onto the bed. The straw mattress rustled under her, and Briar drew her warm cloak more closely about her, as if the woollen cloth could protect her from what was to come. Ivo de Vessey seemed concerned for her welfare, but Briar wasn't deceived.

He was Radulf's man.

Did that mean he had told Radulf who she was, too? Briar did not expect a great man like Radulf to be afraid of her, but she did not want him warned of her presence. Vengeance, justice—how could she extract them if Radulf were forewarned?

Vengeance?

Anna's beautiful face appeared before her,

smiling, always smiling. Her stepmother had hidden her black heart behind her smiles, and Briar had been too blind to see it.

She covered her lips with her fingers, but whether to stop herself laughing or crying, she did not know. At this moment, either seemed possible.

"I do know you, demoiselle. But I knew you before I met Sir Anthony in the north."

His voice was so reluctant that she turned to look up at him, where he stood with head and shoulders bowed beneath the roof that was too low. His black eyes were glittering with emotion.

"How is that so?" she asked, and held her breath.

He pulled the stool closer to the bed, and sat down on it, ignoring the ominous creak as it took his weight. Now he was closer, she could see the black stubble on his jaw, the darker centers of his dark eyes, the firm fullness of his lips. Something coiled in her belly, and this time it was not nausea.

He smiled, as if he had read her mind. "I knew you by this, demoiselle," he said, and reached out and brushed the tiny scar on her cheek with his rough fingertip. "Briar, I was there when it was made."

She opened her mouth to reply, but could not speak. She could not think. What did he mean? *There* when it was made? She did not understand. Her quick mind seemed to have slowed to a crawl.

He recognized her confusion, and leaned closer. He smelled of soap and sweat, man and

horse. She liked it. She wanted to run her tongue
along the crease of his neck, into the hollow there.
Her nails dug hard into her palms beneath the
Lincoln green cloak.

"You were a child," he explained slowly, as if he
realized her wits were befuddled. "I was a young
squire in your father's household. One of the
hounds knocked you over and you cut your
cheek. There was much blood, and you screamed
very loud." He gave her a reminiscent smile, but
his eyes remained watchful of hers. "I came to
your rescue like the knight I meant to be. You followed me about afterward, and others laughed,
but it pleased me and I did not stop you. A short
time later my father died, and I returned home.
The next time I saw you, you were singing like an
angel in Lord Shelborne's hall."

Briar stared at him in wonder. "Of all those who
have known me in the past, no one has remembered who I really am. Until now. How can that
be? Why are you the only one?"

He shrugged, observing her as if he did not
quite know what she would do.

"And you knew from the very first night?
When we . . . I . . . when we sated our lust together?" She forced the words out, purposely
made them as blunt and unfeeling as she could.

He laughed softly, deliberately. "Aye, almost
from that first moment. I had a sensation of knowing you, of having met you before. Mayhap you
had it, too?"

Had she? Was that what had set her on her
wrong course, when she peered through the

smoke and noise of Lord Shelborne's hall? Had she seen Ivo de Vessey, and recognized that long ago boy in him, and taken that sense of recognition for the certainty that he was Radulf?

It sounded plausible, but Briar was not convinced. If she was honest, she knew that it had not been familiarity that drew her to Ivo de Vessey, but something far more basic. She had seen him and desired him. 'Twas as blunt and as frightening as that.

"Have you told your master?" She spoke quickly, breathlessly, to stop the rogue thoughts in her head.

He hesitated. "Not yet."

Briar's eyes narrowed, and blessed anger filled her. "Tell him! Tell him I hate him! In my eyes he stands forever accused of my father's death, and all that has befallen us since. Aye, tell him that!"

Her voice cracked, and horrified, she stopped. Tears were close, but she held them back. She would not cry before him, not now, not again . . .

Ivo touched her shoulder. His hand closed on it, warm and strong, before she could shrug him off.

"Radulf loves Lily," he said gently, as if she were a child again and he the young squire. "He would never betray her, demoiselle. It would be like lopping off his own hand. You must understand that."

"But I don't," she said bitterly.

The hand tightened, and then before she knew it, he had moved to sit down on the mattress beside her, and drawn her into his arms. She should pull away, and she knew it. She should strike at

him with her fists and demand a proper explanation. But she was so weary, so very tired. And he
knew her, he was someone from the old days. That
fact more than any other halted her struggles.

With a shuddering breath, Briar gave way.

"I remember your father well." Ivo murmured
the words she had longed to hear, as if he already
knew what would please her most.

"Do you?" she breathed.

"Aye, Briar. He was a man to be proud of, a
kind man and a good one. He was patient with
young Ivo de Vessey. He understood the secret
longing of a green boy for his home, and the need
not to speak of such weaknesses aloud. He did not
deserve to die in such a way, demoiselle. But
when I heard of it, I regretted more than the manner of his death. I mourned him because of the
man he was."

What had remained of the dark, smoldering fire
inside Briar went out. The pain was intense. Sobs
rose up from somewhere deep, deep in her chest.
Two years of repressed grief spilled out, and with
it all her bitterness and rage. Briar's whole body
shook and shuddered, and she clung on to Ivo as
if she would drown without him. He held her,
murmuring comfort, the feel of his arms so comforting. Probably he had held her thus as a child,
when she had cut her cheek. That thought set her
off again.

When at last the storm had begun to abate,
Briar realized that at some point he had drawn her
onto his lap, where she lay warm in the curve of
his arms. Gasping, catching her breath, she
moved only to hide her swollen, bleary eyes as

their host returned with a tray of food and wine.

The man and Ivo exchanged words, and although Briar did not listen it seemed to go on for some time. When they were once more alone, Briar began to use her sleeve to mop her face, but Ivo stopped her. Lifting her chin with his gloved hand, he dipped a soft handcloth into a bowl of scented water. She realized then that that was what he had been asking for. Water to wash away her tears.

The cloth was cool against her heated skin, and soothing beyond anything she had ever known. Briar kept her eyes closed, letting him minister to her, too weak and drained to do otherwise. She had sworn not to shed tears before him again, after that first night when she had howled in his arms, and now here she was again, ugly with weeping. And worse than that, she had exposed her terrible vulnerability to the man from whom she most wished to hide it.

"Demoiselle?"

Her eyes fluttered open. Something brushed her lips, a fragrant piece of pastry wrapped vegetables. Obediently, she opened her mouth and chewed. The flavors burst upon her, spreading through her body, a pleasure so simple and yet so wonderful. She had not even known she was hungry! Next he lifted the goblet of wine, and placed that against her lips. Briar sipped and swallowed with a sigh, allowing the slightly sour wine to warm its way down her throat. She tingled.

With great care, Ivo continued to feed her, giving her sips of wine between mouthfuls. And Briar let him. His gaze was tender and yet intent, his fingers gentle and yet sensual. It was a heady experience, as if every mouthful he gave her only increased her awareness of him and the world around them. As if she had come alive again, after two years of something very much like death.

She felt raw and new, and very, very confused.

Gradually, Briar grew aware that Ivo was not as untouched by the situation as he pretended. His servile pose was just that, for evidence to the contrary pressed full and hard against her hip.

He desired her.

With a bump of her heart, Briar knew that she desired him, too. Needed him with a feverish urgency. The knowledge frightened her, but excited her, too. This was Ivo de Vessey, her squire, her knight. Her man. And suddenly to desire him did not seem foolish or wrong, just very, very right.

When he placed the last piece of pastry within her mouth, Briar let her tongue dart against his finger. His breath hissed in, his body immediately tensing. Slowly, Briar looked up into his eyes. He searched her face, and she saw the moment when he read her own need. And yet he hesitated.

Waited.

Gently, Briar touched his lips with her fingers, lingering, tracing the texture and shape. He closed his eyes with a groan. And yet still he did not respond with his own fingers. Why did he not respond? Slowly the reason came to her . . .

He is awaiting my lead.

The knowledge thrilled her. No man had let her lead before. To be in charge of such a situation gave her a feeling of power. She paused, enjoying it, but her urgency was too great. Briar leaned closer, searching that stark, fierce face. With his eyes closed she could see him as he must have been before his hard life began to mold him into the warrior he now was. It was Ivo's eyes that were so full of ancient pain.

Briar brushed fingertips lightly over his closed lids, then down over the harsh planes of his cheekbones, to the rough stubble on his jaw.

She felt lightheaded.

Her body tingled and ached. Suddenly it wasn't enough just to touch. Briar wanted to taste him, too.

She stretched up and pressed her lips to his.

Without hesitation he kissed her back, tenderly, brushing his lips slowly back and forth against hers, content to play at innocence. Again waiting for her lead. It was Briar who opened her mouth. With a groan, Ivo followed, deepened his kiss, his tongue finding hers. His hands slid up into her hair, teasing out her braid, shaking the tresses so that they spilled down her back and around her shoulders.

Briar moved closer, her arms circling his neck, her mouth drinking from his. Her breasts ached, and she leaned harder against his broad chest, enjoying the friction between them. His hands caressed her back, moving down, closing briefly on her hips, and then curving to the shape of her bottom through the coarse stuff of her gown.

Briar wriggled around, helping him to lift her, turn her, until she straddled his thighs with hers. They were both in the place they wanted now, the bulge between his legs stroking the sweet, swollen ache between hers. Briar rose up on her knees with a gasp, pressing closer, moving against him, seeking the pleasure she knew he could give.

"Let me inside you, demoiselle." He groaned the words against her mouth. "Let me ease your sore heart."

Briar did not know if he would ease her sore heart, but he would certainly ease something else. And why not? 'Twas only what they had done before. And she needed him now. Just as she had not comprehended how hungry she was for food and wine, before he fed her, neither had she imagined how much she hungered for Ivo.

Should she be doing this?

The questioning voice in her head was faint but audible. Somehow she pulled back. Both of them were breathing quickly, hovering on the brink. He looked dazed with need, but still he restrained himself, waiting, making it her decision whether they took that next step or not. Once again the knowledge that she was in charge soothed Briar's doubts, and gave her the courage to follow her body's urging.

Slowly, still gazing into his face, Briar moved her hips against him, blatantly. Ivo groaned, completely enraptured by the sensation, his head falling back to expose the long masculine line of his throat. Briar leaned forward to run her tongue over his salty skin, down to the hollow there, just as she had been longing to do.

Ivo drew another ragged breath. "Ah, lady, I am about to burst."

She laughed softly and nipped his skin.

He adjusted his grip on her bottom, his fingers digging into her firm flesh, lifting her, changing the contact between them until it was even more urgent. This time it was Briar who moaned, her mouth pressed in a hot, open kiss to his throat. She reached down to fumble with the laces of his breeches, unable to wait any longer. Needing him inside her. Now.

Just as the owner of the hostelry cleared his throat.

Loudly.

Briar leaned back against Ivo's chest, warm beneath the folds of her cloak, while the horse moved smoothly beneath them. Her body was unfulfilled, but the ache had faded somewhat. Ivo had been grumpy when they left, glaring at the man as if he would like to run him through. His display of bad temper had eased Briar's, and she smiled.

"Next time you must find a private chamber that is not so popular, de Vessey."

Ivo grunted and gave her a cross look. "I did not know it *was* popular when I reserved it, demoiselle. I thought you would need a place to recover yourself, that was all."

"Was it?" she mocked, not quite so amused now. "So you arranged with the innkeeper to bring me there? Well, it seems others were also keen to avail themselves of his chamber. There was a queue outside the door, de Vessey. The host had no choice but to hurry us along."

"Curse him."

Briar laughed in delight. The sound surprised her; she had not laughed like that in a long time. She wondered if she should force a frown, suppress her high spirits. 'Twas not wise to feel so alive, not safe—if she had learned one thing in the past two years, then 'twas that. But she did not want to lose this lightness inside her, this new sense of optimism.

Deliberately, she leaned back into Ivo's chest, ignoring his restless shiftings, and put her palm on his thigh.

He jumped as if she had been red hot, and removed her hand.

"Demoiselle," he said through gritted teeth, "it is not safe for you to touch me yet."

"Taking me to Sir Anthony has not altered my mind, you know," she said. "I still believe Radulf arranged Anna's death because she was inconvenient to him. Nothing else makes sense."

"She was inconvenient to many," Ivo muttered, shifting about again. "What of the others? You need to discover who her lovers were, near to the time of her death."

Briar snuggled against him, returning her hand to his hard thigh. She loved the movement of muscle under his skin, but she would never tell him that.

"You are right," she said, surprising herself and him. "Aye, I would know how matters lay between my father and Anna in those last days. I need to know for my own sake as much as theirs."

He was silent a moment, and she pretended to gaze about her at the busy, narrow street, pretended that she was not totally aware of him, close behind her.

"I will help you."

Briar tilted her head back so that she could see

him properly. He glanced down at her, gave her a faint, knowing smile, and then concentrated on the road ahead.

"Why will you help me?" she demanded, not sure herself why his offer was so important to her. "Is it because you believe Radulf to be innocent?"

"There is that, aye," he said thoughtfully, and removed her hand from his thigh. "But that is not really why I want to help, lady. It is because you need to be free of this burden you have placed upon yourself. 'Tis a heavy weight for you to bear."

" 'Tis not so heavy." Briar knew that was the truth. 'Twas only her vow that held her to her task now. The dark, tattered cloak of hatred she had worn for two years was gone. How had he done that? She didn't know, only that when Ivo had come into her life, it had begun to change.

"But you are right," she went on, slipping her hand back onto his leg, smoothing the tight stuff of his breeches. "I do need to know the truth. Anna's murderer must be found and punished. Only then can I and my sisters make a new life, without pain."

"Then that is what we will do."

"You have no doubts, do you, Ivo?" she asked curiously. He sounded so certain, so confident.

"Demoiselle, I have many doubts, but they will not stop me from finding your stepmother's killer." He smiled without humor, taking her hand firmly in his and holding it captive. "I want you, Briar, and until the past is dealt with, until you are free of it, you will never be able to give yourself fully to any man."

Briar gazed ahead, knowing that he spoke the truth.

I want you too, Ivo.

The words sounded in her head, but unlike Ivo she was not yet ready to say them aloud.

Chapter 8

❧❧❧

Lord Shelborne's hall was the same as it had been the first night he saw her. The night he took her in his arms, and made her his. The frustrated ache in his body reminded Ivo of their moments together at the hostelry, and her willingness. He had been so, so close to losing himself once again in her sweet body. And she had wanted him, too. He felt her soft mouth on his skin, her trembling hands within moments of taking hold of him and . . .

And then that lackwit had interrupted them!

Ivo had looked like a fool.

Briar had laughed at him, and set aside her own passion as easily as stale bread. Were her feelings for him so shallow? Or was she just better able to disguise them? Aye, that was probably it. She had been playing a part since Castle Kenton was taken from her, and she had learned well to dissemble.

It had become clear now to Ivo that she had sought revenge upon Lord Radulf because her father had cursed Radulf and blamed him for all their troubles. Briar had taken up the quest in his name. She had planned to punish Radulf and revenge her father, and thought all would be well afterward. Or had she simply failed to consider afterward?

It was a simpleton's way of looking at things, but Ivo did not think Briar a simpleton. She had a clear, concise view of the world; she saw things in simple terms. In her eyes Radulf was to blame, therefore Radulf should suffer, and she looked no further than that.

Sir Anthony had given her another story to mull over, one she had not heard before, and it had confused her and hurt her. But Ivo thought the knowledge, no matter how distressing, was important to her. Ivo was well aware that Radulf would never have forsaken Lily for Anna, and neither was he responsible for Anna's death. So Briar needed to look elsewhere, and she appeared to have already accepted that possibility.

And what if she begins to ask questions of men who do not want to answer?

Ivo well knew that the past could be a murky and dangerous pond, one that was sometimes best left undisturbed.

She needs to resolve this matter or she will never be free. She needs to know the truth, even if it is dangerous. And I will protect her.

Sir Anthony had mentioned Lord Fitzmorton's name. Ivo knew Fitzmorton was presently in the

south, licking his wounds after his castigation by
the king on Radulf's behalf. Anthony had also
made mention of Lord Shelborne, and *he* was
right here.

Ivo glanced over to where Shelborne was
speaking with Radulf. A large, robust man with a
ruddy face and sparse gray hair, his host smiled
often. But Ivo had noticed that his pale eyes remained watchful.

'Twas sensible to be watchful, and Ivo did not
think any less of Shelborne for keeping a close eye
on his guests. Only a fool trusted all men. And
women. Was Shelborne really Lady Anna's lover?
Would such a reputably beautiful woman really
have been interested in such an ugly man? Mayhap it was not beauty that attracted Anna, but
power. To have a strong man like Lord Shelborne,
and an evil one like Lord Fitzmorton in thrall to
her must have given her an intoxicating sensation,
better than any wine.

The idle thoughts continued to spill through
Ivo's head, but they were really only a distraction.
He was not here in Lord Shelborne's hall to decide
what made a woman like Lady Anna what she
was. He was here for quite another reason.

Briar.

Ivo's sense of anticipation grew—his skin tingled, his chest tightened, his heart began to
pound. He was waiting for Briar to appear upon
the little dais. For her voice to once again open
wide his wounded heart.

And set him free.

It was madness, and he knew it. To give in to his
vulnerability, to strip himself bare in these dan-

gerous times! But he could not help it. Briar was
his redemption . . . and mayhap she would be his
destruction.

The crowd began to cheer and applaud. Ivo's
head came up. Briar and Mary had come into the
hall, plainly dressed and with their hair loose
about their shoulders. And yet they seemed to
glow. Ivo watched as they settled themselves
upon the small dais. There was a hush, a sense of
waiting, and then Mary's clever fingers brought
the harp to life, and Briar began to sing.

At the sound of her husky voice, a great wave
of emotion swelled Ivo's heart. It felt almost too
big for his chest. He tried to disguise his feelings,
standing tense and still, but her voice, her words,
pierced him like a lance. How was it possible to
feel so painfully shattered, and yet so wonderfully
released?

"Who is the girl?"

Lord Radulf's voice.

Lord Shelborne answered. "Her name is Briar.
She and the harpist are sisters, and they have become quite famous in York, my lord."

Ivo felt himself bristle, knew it was stupid and
still could not help it. The tightness in his chest increased. He did not like their interest in Briar; he
did not like their casual discussion of her. She
was his, and he felt an urgent need to guard his
property.

He took a deep breath and forced himself to relax, not to do anything foolish. Ivo leaned back
against the wall and swallowed down his ire. Had
anyone noticed his moment of madness? he wondered, glancing uneasily about him. That was

when he saw that Sweyn had moved to stand further around the hall, where he had a better view of the two women. His friend's blond head rose above the crowd; his blue gaze was fixed on Mary, and it was clear that for Sweyn, the rest of the audience had ceased to exist.

Ivo forgot his own problems.

Sweyn, in love?

Surely such a thing was as unlikely as horses taking to the sky? Sweyn was the sort of man who found it impossible to take anything too seriously—everything was a joke to him. He liked women, he enjoyed them often, but if a woman asked more of him than a smile and a good time, then he was gone. There was no harm in Sweyn; he did not hurt anyone apurpose. But he was definitely not the man for a woman to set her sights on if she wanted a husband who came home to only her.

And now there he was, gazing lovestruck at Mary, the youngest daughter of the traitor Lord Kenton. Although Sweyn did not know that, he still thought that the "important man" who was their father was some sort of merchant or tradesman. Perhaps Ivo should warn him? And then again, he thought with a smile, perhaps he would not. Not yet, anyway. The cold harsh reality of Mary's past might give him an excuse to turn and run. Poor Sweyn, how would he deal with falling in love? Run as far and as fast as his legs could carry him? Or simply refuse to accept it?

His smile faded. 'Twas all very well to scoff at Sweyn, but was he not in much the same boat? Briar had crept under his skin like a tick and now he had a constant itch that could not be scratched.

He wanted her, aye, but it was more than that. Ivo wanted to look after her, to protect her, to fight for her. Do those things he had been trained to do from boyhood.

Aye, admit it, I want to be a knight again.

For her.

Briar had started another song. This one was livelier than the last, and the noise level increased. One of the more merry guests clasped the arm of a serving wench, and started a jig. Ivo could see that Briar was enjoying herself, her eyes shone and her skin was flushed.

She was beautiful. There had been someone else, once, who exuded the same inner radiance. Although Matilda had not had Briar's temper, she had been gentler, more trusting. She had trusted her brother Ivo above all other men.

And Ivo failed her.

Ivo felt his stomach clench. He ran his gloved hand over the beads of sweat that had sprung out on his brow. *I am no knight!* A knight saved the ones he loved most, he did not leave them to die miserably, screaming out his name. How did he expect to protect Briar, even should she wish him to do so?

And she didn't, Ivo reminded himself with a grimace of a smile. She considered herself perfectly capable of protecting herself. Ivo remembered again the sword she had held this morning, and the competent manner in which she had handled it. Unlike Matilda, she was fiery and independent, and considered his protection as an interference in her life.

'Twas as well, Ivo told himself bleakly, for she

couldn't rely on him. No one could. For a time he had forgotten that. Pushed the pain deep. Briar's reawakening of his heart had made him believe for a while that all things were possible, that all broken pieces could be healed . . . Well, this was one broken shard that would remain lodged inside his heart, forever.

Briar finished her song, well pleased with the response. After they had made their bows, it was clear the guests in Lord Shelborne's hall would not be content until they sang another. Mary, catching her sister's glance, nodded, and ran her fingers over the harp's strings, plucking forth a series of plaintive notes. Once more Briar began to sing. A sad song this, the tale of a lost maiden and her dead knight. She did not sing it often, but for some reason it seemed appropriate tonight.

When she had sung this song in the past, Briar's thoughts had turned to her father and Anna, of their great love cut tragically short by the jealous Radulf. Tonight those familiar images of them would not come. She had taken a step back from her obsession, and the image she had now of her father and Anna was clearer, sharper, more real. Ivo de Vessey had opened her eyes and her mind to the truth, but in the process he had left her floundering in unknown country.

If she was no longer able to spend her time hating Radulf and swearing vengeance, what was she meant to do?

Her gaze sought out that tall, dark-haired figure who was becoming very familiar to her. She had noted his position as soon as she walked into

the hall. How could this man have become so necessary to her, so quickly? He was holding his hand
up to his face, but as she watched, he straightened
to his full intimidating height and took a deep
breath. Ivo looked pale and grave. As if he were
thinking unhappy thoughts.

Briar faltered on her lyrics.

She caught herself, substituting different ones,
stumbling through the next verse to the chorus.
Color stained her face, and she felt Mary's eyes
boring into her, but she did not turn. Concentrat-
ing fiercely now, Briar sang on. But after a moment, as if she could no longer order her own
actions, she found her eyes fixed once more upon
Ivo de Vessey.

This time he was watching her, too. His gaze
was black, brooding, suffering. Delving into her
mind, interfering in her life, making her weak and
vulnerable . . . Her throat closed up, and she fumbled the words again.

Resentment rolled away, and in its place came a
terrible urge to go to him, to put her arms around
him. To comfort him.

Dear God, what is happening to me?

Ivo de Vessey did not need comforting! He was
big and strong and battle-scarred, and perfectly
capable of looking after himself. Why then did she
have this terrible urge to lock her arms about him
and whisper, *'Tis all right?* Why then did she sense
some appalling hurt within him, that she alone
must heal?

"Sister!"

Mary's hissed admonition brought her back to
herself. Briar soared into the last note of the song.

The applause was thunderous. No one grasped how many errors she had made, or perhaps they were too drunk to care. With a relieved smile, she rose and bowed low, holding tight to Mary's hand, and then the two girls made their way out of the hall.

"What ails you tonight, sister?" Mary demanded. Worried dark eyes examined Briar's for signs of illness or fever. "I have never known you to take so many wrong turns in a song!"

" 'Twas nothing. I was simply distracted." Briar pushed by the tapestry screen into the cool darkness of the passageway.

"*Distracted?*" Mary would not be put off. "Was the hall too noisy? Too crowded? They were more than pleased with us tonight, so what was—"

"Ladies."

That familiar deep voice stopped them. Mary glanced uncertainly over her shoulder. Briar closed her eyes, briefly, gathering her tattered defenses about her. It would never do for him to find out just how much he affected her. Since Filby, Briar had been careful never to rely upon a man, nor had she wanted to. She must not show her weakness to him. That way lay more hurt, and Briar had had enough of hurt. Her emotional defense had always been to attack first, and that is what she did now.

" 'Tis the disgraced knight," she said, her voice light and cruel as she turned to confront him. She saw his face go tight with anger, but would not let herself feel. "And his friend who is no knight," she added, as Sweyn also pushed through the arras.

Sweyn ignored her, his eyes shifting to Mary as

he examined her flushed face and bright eyes, as if
he were satisfying himself of her well-being.

Ivo's expression was hidden now by the shadows and his own force of will. "You have sharpened your tongue, lady. Does it cut deeply enough
for your liking?"

"If you didn't feel it, then clearly it is not sharp
enough," she replied sweetly.

"Oh, I felt it. 'Tis just that I can think of more
pleasurable things to do with it."

Sweyn snorted a laugh at the coarse jest. "She is
a shrew! Find yourself a sweet girl, Ivo, who will
be grateful for your consideration. Not one who
fights your every kindness as if you were binding
her with ropes."

Mayhap Briar deserved it, but the words stung
her far more than she would admit. She flashed
them both a look of disgust, and marched off.
Mary, after a quick glance at Sweyn, hurried after
her, calling for her to wait.

Briar hoped she could reach the safety of the
kitchen, and Jocelyn, without further hindrance.
In truth, she felt less than her tough self tonight.
Her tongue might be sharp, as Ivo had said, and
clearly she had cut him, but there was a shakiness
in her belly, and a tightening in her throat, as if she
might very well weep. And Briar never wept.

Well, she had not done so until she met Ivo de
Vessey. Now it was as if her world had turned to
tears, for she had sobbed her heart out twice in his
presence. And he had comforted her. She remembered again how he had bathed her face, and fed
her tiny pieces of food and tiny sips of wine.

Heat coiled in her belly, ousting the sick feeling

that had begun to gather there. She had wanted him so badly, as they kissed and touched upon that narrow bed. She had been willing to give herself to him. Life had surged through her, and Ivo had been part of that desperate need to experience all that her body could feel. All that it had lacked in the past two years.

She had given herself away, mayhap. Dangerous. He must not know that he was important to her. That she needed him by her side. That she was beginning to think she could not do without him ... *No!* His importance to her lay only in what he could do to help her discover the truth about Anna's death. Nothing else. *I dare not trust or believe in a man, ever again.*

Briar repeated it to herself, feverishly, stubbornly, blindly.

As if by doing so she might begin to believe.

Behind them, heavy steps rang out on the floor, and Sweyn's stifled chuckle echoed against the walls. The two men were following them, Briar acknowledged, grinding her teeth, her hopes of respite crushed. Although, by the look of the soft smile on Mary's face, she felt the exact opposite.

"He will use you and then leave you," Briar said sharply, for her sister's ears only. "All men do."

Mary turned to her with big, hurt eyes.

Briar groaned silently. She had meant the warning as a kindness, to save Mary unnecessary pain, but in her turmoil she had been less than subtle. Mary was young, and she had had little enough in her life that gave her pleasure. Sweyn was not a suitable recipient for her warm glances and romantic dreams.

But it was too late now to take the words back, and there was no time for soothing or explanations. The warm smells of the kitchen were wafting toward them, and the next moment they were within the well-lit room, with Jocelyn's presence as warm as her oven.

"Sisters!" she cried, pleasure lighting her face. "You played and sang tonight like angels in heaven. Come, sit yourselves down and I will fetch you something to eat. I have eel pie and cold ham. And to drink I have mead. Sweet, honey mead, so that you can float home to your beds."

And then her eyes lifted and fixed on a point above and behind them. For a moment she looked comically startled. "What do you here in my kitchen?" she asked blankly.

Mary glanced nervously back and forth between the men and Jocelyn, waiting for Briar to introduce them, or at least insult them. But Briar was busy with her own problems, and when she did not speak, Mary had to.

"Jocelyn, these men are in service with Lord Radulf. This is Ivo de Vessey and this is Sweyn. Jocelyn is our elder sister."

Briar had sat down by the oven to warm her cold hands. She had not made introductions, or insults, because something had just occurred to her. Something that made her heart turn to ice.

Jocelyn must know who Ivo was.

She had been eight years older than Briar at the time he was squire to their father—she must remember him. The day he found her at the market, he had been here to Lord Shelborne's first, and spoken to Jocelyn. Her sister had set him onto her.

What had she said to Briar, that memorable night when she had accidentally taken Ivo to her bed? Every vixen will meet her match? Well, Jocelyn had made certain of it!

"You know him, don't you?" Her voice shook with her effort to check her anger.

Jocelyn didn't even pretend to misunderstand. "Of course."

"You didn't tell me."

Now her hurt and anger were plain in her voice, as well as bewilderment. Why had Jocelyn not warned her that Ivo knew more than he was saying? She could have saved Briar from making even more of a fool of herself than she had already, she could have stopped her from sinking into this pit.

"I thought 'twas best to keep it to myself, Briar. I—"

"*I* asked her to stay quiet."

Slowly, reluctantly, Briar looked up into that dark, intense gaze. Ivo de Vessey still seemed a little paler than usual, his wonderful eyes shadowed.

"You have no right to interfere between my sister and me."

"Not yet, perhaps."

"You are arrogant!" Briar's hands trembled as she folded them about herself. The nausea within her was growing, but she held it back. Such bodily weaknesses would not get the best of her, or stop her from doing as she wished. Briar would simply not allow it.

"I wanted to tell you in my own time, demoiselle, and so I did."

"Oh! You—you—"

"Briar, enough!" Now Jocelyn was glaring at her. "I knew him, but I said nothing because I felt it best he tell you. What is wrong in that? Is it a crime to have known you when you were a babe? Or mayhap you are simply embarrassed to recall the manner in which you followed him about like a lovelorn little puppy."

Mary, who had been watching and listening with great interest, giggled, and quickly covered her mouth. Ivo smiled at her, changing the brooding angles of his face into beauty. For some reason that made Briar angrier than ever.

"I worry for you, Briar," Jocelyn said softly. "I want to see you smile again, laugh again. I want to see you as you used to be."

"Nothing is as it used to be," Briar retorted stubbornly.

"I want to see you happy."

"How can I be happy! After all that has happened?"

"Briar, we must move on. We *must*."

"Aye, go ahead, if you can. I have not finished yet with the past."

Jocelyn threw up her hands with an exasperated sigh. She turned to the two men, determinedly ignoring her sullen, fuming sister.

" 'Tis not often I have such visitors in my kitchen. Next *Lord Radulf* himself will appear and demand to sit by my oven." She spoke the name deliberately.

Sweyn laughed, ignoring the undercurrents. "You would be sorry if he did, lady. He is foul-tempered these days. He misses his wife," he explained, when Jocelyn looked quizzical.

"Ah!" Jocelyn nodded, as if she understood. And she probably did, Briar supposed reluctantly. If Odo were gone, Jocelyn would feel as if part of herself were missing. That was what loving someone meant—not that Briar was willing to admit for a moment that Radulf was innocent of Anna's death. Not yet. But she could accept that he loved Lily, his wife. As her father, Richard, had loved Anna. Love was cruel. Briar knew she would rather bury her heart deep in the ground before she allowed herself to love a man like that.

Jocelyn served the mead in small wooden bowls, and Briar took hers with a stiff thank-you, and ignored the surreptitious glances her sister was sending between Ivo and herself. 'Twas none of her business. Especially now, when Jocelyn had been caught out in her deceit. Briar told herself bleakly that she would never trust her again.

Instead, Briar watched Mary and Sweyn. They stood close, and murmured quiet words to each other. It was as she feared, Briar thought bleakly. Mary was enamored of the handsome Dane, but worse, he was smitten with her, too. How could anyone mistake that dazed smile, that startled expression in his eyes. And Mary, coloring for no reason when he looked at her, or gazing up at him with adoring eyes.

Aye, love glowed about them like a candle flame.

Briar sipped at her mead as though it were poison. This was wrong. Mary was too young. She needed Briar to look after her. What had happened to her world? All she had thought solid and real, had begun to shiver and twist like the leaves that were even now falling from the trees. How could she see her way clear? If she no longer knew what lay ahead of her?

This was Ivo de Vessey's fault. 'Twas all because of him! Until he had come to York, all had been well, and now . . . Briar clenched her hands tighter about her bowl.

He was standing beside her. She could feel his presence without having to turn her head and look. The warmth of his body, the scent of him, the sheer dark presence of him. She could have been locked in a night-black dungeon and still have known when he came through the door.

This new understanding gave her no pleasure.

"Briar?"

She schooled her features, and turned to look up at him. He opened his mouth to speak, then reading her mulish expression, frowned and changed his mind. With an exasperated breath, he reached up and ran his fingers through his black hair.

Jocelyn, who had stopped to watch the byplay, seemed to notice the glove for the first time. "You are prepared to do battle even here?" she asked, nodding to his hand.

Ivo glanced at his leather encased fingers as if he had forgotten them, and then his face turned hard as granite. "My hand was hurt in a fight, once, long ago, Lady Jocelyn. I wear the glove because it is unsightly."

Jocelyn nodded. "But it does not prevent you from your profession?"

"Nay, I am as able to fight and defend myself as well as any other man. I have learned to compensate for the missing fingers."

Suddenly Briar looked up at him with wide eyes. She had not realized, when he said he was hurt, that he meant . . . Sweet Jesu, that he should have lost his fingers in a fight. Fierce, beautiful Ivo! Nausea and pain sliced through her.

With a gasp, she stood up and flung herself toward the slop bucket. The mead and all else she had had at supper this night came back out. Noisily.

Jocelyn's mouth dropped open, but in another moment she had hurried to her sister's side, making soothing noises. Mary started to follow, but Sweyn grasped her arm, murmuring, "Leave her be, she is in good hands."

Ivo did not move at all. He was stunned, and the misery inside him burned like a brand. She was repulsed by the thought of his hand. What else could it be? Indeed, she was so revolted that she had cast up the contents of her stomach into a bucket. He turned on his heel and left the room.

Briar took several gulps of air, allowing Jocelyn to mop at her hot, damp face with a cool cloth. It was not squeamishness that had made her ill— she was never squeamish. The thought of Ivo's pain had jolted her, aye, but never enough to make her physically ill. Mayhap she had a fever— that would explain her odd thoughts during the song, her lack of concentration, her wild fears.

She was not herself.

"I am not myself," she said the thought aloud.

"She kept forgetting the words to the song," Mary piped in worriedly.

Jocelyn nodded, smoothing Briar's hair out of her eyes. "Stay here tonight."

Briar shook her head. "I want to go home. I need to go home." Her voice had an edge to it that she didn't like. Briar took a deep breath, meeting Jocelyn's worried eyes. "I'm sorry . . . for before. I know you mean well, Jocelyn . . ."

"But you saw it as betrayal," Jocelyn replied evenly. "I wasn't taking sides against you, Briar. Not everything is about taking sides."

"Is it not?" Briar's reply was bleak.

Jocelyn squeezed her sister's shoulder. "You need to be home in bed. I will wash your face and make up a hot posset for you while you are here, and then you can take another dose before you sleep."

Briar nodded, not even bothering to argue further. Sweyn glanced from one to the other, and then spoke to Jocelyn. "I will see that they reach home safely."

Jocelyn smiled her relief. "Thank you, Sweyn." She leaned close to Briar, kissing her pink cheek. "You are still feeling ill?"

Wearily, Briar shook her head. "I am well now," she said huskily. "Just tired."

"Then let the Dane take you home. You will be well in the morning."

Briar rose and looked about her properly for the first time since her rush for the bucket. "Where is de Vessey?"

Her sisters exchanged a puzzling glance. "He left when you were ill," Jocelyn said carefully.

"Mayhap he is one of those men who can not bear to see a woman being ill," Mary added.

It seemed a strange affliction for a mercenary, but Briar let it pass.

Sweyn moved toward the door. "I must first tell my lord where I am going. I will meet you both at the stables."

"He is a kindly man," Jocelyn ventured, when he had gone.

"Aye." Mary smiled with pride.

As if the man's character were entirely her doing, Briar thought crossly.

"You like him," Jocelyn went on, with a pleased nod. "Aye, Mary, 'tis about time you found a sweetheart."

Briar stared at her elder sister with disbelief. "She is a child! How can you push her in the direction of such a man as that? A Danish mercenary? Jocelyn, Mary is innocent and gently bred—"

"*She* is a harpist, Briar, with no money and no prospects." Jocelyn's retort was brutal. "*You* are a songstress and *I* am a cook. We no longer live at Castle Kenton."

Briar shook her head stubbornly, but her throat was too tight for her to argue. Tears, again? Jesu! What was wrong with her?

"I am not a child." Mary spoke up softly and with a determination Briar had not seen in her before. "I know my own mind, Briar. I do not need you to tell me what I can and can't do. Sometimes you make me feel as if I can't breathe!"

Mary stopped and the silence was heavy. Briar knew she looked hurt and shocked. She *felt* hurt and shocked. Mary was a child, her little sister— wasn't she?

Warm fingers grasped her own. Briar looked up into Mary's kind, dark eyes. "Come and let me wash your face."

Jocelyn raised an eyebrow as they passed, but she was smiling.

"I hope you're enjoying this," Briar murmured darkly as Mary led the way. "You'll be sorry when Mary is abandoned and ruined. It will be too late then."

"Life is never certain, Briar." Jocelyn held her gaze. "We cannot always wait to have all our questions answered. There is not always time to wait. Sometimes we have to leap, and pray we land safely."

Ivo watched Sweyn make his way back into the hall. The Dane's eyes fixed upon Lord Radulf, and he only seemed to notice Ivo as he drew closer. Clearly Sweyn was a man on a mission.

Ivo still felt empty. Like a large vessel unloaded of its cargo, echoing with a forlorn silence. Briar's reaction had cut him so deep he was light-headed with loss. He knew his hand was ugly—that was why he made sure to always keep it covered—and aye, in his heart, he was ashamed of it, too. But it had never yet made a woman vomit. And that it should be *this* woman, in particular . . .

He shook his head angrily.

Maybe 'tis for the best.

He squeezed his gloved hand into a fist. He should never have let Briar open his heart again.

"The songstress is ill, my lord." Sweyn's voice drifted into Ivo's consciousness. "I beg permission to take her, and her sister, safely home. They are alone and they live by the river. 'Tis not safe for them to walk."

"Near the river?" Radulf replied.

"The songstress is ill?" Lord Shelborne was looking concerned, despite a tendency to sway back and forth, the legacy of too much of his own wine.

"Aye, my lord." Sweyn turned politely to Shelborne, concealing his impatience to be gone. "Have I your permission to escort her and her sister home?" Now Sweyn was looking to Lord Radulf, waiting.

"I will do it! I have men aplenty." Lord Shelborne swayed more violently and had to flop down upon a nearby stool.

"Thank you, my lord, but they have asked for me," Sweyn replied, all smiles and respectful steel.

Ivo straightened and paid more attention. Sweyn was an easy going man, but a man used to getting his own way. Would he get his own way with Mary? And what exactly was it that he wanted?

"You are in a hurry to play the gallant knight, Sweyn." Radulf was no fool. He had seen there was more to this than Sweyn was saying. He grinned, planting a playful blow on Sweyn's shoulder that made him stumble and almost lose his balance. "You are lovesick," he announced. "I well know the signs. Which one is it that you covet? The smaller one who sings so sweetly, or the tall one with the dark eyes?"

"I covet neither Briar nor Mary, my lord," with a betraying gaucheness.

Radulf chuckled at the wary, almost scared expression in Sweyn's blue eyes. "Aye, I believe you, but the heart is not always as obedient as a man would like." His own eyes narrowed, all humor fleeing his face. "What did you say their names were?"

Ivo sensed trouble. He stepped forward and stood shoulder to shoulder with Sweyn. His friend sent him a relieved and grateful glance. Radulf raised an eyebrow and waited.

"My lord," Ivo said, "they are called Briar and Mary. Two simple girls who sing and play like angels."

Radulf raised the other black brow. "What, are *you* being poetic now, de Vessey? You have never struck me as the type. Which one of these sisters do you covet? Briar or Mary?"

Ivo hesitated. 'Twould be easy for him to deny it, to swear he had no interest in either of them. A moment ago he would have done it—mayhap. But now, suddenly, he couldn't. It would be a lie, and Ivo did not want to lie about Briar. He *did* want her, despite all that stood between them now and in the past. Perhaps it was time she and everyone else knew it.

"I want Briar," he said bluntly. "My lord."

Radulf gave a soft laugh. "Aye, I believe you, Ivo. You have the look of a man who's been struck down by love."

Lord Shelborne was turning his head from one to the other, making an effort to follow the conversation with an obviously wine-soaked mind. "Briar and Mary? Aye, Radulf, their names are f-f-famil . . . familiar to me, too."

Radulf nodded, frowning. "I know them from somewhere."

Shelborne hauled himself up by grasping on to Radulf and using him as a ladder, ignoring the latter's sigh. "Kenton had a daughter named Briar," he muttered drunkenly. He wagged his head back and forth. "Poor Kenton. We all take some blame in his death."

Radulf was staring at Ivo, but Ivo refused to meet his eyes. Now was not the time for such confidences, and he prayed God Radulf had the wit to realize it . . .

"Go then," Radulf said brusquely, although he was clearly not happy. "Take the singing sisters home."

"Thank you, my lord," Ivo and Sweyn replied in unison.

"But Ivo," Radulf stopped him in mid-stride, and transfixed him with a look. "I will have words with you, when you return."

Ivo nodded, resigned. He had a fairly good idea what Radulf's words would be about.

Chapter 9

Briar, Mary, and Jocelyn had been waiting at the stables for only a short while when the two mercenaries appeared. It took only a moment for the grooms to prepare the horses, Odo fumbling at the harnesses slowly, clumsily. Briar could never look at him without remembering him as he used to be. Brash and confident, with his big laugh. Women had adored him, but Odo had only ever had eyes for Jocelyn.

His horse ready, Sweyn reached for Mary without a word and lifted her up before him. Ivo turned to Briar. He appeared overwhelming in this dark place, the flare of the torches accentuating his size and looks. His black eyes gleamed red from the flame. Her own face must be strained and white—it had been a long day and she was weary, though thankfully the nausea had passed.

Her head was thudding a little, like a distant cur-
few drum, but Briar knew her bed would cure
that.

"Will you ride with me, demoiselle?"

That deep, soft voice. Briar knew she would
hear it in her dreams, years away from now. And
it would still send tremors of delight over her
skin.

"Aye, of course I will."

He seemed surprised, but the next moment he
had reached out and fitted his big hands about her
narrow waist, lifting her easily onto the saddle.
Then he swung himself up, steadying his mount,
arranging her comfortably before him. At Ivo's
signal, he and Sweyn set their horses to traverse
the narrow laneway, and rode out into Stonegate.
Behind them, Jocelyn raised a hand in farewell.

Cold mist lay milky upon the ground. It drifted
across their path in long tendrils of white, and
stirred at the movement of the animals' hooves.

He was so warm, surrounding her, protecting
her. Briar rested her head contentedly against his
chest, and sighed. "I did not mean to cut you with
my tongue," she murmured sleepily.

"Did you not?" He sounded as if he doubted
her.

Briar didn't like that. "No, I did not."

"And I suppose the thought of my missing fingers did not make your stomach turn inside out."

There was hurt in his voice, but he had made it
into a joke. Surprised, Briar lifted her head to peer
up at him. She could see the shape of his jaw, the
jut of his nose, and the gleam of his eyes as he
glanced down at her.

"Nay," she breathed, stammering in her need to reassure him 'twas not so. "That is nothing to me. 'Tis only that I imagined how you must feel, how it must have hurt you. But it did not make me sick. I was *already* sick. 'Twas the mead, Ivo, that is what turned my stomach inside out."

He stared steadily down at her. Judging her. Suddenly it seemed desperately important that she convince him.

Briar turned slightly and reached up. Her fingers brushed over his firm, shaven jaw until she touched his smooth lips. She let herself explore the texture of them, the shape of them, the warmth of his breath through them.

She felt him smile.

"Lady, you are distracting me," he murmured against her fingers, gently admonishing.

"Am I? By doing this? Interesting." She stretched up, turning her body more fully into his. "What if I were to do this?" Her lips made contact with his neck, tasting his warm flesh. "Or this?" Now she nipped at the lobe of his ear, gently, but hard enough to let him feel her sharp little teeth. His breath quickened.

A great wave of heat swept through Briar.

Am I mad, to do this? What does it gain me?

Nothing was the answer, apart from the moment's pleasure and Ivo's delight. Never once, in the two years since her life ended, had Briar done anything that did not gain her some foothold further up the ladder of survival. But now she wanted to touch him, to kiss him, simply because it made her feel so good.

He turned his face, and claimed her mouth with his.

He tasted of wine and man. She wanted to get closer, she *needed* to get closer. Her hands crept about his neck, into the springy hair that was growing back at his nape, while her lips clung to his.

"Which of you is the real Briar?" he murmured teasingly, his breath warm against her cheek. "Is it this one here, now, in my arms, or the other with her cutting tongue?"

"They are both me," she whispered, and pressed yet closer. "Is it not possible for me to be two women in one?"

He bent again, hungrily, but his mouth paused just before it touched hers. "I like this one better," he growled, and claimed his kiss.

Briar clung to him, returning his passion, her body straining hard against his. Heat poured over her, sizzling her from the top of her head to the tips of her toes. *This* was what she wanted, she thought dizzily. This sense of being part of another, this belonging. Jocelyn was right. Sometimes you had to leap and just pray you landed safely.

"Beware!"

Sweyn's voice, loud and frantic, cut through her heated passion like a sliver of ice.

Instantly Ivo had tucked her in against his chest, in the safety of his arms. His body was rigid and alert, his hand on the hilt of his sword. He was prepared to fight, and Briar was still struggling to catch her breath. Ivo wheeled his horse around, facing the direction of Sweyn's raised arm. Not that he needed to, thought Briar, for she was certain that he too could hear the heavy thud and rattle. An armed troop of men were approaching. Danger, bearing down upon them, leaving them only two options.

Turn and ride as fast as they could and hope to outrun them. Or stand and fight.

Ivo drew his sword.

At his side, Sweyn did the same. The two of them waited, weapons ready, as five armed men rode into Stonegate in front of them. They wore chain-mail tunics and full-face helmets, their identities completely hidden by steel and shadows. One of the men urged his mount forward a little, as if to claim the role of leader. The horse shifted nervously and snorted, the plume of hot breath turning the cold air to white.

They all waited, and although it seemed to Briar an interminable time, it was only a couple of heartbeats. The man stared at them, his body rigid with the effort to control his horse, while his men were as silent and frightening as he.

"*Jesu.*"

It was Ivo's murmur, his voice hoarse and strange. Briar felt his hard body grow even more hard.

And then, without a word, the leader dug his spurs into his mount and came at them.

Briar gasped and tried to make herself as small as possible, curling against Ivo, intent on not getting in the way of the swing of his sword. Her heartbeat was as loud as the galloping horse. Ivo's own heart sounded so solid against her cheek,

and she felt his muscles stretch and harden as he
twisted his body to protect her, and fight off their
attacker. The leader of the troop drew his sword
and shouted a long, wordless cry of rage. The
hairs on Briar's neck stood up at the sound.

Ivo lifted his sword and drove forward.

Steel connected with steel with a hideous clang.
The dull clash echoed about them. Ivo hissed with
pain. And then the galloping horse had passed
them, moving on.

Ivo cursed and swung around, shouting orders
to Sweyn. Briar peered between her fingers. Their
faceless attacker had already been swallowed up
in the darkness, his men close behind. They had
not even unsheathed their weapons, and had
given Ivo and Sweyn a wide berth.

Swords still drawn, faces blank with confusion,
the two mercenaries stared after them.

"Are they gone?" asked Sweyn in a whisper.

"Aye."

"What did you make of it?"

"I know not," said Ivo, and yet . . . There was
something in his voice that made Briar wonder.

Sweyn appeared not to notice. "Who would
play such games? Why make a threat, and then
fail to follow it through? What does a man gain
from it?"

"Our fear."

"He wanted to unsettle us? Why?"

Ivo shifted on his mount, not answering. Briar
decided then that he did have some idea what this
was all about. He simply wasn't sharing it with
them.

Abruptly Ivo sheathed his sword. Apart from

that single clash of blades there had been no fight. Had the sight of two big, armed men been enough to frighten off the attackers? Was it that simple? Had this been some foolish dare?

Ivo reached down and rubbed his thigh, and winced.

Briar's mind froze. Speculation was forgotten and she was suddenly dizzy with terror. "You are hurt?" She ran frantic hands over him, searching for possible wounds.

For a moment he allowed her to do so, confused by her desperation, and then Ivo caught her hands in his, stilling her. "Nay, Briar, stop. I am unharmed." His voice was gentle. " 'Tis an old injury, and sometimes the muscle pulls again."

Briar nodded, feeling foolish. He was still gazing down at her, and when she flicked her own eyes up to his, she read warmth and admiration in his gaze.

"You are brave, demoiselle. You did not swoon, like your sister."

"Swoon!"

Startled, Briar swung around to Sweyn and noticed that Mary had fainted in his arms. Sweyn looked as if he would faint himself, touching Mary's cheek, her shoulder, whispering in her ear. "Sweet Jesu, Mary," Briar gasped, wriggling to escape Ivo's grip.

"She is not hurt." He would not release her. "She swooned when she knew we were safe. 'Twas better than had she done it in the midst of a fight."

"I am glad that pleases you," Briar said sharply, her concern for him forgotten. But she gave up her struggle, content that Mary was in good hands.

"Who were they?" she asked, watching him curiously.

Ivo's mouth went hard and straight. "Friends of the rebels who would take Lord Radulf's lands? Thieves intent on our purses? Enemies of mine?"

"What enemies do you have?" she demanded.

He shrugged. "I am a mercenary and, as you are so fond of reminding me, a disgraced knight. We all have enemies, awaiting their chance to hurt us, whether it be by word or blade. Perhaps I have wronged someone and now they seek revenge. Or mayhap 'tis Sweyn they seek, in retaliation for one of his bad jokes."

Sweyn pulled a face at him, too occupied with Mary to reply.

He was probably right, thought Briar. Enemies were everywhere, and Lord Radulf must have many. She was among their number. The troop of men had been well armed, they looked like soldiers who had killed before, but mayhap they had not expected such seasoned fighters as Ivo and Sweyn. Was that why they had ridden off like that?

Briar shivered, and Ivo's arms closed more firmly about her. Keeping her safe. He brushed his lips against her hair, his voice quiet, "Let us go home, demoiselle." As his horse set off at a slow trot, Briar closed her eyes, suddenly very content to be exactly where she was.

Briar must have dozed momentarily, for when she awoke, they had already reached the cottage by the river. Starlight washed the dark water intermittently as cloud slipped across the sky. Waves brushed the shore in soothing motion. The dwelling was a black shape, silent and faintly sinister.

Swiftly, Ivo dismounted and brought her down beside him. Briar had hoped he might carry her—she was oddly loathe to give up the warmth and safety of his arms—but understood he needed to have both his arms free. In case he had to fight for them.

"Wait here." His eyes were very dark, a warning that he meant what he said. Briar nodded, though her frown told him she didn't like it. He smiled, a faint lift of his lips, and turned away.

He was only gone a moment. It seemed like much longer to Briar, as she waited, her breath held.

" 'Tis safe."

His shadow appeared at the door, but at the sound of his voice, Briar had already followed him inside. Fumbling, she found and lit a candle. The wane light fought with the shadows. Briar wondered how a single candle could give such comfort? The same way in which one man, among all the others, tugged at her heart and made her so weak, so vulnerable.

It was incomprehensible, and very frightening. Once before she had believed in a man and he had failed her. How could she give herself to Ivo? He was near enough to a stranger.

"No one has been here," she said huskily, carefully looking about her. "I would know if they had."

He nodded, his dark eyes glinting in the weak flame. Moisture from the misty night sparkled on his hair as he bent to stir fire from the coals.

"Briar?" Mary's voice trembled.

Her sister was standing within the door, leaning heavily upon Sweyn. Briar hurried to take Mary's hands; to her dismay the girl's fingers were cold and shaking. "Come," she insisted, and with Sweyn's help, lowered the girl onto a stool. Ivo made quick work of turning the smoldering fire into a warm blaze, and dry heat began to chase the cold and damp into retreat.

"Briar, 'tis you who needs care."

"Hush, sweeting, I am quite well again." Briar stroked her sister's dark hair with gentle fingers. "The sickness is past. Truly."

And it was so. She felt perfectly well again, if a little tired. But then what woman would not feel tired after the evening she had had? It was Mary who needed care now—they were back to normal, and the return of their equilibrium was a great relief to Briar. She had begun to fear Mary no longer needed her.

Where would that leave Briar? She would have to begin thinking of life alone, just her, all by herself.

And she did not like it.

Ivo watched Briar while she busied herself making her sister warm and comfortable, and set a posset over the flames to heat.

He had known she loved her sister, of course he did, but to see it so clearly in her actions . . . His firebrand, Briar, seemed suddenly softer, more womanly, very much gentler.

He remembered how she had clung to him on the ride from Lord Shelborne's, her lips sweet on

his. He believed her. She felt no revulsion for his
maimed hand—Briar was not the sort to cringe
and turn faint at the sight of blood or damaged
flesh. His raw feelings where his lost fingers were
concerned had deceived him into seeing something that was not there.

Ivo took a long slow breath and wondered
where he could go from here. He would protect
Briar, he would help her solve the mystery of
Anna's death, but after that? What then?

Matilda.

His sister's name was a bittersweet memory, reminding him of his failure once before. *Not this
time, though. Miles won't win this time . . .*

Sweyn caught his eye.

The Dane looked miserable and uncomfortable,
as if he wished himself far away. Ivo jerked his
head at the door, and Sweyn followed him back
out into the night.

Mist from the river puddled about their feet.
They could hear the voices of boatsmen and the
wash of their oars, strangely muffled by the miasma. From inside the dwelling, the women's soft
murmurs spilled like candlelight.

Ivo spoke. "Radulf has asked to speak with me,
otherwise I would stay. I must leave them in your
hands, my friend."

Sweyn nodded, his handsome, good-natured
face more serious than usual. "I will guard them,
Ivo. I will do whatever I must to keep them safe.
Return to Radulf, and know they are in good
hands."

Ivo nodded. He wanted to stay, but Radulf had
asked specifically for him. Radulf was a good

lord, but even the best of them did not like to be disobeyed.

"Who were they?" Sweyn was watching him, waiting. As if he sensed Ivo had his suspicions.

The knot in Ivo's belly tightened. "Enemies of Radulf, mayhap?" he offered.

Sweyn turned thoughtful. "They wore dark colors—no emblems, no signs as to who was their master, and yet a troop of men like that . . . They were disciplined, trained, not the riffraff who normally set out to steal and plunder. And they were mounted on good horses, too. Aye, Ivo, they belonged to someone. 'Twas some reason to it."

"They were not afraid; that was not why they ran."

Again Ivo remembered how the leader had thrust his sword at him so aggressively before he rode past. Ivo had blocked it easily, but there had been real menace and intent in that blow. More *feeling* than one stranger should feel for another. Personal feeling, *old* feeling, the feeling between those who are well known to each other. Mayhap even *blood* feeling . . .

"Was Miles among them?"

Ivo went still at Sweyn's question. Had his friend read his mind? Sweyn said no more, waiting, until at last Ivo spoke, making his voice slow and measured.

"Miles hates me, 'tis true, but he is in hiding. Why come out into the open and risk being arrested by the king's men? Why show himself for my benefit?"

"Do you really think Miles would balk at showing himself, if it gave him the chance to do you

harm, Ivo? He will know how you tricked him at
Somerford, how you played dead and then escaped from him. He missed his chance to kill you
that day, and he will have been brooding about it
ever since. Aye, what else does he have to think of,
now he is in hiding from the king? If he hated you
before, then he will hate you more now. It could be
that Miles has just set you a challenge."

Ivo flexed the fingers on his gloved hand. Miles
wanted him dead. It was the truth. A strange and
incomprehensible truth to Ivo; his brother loathed
and hated him, and longed to hurt him. Mayhap
even kill him. Did Miles see Ivo as his conscience?
Did he think that the only way to silence that conscience was by crushing it? Ivo knew the evil of
which Miles was capable, although Miles's mind,
even after all these years, was still a mystery to
him. But for all its puzzlement, the fact remained:
Miles wanted Ivo dead.

"I recognized him," he said quietly, as if speaking too loud was dangerous and would make
something that he as yet only suspected into reality. "When the troop leader came riding at me, I
recognized him. Not with my mind, Sweyn. Inside my heart, deep in my belly. I felt his hatred
like hot air on my face."

Sweyn was silent, listening to the boatsman's
oars, the splash and dip drifting over the dark
Ouse.

"And then I noticed the way he held his sword,
the set of his head, the line of his shoulders, and I
knew him. 'Twas Miles."

There, it was said now. Like something bad
forced out of the shadows and into the light. But

Ivo felt no better for seeing it. Tension coiled in his stomach, made his throat ache. Miles was here, in York, just as Lord Henry had said he was. Miles, his brother and his most deadly enemy.

"You can't be sure," Sweyn said mildly, now playing at devil's advocate. "A man might resemble another, it does not mean 'tis him."

"Mayhap."

"Miles would be a fool to pit himself against you here, with Radulf at your back, and me at your side."

Ivo managed a grin, and the knot in his belly loosened slightly. "Fool indeed, Sweyn."

"Good." Sweyn nodded, as if the smile had been his aim. "Go now, and speak with Radulf. Tell him of the troop of men, tell him what you think. It won't hurt to warn him."

"Aye. Stay here, and guard them well. I will return as soon as I can."

Sweyn teased. "Do you plan to sleep at all, then?"

Ivo laughed. "Do you think I have slept since Briar came into my life? I am used to going without."

Sweyn gave a roar of laughter, the sound drifting over the river. The silence following it was eerie. As if someone out there was listening to them, observing them.

"I will say my farewells, then," Ivo murmured.

Sweyn nodded, and set his gaze upon watching the shadows.

Inside the cottage, Briar had settled Mary into her bed by the fire. The girl was almost asleep, her dark head cradled against her sister's shoulder as

Briar stroked her hair. As Ivo stepped forward, Briar looked up and smiled.

Ivo held her eyes, as if he would convey something to her by them alone. "I have to go back," he said softly, mindful of the sleeping girl.

"Oh." She glanced away, but he sensed her disappointment.

"I am called to Lord Radulf." He came still closer, eyes fastened on her profile. Beauty was in the curve of her brow and the straight line of her nose, the stubborn tilt of her chin and the long tendrils of her chestnut hair.

"Lord Radulf," she said, and managed to invest those two words with all her disgust.

He smiled. Here was the firebrand back again. "Sweyn is on guard, demoiselle, nothing will get by him. I will return as soon as I am able."

"You must please yourself, de Vessey."

"So you do not care whether I come back or not, Briar?"

"Not at all."

He reached out and touched her hair, the softest of strokes with his blunt fingers. "I do not believe you," he whispered. And then he turned and went outside.

Sweyn, who had been waiting by the doorway, closed the door and dropped the bar into place. With a half smile, he sank down onto the floor with his back to it and closed his eyes. Briar frowned at him a moment, but he seemed impervious to her displeasure. So, instead, she listened as Ivo rode away.

"I do not need his help," she said softly, firmly.

Sweyn smiled mischievously. "*I* see that, lady. But be kind to him, for *he* does not."

Radulf was waiting for him.

He sat in his chair, a goblet in his hand, a fur cloak wrapped close around his broad shoulders and chest. When he looked up at Ivo, his eyes were almost as intent as Ivo's own.

"Are they who I think they are?"

Ivo came forward, his direction clear. He could not even think of lying to this man; he had complete faith in Radulf.

"Aye, my lord. They are the daughters of the traitor Lord Richard Kenton, outcast from their estates and their home. They play and sing, not for the pleasure of it but because it keeps them alive."

Radulf nodded slowly. "Tell me, Ivo," he said, and leaning forward, prepared to listen.

"I don't know all, my lord, only what I have heard, and what has been told me by Briar. 'Tis not much."

Radulf shrugged impatiently. "Sit down, Ivo—you make my neck ache—and talk."

Ivo sat on the stool by the fire. The heat was so wonderful against his back, after the damp cold of the riverbank and then the road to Radulf's quarters, that he almost groaned aloud. But he stiffened his spine and prepared to tell his lord what he wanted to know.

"Briar, the songstress, knows little of Lady Anna, only that she was murdered. She blames you for that, my lord. There were rumors at the time, and she believed them. Her father swore vengeance upon you before he turned traitor and died, and she has taken up his pledge as her own."

Radulf's eyes were far away, but he nodded for Ivo to go on.

"After Lord Richard's death, the king gave all that was theirs to other barons, and they were declared outcasts. From what I have heard elsewhere, they made their way to York, where you see their life now. Very different from what it once was. Do you remember Sir Anthony Delacourt?"

Radulf blinked, his thoughts returning from wherever they had been. "Aye. He is a prisoner."

"And once vassal to Lord Richard Kenton. I took Briar to see him, at his request. He has much on his mind—he is dying—and he wishes to cleanse himself of sin before he faces God. Sir Anthony told Briar that Lady Anna cuckolded her father with many men, Lord Fitzmorton and Lord Shelborne among them. There must have been others. Briar was distressed to hear it, at first would not believe it, but I think she will grow to accept the truth. It *is* the truth, is it not, my lord?"

Radulf's mouth twisted in what may have been a smile, though not a very pleasant one.

"'Tis the truth, Ivo. This talk of the past disturbs me . . . brings back memories that are not so pleasant."

Ivo said nothing, watching the other man as he shivered, and huddled deeper into the fur cloak. He had never seen Radulf in this pensive mood, and never seen him appear so vulnerable. This man was a long way from the tales of greatness, the legends of immortality and brutality. This was the real man, seated here before him, shivering from the cold. Lonely. If only Briar could see her hated foe now . . .

"Anna was like a dark storm cloud, and she hung over me for many years before I met Lily, but I am free of her now. Not because she is dead," he added, when Ivo moved as if to ask the question, "but because Lily freed me. I am like the legendary creature held under a curse until the beautiful woman comes to break the spell." His eyes shone with laughter now, and something hotter.

"Anna pursued me when I was in York two years ago. She would not believe I did not want her. She thought all men desired her. But I had Lily, and I knew if I did not stop her, she would destroy my wife. I met her and told her, brutally, that I loathed her. She was furious. She tried to ride me down, but . . . well, the saints were watching over me. I was hurt only. My men drove her off, and I did not see her again. I was told, later, that her body had been found and she was murdered, but whoever did it was never discovered. Lord Richard accused me before the king, but the king was satisfied with my replies and dismissed his accusations. Kenton would not . . . could not, believe that. He rebelled, and later took his own life."

Radulf glanced up at Ivo. " 'Tis a grim little tale, is it not, de Vessey?"

"Why could Lord Richard not see what Anna was?" Ivo demanded, impatient with such willful blindness.

Radulf laughed softly. "You did not know her.

She found pleasure in twisting men's hearts inside out with jealousy and doubt, until they would crawl over hot coals for her smallest favor. And then she would swear she loved them and only them, and all the rest was lies. Kenton would want to believe her, *need* to believe her, for his own sanity."

"I see."

"I knew it, but I could not see a way to make Kenton listen. I felt I did not have the right to force such knowledge upon any husband, but my reasons are private, de Vessey, I will not go into them here. However," he drew a long breath, unknowingly echoing Sir Anthony's words, "if I had tried harder, mayhap none of the tragedy would have occurred. And I knew Anna; I knew of what she was capable. Aye, I feel in some way responsible for Kenton's daughters, for their misfortune. If I had known of their plight before now, I would have tried to help, but I was in the south, busy with concerns of my own."

"I think Briar is still set against you, my lord," Ivo reminded him quietly. "She is stubborn, but I hope to turn her from that."

A glimmer of laughter shone in Radulf's face. "I can believe it, Ivo. You are a man who could turn the devil to sainthood."

Ivo frowned. "I am no glib tongue, my lord."

"Nay, 'tis your earnestness, your knightly qualities. You are a man who has a solid core of gold, and it shines through."

Ivo was nonplussed. He did not see himself like that, far from it, and yet it was flattering for his lord to say so.

Radulf laughed at the expression on his face. "Do not let it go to your head, Ivo. And tell your songstress that I am willing to help her, when she asks. Despite legend, I am no monster."

"I know that, my lord."

"Do you love her?"

Ivo didn't know what to say. There was an attraction between them, a desperate, burning need, and she felt it as much as he. But was that love? Ivo did not know, and nor did he want to. He had sworn never to love a woman again, for her own sake as much as his.

Radulf was amused by his silence. Ivo stiffened, annoyed that he was the object of his lord's mirth.

"Love," Radulf spoke musingly, gazing down at the ring on his finger. "It is the cause of so many of our woes, and yet without it . . . Without Lily, I would as soon be dead."

His frankness made Ivo uncomfortable. "You miss her," he said, when it seemed Radulf would say no more.

Radulf looked up, and there was more emotion in his eyes than Ivo had ever seen. But all he said was, "Aye, I miss her."

Chapter 10

The day looked as bleak as the one before. Ivo glared at the weather as if he thought his displeasure might change it. He was tired and his head ached, and the only sleep he had had was when he sat down to take off his boots and dozed off on a bench by the fire. When he finally woke, stiff and disoriented, it was already dawn. He had grabbed a crust and swallowed a mug of ale, and hurried back to his horse.

Briar.

She was all he could think of. She had taken possession of his mind. His stupidity was beyond bearing. Had he not learned he was not suited to matters of the heart? How could he care for her? Emotional entanglements were not for him. Best he remember that now, before it was too late—for them both.

Smoke drifted from the roof of the cottage, and puddles lay everywhere. Ivo dismounted and strode to the door, thudding his fist against the wood. Sweyn's muffled voice called to ask who was there, and when Ivo answered, the door was swiftly opened.

Inside, the air was thick with the smell of herbs.

Mary was up, looking flushed and busy, while Briar stirred something bubbling in a pot resting over the coals. It was from this brew that the strong smell of herbs came, and it looked singularly unappetizing to Ivo. Briar must have felt the same, for her face was white and pinched, her lips pressed hard together.

Stubborn. Determined.

She shot him a sideways look and caught his smile, but didn't return it. She simply turned back to her pot and grimly continued to stir.

Ivo met Sweyn's eyes and raised his brow. In unspoken agreement, the two men moved into a corner and lowered their voices.

"She is sick," the Dane murmured. "She says she will be better when she eats that mess in the pot."

That was debatable, thought Ivo. "Everything quiet?" he asked instead.

"Nothing to be heard or seen."

Ivo nodded. "I am certain last night's attackers were fixed on us, not the women. Even if their leader was not Miles, I do not see the point in threatening Briar or Mary."

Puzzled, Sweyn tilted his head to one side. "Did you ever imagine it otherwise? Why would Mary and Briar be in danger from those men?"

"They are Kenton's daughters."

And yet, he thought, despite their illustrious past, it still made no sense that *they* should be in danger. For what reason? The past was just that. They were paupers now, they had nothing to steal, their deaths would solve nothing. Unless . . . could the attack have something to do with the murder of Anna? Was that murky pond stirring, giving up its secrets?

Sweyn cleared his throat.

Ivo glanced up and knew that before he could think further on the matter, he had some explaining to do. His friend was staring at him hard.

"Lord Kenton's daughters?" Sweyn repeated. "Share this with me, Ivo, and do it right fast!"

But Sweyn's expression soon turned to bemusement as Ivo quickly explained the entire story. By the time he had finished, Sweyn's blue eyes held both sorrow and resignation.

"They are the daughters of Lord Kenton," he repeated, as if to set the fact in his mind. Ivo found he could read his friend's thoughts in his face easily enough. *She is not for me, then. Even in her present state, she is too high for the likes of me.*

Well, Sweyn must fight his own demons; Ivo would not make up his mind for him.

"I still feel a need to guard these ladies, Sweyn," he said quietly, "however great they may once have been. What say you?"

Sweyn nodded, slowly, as if resigned. "Aye, Ivo, I too feel a need to guard the ladies."

"Good."

Sweyn shook himself, his eyes narrowing. "Did

you speak to Radulf about the attack last night? About Miles?"

"Nay, not yet."

"Why in Odin's name not, Ivo? He needs to know."

Ivo looked bleak. "I will tell him, 'tis just . . . I want to make certain first 'twas no random attack. And nothing to do with Briar and Mary."

Sweyn heaved a sigh. "You want to face him by yourself," he said, with a touch of irritation unusual for him. "He means to kill you this time. If you do not mean to kill him, then he has the advantage."

"I know."

But did he? And could he, when the moment came, actually destroy a man who was of his own blood? His own brother?

Briar served up the mess from the pot, and handed a bowl to Mary, who began delicately to eat. Catching the horrified eyes of the two men, Briar smiled as brightly as she was able and filled two more bowls, holding them out.

For a moment neither of them moved, and then Sweyn swallowed audibly and edged forward to take his portion from her. Ivo managed a faint smile as he reached for his bowl. "Thank you, demoiselle, I am grateful," he said with his usual knightly courtesy. Then he just stood there with the bowl in his hand.

"Eat it, sir." Mary was watching him, wry amusement in her eyes. She was, thought Briar, looking much better this morning. The swooning fit had passed, and Mary was full of life again. Or mayhap, 'twas Sweyn spending the night in the dwelling with them that had something to do with that.

Briar still did not believe the handsome, fair-headed mercenary was good enough for her sister, but after last night, seeing his dedication to protecting them, and his obvious fondness for her sister, she had thawed toward him.

"Do you sing again tonight?" Ivo asked, distracting her.

Mary nodded, giving him a shy smile.

"Lord Shelborne has offered us a generous fee," Briar said, forcing down a mouthful of her breakfast. "His daughter and her new husband have returned from London, and he wishes to greet them with pomp."

She chewed and swallowed another mouthful, then scooped up the next spoonful and stuck it into her mouth. Her cheeks bulged. She could feel the blood leaving her face, and suspected by the interest showing in Ivo's eyes that she had turned pale green. She swallowed her mouthful and started on the next, sure that if she ignored it long enough, the feeling would go away.

Her throat closed over. The mouthfuls she had already forced down changed course, and started to make their way up. With a despairing groan, Briar made a dash for the bucket in the corner. Everything she had eaten came back up, and she was utterly powerless to stop it.

Mary made as if to go to her, but Ivo caught her arm and shook his head, and she subsided. Sweyn set his own bowl thankfully aside. It was Ivo himself who crossed to the dejected form.

Briar had stopped retching at last, and seemed too exhausted to do more than sit with her head in her arms. Gently, Ivo lifted her up from the floor. Her arms fell limply to her sides, and he saw the tears running down her white cheeks. Her mouth was trembling with the effort it was taking not to cry, not in front of him. Ivo's heart ached for her, his brave, beautiful Briar.

"Take this," Mary murmured, and handed him a warm, damp cloth.

Ivo smiled his thanks, and sat down, cradling the woman in his arms. She kept her eyes tight shut, refusing to look at him while he bathed her face as he had done once before. Gently, thoroughly. After a little time, her tears stopped running and she was quiet, acquiescent against him and close to sleep.

"You will not sing this even, demoiselle," he murmured the order, and set his lips to her brow.

It was as if he had stuck a pin into her.

She stiffened, her eyes shot open, their color almost completely green, and she glared up at him.

"I *will* sing!" she declared. "Leave me be, Ivo de Vessey. I will sing. 'Tis nothing to you. You cannot tell me what I can and cannot do."

She struggled up, shaking herself free of his arms, and stalked to the other side of the room. Ivo watched her in amazement, her feet bare beneath the ragged hem of her gown, her hands clenched into fists at her sides as she fought him with every fiber of her being. If he hadn't seen it with his own eyes, he would never have believed her to have been prostrate with illness only moments before.

Jesu, she was magnificent! Ivo tried very hard not to grin, but he must have given himself away, because she let out a faint, strangled scream.

"Do not patronize me, de Vessey. You are not worthy, and we both know it."

Ivo's amusement fled. He squeezed his fist about the cloth he had used to cool her face, and tossed it aside. "Your insults grow old," he said, and stood up. "You need to think of new ones, Briar, if you are to hold my attention."

" 'Tis not a matter of thinking up insults—there are so many, I hardly know where to start."

With an impatient shrug, Ivo left her to her sister's care, and beckoned Sweyn outside.

Sweyn grinned. "I'll say it again. She is a shrew, my friend. You will have your hands full if you decide on her."

Ivo glanced sideways at him. "Even if I dared to think such thoughts, what use would the daughter of a baron have for a disgraced knight? She is right, I am unworthy of her."

Sweyn laughed. "Better to ask yourself how the outcast daughter of a traitor can make herself worthy of *you*, Ivo."

Ivo smiled at last, and some of his anger drained from him. "And what of you? If I am worthy, then so are you, my friend."

But Sweyn shook his head, and the bleak look in his amiable blue eyes returned. "Nay, Ivo. You are wellborn, a knight . . . aye, yes you are. What am I? The mercenary son of a Danish farmer. Not even a Viking raider, but a tiller of the soil."

"The son of a farmer? Who would think it? Do you ever feel the urge to go back to the soil? Mayhap Mary can help you sow your seed."

He took off for his horse with speed, but not before Sweyn had struck him a solid and painful blow on his shoulder.

"You are very foolish and very stubborn, Briar. But then so you always were."

Jocelyn stood before her, hands on hips, but there was worry in her blue eyes. Mary had gone to help with the hall—there were never enough hands. The girl seemed full to brimming with energy since Sweyn had stayed with them, as if her thoughts could not be still.

The sickness of this morning had passed again and, although tired, Briar had passed an uneventful day. It was only now, as darkness fell, that her stomach had begun to roil again. As if in sheer bloody-mindedness it sought to upset her plans for the evening. Lord Shelborne had offered them more money than they had yet had for any one performance, and Briar was determined to have it.

"Mayhap Lord Shelborne has discovered who we really are," Briar said now, amidst the bustle of Jocelyn's kitchen. "Mayhap he wants to make amends for the past."

"What past?" Jocelyn retorted, frowning.

Briar chose her words with care. "I have heard a rumor that Lord Shelborne was our stepmother Anna's lover."

Jocelyn seemed to freeze, the curious expression in her eyes slowly draining away. Her voice sounded strange. "Her lover? Lord Shelborne?"

"Aye," Briar replied, watching her doubtfully. "And Lord Fitzmorton. And others. Did you not know this, sister? Did you not know how many others, apart from Lord Radulf, our stepmother was merrily welcoming into her bed?"

Slowly, as if she were in a daze, Jocelyn turned to the table. Her hands shook as she put the finishing touches to a songbird pie, and Briar had the odd feeling she was just fiddling with the elaborate pastry decorations to gain time.

"I wondered." She spoke at last. "When I first saw her, I thought her beautiful, and afterward I heard 'twas all skin deep, and she had never been faithful in her life. I hoped 'twas nothing more than talk, for our father's sake. He was happy, and so blind with love for her—"

"Why did you never tell me!"

Jocelyn flinched at the accusation. "I had no proof, and it seemed unnecessarily cruel to speak of such things."

"I have believed all this time that Lord Radulf was the one who sent her to her death."

"He probably was. I can tell you this, Briar, that of them all, Radulf was the one she cared about. She wanted him to come to her, and when he wouldn't she was furious with him."

Briar shook her head, feeling abandoned and adrift. "You should have told me. Now 'tis too late."

"Why too late?" Jocelyn retorted, a strange bitterness flavoring her words. "I thought you were determined to revenge our father, right the wrongs? Once you could talk of nothing else. What has changed now?"

Briar opened her mouth to defend herself, and promptly burst into tears.

Jocelyn made a wordless cry and moved to comfort, but Briar pulled away. Furiously, she dashed at her cheeks, as if to scrub away the evidence of her weakness before it fell.

"What in God's name is wrong with me!" she wailed. "I am sick, I am well, I am tired, I cry, I think foolish thoughts that I never thought before! Jesu, I beg you, heal me or let me die!"

Jocelyn had stopped to stare at Briar, and now her eyes widened. Purposefully, she grasped her sister's shoulders in hard, hurting hands, forcing her to look up. Even Jocelyn's lips were white, Briar thought in amazement. What had she said? What was wrong?

"When did you have your last flux, Briar?"

Briar moved to shake off that cruel grip, and then she froze. Last flux? She had not even thought of such a thing. She had been too busy trying to survive and being angry at Ivo de Vessey . . . Ivo! The night they had spent together under this very roof, his seed spilling into her, finding fertile ground in her womb . . .

"No." The word stuck in her throat. She shook her head. Her vision wobbled and darkened.

"Aye," Jocelyn retorted grimly. "How long ago was it? Briar?"

Briar pulled herself up, swallowing past the shock and disbelief. "Near to three moons. 'Tis late October now."

"Then you are with child."

The idea was too big, too overwhelming for her to take in. A child. Ivo's child. Her fierce and brooding knight, a father? Briar, a mother? Wild emotions flooded her, each clamoring for their turn, until she put her head in her hands and cried, "Enough!"

Silence, blessed silence.

Jocelyn's fingers were gentle on her hair, smoothing the tumbled locks, comforting her. But Briar knew in her heart her sister could not really help her; she was alone in this. Alone . . .

"There is no need to worry yet," Jocelyn said carefully. "Three moons is not long. Mayhap it has not taken root properly. You will lose it as easily as it was gained."

Did she want that? Briar struggled to make sense of her feelings.

"I cannot talk of this now," her muffled voice was shaky. "I have to sing. I know you mean well, Jocelyn, but I cannot speak of this now."

Jocelyn nodded and stepped back. "Very well, Briar. But you will need to speak of it, and soon. You can not will this away by ignoring it."

Why not? Briar thought hysterically. *Why can I not just wish it away?* She was carrying the child of her disgraced knight. Aye, the daughter of a traitor and a disgraced knight! What sort of parents would they make for a babe?

And how could they be parents, when they were but passing strangers, brought together by a mistake. He would go south again, when Lord Radulf was finished killing rebels, and she would remain in York. Alone.

I have my sisters. They will help me.

But the voice in her head sounded forlorn, afraid, desperate.

She was carrying Ivo de Vessey's child, and despite his claim that he wanted *her*, it was doubtful he planned to settle down and play at husband and father. Would he?

The waiting stillness in her heart gave her no reply.

Ivo watched as Briar climbed up to the dais and seated herself on her stool. She looked white but composed. She clasped her hands in her lap, and straightened her shoulders. There was courage in every line of her. Even at a moment like this, when every face turned to her was welcoming and anticipatory, she was prepared to fight.

Aye, he admired her. While she was cutting at him with her sharp tongue, he admired her. Besides, she did not mean to hurt him—the attack was a defense, he knew that. She was frightened and confused, so she lashed out. And the target she chose was one who she knew would never hurt her, upon whose tough hide her barbs would fall harmlessly.

Because he would *never* hurt her intentionally. Ivo knew it deep, deep in his soul. He would never hurt her, and he would fight anyone else who dared to try.

By now Mary had also settled herself, the harp ready. The two women conferred briefly. Then Briar turned back to her audience. Her eyes searched the expectant faces, discarding each one, looking for someone in particular. Until she found him.

Their gazes held, locked.

Ivo felt the power of it.

What was it in her expression that struck him to the core? He sensed her wildness, her despair. Her need of him. It shimmered between them.

Shocked, Ivo took a blind step forward.

But it was too late. She had begun her song. He stopped, hesitant, suddenly uncertain whether he had really seen such naked anguish in her beautiful, slanting eyes. He stood and listened, while her husky voice and poignant words tore at his heart. Ivo moved to lean back against the wall, his legs unable to hold him and with a deep breath tried to prepare himself for the emotional ride ahead.

The first song was well received. Lord Shelborne's guests cheered until the hall shook with their approbation. They sang again, and again. And then one last time, especially for Lord Shelborne's daughter. The girl flushed with pleasure, and Lord Shelborne looked grateful. As Briar and Mary rose to leave the dais, Shelborne came forward and took their hands in his.

Ivo frowned as Briar stiffened, and then gradually relaxed. But her smile was forced, and she seemed relieved when he released her and took a step back. Once more her eyes searched for, and found, Ivo, this time beseechingly.

Ivo pushed away from the wall, and strode across the hall to her rescue.

". . . remember Lord Richard with fondness."

Lord Shelborne was beaming at Briar. Mary, close by, twisted her fingers around her harp, clearly nervous and upset. What, thought Ivo, is the man saying to them?

"My father was a good man." Briar's chin was up, her back straight. "He did not deserve to be treated so."

Now Lord Shelborne looked a little uncomfortable, perhaps wondering if her words had a personal slant. Ivo prayed Briar was not so foolish as to insult so important a personage, especially when he had just done her great honor by acknowledging her.

"He was loyal to those he loved," he said at last.

Briar opened her mouth. Her eyes slid past Shelborne and found Ivo's. He shook his head once. She hesitated a breath, and then forced a polite smile.

"'Tis a fair assessment of him, my lord, thank you."

"You have pleased my daughter very much, ladies. I thank you for it."

Briar and Mary curtsyed and did not rise until Lord Shelborne had gone. Mary looked frightened, her dark eyes flicking to Briar and back to Ivo. Briar looked angry, her cheeks flushed, her hazel eyes glittering.

"Did you hear him patronizing us?" she said to Ivo, but he was thankful she kept her voice low.

"Briar—"

"As if he had never done anything so despicable as cuckold my father—"

"Briar."

She stopped, gave him a wary glance. "'Tis true."

"Sometimes 'tis wiser and safer to keep one's thoughts to one's self, demoiselle."

She searched his face, and then shrugged one shoulder with pretended indifference. "Very well, I will say no more."

"You would be wise not to, lady. At least, not until you have left this place."

"*Very well*, de Vessey."

He smiled. "Thank you."

"What do you here anyway? Is your lord in attendance?" She looked past him briefly, searching for Lord Radulf. Then, as if a new idea had struck her, she frowned at Ivo. "Who told Lord Shelborne our secret?"

Ivo grimaced. "He had already guessed, demoiselle, as had Lord Radulf. They recalled your name—'tis unusual. A prickly name for such a sweet woman."

She paled, then looked down and said no more. Her hands twisted in her gown.

Ivo reached out and covered her hands with his own. Her fingers stilled, and then relaxed beneath his warm, strong grip. "I am come to take you home, demoiselle," he murmured. "Are you ready to go now?"

"Aye," she breathed, and cast him a secretive glance from beneath her long dark lashes. "Aye, Ivo, I am."

He had known she needed him, and he had come. Briar understood it had been so ever since he returned from fighting in the north. Whenever she was in danger or need, Ivo had been there.

And, oh, she needed him now, in this moment, more than any other.

But did she dare to take what he was offering her?

Briar shivered, leaning back into his warm body as they made their way through the dark streets toward the river. Instinctively, his arms tightened, and he drew her cloak closer to her, and added his own as well. So safe, she thought with a sigh. She had never looked for safety before—she had not thought to need a man in such a way. Briar strongly believed in her own ability to protect herself and her sisters, but nevertheless it was pleasant to have a man like Ivo de Vessey standing behind her. One look at his big body and rugged features, and most people backed away, eager not to draw his ire.

But he was not like that, not really.

They did not know Ivo as she did.

He was honorable and chivalrous, thoughtful and passionate—aye, he was all those things and more. A mixture of impatient hot-bloodedness and loyal self-sacrifice. It did not matter that he was a mercenary and a disgraced knight.

He would make a fine father.

If he stayed.

Briar's heart pounded. *Jesu, how can I tell him? What will he do? Say?*

What if he abandoned her?

Would Ivo do such a thing? She could not imagine it, but then she really did not know him. Was she going to put her hope and trust, her future and that of her child, into the hands of a man who was almost a stranger?

"Lord Shelborne meant well," Ivo said now, oblivious to her agitation.

Briar laughed bitterly, as she was thrust from her new concerns into the old. "He seeks to soothe his conscience, like Sir Anthony, that is all."

"Isn't that something we all do, from time to time?"

"I have never cuckolded anyone."

"Oh? Was not that why you wanted me to be Radulf? So that you could pay him back in similar fashion?"

"That was different!"

"Was it? Well, think hard before you cut Shelborne with that sharp tongue of yours. You will not sing in his hall again if you insult him in front of his family and friends, and he will probably see to it that you do not sing anywhere else in York."

I don't care, at least my father will be revenged!

She opened her mouth to say the words just as she had meant to accuse Lord Shelborne when he came up to her on the dais. And did not. Ivo was right. She could not ruin their lives for the pleasure of insulting Lord Shelborne, much as she might want to. She could not afford to be chased from York. She had more than herself to think of now.

"Someone should pay for what happened to us," she said plaintively. "When my sisters and I were outcast from Castle Kenton, we went to our village, to beg help from our people there, the people whom we had cared for and loved. They would not let us into their houses. They were afraid of Filby and what he would do to them if he discovered they had given us shelter."

"Filby?" Ivo looked down at her; she saw the gleam of his eyes. "You mean Lord Filby?"

"Aye. My betrothed." The word slid over her tongue like barbs of glass. "When my father was declared a traitor and took his life, Filby refused to have me to wife. He took our land instead."

"Not a man of honor, then," Ivo said lightly, but his voice quivered with anger.

"No, de Vessey, he was not like you."

She felt his eyes on her again, curious, searching, but he said only, "Does Filby still hold Castle Kenton?"

"Nay, that is the joke, if your humor is of a grim bent. Filby was killed in an uprising soon after we had gone—his peasants and serfs rose up and murdered him. So perhaps they missed us a little, after all."

Ivo smiled. "Perhaps they did. How did you survive in such a situation?"

How did they survive? Cunning, determination, luck . . . there were many reasons. They had been stronger than they knew, even Mary.

"Each day brought new tests for us. To find food, to find warmth, to find somewhere to sleep. And somehow, most days, we managed. When we were separated from Jocelyn and Odo, it grew harder."

"You were separated?"

"Soldiers came into the village where we were singing, and Jocelyn took Odo to safety one way while Mary and I ran another. We were afraid if we were seen, the men would take us and lock us up. We were the daughters of a traitor, remember, and we did not expect kind treatment."

"Go on."

"Mary and I dressed up in men's clothing. We strode about like men—we would practice the walk until we fell into fits of laughter. We were a little crazy, I think, in those days. When we reached York, we were safer. We began to sing in the market, and that was where Jocelyn found us. She and Odo had been given work with Lord Shelborne, mainly because Jocelyn cooks so well. Odo would never have been allowed to stay if not for Jocelyn."

"Odo was your father's strong arm?"

"Aye. Odo stood by my father, always. He fell ill at the time Anna was murdered, struck down with an apoplexy the very morning her body was found. He could not advise or protect us. My sister was with him day and night, and eventually he regained the use if his body, if not his mind. But by then it was too late for my father, and for us. And he is no longer Odo, not really, but Jocelyn clings to him because she cannot bear to let him go."

" 'Tis hard to let go of those we love."

He said it as if he understood, but before she could ask questions, he went on.

" 'Tis truly a long journey you and your sisters have undertaken, Briar. I honor you for your courage. Do not squander all you have gained with one hasty, vengeful act."

"Even if he deserves it?"

"Even then."

At that moment they reached the dwelling by the Ouse.

She was admirable and brave. What other woman in her position, coming from her privileged background, could have survived such travails? And yet Ivo wished he had been there, that he could have lightened her terrible load, protected her, made her difficult life just a little bit easier.

"You do not have to live in such hard times again," he said at last, halting his horse and tilting his head so that he could see her. "While I am here, I will look after you."

The words had barely left his mouth when she fired up like dry tinder.

"While you are here? What use is that to me! Mayhap you would stay if I paid you."

"I do not ask for payment," he replied stiffly. Was she willfully misunderstanding him? What had he said to make her so angry so quickly?

"I do not want your care if you have no intention of letting me keep it longer than a week . . . a month . . ."

Surprised, he tried to read her face in the shadows, but she pulled away. "I will not leave you in danger, Briar," he insisted. "I will see that you are safe."

He could hear her spluttering with anger and frustration. "I have never asked for anything of you, de Vessey—"

Ivo closed his eyes and said, loudly, "I want you."

She stopped, breathing fast.

"I want you," he said again, and opened his eyes. She was staring back at him, and her eyes shone with tears.

"You *want* me," Briar whispered, "but is that enough?"

"Then what *is* enough, demoiselle?" Ivo retorted, his voice harsh with his own sense of frustration.

Briar didn't know. She was frightened and confused, and now she had the prospect of a child to care for, to feed, to clothe . . . And all Ivo could say was, *I want you.* It wasn't enough.

"Do not come back here again." Her voice shook. "I do not want a disgraced knight following me about. I do not want *you*, de Vessey."

"If you say that often enough, I will begin to believe you mean it, Briar."

"I *do*, I do mean it!"

"Briar." Mary was staring at her sister in dismay. "Ivo and Sweyn have been so kind, and this is how you thank them? You are making me ashamed."

Briar stared at her, mouth open. Mary had never spoken to her in such a way before, never. Ashamed? After all she had done? The threatening tears choked her. She ran for the cottage and slammed the door behind her.

She flung herself onto her bed, head in her arms, wishing she could cry. The sobs were there, in her throat, but now when she wanted to weep, they would not come forth. Trapped, cornered, that was how she felt. Her life had slipped beyond her control, and it had happened the night she first saw Ivo de Vessey.

When she felt the touch on her hair she told herself it was Mary. But it was not Mary's touch. Big, gentle fingers, stroking. He caressed her back, and then lifted her, turning her into his shoulder. She clung there like a burr, a terrified creature, her arms locked about his neck.

"I am with child."

She felt the heavy thud of his heart, his silence, and wished she could read his expression.

"How long have you known?" he said, not quite evenly.

"Since Jocelyn told me, before I sang tonight." She clung even harder, as if afraid that now he knew he would push her away. Or ask her if it was his. He had every right to do so. She had lured him to her bed, a stranger. How could he be certain she did not do that with others? Jesu, she had pretended she did, just to annoy him!

"Ivo," she whispered, "the babe is—"

"Mine."

She leaned back to look at him, laughing and crying at the same time. He gave her a serious smile in return, but something bleak chilled his warm dark eyes.

"Do you still want me?" she asked uncertainly, reining in her wild emotions.

He nodded without hesitation. "You and the babe."

"But—" What was that look in his eyes, what did it mean?

He pulled her close again, so that she could not read him.

"Tonight I will stay here with you. I will send Sweyn back to Lord Shelborne's with Mary. Do you think Lady Jocelyn will mind?"

She hesitated, a tiny spark of rebellion catching heat at the ordering note in his voice. But she quenched it.

"Jocelyn will not mind, Ivo."

He didn't seem to notice her uncharacteristic

compliance as he rose to his feet and went out to give Sweyn his new orders.

Sweyn didn't argue, although Mary insisted on speaking to her sister. When she returned she looked a little dazed, and her glances at Ivo were suspicious. Shortly afterward they were gone.

Ivo stood and stared at the river. The shock of Briar's confession was wearing off. He knew he wouldn't turn away from her. It was not in his character to do so. He would care for and protect her until death. That was what he had been trained to do. But even if it were not, even had he been one of the boatmen out on the river, he would have remained by her side, whether she wanted him or not. Briar was carrying his babe and suddenly his life's choices had narrowed down to one.

Ivo had loved before, and it was not the thought of loving a woman and being responsible for her that worried him. It was the fear that she might be taken from him. And that he might be unable to stop it happening, that he might fail her in some way.

As he had failed Matilda. He hadn't been able to save her, had he? No matter how much he had loved her, his love had not stopped her death at Miles's hands. And it still hurt just as much as it always did, for Ivo's love had not died with his sister. Once Ivo loved it was forever.

To his cost.

He tipped back his head and gazed at the stars, like tiny molten balls in the black furnace of the sky. A babe. His and Briar's. A de Vessey. Ivo did not doubt the babe was his. Did that make him as arrogant as Briar was always accusing him? He thought now that he had known, from the moment his seed spilled into her, he had known that this was meant to be. *They* were meant to be. Struggle though they both might, the fates had already decided. Briar was Ivo's, and Ivo was Briar's, and there was an end to it.

The door opened behind him. He felt the warmth spill out, and the sweet scent of Briar. The stars swam before his eyes, and Ivo turned to her.

Her face was pale from crying, and she looked uncertain, though trying to hide it with an indifferent mask. Sheltering her heart in case he shattered it, even after he had sworn to stay with her. His brave, beautiful love who had been so wounded by others.

He took a step forward, looking down into her eyes, and deliberately bent his head and kissed her. Captured her lips. Passion surged into him, and he felt the answering heat in her.

"Ivo," she gasped, arms clinging, pressing closer.

He lifted her and carried her into the dwelling, closing the door behind them.

Briar felt herself slip into a warm, heady waking-dream. Ivo's lips closed on hers, tenderly, but with a hint of urgency. He had said he wanted her, and she could feel the truth of it in his kisses.

His hands stroked her shoulders, her back, as his mouth drew her deeper into the dream. Briar's breasts felt heavy, achy, and she moved against him, enjoying the sensation of her soft flesh against his hard-muscled chest. He turned and slid his thigh between hers, lifting her with his hands about her waist, bringing her closer.

"Ivo," she murmured. She ran her hands over his shoulders, tugging her fingers through his hair. He bent, pressing his face to her breasts through her gown. It was not enough. She needed his mouth on her bare skin, she needed to feel his tongue on her.

Ivo must have felt the same, for he began hastily pulling at ties and knots, drawing the garment over her head and tossing it aside, leaving her in her chemise, stockings, and shoes.

He stood and looked at her, his eyes hot. Then gently, he knelt down and began to undress her. Briar closed her eyes, her mind full of the sensation of his calloused fingers on her feet as her shoes were removed. Warm, determined, his hands caressed her ankles, her calves, her knees, rolling each stocking down the curving slope of her leg. She opened her eyes and gazed into his.

He smiled up at her, and suddenly dizzy, she placed her hand on his shoulder to steady herself. The other she used to touch his jaw where the bruise still showed, his cheek, his mouth. His gloved fingers fondled her thigh, and she ached with wanting.

Ivo stood, lifting her with him, and carried her to the bed. Briar lay back and watched as he removed his wolfpelt cloak, and then his tunic and shirt. His skin shone bronze in the firelight, while his face was all shadows. He unlaced his breeches, and she reached out to touch him. He felt hard and hot, and at the brush of her fingers he groaned.

"Briar."

But when she would have gone further, he eased back and hurriedly stripped off his boots and breeches. He stood before her now, naked, apart from his glove.

"Will you take that off for me, too?" Briar asked, with surprising shyness.

Ivo hesitated, and then shook his head. "Not now, demoiselle."

Briar did not insist. In truth, she was a little afraid of what she would see, and mayhap this was not the time for such things. He was watching her, suddenly uncertain.

"Do you think our friend at the hostelry will knock on the door tonight?" Briar teased nervously, to lighten the moment.

Ivo bent and slid his fingers along her thigh, seeking her center. He smiled. "He will be sorry if he does."

She laughed and then gasped as he leaned forward and found her nipple through the thin chemise, biting very gently. The bud swelled, went hard, and she clutched at his shoulders, feeling the muscles move beneath his skin.

"Take me, de Vessey," she commanded. "I need you now."

He looked down into her eyes, his own half closed, blurred with desire. "You are very bossy, my lady. Do you always instruct your lovers so?"

She arched as his fingers moved in her again, her reply ragged. "Only you, Ivo."

He smiled, and it transformed him into a

younger, more carefree man. Her handsome, lusty
warrior. Briar reached up and took that mouth
with hers, and at the same time he slid himself
into her, claiming her as his.

"Ivo," she gasped.

He groaned and withdrew, thrusting again,
deeper this time. Briar lifted her hips, eager for
more, quickly spiraling out of control. Could any
other man give her this, this sense of complete-
ness? There *was* no other man . . .

Briar cried out her joy as Ivo pushed her beyond pleasure, and followed after.

Briar lay content by Ivo, her body throbbing
still from their passion. Ivo stroked her arm,
where it lay across him beneath his wolfpelt cloak,
which he had pulled over their cooling flesh.

"Will you wed me, Briar?"

Surprised, Briar viewed the request hungrily. *I
want this*, she realized. I want to wed him and be
his wife, have his child, make him happy and be
happy myself.

Happiness had not had much to do with any
plans she had made over the past two years. Briar
was not sure if she trusted it.

"Is that what you want, Ivo?"

She half sat up, to see his face, but it was closed.
Reminding her that he, too, had his secrets.

"I want you. A marriage between us will give
me the right to protect you and the child, to care
for you. It will bind us together, Briar."

She shook her head, her hair spilling about
them. "No more than we are already bound," she
said seriously.

He touched her cheek. "There are reasons why being a de Vessey may not be such a good idea," he said, as if to himself. "And yet I would call you wife, Briar. I would that our child takes my name."

Warmth flooded her at his answer. "Very well," she whispered. "I will wed you, Ivo. I will be your wife."

He took her in his arms, and his mouth grew hot and eager on hers. They had made a new pledge, thought Briar, as desire built between them once more. And it had nothing to do with vengeance or hate. This was a vow to each other, and it was built upon trust and responsibility and caring. And hope.

Sweyn drew Mary closer to him, the darkness itself like a cloak about them. Their horse moved cautiously through the silent streets of York.

"Will my sister wed Ivo?" she asked him, her voice soft and uncertain. Mary had been deep in thought until now, and Sweyn had left her undisturbed.

"Did she say that?"

Mary rested against his chest, trusting, comfortable. And he allowed it because it felt so good.

"Nay. She told me she was with child, and the father is Ivo."

Sweyn was silent, almost as surprised as Mary. Almost. Ivo, a father? Well, it happened to most men. But most men weren't Ivo. Sweyn knew his friend would not abandon this girl, even if he was not besotted with her. To leave her in such a plight was not in his nature.

"And your sister is happy about this?"

Mary considered. "I think so, or she would be, but she fears the future. You see she has been betrayed before."

"Ivo would never betray her, Mary."

She glanced around at him, trying to see his face.

"She will be well taken care of," Sweyn added reassuringly.

He could see Ivo now, several years into the future, with Briar and a gaggle of children. Aye, his life was like a tale, already told. If, that was, Ivo could best his brother, Miles. If he could do that, then the story would end well. If not . . .

Sweyn turned the horse into the lane off Stonegate. The future was not so clear for him. He supposed he would go on doing as he had always done. Moving from place to place, from woman to woman. As if in rejection of his thoughts, he tightened his hold on Mary's pliant form, and the sweet scent of her hair made him dizzy.

"My sister thinks I am still a child." Her gentle voice came to him from the darkness. "But I am not."

"No, you are not," he retorted. He knew well enough, from the feel of her in his arms, that she was all woman.

Mary seemed pleased with his answer.

"I would like a husband one day, and a babe," she said, her voice carefully, painfully casual.

"Aye," Sweyn replied bleakly, "I feared that you might."

Chapter 11

The afternoon shadows were long, reminding Briar that very soon winter would be upon them. They gave a grim cast to this part of York, making it seem far more desolate than it would have been on a fine and sunny day. These buildings had been burned during the last siege of York, either to prevent occupation by the enemy or in one of their raids. Some of them had since collapsed or been demolished, and those that remained standing looked most unsafe.

Briar ran her gaze down the line of abandoned dwellings, until she came to the one she wanted. It was still there, then—or what was left of it, for as they drew nearer she could see that a good part of it had also been burned. Charred wooden beams rose against the gray sky, dark and gaunt, like clutching fingers.

"This is it?"

Ivo had been watching her. He was unobtrusive in his care of her, helping her to mount before him on the horse, making sure she was warm enough, comfortable enough, but nevertheless he was always there to lend her his hand when she needed it. As soon as she had expressed a wish to visit her father's old home, he had agreed to take her.

If Ivo had been her gallant knight before, then he was doubly so now that she carried his child. To Briar, who was so used to looking after herself, such a state of affairs seemed strange and confusing. And very pleasant, too. She could get used to it, and that worried her.

After leaving Castle Kenton, she had always made certain she did not become too fond of anything. In case she lost it. Now Ivo had asked her to wed him. He had spoken to the priest and they only needed to set the day. But Briar hesitated.

The truth was, she did not feel as if she could entirely trust him. And he knew it. Although it had been Briar who demanded Ivo make a commitment to stay, who had needed him to say yes, it was now she who hovered uncertainly on the brink of the rest of her life. And Ivo had not pushed her; he stood back and waited.

Mayhap he knew her better than she thought.

At night, her dreams were full of him leaving without telling her, or vanishing into the night, back to his home in the south. Or dying upon some lonely battlefield somewhere. Despite all his promises, Briar was finding it very difficult to believe that he would really stay. She could not help it. Filby had abandoned her, Odo had fallen ill and was as much as dead, her father had taken his own life. Her dealings with men, so far, had led her to the conclusion that they were never there when she needed them.

"This is the house your father and Lady Anna lived in, the last time they were in York?" His voice broke through her musings.

Briar blinked around at him, unscrambling her wits. "Aye, this is it. My father built it especially for her—as a gift. I stayed here once or twice, but mostly I remained at Castle Kenton. Jocelyn and Odo spent more time here than I. After my father died the house lay empty for a time, and then it was burned by King William's men, or the Danes—I forget which. It will fall down one day. I don't think anyone wants it. They see it as being tainted, like him."

And me.

"Such things will be forgotten in time," he said, as if he believed it.

She didn't bother to answer him. They both knew that her father must remain a traitor, even in death, until the king forgave him. And that seemed unlikely. So Briar, as his daughter, would remain outcast, forgotten. A creature of the shadows.

Did Ivo really want such a wife? Even a man in his position must have some ambitions. Taking a traitor's daughter to wife could hardly further his career.

She opened her mouth to ask him, but he spoke before her, and the moment was lost. Briar was

SARA BENNETT

not sure whether she was sorry or not. Mayhap she was a coward, but despite her own doubts, she did not want to hear Ivo's.

"Have you seen enough, demoiselle?"

"I would like to walk through it."

Ivo eyed the building uneasily. The burnt part was mostly to one side, while the remainder appeared reasonably sound. Briar firmed her lips, and gazed at him with big eyes, managing to look mulish and pleading at the same time. She hid a smile when he gave a long-suffering sigh.

"We can look inside without danger, can't we, Ivo? And you will protect me, won't you?"

His eyebrows rose cynically. "Very pretty, Briar, but I do not believe that meek pose. You need more practice." He began to dismount. "Come then! But do not move away from me, and if I say we must go, then go we must."

"Very well, Ivo," she murmured, eyes brimming with laughter. He swung her down and she took his hand, and together they moved into the abandoned building.

'Twas hard to believe this was once an elaborate gift, Briar thought wearily. The shrine her father had built to Anna. The air was acrid. Smoke and damp and neglect caught in her throat. Briar had been here rarely, but she well remembered how the candles had shone and the people had laughed. As usual, Anna had been at their center, glowing and beautiful, for such attention was her milk and bread. And her father had been so happy, in his quiet way, because Anna was happy.

Aye, she had thought at the time, this is *love*.

To put someone else above one's self.

Could she do such a thing? Was she capable of it? Not of putting her sisters above herself, for she had done that often enough, but a man. In particular, Ivo. Could she ever love him that much, enough to set him higher than herself?

Aye, there was the test.

Her doubts caused her to pull away from him despite his warning. She set off on her own, making her way farther into the shell of the building. Light shone dully through a hole in the wall, the outline jagged. Birds twittered in the sagging roof high above, where they had made snug homes in the moldering thatch.

Here, where there had been joy and laughter, was only emptiness.

Does that mean I should not put my reliance in love? That it does not last?

The warning rang in her head like a bell, but she ignored it.

Anna's love had been false, just as her father's happiness had been false. Briar's memories of the past were brittle, a false fairytale. What she and Ivo would have must be solid and real . . .

"Demoiselle?" Ivo was standing close behind her and she had not even heard him come up. "Have you seen enough of this place? Whatever there is left of your father, you will not find it here. Let me take you somewhere warmer."

His breath was hot against her nape. Briar shivered and leaned back against him. He was so solid, so safe, and it was frightening how easily she had grown used to him being there. Dangerous, too. For in Briar's world nothing was certain, and she had learned not to rely upon anything or anyone.

Do I dare do so now?

"Do you remember my mother, Ivo? Not Anna, but my real mother?"

She spoke quickly, to still her own fears. Perhaps sensing her inner turmoil, he rubbed his hands over her arms, slowly, as if to warm her through the cloak. As if to comfort her.

"I remember her a little. She was small and hot-tempered, like you."

Briar smiled and rested her head on his chest, content to listen.

"Once, when I hurt myself at training, she tended my bruises. I remember her scolding me, but I knew she didn't really mean it. We both understood that. I remember her kindness—small matters she dealt with, to ease my homesickness."

"And yet my father did not love her, not as he did Anna. He married my mother because it was agreed between their parents. He married Anna for love."

"Did Anna love him?" He sounded curious.

"Perhaps, in her way. I don't think she was able to love anyone very much, but because he gave her everything, she responded to him. I believed at the time that it was love. Now . . . you have made me see the truth, that she gave her body freely."

Ivo continued to smooth his hands over her arms. Briar felt the warmth from his touch, and the comfort, the offering of his support without words.

High above them, through the crisscross of

charred roof beams, the sky looked bleak. This was a grim and depressing place. It spoke of too many lost dreams and shattered lives. Ivo had been right, there was nothing for her here.

"Let us go," Briar said.

It was in that moment they heard the footsteps, the grate of boots against fallen stonework and timber. A dark shape appeared at the far end of the building, silhouetted against the jagged hole in the wall. And stood, watching.

A tall man.

Part of Ivo's battle-trained mind took note of the details, even as he was making swift plans for Briar's safety.

He moves with the easy grace of a fighting man, a soldier . . . No, not a follower. He moves with the confidence of a leader of men.

He set Briar aside, freeing his sword arm, and glanced behind him. *Accomplices?* Nay, there was no one blocking their escape, if such a thing became necessary. Although Ivo had enough confidence in his own skills to doubt he would need to run. Still, there was Briar to consider, and their child.

He reached for his sword, feeling the green stones pressing into his flesh.

He had never had so much to lose before.

"Hold, Ivo! I did not mean to startle you. I have been enjoying your conversation. How goes it with you?"

He sounded almost merry, as if he were greeting an old friend. Only he was not Ivo's friend, he never had been.

Ivo's fingers tightened convulsively on the hilt of his sword. He felt dizzy, disoriented, as though the ground were tipping beneath his boots. Like icy water the past rose up to meet him, cold fingers covering his mouth and nose, making it hard for him to breathe.

"Miles." He didn't know whether he spoke the word, or if it was just so loud in his head.

The tall dark shape stepped forward into the light, and it was no longer just a bad dream. *Miles.* He looked thinner, older. As if recent times had been hard for him. His clothes were still fine, but they appeared frayed, and not as clean as they could be. Miles had been running and hiding from his enemies, and it did not suit him.

The sensation of walking on, and breathing in, frigid water was passing. Miles was here and he was real. And Ivo knew, with a twist of nausea in his belly, that if he was to get Briar to safety he must not let Miles guess what she meant to him.

"I did not think to see you here in York," he said calmly, knowing his lack of emotion would annoy his brother. "Last I heard you were in Normandy."

Briar glanced warily back and forth between the two men. "Who is this, de Vessey?" she asked bluntly. "Another mercenary?"

Miles turned to look at her with sudden interest, his cold gray eyes lighting, and Ivo felt his heart stop. 'Twas not a good thing to draw the attention of Miles de Vessey, not if you were a woman.

"This is no one, demoiselle. Do not concern yourself."

Miles laughed quietly, mockingly. *"No one?*

Brother, you do me a grave disservice." He turned back to Briar and bowed low. "Let me introduce myself, lady. I am Sir Miles de Vessey, the brother who is *not* disgraced."

Wide-eyed, Briar turned to Ivo. He knew he looked white and strained, but he hoped there was nothing more to be read in his face. Their safety depended on him playing a part of indifference. Briar return to Miles with a practiced smile, suddenly very much the great lady. " 'Tis good to know one of the de Vesseys is still in favor, Sir Miles. Tell me, what do you here?"

Miles cast an indifferent look about him and shrugged. "I was passing and I saw you enter. It hardly seems the sort of place for an assignation—though I doubt my brother has ever made an assignation with a woman in his whole life. I was curious."

"This is my father's house," she said bluntly.

And that told Miles who she was.

Ivo saw it in the narrowing of his cold eyes, the twist of his lips. Aye, he knew her, but would he make use of the knowledge? Miles had many schemes spinning in his head, but he always had room for another.

"I have been in this hall," Miles said. "I was in the service of Lord Fitzmorton, so I knew your father slightly. And your mother, the Lady Anna. A most beautiful woman."

If Briar was surprised by his quick understanding she did not show it. "Stepmother," she corrected him haughtily, her polite smile fading.

Take care, thought Ivo, while his own tongue felt frozen. Why was it Miles had this power over

him? A combination of regret and fear and guilt
and hate. Regret, because Miles could so easily
have been his friend, was still his flesh and blood,
and Ivo could not help but remember it. Fear, because he knew of what Miles was capable, guilt
because he always felt as if it was his fault that his
own brother loathed him. And hate, because of
what Miles had done to him ever since they were
children.

Miles was bowing his acknowledgment of
Briar's correction. "My own mother was not Ivo's,"
he said with a smile. "We have that in common,
lady."

Ivo shook his head, and his voice came out like
that of a stranger. "You have nothing in common
with her, Miles. Come Briar, 'tis time to go."

Briar looked as if something had just occurred
to her, and she ignored Ivo, turning again to Miles.
"You say you were in Lord Fitzmorton's service,
Sir Miles? I have heard he was very fond of
Anna—her death must have upset him greatly."

Miles nodded, his gray eyes fixed on her face. "I
believe they were *close*. Is that what you wished to
know, lady?"

Briar looked chagrined that he had so easily
seen through her question. Miles's smile broadened—pleased, predatory. Ivo felt the hairs rise on
his neck. He spoke without thought, attempting
to draw Miles's eyes away from Briar.

"And what of you, Miles? Were you *close* to
Anna, too?"

"I do not tell tales, brother. You should know
that."

"Aye, *brother*, you are too busy telling lies."

Miles laughed. "As you will, but it is you who is disgraced, Ivo."

That made him angry. So angry that there was no way to conceal the flare of pure rage in his eyes, or the iron-hardening of his body. How could Miles do this to him with mere words, after all this time? To his utter frustration, he knew that nothing had changed after all. Despite all that lay between them, he still felt like a child.

"You would know better than I why that is so," he managed, but his voice sounded choked, ineffectual.

"You must try not to blame others for your own shortcomings, Ivo. 'Tis a fault you should have grown out of long since."

Briar's eyes widened. She was clearly fascinated by their bitter exchange. Perhaps she mistook it for brotherly bantering. Miles turned his smile at her, his gaze cold and possessive, as if she were a strange and interesting object that he coveted. But not to love, thought Ivo wildly. Miles could not love; it was an ability he had always lacked.

Ivo felt fear run through him, like a fire in dry grass catching and leaping and burning, unstoppable. He knew better than anyone of what Miles was capable. The thought of his brother with Briar in his hands was enough to make him want to retch.

"Ivo may no longer be a knight, but he has not stopped rescuing damsels in distress." She glanced at him as she said it, her slanting eyes flirtatious, warm. *We are together in this,* she seemed to be saying. And did not know it was the last thing he wanted her to do.

Miles, too, glanced at Ivo, slyly, knowingly. "My brother was always one for rescuing those in distress. It is just a pity he does not always arrive in time."

The world went red. Ivo's rage swallowed him up, and he lost the ability to reason. His words spewed from his mouth.

"You talk as if all that means nothing to you! As if it were a forgotten joke. Why are you here! To torment me again; to make my life a living hell? Go away, Miles! Find a corner and curl up in it and die!"

His voice echoed, raw and shocking. Briar looked astonished at his outburst, her eyes huge in her pale face, her lips apart. And throughout it all, Miles watched him. And then he sighed.

It was the sigh of a man who had suffered, who was deeply wounded by what he had just heard. If Ivo had not known Miles through and through, he would almost have believed it was the sigh of a man who despaired of his beloved younger brother.

"That is what you want me to do, Ivo? To die?"

"Aye!" Ivo managed. His voice was hoarse, his fingers white as he clenched them on his sword. "That is what I want, Miles, above all things. Jesu, you deserve nothing less."

"You disappoint me," Miles said quietly. He looked to Briar, his gray eyes brimming with sorrow. "Lady, Ivo has always been the black sheep of the de Vessey family, but he is still my brother. Forgive him."

Briar frowned from one to the other. "I—I do not . . . Ivo?"

Ivo ignored her, concentrated on his brother. Telling himself that as long as he kept his eyes on Miles, he could not harm Briar.

"If I see you again I will kill you. This time I will not let anything stop me. Do you understand?"

Miles made a face. "How can I not understand such blunt speech, brother? So be it. We will part now."

Before Ivo could do more than draw breath, Miles had taken Briar's hand, raised it to his lips, and released it. All in a heartbeat. Too late, Ivo grabbed Briar's arm and pulled her away, causing her to stumble on the rubble. Miles's gray eyes gleamed, amused by Ivo's tardiness, but his face maintained the expression of sad courage he had affected for Briar's benefit.

He has turned me into a clumsy fool. A vindictive oaf. Just as he intended . . .

Briar struggled in his grip, but Ivo would not let her go. He pulled her after him by force, marching her from the building and out onto the street. There they stood, Ivo still feeling dizzy and ill, Briar glaring at him like an angry little cat.

"What is wrong with you, de Vessey?"

I wanted to get you away from him, Ivo thought. He is evil, and he will hurt you. He will hurt you because he destroys anything I love . . . Aye, he loved her. The truth shone like a torch in a dark hall.

Ivo blinked and turned away. No time for that now. And he could not discuss Miles, either, not with her. His lips were stiff with all the terrible memories aching to spill out, as he prepared to mount his horse.

Briar's voice followed him. "You are a disappointment, Ivo, just as your brother said. Why can you not be as charming as he?"

Ivo started, and then he threw back his head and laughed. But it was a wild laugh, without any humor. "Like Miles? Oh, demoiselle, you would not like me if I were like Miles."

Annoyed at his strange, secretive behavior, Briar sniffed and tossed her head. "Well there you are wrong, for I would like you very much better!"

Does she mean it?

Ivo flinched, and felt the pain of her words go deep, tearing and ripping like an arrow bolt through soft flesh. She could not have hurt him more had she tried.

She doesn't understand, he told himself. You must explain to her.

But he couldn't. The words would choke him. And more than that, when she learned how he had failed his sister, she would look at him with new eyes. She would no longer think him capable of daring feats, she would no longer nestle so confidently into his arms. She would know he deserved to suffer, as Miles was making him suffer now.

So she preferred Miles?

Then God help her.

God help them both . . .

"Come with me, Briar," he said, and his voice had turned dead and cold. He felt both. Miles had come to York to destroy him, and this time Ivo had more to lose than ever.

After a brief hesitation, Briar gave him her hand with a shrug of impatience, and he helped her up onto the horse. She cast him a sideways glance, puzzled, uneasy.

"Are you angry with me, Ivo?"

He didn't answer her.

"Are you angry with Miles?"

"My feelings are my own business, Briar. Leave them be."

She gave a noisy sigh, and subsided into silence. As she settled herself, Ivo found himself remembering what else Miles had said. He had been too enraged at the time to give it any weight, but now he recalled Briar's question about Anna Kenton. Lord Fitzmorton had known her, but they had already heard that from Sir Anthony. It had not previously occurred to Ivo that, if Fitzmorton knew Anna, then Miles would know her, too. And if Miles was involved with Anna, then there was more than a possibility that it was he who had killed her. Miles would not think twice about killing a woman who had displeased him or had made him feel less than adequate.

Death seemed to follow Miles about.

"Sweyn?"

He looked up on hearing Mary's voice, pretending surprise. Upon their return to the dwelling, Sweyn had stayed to guard her. Now the wind from the river blew her long dark hair about her serious face, stinging color into her cheeks. So she had finally gained the courage to come outside and speak to him.

From the corners of his eyes, he had seen her open the door, had felt her gaze upon him. As she drew closer, he had smelt her scent. Aye, he had been as aware of her as if she had run her hands down his body.

Sweyn took a sharp breath at the image, every muscle and sinew tightening with his desire and need.

"Sweyn?"

She was closer now, and he forced himself to relax. He smiled, made it casual and friendly. Nothing too intense, nothing too meaningful.

"Lady?" he said.

Who was he fooling? What he really wanted was to lean down and plunder her soft lips. He wanted to pull her to him, lift her against the wall so that he could better press his male hardness against her soft womanhood.

Madness!

And what was even more crazy, more bizarre, more *frightening*, he wanted to cradle her in his arms and sleep with her every night. He wanted to gaze deep into her dark, serious eyes every morning.

How could he, the famous jokester, the easygoing womanizer, have come to such a pass as this? Sweyn felt completely bemused and dismayed. As if he had wandered into a familiar forest, only to discover the trees had all changed and he could not find his way out again.

"I am no lady," Mary said.

She must be cold; she was blowing warm breath on her fingertips. Without thinking, he took her hands in his and held her cold fingers to his own mouth. She went still, her lips parted, and gazed up at him in wonder as he gently warmed each rosy finger with his own breath.

"You are a lady to me," he said, and wondered if she could read the confusion in his face, matching her own. He could see an image of himself in the mirror of her dark eyes. Big and fair, his tanned face gone a little sallow from the cold, his blue eyes bright in color but dull with tiredness. He was so much older than she, in years as well as experience. How could she look at a man like him with such longing? With such wanting? He could give her nothing; he *was* nothing. Didn't she understand that?

She wants a husband and children.

"Mary—"

She pressed her fingers against his lips. "Do not say anything," she whispered. "Do not try to make sense of it."

He hesitated, on the edge of the abyss, and then he closed his eyes—telling himself that what he could not see did not count—and slipped over.

Sweyn kissed her fingers. It was so easy now, to enjoy the feel of her, the warmth of her, the sweet scent of her. Mary slipped into his arms and rested her body against his, as if she too were savoring those very things.

"Don't trust me," he breathed into her hair. "I do not trust myself. I will hurt you, Mary. I have never been faithful to one woman in my life."

For a moment she stiffened, and he thought her hurt by his honesty, but when she spoke again he could hear the smile in her voice, and with it a steel certainty that awed him.

"I do not know if you can trust me, either, Sweyn. I have been a child for so long, it will be difficult for me to be a woman. I am trying, but . . ." She sighed and cuddled closer. "I don't want to be a child anymore, Sweyn. I think you can help me to become a woman. Even if you do not stay with me forever, I want you to be the first."

What was she asking him to do? Sweyn opened his eyes and met hers. The invitation was there, unmistakable. Sweyn swallowed. Great Odin, she was asking him to . . . ! His rod grew even harder, though a moment ago he had considered that impossible. He imagined bending and devouring her soft lips, plunging his hands into her hair, plunging his body into hers. He imagined sating his need on her, and the vivid images in his head were all wonderful.

And then, just as abruptly, the desire leached out of him.

How could he take her in such a way? Steal her innocence? He was not a man to stay with her, or any woman. He would use her and leave her, and then what? She would be hurt, she would suffer, she would look at him with pain in her eyes. He could not bear that, and Sweyn knew suddenly that for the first time in his whole selfish life, he would rather deny his desires than suffer the consequences.

Cautiously, amazed at his own self-denial, and feeling almost saintlike because of it, Sweyn shook his head. "Nay, Mary," he said gently. "I am not the man for you. You will find someone else, someone who cares for you and will stay with you, always. Someone who is deserving of you. Now go back inside, 'tis far too cold out here."

And then he stepped away from her. Although releasing her was like cutting off his hand, he still managed to do it. Pride at his self-sacrifice surged through him, mingling with his savage pain of loss.

Mary stared up at him a moment, bewildered, tears sparkling in her eyes, and then she turned and walked back to the cottage. When the door finally closed, Sweyn was sure that it sliced his heart in two.

You did a fine thing. You were a knight, like Ivo. Be proud. She will be much happier with a better man.

"Aye, but can I stand the thought of it?" Sweyn muttered, and then cursed and kicked savagely at a pile of debris. "If I've done such an honorable thing, why am I feeling so bloody miserable?"

Chapter 12

Briar had enjoyed the journey to the old house, even though it had stirred up painful memories. But now the pleasure was gone. Ivo had spoiled it with his strange behavior toward his brother, his wild manner inside the abandoned building, and now his frozen, icy politeness.

His silence irritated her beyond bearing, and in the end she had to remind herself of the vow she had made to herself, in case she sought to stir him into response, *any* response, by baiting him.

But still Ivo had said nothing. The raging temper that had afflicted him was gone, turned to frigid ice, and no matter how patient and forbearing she was, he simply gazed at her with dark, tormented eyes.

"Ivo!" she cried at last, beyond caution. "You

must tell me what is wrong, for I cannot bear it any longer."

"There is nothing wrong with me that you need concern yourself with." He looked away, toward the Ouse, and his mouth firmed. "My problems are my own, demoiselle. I will handle them in my own way."

"Ivo—"

"You are home." He slid from the saddle, and reached to help her down. "I have matters to attend, so I will bid you farewell for now."

His voice was stilted and emotionally bereft. How could that be, when before he had been so warm, so real? Briar wanted the other Ivo back; she already hated this icy man. She stamped her foot in frustration. "Ivo!" But he simply ignored her, climbed back on his horse, and rode away.

Briar did not understand it, and it worried her. She did not like the Ivo she had seen today, he frightened her. They were to be wed. This man was to be her husband, the father of her babe. What chance did they have at a life if she did not like or understand him?

She had not even known Ivo had a brother, he never spoke of him. Miles's face filled her mind, that expression of sad resignation in his eyes. As if he had long ago given up on reclaiming his brother. What had Ivo done that was so terrible? Why had he been disgraced? Why did he hate his brother so? Was it because Miles was still a knight? That Miles was a better man?

Nay, I don't believe it. Ivo is a good man. I trust him with my life, with my babe's life.

This surprising revelation ousted all her former

doubts. She had been wrong when she worried Ivo would leave her—she knew it was not in his nature to abandon those in need. But there were still so many questions Briar did not know the answers to. Ivo had secrets, painful secrets, she accepted that. But so did they all. How could she help him if he did not tell her?

Aye, he was angry, but it was more than that. Something was festering and rotting deep inside him. Something was poisoning him, and preventing him from being the man he could be.

It was up to Briar to find out what it was, and heal him.

"Are all men so infuriating?" she asked Mary, when she had finished glaring after him, and gone inside to find her sister returned.

Mary looked up with a vague smile, her face drawn and pale, her eyes distant. She did not even bother to answer.

What is wrong with everyone? Briar felt like screaming.

To add to her misery, an hour later the sickness returned. Despite it, and with fierce determination, she set about dressing and readying herself for their performance that night. Jocelyn had sent word that they were required at the home of a city merchant. Lord Shelborne had been shouting their praises so hard, others were clamoring for them to perform.

It was not until they reached the venue, that Briar understood how quickly the rumor of their real identity had spread. Instead of the story turning patrons against them, it was having the opposite effect. The wealthy of York appeared to be fascinated by them. Having them perform gave a touch of danger to proceedings, Briar supposed. A brush with the forbidden. She was not foolish enough to think that, if it became too dangerous, these same people would not drop them like hot coals and abandon them to their fate.

As Briar knew all too well, 'twas the way of the world.

The merchant's house was opulent, the people enthusiastic, and despite her afflictions, Briar sang well. Tonight it was Mary who made the blunders. At one point she lost the tune entirely, and her lip wobbled, as if she might burst into tears, but Briar simply sang louder and they got through it.

They had come to their final song, and a troop of acrobats was waiting impatiently to take their place, when Briar glanced across the heads of the guests and spied Sir Miles de Vessey. He was standing, watching her from the shadows at the very back of the room.

Her heart gave a great thump, almost as if she was afraid. But that was foolish, for why should she be afraid of Miles, who was Ivo's brother? And then she thought of Ivo, and how cold his behavior had been. Had she not decided she must heal whatever ailed him? If only there was some way to discover just what it was . . .

She looked up again, searching the faces before her, but this time Miles had gone. Vanished into the shadows, as if he had never been.

Sweyn peered around the room, wondering who it was Briar was staring at. The woman was dangerous, and he wished Ivo luck in taming her. Aye, all women were dangerous. He was better off alone.

"They're both bonny, but for my money, I'd have the taller one."

The voice drifted in Sweyn's direction, cocky and confident, and Scottish. Sweyn gritted his teeth. He hated the Scots. In his experience all they did was fight and fornicate, and they never knew when to stop on either count. He had just spent some of the worst weeks of his life chasing them off Lord Radulf's estates and back over the border, and now here was another one, lording it over the locals in York.

"I like tall women," the voice went on, as if everyone was panting to know his preferences. "I like to look right into their eyes when I'm on top of them."

Sweyn ground his teeth. His head was muzzy with drink and now a rush of hot blood added to the mixture. He knew, even as he began pushing his way through the rich sea of fine cloth tunics and silken gowns, that he was making a mistake. He had never fought for a woman before, he had never even been jealous before.

But this was about Mary. And Mary was special.

Amazed, he paused, stood gazing at nothing, forgetting where he was.

Aye, she is special. She's different from all the others. I don't know why or how, but she is. And no amount of my wishing can change how I feel about her . . .

"I wonder if her fingers are as nimble on *other* instruments."

Sweyn groaned. That was it! He could take no

more. Like a maddened bull, he thrust his way
into the group around the Scot and grabbed the
man up by the scruff of his neck, and shook him
hard.

Women screamed. Men cursed and backed
away. The Scot choked and clawed at his hands,
but Sweyn kept shaking him.

"Do not speak about my lady in that way," he
said, drawing out his words, giving the Scot a
good, hard shake on each one. "Do you hear me,
you foul-mouthed beastie? Do you hear me now?"

The Scot nodded desperately, his face turning
blue.

"Let him go, Sweyn."

Someone put a hand on his shoulder. Ivo,
Sweyn realized through the fumes of drink and
rage. His friend's fingers were very strong, and
they pressed down hard, and then harder again.

"He has learned his lesson, and we do not want
to attract too much attention. He might be someone important."

Sweyn blinked, and then promptly dropped his
burden. The Scot landed with an oomph as Sweyn
walked away.

"What were you doing?" Ivo had followed him
to the far side of the room.

Sweyn turned his face away and shook his
head. He had run mad, that was the only explanation. The words spilled out of him.

"She wants me to make her a woman." He tried
to laugh, but the sound cracked in the middle.
"Me! What do I know of faithfulness and . . . and
love, Ivo? I have never looked for such things before, not even within myself."

Ivo appeared to be as much at a loss as Sweyn, although he didn't seem to need to ask of whom Sweyn was speaking. "Be careful," he said at last. "Be very sure before you make any decisions, my friend."

Sweyn groaned and sank his head into his hands. Careful? It was far too late for careful. He was already up to his neck and gasping for air. Odin help him, he loved her, and unless he could think of a very good reason why, Sweyn knew that sooner or later he was going to do just as Mary asked.

The final song was finished. Despite a fight that had broken out in one part of the hall, Briar and Mary had managed to sing it perfectly, together. Pleased, they soaked up the applause, which was long and loud. And then the acrobats came running, darting amongst the crowd, turning somersaults and climbing onto each other's shoulders.

Mary laughed and clapped her hands as one of the acrobats pretended to look under a woman's skirts, causing her to squeal in outrage. A moment later, the humor had drained out of her again, and she looked so sad that Briar reached out to touch her cheek.

"What is it, sweeting?" she asked gently. "You are unhappy. Tell me, Mary, what ails you?"

The girl sighed and shook her head.

"Please, Mary?" Briar whispered. Why would no one let her help! Once she had always been the one her sisters turned to, now they kept their troubles to themselves. How could she help if they would not tell her?

"I am grown, Briar. I can mend my own broken toys."

Briar gave up. She turned again to the crowd, now enjoying the acrobats' performance. *Miles.* The name slipped into her mind like a cool breeze on a hot day, and just as tempting. If she spoke with him, asked him about Ivo, where was the harm? Assuming she could find him in this crush.

"Wait here," she said, over her shoulder to Mary, and started to make her way in the direction she had last seen Miles de Vessey.

Luckily most of the guests were entranced with the attempt by the acrobats to climb, all five, upon each other's shoulders. While the motley column swayed back and forth, Briar was able to find her way to the back of the hall without being accosted or complimented on her singing, or asked if she was really the daughter of the traitor, Richard Kenton.

She glanced about her.

Miles was not here, but there was a doorway, curtained by a tapestry, which led into another chamber. Perhaps he was in there? It seemed unlikely, but where else could he have gone so abruptly? Briar lifted aside the tapestry and peeped through the gap. Shadows, nothing but shadows in a small alcove which contained nothing more than a bench and a table. She turned to go.

"I enjoyed your singing, lady."

Miles.

"Come in, I have been waiting for you."

One of the shadows moved, took the shape of a man. Miles stepped closer, and Briar could see his eyes, pale in the gloom and fixed on her. He had changed his clothing from earlier, the green tunic he wore now was clean and well made, his breeches of fine stuff, and his boots soft leather. His jaw was freshly shaved, accentuating that attractive leanness she had already noted.

There was a resemblance to Ivo. In the shape of his chin, mayhap, and the way he held himself, in his handsome smile, but Ivo was bigger, broader, and not so good-looking nor so cool-tempered. Miles, with his gray eyes and lean face, was the more attractive, and yet there was something about him that repelled Briar. She did not know quite what it was, and even as she thought it, she dismissed it as unfair. He was different, that was all. She should not, she thought guiltily, judge every man by one.

Her guilt made her step into the alcove with him.

"Is my brother here tonight?" His voice was softer, more intimate, as if they were preparing to exchange secrets. Which was what Briar had been hoping to do. Why then did she feel so uneasy in his presence?

"Ivo is not my keeper, sir," she said calmly enough, pretending his gaze did not make her nervous. "I do not know where he is."

Miles smiled Ivo's smile, but it lacked Ivo's warmth and sense of mischief, it lacked Ivo's chivalrousness and protectiveness. If she were handing out counters, Ivo had them nearly all. "I can see he is not your keeper. You are a lady with a mind very much of her own."

She smiled back, pleased he should realize it. Ivo still did not understand that she could take care of herself. Finally she could set a counter in Miles's pile.

He leaned closer, and confided, "You asked me about Lady Anna. I did not tell you all."

"What more is there to say, Sir Miles?"

He hesitated, glanced at her, and away again. "I am ashamed to say, lady. Will you tell Ivo? He already thinks badly of me. And yet he is my brother, my only brother, and I love him. Do you know what it is like, Lady Briar, to be at odds with your own brother?"

That deep sadness had crept back into his handsome, austere features. He had the look of a priest; how could she not trust a priest. Despite her instinctive caution, Briar felt an answering empathy. She loved her sisters, and presently felt out of step with them, and the sense of loss and frustration was uncomfortable. How much worse for Miles and Ivo, who had clearly suffered some terrible fissure? At least, Ivo had cut himself off from his brother, though Miles seemed willing to repair matters.

"He is the only flesh and blood family I have left."

Jesu, there were tears in his pale eyes. Despite herself, Briar's own eyes filled.

"And 'tis all over a misunderstanding," he went on, his voice turning bitter. "A foolish thing.

But Ivo will not speak with me, he will not let me explain to him . . ." He took a breath, pulling himself together. "Well, what is the point of mulling over it? Nothing can be done."

Impulsively, Briar put her hand on his arm. "Perhaps there is something we can do, Sir Miles. Perhaps I can talk to Ivo for you."

He looked at her sharply, and suddenly he had all of Ivo's intensity. "Would you, lady? Would you do that for me?"

His eagerness was heartwarming, and Briar smiled, forgetting any doubts she may have had. "Aye, I would. But first you must tell me what it is that keeps you and Ivo apart . . ."

Miles stiffened, looking past her to the tapestry. Light spilled through the narrow gap where the cloth was not flush against the doorway. "I do not want Ivo to find me here with you. It will be another mark against me, in his eyes. Can you meet me tomorrow? Can you meet me at the house of your father?"

It seemed an odd request, but he was staring at her so fiercely, so pleadingly. As if he had put all his hopes in her.

"Will you trust me, lady? I want so much to reconcile with my only brother. In his heart, I know that Ivo wants that, too. We need someone like you, someone who cares for him, to help us take the first step. Will you do that for Ivo and me, Lady Briar?"

Briar already knew that she would, but she pretended to consider. Ivo would be cross with her, but surely he would understand when she explained to him that she had only wanted to help? And he would be pleased with her, wouldn't he, when he was friends again with his brother? It would all be worthwhile, then.

She nodded her head.

"So, you will come? Tomorrow?"

"Aye, Sir Miles, I will come to my father's house tomorrow."

He smiled with relief, and took her hands warmly in his. "I thank you, lady. Ivo cannot thank you, yet, so I will do it for him. And I thank you with all my heart—"

"Briar?"

It was Mary's voice, beyond the tapestry. Briar pulled away, moving toward it, saying, "My sister is looking for me . . ."

"My brother will not let you come and meet me, if you tell him of our plans. He will stop you, lady. Be aware of that."

"Sir Miles—"

Just then Mary lifted the stiff cloth aside and peered into the alcove at them. She frowned, eyes going suspiciously from Miles to Briar. "Briar? I want to go home now."

"Of course." Briar shot a warning glance over her shoulder at Miles. "Thank you for your compliments, sir."

Miles bowed, his gray eyes like quicksilver. "Remember what I have said, lady."

"I will."

Mary was still frowning when they returned to the hall. "Ivo is looking for you," she said. "I told him I would find you. I saw you go into that room, but I did not tell him so. You were very sly. What are you playing at, Briar? He is to be your husband, and yet you go off with other men."

A lecture from Mary! Briar felt bemused. Who would have thought it? Clearly her younger sister was growing up.

"You don't understand," she began, but Mary wouldn't listen.

"No, I don't! And I don't want to. You are so lucky, Briar, and yet you play with fire. I do not want to know why you would want to spoil all the good things that have fallen in your lap. Mayhap you don't deserve them."

"Mary!"

Mary pulled away from her outstretched hand, flushed and angry and upset. "Ivo is waiting for you. Go to him, Briar. I will be there in a moment."

Briar stared at her sister's back, more bewildered than angry. When had Mary grown a temper? And why had she exploded with it now, almost as if she were . . . jealous?

With a sigh, Briar went to find Ivo.

He was standing by the door—no doubt planning to escort her home. Of course he was. How could she have thought he would have forgotten her? She was carrying his child, and he would smother her with attention if it kept her safe. Fate had brought their lives into collision, and whatever this feeling was that kept them together, it was strong. Ivo, despite his odd behavior since he saw Miles, would never hurt her. Briar owed it to him to force a reconciliation between him and his brother.

It was the least she could do for him.

* * *

She looked as if she had been telling secrets. There was something about the expression in her hazel eyes, the flush of her cheeks, the curl of her lips. Ivo realized he didn't trust her, and it frightened him. His belly clenched.

"Where were you, Briar?" He tried to ask her gently, but his voice came out harsh and demanding. Like a captain ordering his troops.

She ruffled up, shooting him a sideways glance. "I was speaking to my admirers, Ivo."

"Are they many?"

"Aye, legion!"

"Briar—" He had gone too far; his fears for her safety had eroded his good sense. It was Miles's fault. Miles had always managed to destroy his equilibrium. Now he was working on corroding Ivo's feelings for Briar, and he was not even there.

"Do you not think I sing well, Ivo?"

She looked so cross, and yet there was a vulnerability in her eyes that broke his heart. His woman had suffered, and it made him so angry and determined that it not happen again. He forgot for a moment what Miles's presence meant to his ability as Briar's protector, and concentrated on soothing her feelings.

"No, demoiselle, I do not," he began.

"Oh!" She glared up at him. "At least your brother knows how to compliment me properly."

His heart went cold. He felt it turn to ice in his chest, and knew his face was white. Whatever she saw in him frightened her, for she backed a step, catching her breath. But in a moment she had lifted her chin, trying to be brave.

"What do you know of Miles, demoiselle?" he asked her, and his voice was deadly quiet.

If you tell my brother you are meeting me, he will stop you from coming.

Briar knew now that Miles had spoken the truth. Ivo would never allow her to meet Miles alone. But her curiosity was now too strong for her not to do so. There was something putrid, something foul between Ivo and his brother, and it was time it was brought out into the open air.

"Demoiselle?" He was waiting, and his black eyes burned.

"Nothing," she retorted. "I know nothing about your brother. I only meant that he was chivalrous."

"Miles is nothing to do with you. Leave that matter alone."

"Leave what matter, Ivo?" she cried, and to her shame her voice broke. Now he had made her cry! She turned her back on him and walked out into the night. She would walk home, alone with her hurt. She would never trouble him again. Aye, he could drown in his own bad temper.

"Demoiselle?"

He had followed her, his voice warm in the darkness, almost tentative. Was he sorry? Had he come to apologize? Briar slowed and stopped, but did not turn around.

"Demoiselle, when I said I did not think you sang well, you misunderstood me. 'Well' is too mean a word for your voice. You sing like an angel. Each time I listen to you, it is as if my heart overflows and washes me clean."

He meant it. Briar felt emotion well up within

her, and the easy tears trickled down her cheeks. How could she doubt him? How could she deceive him, even if she meant only good by him? He needed her help, aye, but she should not go about it behind his back.

Briar turned, stiffening her own back and preparing to tell him about Miles . . .

He slid his arms about her and held her against him. Just held her. As if she were the most precious thing in his life.

Briar could not remember being held in such a way, not since she was a child. And she liked it, she liked it very much. 'Twas a fine thing to be strong, to be the shield behind which everyone else sheltered, but there were times when even the strong needed to be held and comforted. And Ivo seemed to understand that. There was no weakness in leaning against his big body, no shame in it.

For he needed her as much as she needed him.

"Ivo?"

Sweyn was approaching, and Ivo sighed. He looked a moment into her eyes, as if trying to memorize her face, then he turned to his friend. Briar noticed that Mary was also there, wrapped in her cloak, standing a little behind the Dane. As if she were using him as a shelter against the wind, Briar thought with weary amusement.

"Mary is tired," Sweyn said. "Will we take them home now?"

Ivo nodded. "Aye. I will leave that to you and Lord Radulf's men." He glanced at Briar as he spoke, adding, "We have more men at our disposal, so you will be safely guarded until we can wed."

Extra men? Briar wondered at it, but she had more important things to speak about.

"Will you not take me home, Ivo?"

He stroked her cheek, gently, sadly. As if he were saying goodbye. The thought terrified her.

"I have something to do, my lady. Do not worry, I will see you tomorrow."

"Ivo . . . ?"

But he had turned away, moving back into the hall.

"Where is he going?" Briar demanded of Sweyn, making the question an order.

Sweyn hesitated, before answering, "He is seeking his brother, lady. They have unfinished business."

Doubts assailed her once more, but she forced them back. *Unfinished business* could mean anything. And Ivo had looked so sad, as if more than anything in the world he wanted to find Miles and make up the rift between them. Briar hugged her arms about herself, shivering in the cold. She would feel the same, if she were at war with one of her sisters. She would be grateful to anyone who could help her repair the damage. 'Twas as well she had not told Ivo after all. Aye, she was doing the right thing by agreeing to meet Miles tomorrow.

She was certain of it.

Briar was still certain next morning, when she set out on foot. Her sickness had eased, and she told herself she was actually beginning to feel her old self again. Strong, sure, and determined. Ivo needed her help—there was something very wrong between him and his brother. Briar knew she was doing the right thing. This wasn't deceit, not at all.

She had been up since Terce rang out over York, thinking of Ivo's words to her last night. They had touched her deep. She wanted so much to help him, to reconcile him with his brother. Aye, Briar longed to heal the anguish she sensed in him. And if that meant meeting Miles behind his back, then so be it.

The day was fine, though cold. Briar followed the line of wooden ramparts upon their earthen walls, broken only by the heavily guarded bars that gave entry to the city. A vendor was selling parcels of cheese and herbs wrapped in crisp pastry. They smelled good, and suddenly Briar was aware of how hungry she was. Another sign that her sickness was passing, and her babe was thriving. She handed over her coin, and munched as she walked.

Over by the Minster, where Ivo had kissed her and she had pretended to make him part of her plot, the carpenters and stonemasons were hard at work, restoring the damaged church. Briar walked by. There was no plot anymore, unless it be to solve Anna's murder so that she and Briar's father could finally rest in peace. Her concerns were for Ivo now. Ivo, who was clearly in desperate need.

She did not ask herself why that was. Why her whole life had become focused on making Ivo happy, when before she had claimed to be using him only for her own ends. That was unimportant, she told herself blithely. What *was* important was meeting Miles. Whatever he might tell, she

must listen. Ivo was a good man—she truly believed that. Whatever he had done in the past did
not matter, not now, not to her.

They would look upon it, and then put it behind them.

Briar took a deep, sustaining breath, and kept
walking.

"Where is Briar?"

Mary looked up at Ivo's question, and then
down again as swiftly. Ivo frowned, flicking a
glance at Sweyn. Sweyn shrugged.

"Mary?" Ivo repeated, stepping closer. The
girl's cheeks were bright red, and her fingers
clutched at the cloth she was mending as though
she would strangle it. "Do you know where Briar
is, Mary?"

She sighed and looked up again. The guilty expression in her eyes made him uneasy. Why
should sweet Mary be guilty about anything?

"I think she's gone to meet someone," she whispered. "I'm sorry, Ivo, truly I am. I would have
stopped her, but she slipped out while I slept."

Ivo sank down on his knees before her, and
Mary's eyes widened in surprise. He caught her
hands in his, trying not to hurt her. A frantic pulse
was beating in his jaw, and he had to blink away
the terror he knew was in his eyes.

"Mary," he said, his voice trembling, "who has
she gone to meet? Who is this person, Mary?"

"Ivo, you are frightening her!" Sweyn was behind him, but Ivo ignored his friend's admonish-
ment. There was no time for it.

"I . . ." She glanced to Sweyn, and back to Ivo.

She took a steadying breath, and straightened her shoulders very like Briar was wont to do when she was preparing herself for something unpleasant. "I don't know who it was, Ivo. He was in the alcove, off the hall, last night, and she spoke with him there. I wanted to go home, and I came to fetch her and . . ."

She flicked another look at Sweyn, the color returning to her cheeks.

"Go on, Mary," Ivo insisted. " 'Tis important we know."

"I listened, a little. They spoke of meeting today, at my father's house. That is where she has gone. She made an assignation. Ivo, I am so sorry."

Her fingers squeezed his, but Ivo did not notice. He was frozen in place, slowly being suffocated by a sense of terrible foreboding.

"You do not know it was Miles," Sweyn said sharply, pressing his shoulder. "Ivo?"

"Did you see this man?" Ivo asked Mary, and his voice was not his own. "Did you see what he looked like?"

Mary swallowed, frightened now. "I did, just for a moment. It was dark, but . . . he was tall and dark-haired, and handsome, too. But I did not like him. There was something about him, something cold. Mayhap it was his eyes. They were pale and even when he smiled, they did not . . ."

She had barely finished the words when Ivo was on his feet, brushing by Sweyn and running for the door. Cursing, Sweyn ran after him, shouting orders to Radulf's men, who waited outside.

"Watch her! Do not allow anyone near her!"

Mary stood in the doorway, her mouth agape as they rode off.

The house that had once belonged to her father was just as abandoned. Only this time Briar had no Ivo to hold her hand and make her feel better. 'Twas strange, how she had felt so irritated by his care of her before, but that now she missed it. She missed him.

Briar stomped her feet, trying to thaw out her cold toes. She could see no sign of Miles. He had said he had something to tell her about Anna? What could that be? Before she could get the information from him, he had changed the subject to Ivo, and then Mary had come. Perhaps it was only that Lord Fitzmorton was another of Anna's lovers?

How could her father have loved his wife, and still she had shared her favors among so many others? It was incomprehensible to Briar, and unforgivable.

If I loved a man I would not betray him for a moment's pleasure. I would not betray Ivo . . .

Her mind stilled at the thought. Love? Did she love Ivo de Vessey? Was that what this warm glow around her heart was? But Briar was not sure she wanted to explore that thought, not yet, not now. It was not the place or the time for thoughts of love.

The house stood silent, waiting.

Briar peered at it, swinging her arms now. The air was getting colder. If she waited much longer she would surely freeze to death. She may as well go inside and wait there. Mayhap Miles had left her a message? Mayhap he had already come and gone?

Again that strange thump of her heart.

As if it were warning her.

As usual when something interfered with her plans, Briar ignored it. Instead she gathered her skirts in her hands, and picked her way over the fallen debris to the door.

Inside the air was stale, and the smell of smoke seemed stronger than it had been yesterday. Briar wrinkled her nose in distaste but continued forward, mindful of the uneven floor. The twittering birds were silent, but Briar didn't mark it. In fact she was so busy watching her feet, it was not until he cleared his throat that Briar sensed she was not alone.

"Oh!" She looked up, startled, and then laughed nervously. "You are here after all, Sir Miles."

"It would seem so, lady," he said easily, and his bow was slight.

Briar could not see his face properly, the light from the jagged hole in the wall was behind him again. However his voice was mild, unthreatening, and she forced herself to relax. *This is Ivo's brother. What have I to fear from Ivo's brother?*

As if he had read the name in her thoughts, Miles said, "My brother is not with you?"

"No, he is not. You told me not to tell him, remember?"

"I remember." He smiled. "I am grateful."

Comforted, Briar took a step closer.

"Ivo would never have allowed you to come here on your own, lady. He would have brought a dozen men with swords. He doesn't trust me, you see."

Satisfaction permeated his voice, and something more, something that oozed through his words, chilling Briar's blood. Like evil.

Briar's heart gave that hard thump, more urgently this time. She tried to remember who she was, to restore her courage. Lady Briar, daughter of Lord Richard Kenton. Aye, she was quite capable of dealing with a mere knight. And her feelings might be a little confused right now, but she would not let them overwhelm her. She was here on a matter of importance to Ivo, and the sooner she found out what she needed to, the sooner she could leave.

"You said you had something to tell me about my stepmother, Sir Miles," she reminded him, as calmly as she was able. "And about Ivo."

He walked forward, and he was not smiling. His gray eyes were as cold as the Ouse in winter. As he drew closer, his face no longer seemed handsome, but instead had the lean, unpleasant look of a weasel or a stoat. A killing animal, an animal without pity. Why had she ever thought him charming?

Briar shivered. It was very cold in here. Her breath puffed white and her toes were going numb.

"Sir Miles? Lady Anna?" she reminded him.

"What can I tell you about Lady Anna? She was a wellborn whore."

Briar heard her own gasp. "I—that is brutal, Sir Miles," she managed, but her face betrayed her.

He smiled then, enjoying her fear. "I prefer brutal, Lady Briar. You asked me to tell you, and I have. She lay with my master Fitzmorton, but then her eye turned to me, and so she lay with me, too. She was beautiful, but even beauty loses something when you are made aware so many men have used it before you. Don't you think?"

"I am not schooled in such matters."

Her voice was frigid, but it took all of her willpower not to stumble backward, away from him. Briar sensed that if she ran he would give chase, and enjoy the hunt, so she stood still and brave before him.

"Did you . . ." Her throat had gone dry, and she cleared it. "Did you kill her, Sir Miles?"

The look he gave her was astonished. "Why would I? Put myself at risk for such as she? Nay, lady, I did not kill her. She was not worth the effort."

Briar felt the nausea in her belly, threatening to sap her strength. Not now! Please, sweet babe, not now! She must not be weak. She must talk her way out of this place, then escape and run. Run all the way home, if necessary. *Dear God*, she thought, *let Ivo forgive me. What have I done, what have I done . . .*

"Ivo wants you." He said it like an accusation.

"Nay," Briar laughed brightly, as if he had made a nonsense joke. "He does not want me, Sir Miles. I am a diversion to him, that is all. The traitor's daughter who sings songs. He thinks me an oddity."

He didn't believe her. She saw it in his wolfish smile. And she knew, in that single moment, what her heart had been trying to tell her all along. He would hurt her, but not because he had any grudge against *her*. He would hurt her because by doing so he could make Ivo suffer.

"You were riding with him the night I tried to frighten him," he went on accusingly. "He knew it was me. I saw the fear in his eyes."

Briar remembered the night in question well, the journey from Lord Shelborne's house, but she had not realized until now that it was Miles who came out of the darkness, screaming like a devil.

"Ivo is afraid of nothing," she said with complete certainty.

Miles's pale eyes narrowed. "Ivo was always the brother that people preferred," he said, and it was a statement. "That people loved. Do you love him, lady?"

Aye, I do love him.

Briar shook her head, her eyes on him. She dared not look away, in case he sprang.

"I think you are lying," he said, and shook his finger at her as if she were a wayward child. "I think you do love my brother. I am going to enjoy this. I wondered whether or not I should finish you in the alcove last night—I had a dagger, nice and sharp—but then I decided I needed more time. There are so many things we can do together, lady. Oh yes, I am going to enjoy imagining Ivo's face—when he finds what is left of you . . ."

The bird flew up.

It must have been nesting in part of the wall and their voices had disturbed it. It was the only chance she had, and Briar used it. She turned and ran for the door. It seemed leagues away. A patch

of brightness in the shadows. She heard him behind her. His fingers tugged briefly on the back of
her cloak, and then he was cursing foully as he
stumbled on loose stone. Next thing she was out
in the light, gasping as if she had run the entire
length of York.

The man stepped in front of her so suddenly
she cannoned into him.

Briar screamed, backing away, her feet stumbling on the uneven road. He caught her in his
arms, and something in his touch, his warmth, his
scent, spelled safety. Wildly, she looked up into
his face. Savage dark eyes, hair growing back
some of its riotous curl, and a grim, white face.

It was Ivo.

Briar's limbs turned to water.

He gripped her arms a moment longer, holding
her until she had steadied herself, and then he
looked past her. Briar also swung around, trembling for what she might see, but there was no
one. Only the abandoned house as silent and forbidding as before.

"But . . . where did he go?" she gasped, eyes
huge.

"You mean Miles." It was not a question.

"He was inside. I . . . I was frightened of him."

"At least you have that aright." But his dark
gaze slid quickly over her, assessing any damage,
and if possible he grew even more angry. "Briar,
stay here with Sweyn. Do not move. Do you understand me?"

For the first time, Briar noticed Sweyn standing
to one side. Instinctively she wanted to protest.
She didn't want to stay here, she didn't want him

to go inside alone. But his intensity was such that she bit her lip and nodded her head. He walked toward the building, his head moving slowly from side to side as he surveyed his surrounds with all the care of a prospective purchaser. And then he reached down and slid his sword from its scabbard and walked through the doorway into the darkness.

Briar held her breath. She expected to hear shouts, swords clashing, a dying scream . . . Ivo came out of the house with a quick, easy stride, resheathing his sword as he approached.

"There is no one there now," he said shortly, with a glance at Sweyn. "Miles must have found another way out—there are plenty of broken walls. He was always good at running away."

Sweyn gave an edgy laugh. "This time you'll catch him, Ivo. This time you'll beat him."

Ivo nodded, but he looked bleak.

Briar closed her eyes, weary beyond imagining. "I do not understand. He said he had more to tell me of my stepmother, and to meet him here. He said he would talk to me of you. I thought it would be a good thing, to bring you together again, to reconcile you with all that remains of your family. If it was me, then I would want that very much, Ivo, and he . . . he seemed to want that."

The expression in his eyes hardened. Turned into a dark and burning fury. "What happened, Briar?" he asked her, and she could feel the tension in him as he waited for her answer.

She spoke slowly, halting over her words as she

recalled her terror. "Once I was inside the house, I knew it had all been a lie. A reason to bring me to him, alone. He wanted me because he thought I belonged to you. He planned to use me, to hurt me, to hurt *you*."

Ivo took her arm in strong fingers. "You spoke to him last night. Was that when you hatched this plan?"

"Aye," she whispered, casting him an anxious glance. "I saw him at the back of the hall, and when I went to find him he was waiting in a chamber there. He asked me to meet him here, to-day. He said not to tell, that you would not like it, that there were reasons and he would explain to me. He . . . he wept. He was so plausible, Ivo. I did not think to doubt him."

But Briar remembered she *had* doubted; she had simply pushed her inner warnings aside. Briar the impulsive, with her mind set on doing what she thought was best. Would she never learn? Had not the night she mistook Ivo for Radulf taught her that she was not always right?

Ivo was watching her, mayhap thinking the same thing. Was she too much trouble for him, too much of a bother? She did not want to be a burden. The thought of being seen in that light made her squirm. She *loved* him, and during those moments with Miles, she had wanted nothing more than to have the opportunity to tell him so.

And yet now she said nothing.

"Miles has a warrant on his head, lady," Sweyn said, glancing between the two of them with curious blue eyes. "That is why he was hiding last night, why he cannot walk about like a free man. He led a rebellion against Lord Radulf in Somerset, and the king wasn't best pleased."

"I did not know," she whispered. "You should have told me."

Ivo spoke. "Would you have listened, Briar? When I went to your dwelling and found you missing, I had a feeling 'twas Miles's doing. He ever had the smoother tongue. There were always women eager and willing to fall into his lap like ripe plums. And then he would suck them dry and spit them out."

"I'm sorry," she said, not sure whether she was apologizing for her own actions or those of his brother. "How did you find me?"

"Mary overheard you last night, lady, and unlike you she did not like Miles's looks. You are lucky to have a sister who loves you and watches out for you. If I had not come, Briar . . . How could you be so foolish?" He stopped, and pressed his lips tight together.

She took a breath, feeling some of her uncertainty ebbing away. She had acted in good faith, after all. "I meant to help, Ivo. I thought if I could heal the rift between you and Miles, you would forgive my lack of . . . of honesty. That the end justified the means." Her eyes narrowed. "You should have told me. I asked you again and again, but you wouldn't explain to me."

"So now 'tis *my* fault?" Ivo drew a deep sigh and looked away from her tear-filled eyes, staring down the once lively, and now forlorn street.

"Nay, not entirely . . ."

Ivo looked as if he would have liked to smile,

but didn't have the heart for it. "You are right. I should have told you. I should have made you aware of what he was. I thought I could keep you safe by keeping you in ignorance. And I thought . . . I hoped I wouldn't have to tell you, Briar. I didn't want you to know about the past. There are matters, there are things I do not tell many people."

Briar stared at his profile, the sharp nose and strong chin, the dark stubble on his jaw and the curls beginning to grow longer at his brow. *He is going to tell me something horrible,* she thought, her heart turning cold. *Something so horrible that I won't be able to love him anymore.*

"I am a fool, demoiselle. Your opinion of me cannot matter if you are dead by Miles's hand. Better you look upon me with loathing than I never see your smile again."

Briar stared at him in dismay. "Ivo? You make me uneasy with such talk. Tell me what you mean?"

Dark eyes moved intently over her face. As if, she thought, he were fixing her in his mind, remembering every little detail, as if he expected never to see her again. Briar's fear grew, trembling over her skin like butterfly wings, until she barely felt the cold outside for the cold inside herself.

At last he seemed to make up his mind.

"Come," he said abruptly, and held out his hand. "I will take you to Lord Radulf."

Radulf!

Briar could not hide her shocked surprise. Radulf, her enemy, the man she had hated for so long, had wanted to revenge herself on for so long. Could she go there now, and look upon him, without all those old memories surfacing? But Ivo needed her, and he was waiting. Ivo, her husband to be, the father of her child, was in some desperate trouble. Ivo, the man she loved above all others, even above herself.

Which was the more important? Her old memories and longing for revenge—the past—or Ivo, her future?

Briar reached out and placed her fingers in his.

Chapter 13

Lord Radulf was surrounded by important men. Some were allies in his fight with northern rebels, some were vassals, and some were simply there to hear what he had to say.

Ivo recognized a dozen or more as he passed, his hand firm on Briar's arm. Lord Henry clapped him on the back, and gave Briar an interested stare. Ivo drew her protectively closer, feeling the tension in her body thrumming through her, as if she were one of the strings on Mary's harp.

She was afraid. This was not safe ground for her. But despite that, she straightened her back and lifted her chin and prepared herself to face her father's old enemy.

Ivo admired her more than he could say. She was beautiful and brave, and she deserved to be held close and dear, to live a long and happy life.

She deserved to be cherished, to have her children about her. But Ivo also knew, with an impotent sense of rage and frustration, that if Miles got hold of her, he would kill her. Kill her despite all her courage and fiery temper. Aye, Miles would kill her and enjoy doing it, and he had come so close to doing it today.

Today, when Ivo had finally accepted that he was no longer able to protect her without help. As much as he wanted to do this alone, he could not afford his pride. It was a risk too great.

Miles almost took her from me.

The rage was deep inside him, a core of molten fury, but he held it back, kept it in check, surrounded it with ice. There would be time enough to let it free when he came face-to-face with Miles. This time, he swore to himself, Miles would not win. This time he would be ready for all his tricks.

But for now Ivo needed to bind Briar more tightly to him, and right soon. And he needed someone to stand behind him. Someone with a great deal of power, someone who was not afraid of anything or anyone.

Lord Radulf was that man.

Radulf would watch over her, if Ivo should perish—and the doubt was there, that little niggling voice, no matter how hard he tried to shout it down. For every other time they had met, Miles had won. Aye, it was possible he might die, and if he did, then Radulf would make sure that Briar did not wander starving in the hedgerows as she had done these two years past. The thought of leaving her worse off than he had found her was far more painful than the thought of Miles ending his life.

Radulf glanced up from his conversation. When he saw Ivo and Briar, his gaze sharpened, and then he simply waited for them to reach him.

Briar saw a man with dark hair and eyes similar to Ivo's, but other than that they were not at all the same. Whereas Ivo's face was angular and fierce, Radulf's was battered and brutal.

This was the great Lord Radulf, the King's Sword. She swallowed in her dry throat. Aye, here was a man to scare children up and down the countryside. Mayhap the legends were true . . .

Ivo spoke. "My lord, this is Briar, once Lady Briar, daughter of Lord Richard Kenton."

Radulf nodded to Ivo, but he watched her. And while he watched, he stroked his chin with one long finger. There was a ring upon his hand, a heavy red and black ring.

"Lady, I knew your father," he said at last, in a voice low and husky, and she waited, heart thumping, for the accusations to begin. "I deeply regret what happened to him."

Surprised, Briar faced him in silence. She had been ready to retaliate, to accuse him in turn of destroying her father and her family. Now he had made her think again.

For so long she had believed one thing, but gradually Ivo had turned her mind to other possibilities, and clouded her certainties with doubts. Nothing was as simple as she had believed it. Just as the fairytale love affair she had thought existed between her father and Anna wasn't real. Anna had never loved him, she had used him, and he had clung to her despite all.

"You knew my stepmother," she said, and the words were harsh and uncompromising. Ivo's fingers tightened a warning, and she added, "My lord," with a reluctance that made Radulf's lips twitch.

"Anna was my stepmother, too, lady. Did you know that?"

Briar had not. She stared, startled by the revelation, and not quite sure what to make of it.

"She married my father and destroyed him, although I take some blame for that. Do not mistake, I was not innocent in the matter. She cast her lure, but I was quick to take the bait. My father never forgave me. He was blind with love for her, and did not want his face pushed into the reeking truth. Aye, lady, my life was a ragged thing, until I met Lily."

He smiled, and it was a smile at once sweet and sad, and suddenly he did not look so much brutal as tired.

" 'Twas Lily who gave me the strength once and for all to break with Anna, for even though I had not seen her for many years, she had remained a part of my mind. Hatred for her, and myself, had worked on me, eating into me." He leaned closer, as if confiding in her. "I know what hatred is, Lady Briar."

Briar tried to meet his eyes and could not. He *knew*. He had looked into her heart and read it so well, as if she had told him exactly how she had spent the last two years of her life. Radulf *knew*.

And it was a terrifying thought . . . but it was also a relief.

Her own voice came out a little hoarse, but still strong. The loss of that final strand of her dark plot had not diminished her, if anything it had strengthened her and set her free.

"I have learned there were many who had reason to hate Anna, or wish her out of their way. She played with the emotions, my lord, and sometimes that is a dangerous thing to do."

"Aye, Anna enjoyed danger," he said, thoughtful, frowning a little. "Some men are more vulnerable inside than others, and because of that they are more likely to strike, to kill rather than to wound. But I did not hurt her, lady. I did not need to. I had Lily, and I had put Anna's evil behind me. You must look elsewhere for your murderer."

Ivo shuffled his feet, and Radulf glanced at him questioningly.

"You have someone in mind, de Vessey?"

"Miles, Lord Radulf."

Radulf stroked his chin, and the red stones in the black ring dazzled in the candlelight. "You see Miles in the role of Anna's murderer? Would he kill a woman?"

Ivo's face turned grim, but there was resignation there, too. As if the extent of his brother's evil was so well known to him, it had ceased to surprise him.

"Miles would cut a woman's throat as easily as he would snuff a candle, my lord. If she threatened him, or he felt he had made a mistake in joining with her, then he would kill her. If he was tired of her, or she had made him angry, or inadequate in some way, then he would kill her. My lord," and his voice was so heavy with bitterness that Briar tightened her grip on his hand, "if a woman failed to smile at Miles when he smiled at her, he would kill her."

"He has caused you great suffering," Radulf said, and there was understanding in his voice. " 'Tis time you dealt with your brother, Ivo."

"I know it, lord. That moment is fast approaching, and I think even had I wanted to, I would not be able to avoid it. I must fight him, and this time the fight will end with one of us dying."

Briar made a little sound, but neither man glanced at her. They were intent upon each other, and the words Ivo had just spoken.

"I think I would prefer it if you lived, Ivo," Radulf said with grave humor.

"So would I," Ivo agreed, "but Miles is cunning, and he has no conscience. He has always beaten me before."

Radulf grew intent. "But not this time. You are ready for him now, Ivo, and you will give no quarter. You will destroy him."

Ivo nodded, but Briar felt his uncertainty like a dark cloud about him. Jesu, did he really think he would die? Was that why they were here, so that he could give her into Radulf's keeping? Suddenly she knew it to be true.

"I would ask something of you, my lord," he was saying now. "I wish to wed the Lady Briar as soon as possible. I need to keep her close, and I can only do that if she is my wife. But if I do wed her, if I show him by doing that how much I treasure her, then Miles will hunt her even harder.

And if I am dead, my lord, if I can no longer protect her from him, then I beg that you will take her into your care."

"Ivo," Briar whispered, longing for him to stop speaking as if he were already cold and in his grave. It would not happen, it would not! Not if Briar had anything to do with it.

Radulf smiled. "I know that desperate feeling well, de Vessey. Aye, marry her on the morrow. We will have the wedding here, and then we can make a celebration of it. That should show Miles you expect to live a long and happy life, and do not even think of failure. Does that suit you, Lady Briar?"

"I will not wed just to be safe, my lord," Briar said, her face stiff with the effort not to cry.

"Briar," Ivo murmured, and turned her to face him, ignoring the interested stares of Radulf's men. "Miles hates me, and he knows you are my weakness. Wed me, please. Let me protect you and the babe. Let Lord Radulf protect you. I *need* to know you are safe."

She gazed unflinchingly into his dark eyes. "Will you tell me what is between you and Miles, if I agree?"

He didn't want to, she could see he didn't want to, but he would. Resignation drained his face of emotion. "Aye, demoiselle, I will tell you all. I swear it. I should have trusted you before. Between us there can be no secrets."

Secrets.

He was right. No secrets. And yet Briar had kept one vital secret from Ivo all this time. Filby. He knew who Filby was, she had told him, but he did not know the whole story. She had not trusted

Ivo enough to open up her sore heart to him.
Could she really demand honesty from him and
not give him the same?

She was a woman despoiled. She must in all
honor give him the chance to step away from her,
if that was what he wished. Though it broke her
heart and made her babe fatherless, she would not
wed Ivo if he did not truly want her.

They were all waiting for her to speak, but it
was to Radulf she turned.

"I would beg some moments alone with Ivo,
my lord, before I answer."

Radulf nodded. "Very well. There must be a
chamber free for your use in this large house.
Sometimes it feels very empty to me, but then I
miss my wife. Girl!" he called out, impatient with
the servants, or himself. A maid came scurrying
forward for his instructions.

"These two require privacy, see to it."

The maidservant had lit a candle, but its yellow
light did little to hold back the shadows.

Filby.

Tears filled her eyes. Not for remembered hurt,
although that was certainly there. Tears of self-
pity, and for what Ivo would think of her. Until
now he had thought so well of her, despite her
foolish mistake where Miles was concerned. Briar
was vain enough not to want his admiration
eroded by such a one as Filby.

"Demoiselle."

That wonderful voice, the heat of him at her
back, his strong hands coming to rest upon her
waist. Briar had not comprehended how much

she had missed his care and concern until he had withdrawn it from her, and now it was back in full force.

Or was he just being kind?

She had not understood until now how very kind Ivo was. He smiled at shy Mary, and took time to bolster her confidence; he indulged Briar with her swordplay, when he could have put an end to it with one thrust of his blade. He made certain she was safe, and when she was ill he held her and bathed her brow.

Aye, he was kind. But was kindness what she wanted from him now? Did she want a marriage based on kindness? Or would guilt and unhappiness destroy them?

Briar knew she would rather know the truth now, that he had not really wanted her, than marry him and live in dread ever after . . .

"What is it you need to tell me, Briar?" he asked her gently, his breath warm against her chestnut hair.

She turned and looked up at him, trying to be brave, trying to be calm. "I will speak, Ivo, but afterward you must promise me that if you do not wish to wed me, that you will tell me so?"

He laughed shakily, as if he had never heard anything less likely. "Aye, never fear, I will tell you so."

"This is something," she began, but to her dismay her voice wavered. But no tears; she would not cry. She would not gain his consent through pity. "Do you remember Filby? My betrothed?"

He frowned. "I remember he would not help you when you needed help most desperately."

"When word of the gravity of our situation reached me, I believed I had no option but to beg Filby for his help. I went to his gate and pleaded with him to support us. We had been abandoned and he was to marry me. I believed he would come to our rescue. I could not understand why he was suddenly so cold."

Ivo was watching her, and a sour smile twisted his mouth. "He was concerned for his own skin. Go on."

"When he refused to help us, I thought . . . I *believed* that if I gave myself to him, then he would feel obliged to help. He would owe it to me. And mayhap he would remember what he had felt for me, before my father turned traitor against the king. So I offered him my body, and he agreed."

Ivo's eyes were burning like black stars. Was his anger for Filby, or herself? Briar flinched beneath their stare, turning her face away so that she would not see the expression in them.

"I did not enjoy it, do not think that. It was not like you and me. He took me without care or consideration, not brutally, I will say that, but without feeling, as if I were no longer a person to him. Afterward I thought 'twas the way of all men. And I believed that, although I had been humiliated and soiled, at least Filby would have to help us. He would *have* to."

She bit her lip, waiting until the tremble in her voice had subsided again.

"But he didn't help us. He sent me away instead. And then, when he came to Castle Kenton, to take our home from us, he offered to let us remain there as his prisoners. But I knew what he meant to make of me, and that I could not stay. So we left."

His breath sounded quick and shallow. When Briar dared at last to look at him, she saw that he had closed his eyes, and his skin had paled. He appeared to be suffering under some terrible affliction. Jesu, was he ill?

"Ivo?" she cried, and reached out. But she did not quite dare to touch him. She did not know if she still had the right. The tears clogged her voice, and made it difficult to speak. "I am so sorry, Ivo. If you do not want to wed me now, I will understand it. I will do as you wish. Ivo, please speak to me. Ivo . . . ?"

He opened his eyes. They blazed with black fire. He was so *angry*! That was the terrible emotion he was struggling with—anger. Swallowing, Briar stared, wondering if he meant to kill her on the spot.

"Do you know what I wish, Briar?" he said, and he leaned forward so suddenly that she jumped. But he only took her hands hard in his. "I wish Filby were not already dead, so that I could kill him over and over again for what he did to you. And then I wish I could turn time back and come riding to Castle Kenton with my friends, Gunnar Olafson and Alfred, Sweyn and Reynard and Ethelred, and save you and your sisters from the past."

He wasn't angry with her, Briar realized, relieved. Of course he was not! He was angry with Filby, and her heart soared with joy. She gave a hic-cupping laugh.

"You cannot save me from the past, Ivo, though

that would be my wish, too. If I had seen you come to save me, two years ago, everything would have been different."

"I know," he whispered. He drew her into his arms, gently, yet both of them trembling with emotion. "Ah God, I know it."

"You might not have liked me then," she began, tentatively. "I was very arrogant, Ivo."

He smiled into her hair. "I would have loved you, demoiselle, just as I do now."

Briar clung on to him, weeping softly, until Filby had finally been cried away. *Ivo does not want to abandon me. He is angry at Filby. It does not matter to his pride that I gave away my body in good faith to such a man. He cares only for me, that I was hurt. Me!*

He loves me.

Briar pressed her lips to his throat, and Ivo groaned softly, drawing her yet closer.

"Ivo?"

"Aye, Briar."

She kissed him again, then took a deep breath. "I have told you my last remaining secret, Ivo. You know them all. I have no more. Now you must share yours with me."

Ivo tensed but did not let her go. If anything, he held her tighter, clinging to her now, as she had clung to him.

"Ivo? You have said that you love me, Ivo. You must tell me. Whatever it is, it cannot be as bad as Filby."

Ivo sighed, opening his eyes to stare into nothing, into the past. And Briar could tell that it was more dark and bitter than any she could imagine.

But she was right, she knew it. The time had come for him to share with her the darkness of his soul.

"Mary?"

Mary looked up, wane-faced and miserable.

"Are you all right?"

She shook her head, tears sparkling in her lashes like pearls. "Where is Briar?"

Sweyn moved closer, carefully, as if he were afraid of what she might do. Or was it himself he was afraid of? "Ivo has taken her to Lord Radulf. All will be well, Mary. Ivo will take care of your sister, never doubt that. He is an honorable man."

"But why are they gone so long?"

Sweyn sat down beside her. "They are arguing. You know what they are like. Or else they are making up their argument, with kisses and cuddles."

Some of the anguish left her eyes as she considered that. Then it returned. "I should have stopped her from going to meet Ivo's brother. What if he had hurt her?"

Sweyn brushed her cheek with his thumb, feeling her soft, silky skin against his own rough flesh. "Stopped Briar?" he teased her gently. "Can any of us do that, Mary?"

She met his eyes, a steel determination in her own he had never seen before. "*I* could, Sweyn. I am stronger than I thought."

Sweyn looked into her sweet, serious face and knew in a single instant that he was doomed. His carefree, roving days were done. Over. For all time.

The words formed in his throat and he tried to

hold them back, but it was like sweating chain mail. If he did not speak them, he would choke.

"I love you, Mary."

She stared, as well she might, and for a terrible moment he wondered if she would reject him. And then she gave a brilliant smile and said, "Are you sure?"

He nodded, jerkily, feeling light-headed with relief. "Aye. I don't understand why this has happened now, after all these years, but I love you, Mary."

She reached up and cupped his face, smiling into his blue eyes.

"Then all is well, Sweyn."

"I hope so, Mary," he said, leaning forward to press a chaste kiss to her lips. "You have turned me into a new man, and I am not sure about him yet. But I know one thing, my lady. I will not take your innocence without a priest's blessing."

Mary sighed and shook her head with mock disappointment. "Where is the adventure in that, Sweyn?"

"The old Sweyn would not have hesitated to bed you, lady, but the new one will not. Take it or leave it, the choice is yours."

Mary smiled, a slow and very satisfied smile. "I will take it. Now please kiss me, and properly this time."

Sweyn laughed, and some of his old arrogance was in it. "Oh, I will kiss you *properly*, Mary. I will do that."

Bending his head he captured her mouth with his, drawing his last and forever love into the heady world of passion.

Chapter 14

She did not know what she asked.

Ivo leaned back, so that he could see the yellow candlelight reflecting in her hair. Her eyes were so deep, like a forest glade, somewhere to take shelter and to rest. If only that were so, Ivo knew he would remain here with her forever.

But she was watching him; she was waiting.

Briar had made it sound so simple a thing, for him to tell her his secrets. But it was not. There was nothing simple about it. Ivo rarely shared those most painful of memories with anyone. The past was messy, and his was messier than most.

"Ivo," she said gently, reaching up to touch his cheek, where the bruise was fading to a dull shadow. "When I was a little child you came to my aid. You picked me up and held me in your arms, and I loved you. I followed you about, do you remember?"

He half smiled at the memory. "I do, Briar. You were beautiful then, too. I gave you my heart, and you have it still."

"Then do you really think I would harm your heart? Do you really believe I would do that, after you have given me so much? What could be so bad that it would make me turn from you now?"

He tilted his head and kissed her fingers, but the bleakness had returned to his eyes.

"My brother hates me," he said, as if with an effort, and drew her close against him so that he could rest his chin upon her soft hair. "I don't know why he hates me, but he always has. I used to think that it was my fault, that I had done something wrong, and I tried harder to be a better brother because of it. But it didn't matter what I did, he found fault, he derided me, he looked at me with the eyes of loathing. I learned at an early age, that no matter what I did, Miles would still hate me."

The words were coming easier now, as if a door had opened inside him. Ivo let them flow, forgetting where he was and who was listening, letting himself journey back into his boyhood.

"Miles is the elder son, and our father loved him. I was never favored above him, I was never given more than he. There was no reason. He could have made so much of his life, and instead he had made it his ambition to torment me. Sometimes it was as if my mere presence was enough, and he bitterly resented me for it. Perhaps he wanted to be the only son, perhaps it was as simple, as impossible, as that.

"I was told once that, when I was a babe and he was a boy, he took me up onto the roof and held me over the drop to the ground. 'Twas only my mother's threats to tell our father that made him spare me. Afterward, she kept a closer watch upon me, and our father told Miles that if anything were to happen to me, he would send him far away and I would inherit all. But there were still accidents. Small things—a cut here, a fall there, a knock—nothing that could be proved as being done on purpose. One of Miles's tricks was to ride at me with his pony, and miss me by a hairsbreadth. After a time I learned to stand perfectly still and pretend not to mind. He did not intend to knock me down, not then, he feared our father still. His pleasure was all in frightening me, terrifying me, making my life a misery. I learned to be brave from an early age.

"Perhaps that was one of the reasons I was sent away to be a squire in your household." He squeezed her gently, feeling her living warmth in his arms. She returned the pressure but said nothing, afraid perhaps to interrupt him now that he had begun.

"Though I missed my home, after a time I grew to love being in the Kenton household. Your family was so different. No one was favored above any other; no one was hurt for just being themselves. And there was no Miles."

"I am glad you were happy," she murmured, her voice husky. "I am glad my family gave you that, Ivo."

They were silent a moment, remembering. And then Ivo sighed, and said, "But then my father

died, and I returned home. And my happy days
were done. Miles was waiting for me, and now
there was no one to rein him in."

"But *why*, Ivo? Why does he hate you so?" Her
eyes were wide, compassionate, as she leaned
back in his arms to look up at him. Briar, the pampered daughter, the beloved of her father, would
never have understood, although she may have
sympathized. But this Briar had suffered too—he
had seen it in her eyes that first night. She had
been hurt, and she had survived. Just like Ivo.

Mayhap that was why he loved her so much.

He drew her gently back against his chest,
smoothing the fingers of his gloved hand through
her hair, soaking up her warmth as if he were
frozen. She had opened his heart once, when he
had thought all chance of love was dead. Perhaps
she could do it again . . .

"When I was eleven, Miles and I were mock-
fighting with our wooden swords. I could beat
him, and he hated me all the more for it. And the
more he showed his hate for me, the better it felt to
beat him. The old soldier who watched over us at
such times took sick, and in the confusion we
were left alone. That was when Miles thought it
would be a good idea to use real swords.

"I was not afraid of him when it came to swordplay—I was bigger and stronger than him already.
So I agreed, and we found our swords, and we began to fight. But it was no longer a game, Briar. It
was no longer practice. Miles was fighting me in
earnest, and I realized I was not as good at defending myself as I had thought. He beat me back,
and when I held up my sword to block him, he

sliced not at the blade but at my hand upon the hilt. I lost three fingers."

"*Jesu*, Ivo . . ."

"I was half fainting with the pain of it, sure he would kill me now. But instead he lifted me up from the ground, and called for help, as if it had been an accident. I was in agony, swooning, blood soaking into my clothes and dripping onto the ground. I looked up into his face and he was smiling. *Now*, he said, *there can be only one knight in the de Vessey family*.

Briar, face pressed to his chest, was trembling violently. "He was a monster."

"Aye, he was. But he was content afterward, he left me alone. He thought he had won, at last."

"But he had not?" She asked the question eagerly, and despite himself, Ivo smiled.

"No, he had not. I healed. Everyone doubted I would ever wield a sword again, but that only made me all the more determined to do so. I practiced and my mother had a glove made, of steel and leather, that helped me to grip the hilt of my sword without it slipping. And in time I could fight just as well as any man, and better than most. When Miles understood he had failed, he was furious. And he became even more determined to best me, to hurt me, to wound my mind and my heart, as well as my body."

"Because you conquered him, Ivo. You were too strong for him, and he hated you for it."

Ivo felt her tears on his skin, warm and wet, like a benediction.

He could stop now, he thought, and she would never know the worst part. But he would know,

and suddenly he could not bear it. He wanted her
to hear all, he wanted to rid himself of the taint of
his brother. More than anything, he just wanted to
be free.

"I had a sister. She was *my* sister, the child of my
mother and not Miles's mother. She was older
than me but younger than Miles, and he seemed
fond of her, or perhaps he was just indifferent.
Whatever he felt, he had never tried to hurt her as
he did me. Her name was Matilda, and she was
sweet and gentle and serious. A little like your sister Mary.

"When my mother died, Miles decided Matilda
should wed. She was fifteen years, and old
enough. He took me aside and told me what he
had planned for her, and when I wept and begged
him nay, he laughed. He had discovered my
weakness, you see. He had known that he could
threaten and hurt me all he wanted, but I would
always survive and grow stronger. He had realized it was more painful for me if he turned his
evil attentions to those I loved. And I loved my
sister."

Ivo's voice was bleak, as though he stood on the
brink of an abyss. His chest ached, and even the
feel of Briar in his arms could not stanch the
agony of his memories.

*Get it over with. Say it, and then you will know if
she loves you enough to stay . . .*

"He had found a man who was rich and powerful, someone whose suitability no one could object to on those grounds. Indeed, it was a good
match for Matilda. But this rich and powerful
man was brutal. He was a man who knew only

how to kill and had lost the ability to love, if he had ever known it. Matilda was too young and gentle to deal with a man like that, and she begged him to change his mind. But Miles was now the head of the family, and he insisted. She fought him with tears and pleadings, but he stood firm. He probably enjoyed that."

Briar had gone still in dread, and yet still she hoped the outcome of his story would be different. He heard it in her voice when she asked, "Could you not have stopped this marriage, Ivo?"

"I tried. We ran away. We got several leagues before Miles caught us and took us home. He ordered his men to hold me and he beat me until I was unconscious, and while I was helpless, he forced Matilda to marry her brutal husband. He told me, when I woke and she was gone, that he had threatened her with my death if she did not comply. So he used our love against each other."

"She sent me messages," he went on, absently stroking Briar's long hair. "She said it was not so bad. But I heard from others that her husband treated her like an animal, worse, for he believed his animals to be of some use and so he kept them in good health. Matilda was nothing to him, once he had her. He saw her gentleness as weakness and tried to beat it out of her. When she could stand it no more, she ran away and came home, seeking sanctuary."

"Thank God . . ."

"Miles wouldn't allow it. He was angry, and he sent word to her husband to come and fetch her. Matilda was frantic. She begged me to help her. And I tried, Briar. I tried. I made plans for her to go into hiding, and I had horses ready. But her husband came too soon. When we heard him at the gate, I saw the look in Miles's eyes and I knew if we fought he would kill one of us. I told Matilda she should give herself up. I thought, as long as we lived, I could save her. But she screamed that I had forsaken her, and ran and locked herself in her bedchamber and refused to come out."

Ivo's gaze blurred, and he had to swallow the lump in his throat to continue. After all these years, the anguish, the guilt, were as fresh as ever.

"Miles laughed and said that would not save her. So then I fought with him, Briar. I did my best. But there were too many of them. Miles always had his loyal followers—the dregs of the district, those willing to do anything for coin. He laughed again when they held me, so I could see when Matilda's husband came for her. Miles set him onto her, urging him to do his worst. He didn't need any urging, he was like a maddened bull. He smashed at the door with his fists and his sword, roaring, while Matilda screamed out her terror. When he finally broke down the door, he was so full of rage and bloodlust, that he couldn't stop. He killed her in front of us."

"Oh, Ivo, oh, Ivo," Briar whispered brokenly into the warm skin of his throat. Her hands clung to him, but he didn't take comfort from that. She would soon be pushing him away.

"Miles explained it to me, when I could listen again. It was simply bad luck, he said. A husband had a right to take his wife home, and if Matilda had not refused, then she would be alive now. So, he told me, it was her fault, really. And mine, for making her believe I could save her when . . . when I could not. When I was just too weak to help my only sister. And she had seen it, at the end, and hated me for it."

Briar wiped her eyes and shook her head.

"If I'd been able to get her away sooner, perhaps I could have saved her," Ivo whispered, speaking the words that had been with him for so many years. "If only I hadn't forsaken her at the end, if I hadn't told her to go with her brute of a husband. She looked at me in such a way, with such betrayal in her eyes. And I did betray her. I know it now, but at the time I thought only of saving her life. But now I know that there are worse things than dying."

Her eyes flew to his. He saw the very moment the doubt appeared in them. As he turned away, Ivo felt as if his heart had quietly broken in two.

"I am not fit to be a brother or a husband or anything else. Think twice before you promise to wed me, for though I might swear to protect you, I cannot know what I will do when it comes to the point. Miles might come and I might fail you. Fail you, as I failed Matilda."

Her step behind him, her hand on his arm. "Ivo," she whispered, her voice shaking with tears. "Ivo, you will not fail me. You have *never* failed me. I trust you with my life, just as Matilda did. It was neither your fault nor hers that such a tragedy happened. How can you blame yourself for it?"

"Nay!" he said, and his voice broke with emotion. "She is dead because of me."

"She would not blame you—"

"You do not know the rest, lady. Let me tell you the rest," he blurted out, bitterness curdling inside him. "After I had left my home, Miles squandered all he had, and was forced to hire out his knightly services for money. One day I arrived to take my place with a baron hiring men, and found my brother also there.

"He begged me to forgive him. He said he wanted the past forgotten. He said his heart was sore because of what had happened to Matilda. And I believed him."

"You wanted to believe him, Ivo," she said quietly, her fingers stroking his sleeve. He could feel her trying to see his face, but he turned it into the shadows.

"It was all a lie," he went on bleakly. "He just wanted to destroy the only thing of value I had left. He tricked me, and lost me my knighthood. He lied, and I believed him. I betrayed Matilda all over again." His voice rose and broke.

"He lied, Ivo. Aye, he lied."

"I should never have believed him . . ."

"You cannot help your nature." She slipped her cool fingers under his chin and gently but firmly turned his face toward hers. The tears were hot on his cheeks, and he tried to pull away, but she would not allow it. She gazed up at him, compassionately, lovingly, understandingly. Ivo went very still.

"Ivo, you think the best of people. You want to believe in them. You wanted to believe that Miles had changed, because you are yourself a good man. Evil is as foreign to you as cowardice. It defeated you because you could not comprehend it.

Oh my love, Matilda came to you because of who you were, who you are. Do not condemn yourself and her because a single moment of fear made her say things that were untrue."

She stretched up and kissed his lips, her own so gentle.

"You are a *good* man, Ivo, and that is the reason that Miles hates you. Because you are good, and people love you, and they will never love him."

Suddenly the strength went out of him. He sagged, and she caught him in her arms, steadying him. Ivo gave a ragged sigh, and dropped his head to her breast, and she wrapped him close, rocking him gently as if he were a child.

"I nearly died then," he muttered. "I wandered in the forests with the outlaws. If Gunnar Olafson hadn't found me, I would have died. He gave me back a life. But, lady, you have given me back my heart."

For a long time Ivo lay his head against her, savoring her comfort, feeling the bitterness leaking out of him. It was not something that she could repair in an hour, or a day, or perhaps not even a year. But Ivo knew she would make him whole, one day. And the knowledge gave him a wonderful sense of peace and tranquillity, something he had not felt since he was a young squire, in the Kenton household.

After a time Briar took his face in her hands, lifting him so that she could look into his eyes. He blinked at her as if he had been sleeping, and she shook him gently, to catch his full attention. Her voice when she spoke was deadly serious.

"You must not trust him again, Ivo. No matter

what he tells you, no matter what he says, you must not believe it. You must never soften to him. He is evil through and through, and for such as he there is no redemption in this world."

Ivo's eyes were alert and fierce, staring into hers. "He has maimed me, murdered my beloved sister and had me disgraced, and now he has turned his attentions to you. It is enough. I will not risk your life, Briar, that is why I have asked Lord Radulf for his help. I do not trust myself alone, but I trust him."

She stroked his cheek.

"I have wondered often why he wants me dead. It may be as you say, and he hates me because he cannot be me, and yet . . . Perhaps, until I am dead, he will never be free of our joint memories. I know him better than any other person, and while I live he cannot pretend to be other than what he is. I am his conscience, Briar, and while I am alive, I will always be watching him and judging him and reminding him of what he is."

Briar nodded slowly, tracing the shape of his lips with her fingertips. "He is so much lesser than you, Ivo, and he would resent it, and in time resentment might grow into a hatred so intense it becomes unstoppable."

"I will have to kill him," Ivo said quietly. "My brother, my own blood. I will have to fight him and win. He must die, for your sake, and the sake of our babe."

He leaned forward and kissed her mouth, slowly, gently. Worshiping her. He tasted the salt of tears and the warmth of her love. She came into his arms, willingly, and it was as if there were no boundaries dividing them. No secrets.

He was free. And it was a heady thought, after all these years.

The rain was light outside, but here inside their cozy dwelling by the river, it was warm. Briar drank down the brew Jocelyn had concocted for her, and felt her stomach settle. Her nausea was passing, or mayhap she was just growing more resigned to it.

Ivo had brought her back to her cottage, but there were men to guard her. He had not wanted to let her out of Lord Radulf's house, but she had insisted.

"We are not wed yet, Ivo. It will be soon enough then for you to manage my life. But for now, I will go home, thank you, and prepare myself to become your wife. Besides, I have my sisters to tell. I want to spend my last evening with them."

And she had had her way.

Odo sat by the fire, silent, staring into the flames with his lopsided face as if he were a foreigner in a foreign land and they were all strangers. Against the door, two of Radulf's men sat, trying to look alert as they did guard duty. Mary was asleep by the fire, her face peaceful. Earlier, she had glowed with happiness, exchanging foolish grins with Sweyn, as if they were all alone.

"He loves me," she had whispered to Briar.

And Briar had finally pushed aside her doubts. Sweyn was a good man—he must be, if he was

Ivo's friend. Mary would be all right, and she was strong. Briar had not realized how strong her sister was, how quickly she had grown up since they arrived in York.

'Twas just as well perhaps, for soon Briar would have a family of her own to take care of.

Mary had been overjoyed at Briar's news, but a little sad, too. "But does that mean you will leave York now, Briar? That you will go south with Ivo?"

Briar had not thought that far ahead, and did not intend to. Time enough later to worry about where they would finally settle. And somewhat to her own surprise, she comprehended that although she would miss her sisters, it was Ivo she wanted to be with, needed to be with. Wherever Ivo was, that would be her true home.

Tonight Ivo had been required at Radulf's hall, to drink ale with Sweyn and pretend to commiserate over his soon to be vanquished single days. He had gone for Sweyn's sake rather than his own, and to discuss with Radulf plans to trap Miles into coming into the open. Radulf had begun to turn York inside out in the search for Ivo's brother, but as yet there had been no sign of him. However they had discovered the men Miles had hired the night he rode at Ivo in the laneway. They were part of the castle garrison, and were to be punished for lending themselves out to a felon.

"You are fortunate in your Ivo." Jocelyn met her eyes now with a smile. She had hugged Briar tightly when she was told of the impending wedding. "You see," she had said. "My plan was a good one after all. You made the man so crazy for you, he wants to marry you."

"How am I fortunate in Ivo, sister?" Briar asked dreamily. She presently felt so content that she felt as if she might actually float. How had it happened that the most terrible mistake of her life had turned into the best decision she had ever made?

"He wants to wed you, and not just because of the babe. He wants to wed you because you are Briar. The man is wild for you. I see it in the way he looks at you. I have seen looks like that before. Possessive, wanting, barely restrained. Aye, sister, you are fortunate indeed."

Briar turned to her in surprise, for Jocelyn's voice had been trembling. She did not doubt Jocelyn was pleased for her, but mayhap her happiness had brought back memories of Jocelyn's own early days of marriage. Days that could never now be repeated.

"Is that how Odo once looked at you, sister?" she asked quietly.

Jocelyn smiled. "Once, aye." And then her eyes went hard. "Trust me in this, Briar, when I say you must take hold of your good fortune with both hands. Do not hold yourself back. Do not be afraid to give yourself wholly to him, to take what he offers you. Sometimes your time is much shorter than you imagine."

It was a warning, but well meant. And yet Briar, lying upon her bed later, wondered at her elder sister's strangeness. Had Jocelyn really been thinking of her own happiness, when Odo was whole? Odo had loved her, Briar was certain of that, and Jocelyn had loved him. Then why had her sister's eyes been so angry, so unsatisfied? As if she felt she had been duped of her full share.

Am I holding myself back?

Briar didn't think so. Ivo knew about Filby now, and she knew about Miles and Matilda. Briar's need for vengeance had vanished, erased by other more important matters. She didn't want to spend her life hating, or wasting her precious moments of happiness in dark thoughts. She had Ivo and their babe. Out of hatred she had found love, and it was enough.

Selfishly she didn't want to think about her sister's unhappiness. She didn't want to begin imagining what pitfalls lay ahead.

Miles.

The name was like an ill omen. One day Ivo's brother would appear and try to destroy all her happiness.

Jesu, let Ivo win.

If Ivo had been as unscrupulous and evil as Miles, then he would easily win, but he was not like that. Of course, if he was another like Miles, then Briar would not love him so dearly.

But Briar didn't want to think beyond tomorrow, her wedding day. She opened her eyes wide into the darkness: Tomorrow, when she would wed Ivo, who had come into her life like a tempest, tossing and turning her about until she did not know up from down. Winning her over despite her own stubbornness.

She loved him.

And it felt as natural to her as breathing.

With a smile, Briar curled up and closed her eyes. Tomorrow would see her joined to Ivo before God and the law and Lord Radulf. But in her heart she knew she was already his.

Dawn was breaking over York on the day of Ivo and Briar's wedding. Bleary-eyed and cold, the guards at Micklegate Bar looked up at the thunder of hooves approaching from the south. They kept watch day and night at the stout bar that gave entrance through York's solid walls, and the punishment for dozing off on duty was banishment for a year and a day.

One of them shouted out a warning.

A large troop of men had appeared on the road. They were tough men who looked as if they had ridden far, and they carried a banner at their forefront, an azure banner with a sword upheld. Lord Radulf's banner, the famous King's Sword.

"Open up for Lord Radulf!"

The head guard frowned, standing firm. "Lord Radulf is already within."

"We are here to join him. Open up for Lady Lily, wife of Lord Radulf!"

The guard blinked, uncertain, and then one of the riders urged their horse forward. It was a woman, heavily cloaked, but beneath the furs he caught a glimpse of her famous beauty. He bowed low, and then turned and shouted orders for the bar to be opened. Shortly afterward the cavalcade passed through into the city of York.

Radulf was dreaming.

He was at Crevitch, and it was summertime. The green fields stretched before him, and he rode his black horse, bare-chested beneath the sun. Lily sat before him, soft and warm, her laughter a balm for his soul. She looked up at him with her gray eyes, and he bent to kiss her, whispering, "My love . . ."

And she promptly vanished into the chill York dawn.

Radulf awoke in his lonely bed and groaned miserably. Another dream. Another disappointment. When, when could he go home!

"My love?"

He opened his eyes. And she was there, leaning over him, her silver blond hair brushing his chest, her long fingers stroking his cheek. Gray eyes full of love, and sparkling with tears. The dream and reality suddenly merged, and Radulf sat up.

"You are real," he managed hoarsely.

Lily laughed. "I am real, Radulf. I missed you so. I have come north to be with you, my love."

"*Mignonne*," he groaned, and took her into the shelter of his arms. "I have longed for you so."

"Radulf," she murmured, after a time. "Radulf! You are squashing me."

He leaned back with a reluctant sigh, and she smoothed his rough cheek, her fingers tender.

"My lands? The rebels? Tell me what has happened."

"All is well again, for now, but other matters have kept me here in the north. Ivo de Vessey's brother, Miles, is on the loose and must be tethered, and Ivo is set to wed Richard Kenton's daughter, Briar."

Lily opened her mouth to demand more, but he stopped her with a kiss.

"What of our children?" he murmured against her lips. "How are my daughter and my son?"

Lily smiled. "They are both safe and well. Strong and healthy, and very arrogant, as befits children of such a sire. I have left them in Gudren's care."

His mouth teased hers, his body tense with need, and yet he held back. "You are weary, Lily. You must rest. 'Twas selfish of me to want you here with me—you should not have come."

Her arms circled his neck and she smiled into his eyes. "Then I am selfish, too, my lord, because more than anything I wanted to be here by your side. Can it be that now I am here, in your bed, you plan to play the martyr with me? If that is so, Radulf, then I am not at all happy with you and I will turn around and ride home again—"

With a soft growl, Radulf caught his wife to him and tumbled her down into his bed. Lily gave a sigh of pleasure, and did not offer any resistance.

Chapter 15

❧

Briar did not think she had slept at all, but she must have, for the sudden banging on the door made her jump awake.

Mary also sat up, her dark hair cascading all about her. "Who is't?" she gasped, as the two guards sleeping on the floor just inside the cottage struggled to draw their swords.

"I am come from Lord Radulf!" a voice outside informed them.

Mary pushed her hair out of her eyes and looked at Briar. Briar crept gingerly out of bed, wincing from the cold, and moved toward the door. The two guards gestured for her to stay back, and flung it open, swords at the ready.

The morning air crept in. The faces of Lord Radulf's men looked pinched with cold as they stood waiting, one of them holding a largish cloth-wrapped bundle.

" 'Tis a gift," the hard-faced soldier explained. "To the Lady Briar, from the Lady Lily."

"Lady Lily?" Briar looked bewildered. "But is she not still in Somerset?"

The hard-faced soldier smiled, and suddenly he did not seem so very hard. "She arrived in York at dawn, lady."

The bundle was placed on the floor inside the room, and the door was closed firmly. Mary came and stood beside Briar, both women looking down at it in some bewilderment. "What can it be?" Mary asked uneasily.

Briar did not know, but a stab of guilt reminded her that she had wished Radulf and Lily only ill until a short time ago. Perhaps Lily had discovered it. But that was silly—Lily couldn't read Briar's mind. Mayhap it was a gift for the home she would make with Ivo?

She bent and slowly, cautiously, undid the ties, and rolled open the cloth to reveal the contents.

It was a gown. Made of the finest velvet, and colored a deep, luscious green—Briar's favorite color. The skirt and bodice were embroidered with small gold and silver beads, and in the gloomy dwelling, they glittered like distant stars.

"She has sent your marriage dress," Mary breathed, reaching to touch the luxuriant cloth with a reverent finger. "Oh, Briar, 'tis so beautiful! You will look like a queen."

Briar, stunned at the extent of Lady Lily's generosity, gasped as her sister hugged her tightly in her excitement.

" 'Tis a pity you have only your old stockings and shoes to wear with it," Mary added, practically.

And wondered why Briar began to laugh.

There had been little time to prepare Lord Radulf's York house for the ceremony, but with the roaring fire in the hall and the succulent smells of a banquet cooking, it did not really matter. The big room spoke of welcome and celebration, a haven against the threatening weather outside.

The priest spoke the words to bind them together, and Briar clung to Ivo's hand, still a little dazed by all that had happened. And so quickly. Ivo was pale, with shadows under his eyes, but there was no hiding the steady glow of happiness in them.

Radulf and Lily watched on, and although Briar was introduced to Lily, she barely remembered what she said. Afterward, it was always Ivo's words that she recalled, when he first saw her in her green velvet wedding gown.

"Demoiselle, you are an angel," he had breathed, taking her hands and staring down at her in wonder. The gown did suit her well, seeming to capture the secrets in her hazel eyes and causing her chestnut hair to glow where it had been combed over her back and shoulders. "My heart is too full for words," he had added, and 'twas true, for tears filled his dark eyes.

Ivo wore a deep blue tunic with a fine linen shirt beneath, and dark breeches and soft leather boots. With his height and breadth of shoulder, he looked like the knight he had always been, in his heart. A man to be proud of.

When the priest had finished, Ivo drew her to him, carefully, as if he were afraid this were a dream and he might wake up, and kissed her lips, chastely, as befitted the solemnity of the occasion.

There was a smattering of applause. Briar's sisters were there, their eyes shining, and Sweyn, grinning, as well as two other big men, whom Ivo had introduced as Reynard and Ethelred. They all wished her and Ivo well, and the warmth of their smiles washed over her like a happy tide.

And then Ivo laughed, losing some of his awe, and picked her up in his arms, spinning her around to the delight of the guests, until Briar's stomach dipped, and she whispered in a soft voice that he had better stop.

"Briar?"

Briar looked into the beautiful, gentle face before her. Lady Lily was everything the rumors promised and more, ethereally fair, with gray eyes that saw straight to her heart. Briar had already stammered her thanks for the dress when she arrived at Radulf's house, but Lily had brushed her words aside.

"Someone did the same for me when I was wed," she said, with a little smile. "In my case 'twas not done with the best of intentions, but still I felt special. I wanted you to feel special, too, Briar. I know what it is to be poor and put upon."

Now the ceremony was over, and the feast had come and gone. The day was dwindling into

night, and still no one wanted to leave. Ivo was
reminiscing with his friends, and Mary was leaning against Sweyn as if she belonged there. Jocelyn and Odo had retired long since. Tired,
longing only to fall asleep in Ivo's arms, Briar had
found herself a quiet place in a corner to wait until she could retire. It was there that Lady Lily had
found her.

She sat down on the bench beside Briar. "Radulf
has told me of your troubles," she said softly.

"Oh," Briar replied, and could think of nothing
else. The familiar guilt roiled inside her as she remembered what she had planned to do to this
woman and her husband. Of course, her plan had
been doomed to fail from the start because, as Ivo
had said, Radulf would never have taken another
woman in Lily's place, not even for a moment.
Still, that did not make what Briar had meant to
do any less wicked, or make her feel any more
comfortable with her own conscience.

Lily was still smiling, but her gray eyes were
flinty. "Radulf tells me you hated him for your father's misfortunes."

Obviously, Lily did not believe in creeping
around the facts. A woman after my own heart,
Briar thought wryly.

"My lady," she said firmly, "I did hate him. 'Tis
true. My father vowed revenge upon Lord Radulf
before he died, and I believed that I must take on
that vow as my own. For two years I hated Lord
Radulf and believed him solely responsible for
my family's downfall. I know now that that belief
was false. Lord Radulf was as bound up in Lady
Anna's sickness as my father. I do not hate him. I

do not think, on this wonderful day, that I could hate anybody."

Lily laughed. "I am delighted to hear it." Then she sobered and leaned closer, her gaze intent. "I wished to give you some advice, Briar, something I have learned over the years. Trust your heart. The mind is so much more insistent, so much louder. But listen hard to the soft whisper of your heart, for 'tis the heart that speaks true."

Briar smiled, for she had done just that. Followed her heart. "Thank you," she said softly. "I will try to do so, always."

"You will never regret it." Lily glanced across the room to where Radulf was standing, and as if he had felt the brush of her gaze, he looked up. Their eyes met in perfect understanding.

"Wife," Ivo murmured into her ear, "are you awake?"

His hands slid around her, to cup her breasts, his body aroused against hers. Briar lay half asleep in the warm, soft bed and smiled. She was perfectly content to allow Ivo to wake her.

His hand slid over her belly, pausing briefly, as if he thought of the child growing there, and down to the soft place where her thighs joined. Briar bit her lip on a groan. She was ready for him, and he knew it now. The game was over.

He turned her onto her back and gazed down with hot black eyes into her own loving ones.

"You *are* awake, wife."

"I cannot be. 'Tis too wonderful to be real, and I do not want to wake and find it has been nothing but a dream."

He kissed her mouth, his hands caressing her pliant body. "This no dream, Briar. Never fear you will awake and find me gone. I intend for us to grow old together."

She arched against him as he delved deep inside her with his finger, clinging to his shoulders, her eyes closed. He lifted his big body over her, opening her legs with his hard-muscled thigh. She eased herself against him, enjoying the rough feel of his skin on that most sensitive part of her.

"Ivo," she gasped, and reached down to take him in her hand.

He shuddered, suddenly on the verge of losing control, and settled himself more fully between her thighs. She guided him, urging him to complete their joining. But Ivo didn't need urging. He thrust inside her, deeply, feeling the tremors of her body as she adjusted to him.

"Wife," he whispered, and thrust again.

Briar gasped, and gently slipped over the edge into the warm, wonderful sea of completion. A short time later Ivo joined her, and together they lay entwined, dreaming of a life together.

"My love?"

Ivo blinked, too happy to speak.

Briar came up on one elbow, gazing down into his face, her hair tickling his skin. One breast brushed his shoulder and he reached to fondle it, thinking, *This is mine. She is mine. Truly mine.* Miles will never hurt her, not while I live.

She gasped as he found her nipple, gently tugging at the swollen flesh with his gloved fingers.

Suddenly he did not feel like sleep, and reached to pull her on top of him. But she held her palms against his chest, firm and unyielding, and surprised, Ivo stared up at her.

Her face was uncertain, the smile curving her lips a little strained. As though she did not know how to say what she wanted to say.

"Briar? Is something amiss, my angel?"

She shook her head, but her lips trembled.

"Briar," he said, more loudly, "you are frightening me. Tell me, what is wrong?"

She put a finger against his cheek, smoothing the stubble that grew dark against his skin. "Nothing is wrong, Ivo. I want . . . I want to see your hand now. We are wed. Nothing will make me love you less. You must take off your glove."

Shocked, he said nothing, just stared up at her. Take off his glove? Show her what Miles had done to his hand? It would be like bearing his soul. And then he remembered that he had already done that; she knew the worst of him already. What did one more thing matter?

" 'Tis not a pretty sight."

She laughed and then bit her lip. "I don't care about that, Ivo," she assured him, reaching to take his glove in her own warm fingers. "I love you for what you are, and your hand, and all it means to you, is part of that."

Love. She loved him. Aye, the love was there in her eyes. His Briar loved him, and she had wormed her way into his heart and his life, until she *was* his life. He could deny her nothing, and she knew it.

Keeping his eyes on hers, Ivo began briskly to unlace the glove, tugging hard on the leather ties. When that was done, he peeled back the leather, loosening it, and then pulling it from his hand.

Her eyes were still on his, as if despite her brave words she didn't quite dare look down. And then her gaze slid away, toward his naked hand and the scarred, ugly mess that Miles had made of it. And Ivo realized he couldn't bear to watch her, in case he saw the horrified rejection there.

There was silence. He felt dizzy with doubts, and turned away. "Jesu, Briar, say something!" he cried, his anguish plain in every word.

"Ivo," she whispered, and her lips brushed soft and healing against his hurt flesh. "My love, my dearest love. Look at me."

Slowly, he did so. She held his hand in hers, but he looked into her eyes. They were smiling, and there was no disgust in them, no horror and no pity. It was Briar and she was unafraid. He should have known she would accept his hand, just as she had accepted his past.

He sat up, pulling her against him, his mouth hard on hers. She gasped at the suddenness of his passion, but a moment later had relaxed into his kisses with perfect contentment.

"I love you, my angel," Ivo whispered against her lips. "I love you."

"And I love you," she replied.

At that moment, Ivo knew his happiness was complete.

Chapter 16

Briar pushed away her crust and cheese. Breakfast was no longer a meal she enjoyed, but it was necessary to take a few mouthfuls of something, to settle her roiling stomach. She glanced about her at Lord Radulf's household, which was barely stirring after yesterday's celebrations.

Radulf and Lily were still abed, but Ivo had risen early to go with Reynard, Ethelred, and Sweyn to search an area of the city where runaways were wont to gather. Briar had been left to her own devices. Not that she minded, for while Miles roamed free they were not safe. She wanted Ivo's brother captured as much as anyone.

Radulf had decided that both Briar and Mary would be safer under his roof, and Mary had gone to the cottage with Jocelyn and Odo to fetch some of their belongings. It was only after she had gone that Briar remembered she had not asked for Mary to bring her sword, hidden under her bed. She had carried the sword with her, sometimes concealed under her clothing, since she left Castle Kenton two years ago.

She did not intend to leave it behind now.

Besides, it had been a gift from her father, and so was precious to her. Nay, she could not leave it in the dwelling by the Ouse to be stolen. It would take her but a moment to ride there and fetch it, and then she and Mary could return together.

Briar glanced at her crust again, but could not face it. There was no time like the present. Mayhap Ivo would be there when she returned. At the thought of Ivo, her body softened and burned, and she found herself smiling.

He loves me.

She hugged the knowledge to her heart, feeling supremely optimistic. Aye, he loved her, and all would be well. Radulf would find Miles and destroy him, and she and Ivo would live long lives without fear of what Miles might do.

Full of happiness, still smiling, Briar rose and went out to the stables to find a horse. In moments, she rode out into York.

Her cloak did not seem to warm her as it should. The day was bitter cold, the sky a steel gray without pity. The Ouse reflected the colorless sky, while a few dippers, their feathers ruffled, floated disgruntled upon its surface.

Smoke trickled from the sagging roof of her old home. Mary had lit the fire, then. Briar hurried to dismount and tether her mount, thinking how warm it would be inside. The door opened to her touch, swinging back in the dim and shadowy room.

A shape sat on a stool by the fire, hunched, dark, silent. The hairs rose on the back of Briar's neck, and she stumbled back, gasping. And then her mind recognized Odo, and she gave a surprised laugh instead.

"Odo?" she said, moving into the room. "Where are Jocelyn and Mary?"

But of course Odo did not answer her. He had not spoken in two years, since he had been taken ill on the morning after Anna's murder, and it was unlikely he would do so now.

Briar walked toward her bed, lightly touching Odo's shoulder as she passed. Her sisters could not have gone far, or they would not have left Odo by himself. Briar had time to collect her sword and a few of her other belongings, and be ready for them when they returned. And perhaps she had time to stand a moment, and remember all that had happened in this place, the small griefs and the larger ones, as well as the happiness she had shared . . .

"My brother's wife."

She did not even hear him arrive, just his words ringing in the silence. So smug, so satisfied, so victorious. His voice came from behind her, in the doorway, blocking off her only escape.

Miles.

Briar froze. Her heart gave that heavy thump. She knew she was in the presence of evil, and with only Odo to protect her. Slowly, gathering all her courage about her, Briar turned to face him.

He was standing just inside the room, and his smile told her the worst. He had been waiting for her, and he was planning to enjoy this.

"Do you know, I have been watching you from across the river," he said, as if he wanted her to hear how clever he had been. "I have been watching you and my brother. Kissing, cooing like doves. I've seen everything. He was playing at protecting you, playing at being a knight. But he isn't much good at it, is he? He never was."

"Ivo will be here soon," she said, as if he hadn't spoken, and to her amazement her voice hardly trembled at all.

He grinned. "I doubt that, my brother's wife. He is caught up with important matters. He is looking for me, but as usual he is looking in all the wrong places. By the time he recognizes it is you who is missing, it will be too late, you will be gone."

"Gone where?"

"Somewhere safe, and quiet, where we can get to know each other better."

I won't think of that, Briar told herself, gritting her teeth. *I won't let my imagination take me down that narrow road. He has not hurt me yet, and if I am strong and clever, then he will never hurt me.*

Her eyes slid away, down to the floor, and she saw the dull curve of the hilt of her sword edging out from beneath her bed. Quickly she looked away. Odo had been staring blankly into the fire, but now Briar noticed that he had lifted his head and was staring instead at Miles.

For a moment Briar thought she read intelligence there, understanding, but it must have been a trick of the light. As she peered closer, she saw his eyes were just the same as always, that empty blue Briar had grown used to. No help there, then.

If she wanted to be saved from Miles, then it was up to herself.

"Why do you hate Ivo?" she asked him, as if she were really interested.

He smiled, but there was nothing of laughter or warmth in it. "When Ivo came into the world he made it brighter. Everyone seemed drawn to him, as if he were a lantern in a dark place. I felt myself disappearing into the shadows when he was nearby. So you see, lady, it was a matter of life or death, me or Ivo. And naturally I chose me."

She sank down on the bed, as if her legs had suddenly given way, aware that he was watching her like a hawk a field mouse. Her heel brushed the sword hilt and carefully, praying he could not see her movements beneath the hem of her drab gown, she edged it closer.

"Why didn't you just kill Ivo years ago, Miles? Why draw it out like this? Was he too clever for you? Aye, that must be it, he was just too clever for you—"

"Because he has to suffer," Miles cut in, and something sparkled in his pale eyes. "I want to break him, I want him to beg and grovel and accept I am his better. Only he never does. He just keeps coming back, stronger than before." He leaned toward her, breathing quickly, a faint flush in his lean cheeks. "Why does he do that? Why doesn't he break?"

Briar shifted the sword closer, close enough that if she reached down she could clasp it in her hand. And once she had done that, it was up to her.

"He is better than you," she said coldly. "That is why, Miles. He is the better man, and he always will be."

It was a mistake.

With a growl, he stalked toward her. Too soon. Briar fumbled for her sword, snatching it up, but not fast enough. He had grabbed at her arm, twisting it, hurting it. But she would not drop her weapon, though the pain made her feel faint. They struggled together, grimly, making hardly any sound in their battle of life and death.

The sword fell from her fingers.

"Oh, I will enjoy killing you," he whispered into her ear, and she knew it was so. Briar felt sickness building in her throat.

She tried to pull free, but he caught her hair and jerked hard. Briar spun around, slapping at him, trying to make him let go. But he laughed and began to reel her in by her hair like a fish on a line. And then Briar's gaze moved beyond him, and widened.

Odo.

Odo was standing there. The big man had risen up to tower over Miles. Briar cried out, just as Odo slipped his meaty arms around Miles's waist, lifted him, and began to squeeze.

Miles went still, his face slack with shock. And then he began to writhe and struggle, pushing with desperate hands at those powerful arms. Briar stumbled away backward, tripping over a stool. As she fell to the floor, she noticed her sword lying on the ground nearby. Half crawling, she made her way to the weapon and snatched it up, at the same time turning to see what was happening with Miles and Odo.

"You brainsick oaf!" Miles's face was flushed and furious. He had managed to get one arm out of the death grip, and now he swung his elbow around, into Odo's face. Blood gushed from the big man's nose. Odo let him go and sank to his knees, clutching at his face with his hands and making a soft keening sound.

Miles stumbled and half fell onto the bed. Immediately he rolled and stood up, looking around and finding her crouched on the floor. His gray eyes glittered with triumph.

"You have proved surprisingly hard to capture, lady," he said, a little breathless from his struggle with Odo. "But the game is over now."

Briar straightened, her sword held before her, and tried to keep her hands steady. "Ivo is going to kill you," she said, her voice strong and unwavering. "But only if I don't do it first."

He raised his eyebrows in mock surprise, and then grinned as he reached to his side and unsheathed his own sword. Briar stared blankly at the length of sharp steel. She could fight him, and perhaps keep him busy for a short while, but he would beat her and likely kill her in the end. She was no match for a trained fighting man—Ivo had taught her that, and she was grateful now.

But she could run.

Briar lifted her sword and flung it at him like an oversized dagger, then turned and fled through the open door.

She had taken three steps into the open air when he caught her. It wasn't far enough. She screamed, and some birds flew up from the river, echoing her cry. Again Miles twisted his hand in her hair and pulled her back against his body. Briar felt the cold, heavy blade of his sword come to rest against her tender throat.

"Perhaps I'll kill you here," he said through gritted teeth, and she knew she had made him angry. "Then Ivo will find your body when he finally comes to save you. Poor Ivo. He is always too late. Did he tell you that? If you are pinning your hopes on Ivo, lady, then you will be disappointed."

"Will she, brother?"

"Ivo!" Briar struggled and tried to run, but Miles held her fast. The blade pressed harder, and she was still.

Ivo, mounted upon his horse, walked it from around the side of the dwelling. Slowly, carefully, as if there was no hurry. Briar gazed up into his face, seeing the grim determination. There was a deadly look in his black eyes, and after one swift glance at Briar, to assure himself she was all right, they settled upon his brother.

In turn Miles watched him, his body still as a snake about to strike. Excitement and anticipation thrummed through him—Briar could feel both. "Brother, you surprise me. You are usually so tardy when it comes to saving those you love."

"I'm going to kill you, Miles. Let her go, and we can fight. That's what you really want, isn't it?"

Miles bared his teeth. "You'd give your life for hers, wouldn't you? Good and noble Ivo! You make me puke. I've hated you all my life, but never so much as I hate you now."

"Then fight me!" Ivo shouted, and Briar understood then that he knew. Knew that Miles was going to kill her, there in front of him, and then Ivo would not care whether he himself lived or died.

"Let her go."

The voice sounded rough, as though it had not been used for a very long time. It came from behind Miles, from the door of the dwelling. Briar tried to turn, but even as she struggled, Miles was spinning her around. Odo's fist struck empty air. Miles brought his arm back and then thrust his sword into the big man with a satisfied grunt.

Briar slipped out of his grasp and fell to the ground. She knew she should run, get away, but she seemed unable to move from the spot. Odo sat down, hands to his wound, staring up in surprise at Miles.

"I should have done that before," Miles panted, annoyed with himself, and then turned to look at Briar. "And now for you," he said.

Briar felt the air stir, the tremor of the horse's hooves on the ground. Miles looked up, his eyes widened. The horse, already in motion, came in a rush between Miles and Briar. Ivo swung his own sword, the blade arching gracefully.

Miles fell without a sound.

Briar rose on shaking legs. Ivo had dismounted, reluctantly, and was staring down at his brother. Miles's chest rose and fell wildly, as if he couldn't get enough air, the bright blood spreading across his breast. He gazed up at Ivo, gray eyes dulled now, fading. His mouth curled into a smile—Ivo's smile.

"Ivo," he whispered. "I want to . . . I want to . . ."

Ivo dropped to one knee, leaning closer. "What is it, Miles?"

Miles gasped, swallowed, and said, "I want to tell you that I'll beat you yet," and then the air rattled from his throat, and he was gone.

"Odo!"

Jocelyn's screams echoed savagely about them. She came running toward her husband, Mary close behind her. Ivo was still kneeling, staring blankly down at his brother's body. Briar touched his shoulder, gently, and he looked up at her.

"He was going to kill you," he said fiercely.

"I know, Ivo."

"He was evil."

"He was."

"But he was still my brother."

She wanted to hold him, to comfort him, but what could she say that he did not already know? Miles had hated him, aye, but Ivo had still hoped that one day matters might be as he longed for them to be. But now Miles was gone. The dream was over.

Mayhap, in a way, Miles had beaten Ivo. But it was not a victory Briar begrudged him.

"Odo!" It was a wail of sheer anguish. Briar froze, goose bumps rising on her skin. Odo was lying still and pale upon the ground, his wife bent over him. Mary, standing nearby, wept silently.

"Briar," she whispered, "oh, Briar . . ."

Briar went to her sisters.

* * *

"I am very sorry."

Briar spoke softly to Jocelyn, but she was gazing down at Odo. They had carried the big man into the dwelling and laid him upon the bed. Though his face was pale and drawn, he appeared peaceful and, strangely, he looked more how he had used to look, before his illness.

Ivo had led Mary outside to Sweyn, and the rest of Radulf's men. This morning when Ivo had returned to Lord Radulf's house, and discovered Briar missing, he had been like a madman. When he had finally found where she had gone, from the groom in the stables, he had ridden off alone to find her. It had taken some little time for Sweyn and the others to track him down.

Jocelyn sighed. "If only I had not gone to get food. I only meant to be a moment, but then there was no mead, and Odo likes his mead, so we went farther afield. I never planned to leave him alone so long. I never dreamed he would be in danger."

"He saved me," Briar said, and nodded as her sister turned to her in wonder. "He tried to stop Miles twice, and he spoke. Jocelyn, it was the strangest thing . . ."

Jocelyn wiped the tears from her cheeks. "He was a hero, then, in the end."

"Aye, he was."

Jocelyn took a breath and straightened her shoulders, as if she had set herself a very difficult task. "I have something to tell you, Briar. Please, do not judge me. I should have told you long ago, but I did not know until it was too late, and then I could not bear to speak of it. I hoped you would forget, that you would put it behind you. But you were always so stubborn . . ."

Briar took her sister's agitated hands, leaning closer. "What are you talking about? Forget what?"

"About Anna."

Jocelyn was staring at her so intently, trying to tell her something, but Briar did not know what it was. It had been a long and exhausting day, and her mind was less than sharp.

"What about Anna?"

" 'Twas Odo who killed her."

The words ran through her head like a runaway horse, making no sense at first, only a lot of noise. "Nay," she whispered, half inclined to laugh.

But Jocelyn looked white-faced and furious, her blue eyes blazing. "Aye! She always took the men she wanted, Briar. You discovered that, did you not? And when she decided she wanted my Odo, then she took him too. She had him in such a state, he was besotted with her, crazed for her, the way he used to look at her . . ." She gulped. "He really thought she would be his forever. Only she preferred Radulf—I think Radulf was the only man she ever truly loved. The others were puppets to play, strings to pull. When Radulf came to York, she told Odo she did not want him anymore. That it was over. He begged and wept. He told me so. He had so little dignity left, Briar. And she laughed in his face."

Briar sat down, her legs too weak to hold her. Odo and Anna? Jocelyn's Odo, whom she had loved with all her heart and who had loved her? How terrible, that Anna had destroyed them, too, with her greedy grasp.

And Jocelyn had suffered all this time, alone.

"I did not know, at first," Jocelyn said, her blue eyes blurring with tears and time. "I didn't know what he had done. When the messenger came to say she had died I was glad, *glad!* I thought 'twas Radulf's doing, but I didn't care. We were finally free of her, and that was all that mattered to me. And then I turned to Odo and he had such a look on his face. Guilt and pain, Briar, and remorse. He gave a great cry and fell to the ground.

"For a long time I thought he would die, too. It was my punishment, I told myself, for celebrating Anna's murder, and I prayed for forgiveness and nursed my husband like a good wife. I realized then that I couldn't let it happen. I couldn't allow Anna to have my Odo in death as well as life."

"Oh, Jocelyn . . ."

"I was so sick with fear and rage and worry, so caught up in my own life and Odo's illness, that I let our father go out and die for that woman. But I swear to you, Briar, I swear upon all I hold dear, that it was only after our father was dead that I discovered the whole truth. Odo spoke in his sickness, the last time he spoke until today, and what he said chilled me to my soul. He was in the darkness, in the rain, waiting. He was waiting for Anna. She rode by him, and he followed her and stopped her. He begged her not to leave him. But she laughed and said he wasn't man enough for her.

"And he killed her."

Jocelyn sat quiet and still, pale but composed, her thoughts far away. After a time she went on, staring down at her hands as if she could not bear to read what was in Briar's eyes.

"It was too late to tell our father. He was already dead. I sat all night, thinking and thinking, and I decided there was no point in giving up Odo. He was ill and may even die, I told myself. And despite everything he had done, I loved him still. I had lost so much, suffered so much, it did not seem fair that I should have to give up my husband as well."

Briar sat, bewildered and numb. All this time it had been Odo, not Radulf. All her hatred, all her cries for vengeance, misdirected. Odo had killed Anna, and Jocelyn had known and said nothing.

"I hoped you'd forget," Jocelyn said again, as if she had read Briar's mind. "I just hoped you'd forget."

Briar turned to look again at Odo, where he lay so peaceful and still. He had just saved her life, saved it as surely as Ivo had done. What had such an action cost him? What amazing feat of strength had that been for him? And was that enough to make up for all the bad things that he had started when he killed Anna?

Only God could answer that, thought Briar. She would not even try. It was over. At last, the past was behind them, laid bare as the moors around Castle Kenton, but behind them. They could walk away.

Briar slid to her knees before Jocelyn, and gently took her sister into her arms.

The River Ouse caught the dying rays of the sun, like molten gold between its muddy banks. Ivo tightened his grip about Briar as if he would never let her go, and she settled in against his side, molding her smaller body to his larger one. Smoke from the dwellings of York settled low over the city, broken by roofs and church spires and the grim Norman castles.

The day was ending. Odo's body had been taken to Lord Radulf's, as had Miles. Jocelyn and Mary were also there, being comforted by Lady Lily.

"Can you forgive her?"

Briar glanced up at her husband, and found a smile. "Jocelyn? Aye, I think so. I would not have done so once, but now I understand better what she must have felt. Jocelyn has loved Odo all her life, and she will continue to do so. I would not deny her that. In a way . . . 'tis strange, but I think his death is a relief to her. I always believed she would be unable to cope, but she is strong, Ivo. We are all of us, Kenton sisters, strong."

He squeezed her gently, bending to kiss the top of her head.

"And we are safe," he said.

"Aye, we are safe."

"The past is done with, and we can start anew. Make a beginning, you and me."

"You and me," she murmured, and together they watched the sun go down.

Epilogue

⟪◦◦◦⟫

"**L**ady Briar?"

Briar stepped forward at the speaking of her name, curtsying before Radulf and Lily as low as the babe in her belly would allow. Her heart was thumping with fear and hope. This day was as special as her wedding day. The wheel had come full circle.

Radulf held a single sheet of paper in his hand, much creased and stained from its journey, and there was a seal dangling from it. A very official-looking seal.

"Lord Henry has brought this to me from London," Radulf went on. "Do you know what it is?"

Briar glanced sideways at Ivo, trying to keep a straight face when she was longing to smile. "No, my lord. At least, I dare not hope it is what I have longed for these many months . . ."

"Well, perhaps your wishes have come true, lady. This is a decree from the king to say he has removed the taint of traitor from your father's name. You and your sisters are no longer outcasts. The Castle Kenton estate will be returned to you. You have your name back, Lady Briar, and you can go home."

Briar was trying not to cry.

Home. She could go home to her beloved Castle Kenton . . . As if it felt her joy, the babe moved inside her, kicking strongly. She would be able to have her child at home!

"Ivo."

Ivo stepped forward beside her, making his bow and awaiting Radulf's instructions.

"Ivo, the king has also decreed that because of your loyalty, honesty, and bravery, you be returned your knighthood. You will henceforth be known as Sir Ivo de Vessey."

Ivo's dark eyes widened, and he seemed unable to reply. Briar swallowed her tears, knowing if a speech was to be made then it was up to her.

"I thank you, Lord Radulf," she began, her voice shaking. "You have done a wondrous thing, and I cannot express my-my—"

"Then do not try," Radulf interrupted uncomfortably. "I have righted an injustice, that is all."

Lily reached to grasp his hand, her beautiful face full of love for her warrior husband. Briar, too, glanced at her own husband, and found her eyes locked with his.

"We will live there together," she said firmly, as if she were afraid he might say her nay. "I need your help, Ivo. I cannot do it on my own. I would not want to."

"You will have my help, demoiselle," Ivo replied softly. "I give it gladly. Now and forever."

Prepare to be swept away by these unforgettable romances from Avon Books

LONDON'S PERFECT SCOUNDREL by Suzanne Enoch
An Avon Romantic Treasure

Evelyn Ruddick knows she should avoid the Marquis of St. Aubyn at all costs, but she is determined to teach the charming, arrogant rake a lesson in compassion. It won't be so easy—especially since his touch is setting her desires aflame, making Evie yearn to submit to *his* passionate instruction . . .

~

IF THE SLIPPER FITS by Elaine Fox
An Avon Contemporary Romance

Anne Sayer learned long ago that fairy tales don't come true and evil stepmothers do exist. Now dashing and successful, Connor Emory has returned, and this "Cinderella" intends to win back her prince. Because the glass slipper that would never have fit a decade ago, is the perfect size now.

~

KISS ME QUICK by Margaret Moore
An Avon Romance

The instant Lady Diana Westover spies Edmond Terrington across a crowded room, the lovely, sheltered miss believes she's found the man she's been searching for. Though she knows nothing of men, Diana longs to pen a romantic novel. So she resolves to study the handsome, seductive lord's every move, and to experience the pleasures of his kisses . . .

~

CHEROKEE WARRIORS: THE LONER by Genell Dellin
An Avon Romance

Black Fox is determined to hunt down the notorious Cat—a thief who robs from the wealthy to give to the poor. But his satisfaction at finally capturing the outlaw turns to shock when he discovers The Cat is a woman! This breathtaking hellion stirs his sympathy and his desire, yet surrendering to a fiery passion could be disaster for them both.

REL 0403

Avon Romantic Treasures

Unforgettable, enthralling love stories,
sparkling with passion and adventure
from Romance's bestselling authors

Discover Contemporary Romances
at Their Sizzling Hot Best
from Avon Books

THE DIXIE BELLE'S
GUIDE TO LOVE   by Luanne Jones
0-380-81934-1/$5.99 US/$7.99 Can

TAKE ME, I'M YOURS   by Elizabeth Bevarly
0-380-81960-0/$5.99 US/$7.99 Can

MY ONE AND ONLY   by MacKenzie Taylor
0-380-81937-6/$5.99 US/$7.99 Can

TANGLED UP IN LOVE   by Hailey North
0-380-82069-2/$5.99 US/$7.99 Can

MAN AT WORK   by Elaine Fox
0-380-81784-5/$5.99 US/$7.99 Can

WHEN NIGHT FALLS   by Cait London
0-06-000180-1/$5.99 US/$7.99 Can

BREAKING ALL THE RULES   by Sue Civil-Brown
0-06-050231-2/$5.99 US/$7.99 Can

GETTING HER MAN   by Michele Albert
0-380-82053-6/$5.99 US/$7.99 Can

I'VE GOT YOU, BABE   by Karen Kendall
0-06-050232-0/$5.99 US/$7.99 Can

RISKY BUSINESS   by Suzanne Macpherson
0-380-82103-6/$5.99 US/$7.99 Can

Avon Romances—
the best in exceptional authors
and unforgettable novels!

Have you ever dreamed of writing a romance?

*And have you ever wanted
to get a romance published?*

Perhaps you have always wondered how to
become an Avon romance writer?
We are now seeking the best and brightest undiscovered
voices. We invite you to send us your query letter to
avonromance@harpercollins.com

What do you need to do?

Please send no more than two pages telling us
about your book. We'd like to know its setting—is it
contemporary or historical—and a bit about the hero,
heroine, and what happens to them.

Then, if it is right for Avon we'll ask to see part of the
manuscript. Remember, it's important that you have
material to send, in case we want to see your story quickly.

Of course, there are no guarantees of publication,
but you never know unless you try!

*We know there is new talent just waiting
to be found! Don't hesitate . . . send us
your query letter today.*

*The Editors
Avon Romance*